Girls in Tin Hats

ANNIE MURRAY
Girls in Tin Hats

MACMILLAN

First published 2020 by Macmillan
an imprint of Pan Macmillan
The Smithson, 6 Briset Street, London EC1M 5NR
Associated companies throughout the world
www.panmacmillan.com

ISBN 978-1-5290-1175-3

1 3 5 7 9 8 6 4 2

A CIP catalogue record for this book is available from the British Library.

Typeset in Stempel Garamond by Jouve (UK), Milton Keynes
Printed and bound by CPI Group (UK) Ltd, Croydon, CR0 4YY

Visit www.panmacmillan.com to read more about all our books
and to buy them. You will also find features, author interviews and
news of any author events, and you can sign up for e-newsletters
so that you're always first to hear about our new releases.

To the people of BARRA, the Birmingham Air Raids Remembrance Association, who have worked so hard to make sure that the long silence over Birmingham's bombardment during World War Two was broken and a memorial set up in the name of the many people of the city who died during those dark years.

Pay attention, Hitler. You have the insight of a genius. You cannot pretend that you do not know it is either you or them. You must break them or be broken by them. Therefore, send your bombers, and more and more of them. Spare no means. Spread the wings of the Luftwaffe. Fling down fire. All is at stake.

But you must make haste: for hitherto they survive. Hitherto, they do not change. Make haste. If you leave them living it will be thought that there is something in the world that detonations do not shatter. Make haste, or their quietness will echo round the world; their amusement will dissolve Empires; their ordinariness will become a flag; their kindness a rock; and their courage an avalanche. Make haste. Blot them out if you can.

John Strachey, Post D, *published 1941*

I

Small Heath, Birmingham

1940

One

Night, 26–27 August

'They're coming for us . . . They'll herd us all into camps and we'll all be slaughtered . . . Oh – ohh!'

Violet longed to pull her arm away but the voice of her mother, May Simms, rose to a scream. Her scrawny fingers grabbed at Violet's arm, the nails digging into her flesh. They were squeezed in side by side under the flimsy staircase.

Violet pressed her forehead to her kneecaps, the bridge of her specs hurting her nose. Everything shook. The candle was blown out and they were left in darkness.

'Where're you going? Don't leave me!' Mom's fingers jabbed into her arm again, but she managed to pull away.

'I'm just lighting the candle . . .'

Violet groped for the matches, flared one into life and brought it to the wick of the candle. Its light crept around the cramped, shabby living room of their back-to-back house. For a second it felt peculiar to see everything looking so normal: the familiar table and chairs, the range with their undies hanging on it to dry, the bodged rug on the floor and dark rectangle of blackout over the window. For now, the planes had passed over. She heard shouts coming from outside.

'Get back here!' her mother insisted.

Even in the middle of this raid, frightened as she was,

3

Violet wanted to resist. *Come here, stay with me . . .* That was all she ever heard from her mother. If she tried to get out, to have more life of her own, it would be, 'You're a *selfish* girl! I don't know how I brought you up to be so selfish.'

But hearing the drone of the planes overhead again she scuttled back under the stairs. Crammed in beside her mother was the last place she wanted to be – Mom with her sharp elbows and constant fretting – but her belly was churning with fear and it felt as if every hair of her body was standing on end.

'Don't go and leave me on my own . . .'

Violet shut her mind down, the way she had learned to.

'Everyone leaves me – everyone. Your father . . . Left me to bring you up all on my own . . . It's been a terrible, hard road . . .'

Well, I suppose he didn't die on purpose, did he? Frightened as she was, Violet felt rage swell inside her. And did I ask to be born?

Here she was, twenty years of age, with Mom watching like a hawk as always, her life passing her by. She'd been a good girl, done as she was told, and in her drab little life she had hardly been anywhere, never once walked out with a boy, never been kissed! And it wasn't just that she was small and shy and wore specs. How was she ever going to meet anyone nice when she was hardly allowed to budge from home except to go out to work at the biscuit factory? Their neighbour, Mrs Baker, said it wasn't right – and it wasn't.

The next thing was Mom'd be all sweet and sickly. 'Aah – you're my little baby girl, you are. You're all I've got, Vi . . . Don't go away and leave me . . .'

There was no point in saying anything. Not now. Even though she was getting to the point of being fit to burst

4

with the need for freedom. Instead, she strained her ears to hear what was to come outside.

The raid last night had been the first really big one over Birmingham and this morning a sense of shock had spread across the city. The light of dawn brought the terrible sight of the Market Hall at the city's heart – the much-loved, bustling arcade where they all loved to shop for fruit and veg, meat and fish, even live pets – now left a charred shell.

'They'll be going for the BSA and the Singer factory,' people in Small Heath said fearfully. Birmingham Small Arms, a mile away from where Violet lived, was the main factory in England producing rifles and Browning machine guns – as well as bicycles and motorbikes for the war effort. And the Singer Works made engines on Waverley Road, just the other side of the canal. They had to be some of the city's prime targets, as well as all the road junctions in the area.

And now, tonight, here they were again. Another wave of engines was drawing closer. Violet looked up at the staircase, flimsy as matchwood, which seemed to waver in the candlelight. Was this how it was going to be now, her here, night after night next to Mom? Violet took her specs off and pressed her head to her knees again, feeling a scream rising in her as the sounds built outside.

Further up along the other side of Archibald Street, Grace Templeton was squeezed with most of her family into the Anderson shelter Dad had put up on their little patch of garden.

Grace, twenty-one, strawberry blonde, pretty and full of life, had been more than ready to spread her wings –

until the war came along and put the lid on all that. As the eldest of Cath and Bill Templeton's nine children, she felt responsible for everyone, especially with Dad not here at nights.

'Sure, it's like trying to catch a sleep in a tin of sardines,' Cath complained. As if anyone would have been able to sleep during this racket anyway.

Two of the Templeton children were in the neighbouring garden with an elderly couple whose own family were grown and gone. Grace longed to be one of the ones to go in next door with the Josephs. Imagine being able to stretch out on one of the narrow bunks with no one kicking her!

Marie had been chosen to go next door – of course. Out of the nine of them there were only three girls. Marie, at fourteen, dark-haired and pretty, was deemed the most acceptable to kindly old Mr and Mrs Josephs. Patrick, nineteen, and not just the oldest boy but the tallest, had gone with her. And anyway, Mom wanted Grace there as the eldest and she was in a state because Dad was working nights at the BSA.

Their father had put one narrow wooden bench in on each side so Grace was propped in a corner with two of her brothers beside her, while the other three lads were squeezed in on the opposite side like a row of ornaments in descending order of size. Cath Templeton sat on a chair in the middle holding baby Gordon, who was just over a year old. Being the summer, it wasn't too cold, but Grace hated to think what it would be like if they had to be out here in winter. She sat longing for a cigarette, but she had promised Mom she wouldn't smoke in the shelter.

'Mother of God,' Cath kept exclaiming as the sounds of the planes' engines grew and seemed to be heading straight for them personally. 'Mother of Mercy, spare us – and keep my Bill safe . . . Come on now, Grace, and the rest of you, we'll say the rosary.'

Grace murmured along with the Hail Marys, but all she could think about was Dad, her lovely Dad, being at the BSA. It was in Armoury Road, at the heart of the old Gun Quarter in Small Heath. When France fell under German occupation in June and during the withdrawal and rescue at Dunkirk, the servicemen who had pulled out had left behind their equipment – a host of motor-bikes and cycles as well as guns – on French soil. The Birmingham Small Arms company had stepped up pro-duction even more and were working a seven-day – and night – week. Grace's father worked on the motorcycles. It was terrible thinking about them dropping bombs on the works, with all those people on shift there through the long hours of darkness . . .

Grace straightened her aching back. Mom had drifted into silence. It was too uncomfortable to sleep even when the night was quiet. Tonight, they had all been in their beds until midnight when she was woken by shouts from the street outside.

'Take cover! Get in the shelters! Air raid . . . Move, all of you – come on, wake up!'

A policeman had cycled frantically up and down the street blowing a whistle and he was soon joined by Jim-my's dad, Mr Oval, from across the road, who was in the ARP. Shortly afterwards came the blood-chilling howl of the air-raid siren.

'Lord above!' Mom cried, jumping out of bed. They were all shocked out of sleep, blithering about like scared rabbits. 'What do we do? Holy Mother of God – Grace, what is it I'm to be doing?'

'Get Gordon, Mom!' Grace shouted, rounding up her brothers. 'Let's get to the shelter!'

'What about clean underwear . . . ? Have I time to boil some water?'

'*What?* No! Let's just get down the garden!'

Even after last night's raid they were not at all in the swing of it. Joseph fell over putting both feet down the same trouser leg and they had a heck of a job finding the torch. Mom kept muttering because she had forgotten to make a flask of tea.

Grace grabbed two blankets along with a couple of candles and the box of matches.

Just as they got settled in, there was a knock on the side of the shelter.

'It's only me, Mrs T,' they heard Mr Oval's voice. 'Just checking you're all safe in there?'

'Oh, hello, Mr Oval!' Mom stuck her head out. Grace caught a glimpse of the barrel-like figure of Arthur Oval in his ARP uniform. Mr Oval . . . Guilt prickled through her. The man who, by now, could easily have been her father-in-law . . .

Mom exchanged a few words and drew her head in.

'Ta-ra-a-bit then – keep safe,' Mr Oval said, departing.

'Oh, he's a good man, so he is,' Cath said.

Grace said nothing. She knew that under Mom's words lay others. *You could be married to his lovely son Jimmy by now, if you weren't such a silly girl and too fussy for your own good . . .* Brown-eyed, handsome Jimmy, who was undeniably also a good man . . . And Grace was left feeling as if she had been rubbed up the wrong way and didn't know what to do about it.

'Holy Mother,' Mom said again. 'Protect my Bill, dear Lord . . . Please let him be all right . . .' After a while she sat up to shift Gordon's weight a little, then said, 'God, it's funny to think of all his marrows up there above us.'

Grace smiled. Dad had shovelled soil on to the shelter

and planted marrows. They were big this year – even bigger than Mr Oval's, which Dad was quietly satisfied about. She pictured the long, green vegetables lurking out there while the searchlights jittered about and the guns were banging away. The thought of them was strangely comforting.

Mr Arthur Oval found himself breathing very heavily as he hurried back to the street from the Templetons' Anderson shelter. He was a man who, having passed the age of fifty, already stout of build and never knowingly underfed by his wife Mildred, was not at the peak of physical fitness. By day, he worked at Gillott's in Sparkbrook, a small firm making machine tools and, as a strong patriot in the face of what that German feller Hitler was up to, had joined up for Civil Defence training in the ARP long before the war began. They'd all known this was coming, of course – all the preparation for gas attacks and bombing raids. But knowing about it didn't get you ready for all this lot – not really. All this rushing about. He was puffing like a train.

Must go and see my Old Lady, he thought. 'Er'll be frightened to death in there.

He half-ran, lurching along to his house a few doors up and along the entry. Bombs were dropping some distance away. Not here at the moment, thank the Lord. Marrows gleamed faintly in the streaks of light.

'Mildred – old girl? 'S'only me. You all right?'

He pulled the shelter door open. Their old dog, Ginger, gave a warning woof, which pleased him. You never knew who might be creeping around in people's gardens during this lot.

'All right, girl,' he said, stroking her head as it emerged from the shelter.

'Oh – Arthur!' Mildred's fleshy face peered out anxiously at him in the shuddering light of a candle. Her face – always there, always the same. Arthur felt a rush of love for her. His Old Lady. The best, she was. Pure gold.

'Oh, I'm glad to see yer.' She was barely talking above a whisper. 'I've only just got our John to sleep – 'e don't like it out 'ere one bit. Frightens 'im.'

John, their youngest of seven children, was a frail boy, handicapped from birth.

'Poor little mite – I'm not surprised,' Arthur said.

'Hello, Dad!' Dorothy, who was twelve, called to him. He couldn't see any of them in the dark behind Mildred. His older boys had joined up, leaving the four younger children. They were good kids. He knew they and the wife would look after each other.

'I think we'll have to get a Tilley lamp, Arthur – the candle keeps blowing out.'

'All right, bab, we'll do that,' he said. 'Can't stop now – long as you're all right. Anything you need – pop over to the post, all right?'

'I don't like you being out there,' Mildred said, pulling her shawl close round her matronly figure. 'You go careful, Arthur.'

Arthur nodded. He felt suddenly emotional, as if he wanted to tell the Old Lady he loved her – but he didn't feel he could bring that out in front of the kids. He turned and stumbled away to check along the street.

Grace knew her mother was worried to death. She kept thinking to herself, over and over, Let Dad be all right, please let him be all right . . . With another pang of guilt, she wondered where Jimmy was – Jimmy Oval, who loved her. He's probably safer than us, she thought, even

10

though he's in the army. The rest of the Oval family would be in their shelter, under their own marrows.

Trying to snap out of her thoughts, she looked round at her brothers, hunched up together, all awake except five-year-old Adie, their faces hollowed out by shadows, dots of candlelight reflected in their eyes. This was about the quietest she had ever seen them. They were scared and exhausted. Suddenly she was filled with tenderness for them all, no matter how much they drove her mad most of the time.

Dennis, twelve, was sitting up between her and little Adie. Dennis was a sweet lad, one of the quieter ones in the family. He was rocking slightly back and forth and after a time Grace felt his hand slip into hers. Touched, she reached out and put her arm round him, something he would never normally have stood for at his age. He didn't say anything; but he cuddled up close, his bony shoulder digging into her.

'All right?' she whispered.

'Yeah.' He nodded, his dark hair rubbing against her. Dennis was a good lad and she was moved by his sweet-ness, his wanting the comfort of her. That was how she had felt about her dad when she was his age – still did, in fact. Just wanted Dad there because he was kind and reassuring. Mom was reassuring too but Dad would just sit, quiet and solid, and she liked that. Or he would pull her on to his lap as he sat at their old piano picking out jolly little tunes he had taught himself, like 'Begone Dull Care!' and 'The Vicar of Bray'. She had always been a Daddy's girl.

Putting her lips close to her brother's ear, she whispered, 'It's all right, Den,' and then, leaning forward, said more loudly, 'What shall we sing, eh, boys? We'll show those pesky Germans we're not scared, won't we?'

'Ten Green Bottles?' Joseph said.

'All right – come on then.' She started singing. 'Ten green bottles, hanging on the wall . . .'

When she was the only one left awake, Grace got up quietly and pushed open the little makeshift door.

Pulling Mom's old shawl round her she took in gulps of air. But though it was cooler than the fug in the shelter, it was thick with the stink of burning. She twisted round and dared to stand upright outside. Searchlights moved like restless wands about the sky. It was much less dark than usual and she could see no stars – the night was full of smoke and the baleful copper glow of fires coming from the middle of Birmingham.

So this is it, she thought. The raids they'd waited for all last winter and all through this strange, hot summer as Germany invaded country after country and France fell and the scramble to escape at Dunkirk had begun . . . The first raid on Birmingham had been a couple of weeks back, on 9 August, a lone bomber dropping two bombs on Erdington, killing a young man who was home on leave from the army. Since then, bombs had fallen on the Castle Bromwich aircraft factory, where they were building the Spitfires, killing five workers. Last night had been the first real shock – they were saying there had been fifty bombers over the middle of town. And here they were again – was this how it would be now, night after night? It was terrifying, but above all it was exhausting. All she really longed for was to be able to lie down and get some sleep.

Standing out in the horrifying night, beside the vegetables and the little corrugated-iron shell which contained her family, Grace thought, I can't just keep sitting here like this when all these other people are out risking their lives – I've got to do something. At that moment, she felt like the only person left in the world.

Violet thought she had never known a night as long as this one. She felt as if her nerves were fit to snap. I can't sit here like this night after night, she thought. Not with her, like this. It felt as if they were the only people left in Birmingham.

She must have dozed because the next thing she knew was the rising blare of the 'All Clear' and, almost immediately, someone knocking at the door. A correct-sounding, familiar woman's voice called out in the darkness.

'Are we all right in here?' The knock was repeated. 'This is your warden – everyone all right?'

Violet scrambled to her feet and opened the door. Outside, holding a torch, stood Miss Holt, in her ARP warden's uniform, a coat with brass buttons and a rounded black steel helmet. Miss Holt, a retired elementary school teacher, lived along the street at number sixty-one and had offered her little terraced house as the warden post for Archibald Street.

She was a tall, grey-haired, unbending woman in horn-rimmed spectacles, who had taught Violet in her earliest years. Violet had always been in awe of Miss Holt, with her stiffly shingled hair, upright stance and the piercing stare some teachers seem to develop during their years of terrorizing infants. But Miss Holt had also been capable of kindness under her severe exterior. And at least she hadn't been one for the cane – she'd never needed it, the way she looked at you. At that moment, Violet felt she had never been so pleased to see anyone in her life.

'Ah – Violet,' Miss Holt said, becoming stiffer again at

the sight of one of her old pupils. 'Are you and your mother all right?'

'Yes, thank you, Miss Holt,' Violet said, praying that her mother would stay out of it. She sometimes thought Mom didn't always exactly mean to be rude, but she had a habit of saying the wrong things to people. 'We're all right, thank you.'

'Who's that?' She heard her mother's voice, muzzily from within.

'It's Miss Holt, Mom.'

'Oh – Miss Holt!' May Simms had no time for teachers. *Those who can't do, teach,* was her view. But to Violet's relief she managed to sound quite polite. 'Morning, Miss Holt. What a night.'

'Yes,' Miss Holt said. 'I gather the BSA has suffered a bit – no one injured, so far as we know. Some damage to a couple of houses at the bottom end of this street, though . . .'

'Oh . . . Oh, dear.' May finally crawled out from under the stairs, a blanket wrapped round her neat little form. With her clear blue eyes, wavy hair a deep brown against her porcelain-skinned face, she looked like a little doll. 'That's terrible. The damage, I mean. I was sure we were all going to die – I said to Vi, this is going to be the end of us . . .' She had a high, whiny voice.

Oh, do be quiet, Violet begged silently. *Please, Mom.*

Violet felt Miss Holt sizing them both up.

'Well, you can get to your beds for a while now, I think,' she instructed, before adding briskly, 'Since you have no cellar or garden, I would strongly recommend that you go into the public shelter. You have one in your own yard, so I really can't imagine that squatting under the stairs is beneficial either to your safety or your nerves.'

14

'Yes, Miss Holt,' Violet said, though she knew Mom was snootily against the shelter. Violet hadn't been sure about it either, the things you heard about what went on in them. But almost anything now seemed better than sitting here on her own with her mother.

'I shall be coming round regularly, of course,' Miss Holt said, looking severely at May Simms. 'Do think about what I've said. The government has not had these shelters built for its own entertainment.'

Miss Holt was moving away to check on the rest of the yard, but she turned back.

'And Violet –' Even in the torchlight Violet could feel Miss Holt's penetrating gaze. 'We need more volunteers for this sector for the ARP. You might think about lending a hand.'

'Me?' Violet said, astonished.

'Yes, child – you! Who else? There's a lot a girl like you could be doing – the country doesn't just defend itself, you know!'

As soon as Miss Holt had left, Mom said, 'Shut that door, will yer? I can't stand these dried-up old biddies coming and telling you what to do. I'm not going in that shelter with all those oily rags from the yard for love nor money.'

Violet said nothing, but her mind was reeling. Miss Holt had asked her – *ordered* her, practically. What an excuse she had now! Even Mom wouldn't dare go against Miss Holt – especially now these awful raids had started. She could get out – get away!

Could I . . . ? *Shall I?*

Two

'Come on, Titchy Vi, get yer bits and let's get out of 'ere!'

June Perry's voice blared across the throng of chattering women. Violet's shift had just ended at Alfred Hughes's Biscuits the next day and everyone was hurrying to get out into the remains of the afternoon sunshine.

Violet ducked her head. Who did June Perry think she was, bawling at her like that? And calling her Titch like she used to do at school.

It was true that like her mother she was barely five foot in shoes. But she had not inherited her mother's striking looks. She was a more muted version of May – though prettier than she knew – sweet-faced, with soft brown hair that barely waved at all and wide pigeon-grey eyes, but they were hidden behind embarrassingly thick lenses. Mom sometimes told her she looked like a mouse in specs. Even at the age of twenty, people still took her for a young girl. And she was shy with people. But that didn't mean she was going to be pushed around by June Perry – not any more!

'Oi – stop shoving, June,' she heard the others saying. Everyone was tired out after last night. 'We all want to get out.'

Ignoring June, Violet turned to the girl on her left as she hung up her overall.

'See yer tomorrow, Bett.'

Bett, red-haired and freckly, was a quiet soul, but friendly when you got talking to her. Violet had been at

Alfred Hughes's for nearly two years now and was still shy of some of the women, but she always got along well with Bett.

'Yeah – see yer, Vi,' Bett said. 'Let's hope to God it's quiet tonight!'

'Well, we can hope,' Violet said, smiling.

'It's funny how a night in your own bed starts to feel like the best treat you can have,' Bett said, rolling her eyes. 'Still, no rest for the wicked – I'm off doing First Aid tonight, at the Baths.'

'*Are* you?' Violet felt an immediate pang of envy. Everyone seemed to be getting stuck in except her.

'Thought I'd better do my bit.' Bett gathered up her bags. 'Beats just sitting there waiting for them to come and get us, don't it? – Oh-oh, old face-ache's coming . . .'

Violet didn't need to look round to see that June Perry's sizeable form had elbowed her way almost over to her, causing some of the other women to tut in annoyance. June had a head of magnificent black hair, which was pinned back in thick waves from a thunderous-looking face. It had once been a bullying face, which had pursued other girls – including Violet at times – through elementary school, mercilessly, seeking out their weak points. Violet had tried to keep out of June's way ever since, even though she only lived round in the next street. But then, just a week ago, June had turned up to work at Alfred Hughes's and seemed to have changed her tune completely. She acted as if she was Violet's best friend all of a sudden.

Doesn't the stupid cow remember *anything*? Violet thought furiously. Why would she think I'd want to walk home with her?

'C'mon, Vi!' June called again, as if they were the best of pals. She was latching on like a leech. Just so she's got

17

someone to moan at, Violet thought resentfully. It wasn't as if June ever listened to a word *she* said. And she had quite enough of being moaned at by Mom.

'I'm just going to the lav . . .' she called over her shoulder, vaguely, in June's direction.

With her bag strap over one shoulder, the string of her gas-mask box biting into the other, she swam as fast as she could back through the crowd and tore out to the lavatories. She'd be late home now and Mom'd be on at her, but that was too bad.

Shutting herself in, she dumped her things on the floor and leaned against the grubby door. She took her smeary specs off and rubbed them on the edge of her cardi – which only gave her a clearer view of the fag ends trodden into the brick floor and the remains of a roll of Izal paper on its side by the lavatory. It stank in there, but it was worth it to get shot of June Perry.

There was a niggling pain in her right shoulder as if everything in her body was tense. All day she had been filled with a desperate feeling. In the last year, everything had come to be about the war. That Sunday morning when Mr Chamberlain – *their* Mr Chamberlain, a Birmingham man – had finally announced that they were at war, seemed a world away now. A lot of jobs were reserved in Birmingham, the factories all going flat out on war production of one sort or another, but ever since there had been men – and women – joining up, some going into the forces, but a lot into the Home Guard or on fire watch or Civil Defence. All day she kept thinking about what Miss Holt said this morning. She was desperate to get out of her home somehow – now she had a perfect excuse!

Most of her working life, all Violet had ever wanted to do was stick her nose in a book when she got home, to

18

escape her mother's mithering. *Do this, Vi, do that, Vi, poor me, my life's so miserable, Vi* . . . Of course she felt sorry for her mother, being a widow and having to struggle so hard, but she was so full of self-pity, always trying to make Violet feel guilty.

And now she had June carrying on at her as well! It wasn't that June was frightening any more – she just resented being forced into listening to her all the way home. Why did everyone try and make her do what *they* wanted? June would soon get fed up and push off, surely?

After spending what seemed ages staring alternately at her old brown lace-up shoes and a dead spider, crunched up in a web in one corner, she unbolted the door and peered out. And who should be waiting a little way away, leaning against the wall and smoking a fag as if she had all the time in the world . . . ?

'Took your cowing time,' June remarked, smoke streaming out of her nostrils. 'What was you doing in there? You never even flushed it – you always was a little liar, Titchy.'

'Don't call me that,' Violet snapped. She felt very daring standing her ground with June Perry. At school, she'd pull your hair or shove you so hard you fell over if she didn't like the way you looked at her. Now she was sucking up instead.

'All right, no need to get mardy,' June whined, as if she was the injured party. 'You're still only the size of a shrimp.' She tagged along as Violet marched off down the road.

It was nice to be outside, feeling the sun warm on her face. A bitter, tarry stench mingled with the usual smells along the Bordesley Green Road: the sweet, baking biscuit scents of Alfred Hughes's, tinged with cinnamon and ginger, mingled with the acrid stink from Arthur Holden's, the paint and varnish factory across the way.

She and June each lived in one of the 'courts', or cramped yards of houses – June's at the top end of Arthur Street, one over from Archibald Street, where Violet lived at number three, back of twenty-four. Arthur Street, Archibald Street and Herbert Road ran roughly parallel to the main artery of the Coventry Road. It was only a ten-minute walk away, but that felt like an eternity with June rattling on at her.

Then she'd have to relieve Mom in the shop, but at least she could stand behind the counter with her book propped up and have a good read . . . She was just getting into a new book from the library in Green Lane. *The Way of an Eagle* by Ethel M. Dell. It was a lovely story – full of passion and nothing like real life whatsoever.

Today though, the thought made her feel discontented. She was fed up to the back teeth of escaping from life all the time – she wanted to *have* some life!

June managed to make thorough use of that ten minutes. After stubbing out her fag on the wall as they set off, she launched her heavy body off along the road and set her mouth in gear.

As ever, she was one long moan. June was from a family of thirteen children. She had arrived somewhere in the middle of all the Perry offspring and had scarcely a good word to say about any of the others. Some of them had been evacuated, but all somehow found their way like cats back to Birmingham during the first months of the war.

I don't know why she's always complaining, Violet thought, as June took a breath amid a diatribe about her elder sister Hilda, something to do with stockings . . . I wish I *had* some brothers and sisters.

June leaned over to light another fag. 'I see the end of your street got hit last night.' Two houses had been smashed to pieces at the bottom end of Archibald Street. Pausing to inhale, she went on lugubriously, 'Them Germans are gunna come and take over soon, any road – you mark my words. That's what they want. They won't be happy 'til they've finished off every one of us . . .'

Violet rolled her eyes. God, she thought, this one's another little ray of sunshine. She didn't want to hear any more of this sort of talk because it was truly terrifying.

'I mean – what if they come over 'ere – kill us all in our beds and there'll be no one left . . . We'll just all be Germans.'

'Well, we won't if we're all dead, will we?' Violet pointed out. Not that June was listening.

Suddenly June announced importantly, '*My* Sidney's taking me out tonight – says 'e wants me all to 'imself – so I says to 'im, "You dirty devil! I know what *you're* after! *All to yourself!*" She gave a loud, filthy chuckle but then her face sobered. 'I 'ope there's no raid or 'e won't come . . .'

Violet had been wondering when '*my* Sidney' was to make an appearance in the monologue. Sidney who only ever wanted 'one thing'. Violet was starting to wish that whatever it was Sidney wanted, June would just flaming well hurry up and give it him.

'How come he hasn't joined up?' she asked.

'He works for the Wolseley,' June said importantly. 'That's why he's got his own car!'

Oh, yes. The car. There was just no way to shut June up so she thought about *The Way of an Eagle* again. Did real people ever feel all carried away by love like that or was it just in books? Home life had given her nothing to go on. She had never known her father and according to

Mom, men were all wicked filthy beasts and best kept well away from. June and '*my* Sidney' didn't seem in the same league as Ethel M. Dell.

''Ere, I'll walk yer down your road,' June said, as if dispensing a great favour. They had reached the tramway depot, where they would separate to go down Archibald or Arthur. 'I ain't in a hurry to get home, what with the old man gobbing his guts up all day.'

June's grandfather also lived with the already large family in Arthur Street. By the sound of things, he had become like an immovable bit of furniture in the only downstairs room, existing day and night in the same chair, whether or not there was an air raid.

Three

They walked along the sunny side of Archibald Street, a long, cobbled, curving vein through the heart of Small Heath, a neighbourhood tucked into the south-east side of the heart of Birmingham, between Bordesley to the north and Sparkbrook to the south.

Many of the soot-faced terraces housed small business, from Paine's Undertaker's at the top near the tram depot, to Strong's Ironmonger's nearer the middle. Some were the premises of small, often one-man, manufacturing businesses, bringing forth a range of items either for individual sale or components supplying larger firms. Others held a rich variety of shops: general hucksters' stores, bakers and butchers, a fried-fish shop, beer shop, watch repairer, tobacconist and boot-repairer. And, in a cramped front house near the top end of the road, Quinn's Pawn-broker's, now run by Violet's mother, May Simms.

Between the clusters of shops were dwellings, some whole houses, others in groups of courts, side by side – which consisted of houses built back to back. What looked from the front like one house was in fact divided in two: a front house facing the street, like Quinn's, with a downstairs room and scullery and two poky upstairs rooms. The ones above Quinn's were dark and cobwebby and in terrible repair. Backing on to it was another half house much the same, only facing on to a yard. Number three, where Violet and her mother lived on the yard, backed on to number twenty-four, a 'front house' facing over the street.

Threaded between every four or five houses was a narrow alley, or entry, leading to these yards, on to which opened the doors of the 'back houses'. All the dwellings, front and back, shared the facilities of the yard – a tap on one wall, and three odorous lavatories at the far end, set close to a ramshackle brick wash house called the 'brewhouse', with a copper inside for heating water. There was no running water inside any of them.

And now, since these basic houses had no cellars, brick air-raid shelters had been put up wherever a space could be found, some in parks and on playing fields and in this case in a back alley behind their yard and the one next door.

So many things to do with the war were now so normal after all these months that they hardly noticed them: the blackout, sandbags piled against buildings and the white edges of kerbstones, which Mr Strong and Mr Oval and some of the other locals had helped paint to help people see in the blacked-out streets. The gently swaying barrage balloon in the park had become something so usual as never to be remarked upon now, as had the frequent arrival of government leaflets full of advice about gas attacks and air-raid shelters. But now it was the long-awaited bombing they were having to get used to.

'Right, got to go,' Violet said quickly as they drew near to Quinn's. 'Mom needs me in the shop.'

'Oh – I'll put in my head and say hello to her,' June said unctuously.

Blimey, Violet thought, does she *never* take the hint? She was feeling all keyed up. How was she going to tell Mom she wanted to volunteer? Mom'd go mad!

The sign over the little shop said, 'Quinn's Pawn-broker's', with the three golden balls hanging majestically at one corner. The windows, like others in the street, were criss-crossed with tape to protect against the shattering caused by bomb blast. Mr and Mrs Quinn were long dead and Violet's mother had taken over running the shop from them. She never changed the name – it was what people were used to. *And anyway*, she said, *would I want my name plastered across a pawnshop?*

Apart from regular visits to the library, the shop was where Violet spent all her time away from work. Behind the counter were shelves stuffed with objects and bundles wrapped in scraps of old sheet or sacking, some of which came in and went out each week on a regular basis. Some things never changed, war or no war. Others had been long abandoned and were stashed in the grim little rooms upstairs until May had a clear-out and sold them off.

June went breezing up to the door and stuck her head round.

'All right, Mrs S?'

'All right, June,' Violet heard her mother say, managing to drag her voice into a pleasant tone. She had her affected voice for customers and June's mother was a regular. But in any case, it didn't do to get on the wrong side of the Perrys. June's brothers were feared in the neighbourhood; even the very young ones would get into a scrap with anyone. 'Just back from work are yer? Where's Vi? I need her in here.'

Violet, attuned as she was to Mom's moods, could hear the chill edge to her voice. As she stepped into the musty stench of other people's old clothes, the swelling, rebellious feeling that had taken her over all day, boiled over. All these evenings of her life she sat in with Mom, reading at the table while Mom smoked, or they had the wireless on – as the mantel clock ticked her life away . . .

I'm going to do it! she raged in her head. I'm going to do what Miss Holt said. She can't go against Miss Holt!

'Mind the shop for me, Vi,' Mom said, rushing towards the door. As usual she looked very nice, her petite figure – she was an inch taller than Violet – in a blue-and-white flowery frock, her hair pinned back so that it waved prettily round her cheeks.

'Mom –' Violet blurted quickly, her heart picking up to a crazed speed. Her mother wouldn't be able to argue, not with June there. 'You know what Miss Holt said – about me volunteering – you know, joining up . . . ? Well, I've gone and done it!'

Her mother stopped abruptly, head snapping round.

'What d'yer mean – what, the army? You can't go into the army!'

'No – oh, no!' Violet almost laughed. The army – now there was a thought! Imagine if she'd decided to just take off and leave home! 'No – the ARP. Like Miss Holt said.'

Mom gaped at her, then her eyes narrowed into a mean, calculating look all too familiar. But June was still standing there gawping, her mouth slightly open.

'So I've already done it, Mom. I'm in the . . .' Violet groped around for the right term. 'Civil Defence – that's it. I'm going to work in that. You're going to volunteer as well, aren't you June? First Aid, I think you said? People have been joining up for months – we all have to do our bit,' she ended virtuously.

June was obviously having a job keeping up with all this. But wanting to remain in Violet's good books, she didn't argue.

'We'll talk about this later,' her mother said. She went storming out.

June leaned against the door frame. For a moment she didn't speak, which was restful. Violet looked down at the counter for a moment, the ledger with its lists in Mom's careful, looping hand, of people's pawned goods. Beside it was a leaflet.

City of Birmingham Water Department
In the event of an Air Raid . . .

'You haven't really gone and done that, have yer?'

Violet made a split-second calculation. She needed June on her side. Raising her head, she kept her eyes fixed on June's. 'Not yet. But I'm gunna.'

'Your mom's not gunna like it, is 'er?' She shrugged. 'I ain't gunna tell on yer.' June stood there, like a young heifer, shifting her weight from one chunky leg to another. Violet suddenly felt sorry for her.

'Why don't you then?' she said. 'Sign up for summat?'

'Me?' June said gloomily. 'What'm I gunna do? I can't do nothing much, me.'

'Course you can. Like I say – First Aid.' Something not the same as me, she thought. She could only put up with so much of June Perry. 'Bett Carter's doing it – at the Baths. You'd be good at that, I reckon.'

June seemed to be taking the bait all right. And Violet softened at the sight of her face. June seemed a bit nicer than she used to be and she felt generous towards her. The girl's heavy features had taken on a look of amazement, honour even.

'What, *me*? You think *I* could do that?'

'Yeah.' God knew, they both needed to get out of home somehow. 'Course you could.'

June stood, looking stunned.

'You'd best find out, hadn't you?' Violet said.

27

'First Aid!' June appeared all lit up. She left the shop looking ready for anything. Violet watched her go, a little smile on her lips, then idly picked up the information leaflet from the counter.

'"Draw sufficient water in clean receptacles for immediate drinking requirements,"' she read. '"If the house is fitted with a bath . . ."'

'"Fitted with a bath!" Ha, flaming ha,' she said and went back to Ethel M. Dell.

Half an hour later, the clip-clip of her mother's best white shoes – a find in Rag Alley, with Cuban heels – sounded across the shop floor and suddenly the book was snatched from in front of her.

'What've I said about reading in the shop?'

Violet did her usual, automatic calculation of what mood her mother was in. Often she was cheerful enough, always busy and competent about the house. You couldn't fault her when it came to practical things. But today, after the night they had had, was one of her low days when she was crabby and all pent up about things. And now, what with this bombshell Violet had dropped on her . . .

'What's all this then?' She rapped on the counter. 'You come in here, dump this news on me in front of *her*, of all people.'

Violet looked up at her carefully. 'If I hadn't done it now, she'd keep on – you know what Miss Holt's like.'

Mom's cold blue gaze bored into her. She gave a shrug. 'Well?'

'I . . .' Violet wrestled with getting her story straight. She'd had to say she'd already volunteered or Mom would have tried to stop her. 'Civil Defence, like Mr Oval. Air-raid warden. It's only an evening or two a week,' she guessed. All official – an order. Mom couldn't argue.

'Leaving me all alone, I suppose? Selfish, like you always are.' May folded her arms, her mouth hard and tight.

Violet lowered her gaze to hide the gleam in her eyes. There was nothing her mother could do about it. 'Sorry, Mom.'

Four

June Perry drifted back along the street.

'Out the way, yer little bleeders!' From habit, she bawled at a group of girls blocking her path. The road was full of kids – skipping, marbles, hoops coming flying at you, games of tag – it was a right dodgem trying to get along.

The children scattered. She knew they'd be pulling faces behind her back but sod 'em. She had things to do. In fact, she felt heady with excitement. First Aid. Violet Simms thought she ought to do First Aid!

Some women near the top of Archibald Street were perched on the front steps they had scrubbed clean that morning, peeling vegetables or knitting and having a natter with their neighbours. It was the only way to get some sun on your face, living in those dank little houses.

'All right?' June said to everyone, but quite a few of them never answered. Too good to speak to me, are yer? she thought.

She saw Susan Crosby coming towards her with a bag in one hand, three kids all strung out holding hands from the other, and well out at the front with another baby. Susan lived up that end and there was nothing stuck up about her.

'All right, Susan?' June said. Susan was only a year older than she was.

'All right, June,' Susan said distractedly.

'They've said I've got to go and do First Aid,' June said.

'Oh – well, that's good.' Susan seemed startled by June beaming at her all of a sudden. 'Good for you.'

June walked on, still smiling. She didn't want to go home. It was a right barnyard in the house. They were a family of fifteen, plus Grandad, and lived in a two-up, one-down back house on a yard, the family spilling outdoors whenever possible. The house stank of damp and mould, of stale food and wee in brimming po's forgotten under beds, of the sulphur candle Mom burned to try and shift the bugs in the walls.

June's two eldest sisters and one of her brothers were now married, so they'd been down to twelve before the war and then another brother went into the army. But she still slept crammed into a bed with Hilda, her bossy older sister, and the three younger girls with their bony knees.

June dawdled, then stopped in the entry and lit a fag, drawing on it nervously. Could she really go and volunteer for First Aid training? The thought made her nervous. More bothersome at this moment, though, were her worries about Sidney.

If only Sidney truly acted in the way she wanted mousey little Vi Simms to think he did, like the pinnacle of a woman's dreams: handsome, full of desire, his dark eyes fixed on her with constant attention.

Because attention was something she had never had in her life – least of all, truth be told, from Sidney Bowles. The males who did pay her attention – her elder brother Bert for a start at one time, the dirty sod – were all . . . Well, they weren't the mooning romantic heroes she dreamt of. They were lads who were always after one thing, with pawing hands and filthy minds to match. She'd tried belting one or two of them when they started and

31

that put some of the lads off. She'd got herself a bit of a reputation. 'Flaming June' they'd called her, sniggering.

And then Sidney had come along.

The corners of her mouth turned down. Sidney was almost twice her age. She knew all about him now. Not just that he was an agent for the Wolseley, liking to show off his car – but that he also had a wife somewhere in Warwickshire, two kids – and a seemingly endless desire for . . . It.

June still never knew what to call *it*. Sidney would turn up about once a fortnight, now. This had been a regular thing ever since he'd drawn up beside her in his motorcar last winter, raised his hat through the window and she had seen his round pink face, bristly black moustache and dimply chin.

'Afternoon, my dear!' he said. 'Well, aren't you something?' At the time she had been on her way home from work at the biscuit factory. Sidney's voice made it sound as if she was a walking miracle.

Just shows how green I was, she thought now, sourly, as she stood propped against the wall. Sidney sweet-talked her into getting in for a lift, which turned out to be in the wrong direction. Before they had gone more than a couple of miles, he'd pulled up by some ware-houses where the street was quiet, his hand reaching round to thrust down the front of her blouse.

'My God, you're the woman of my dreams,' Sidney breathed on her, a pronouncement laced with raw onion. Soon both hands were up inside her camisole. Sidney was obsessed with – well, with titties. Every time she saw him, he fell on her as if she was a meal.

She'd never actually done *it* with Sidney. Not the full thing. She wasn't that stupid. In a family as big as hers she knew what brought a baby on. But gradually Sidney drove her further afield, to quiet lanes on the edge of town, where he persuaded her to do a range of things exciting at least to him, which left him sweaty and out of breath. And it *was* exciting in a way – then. She even imagined that Sidney bringing her little presents – a thin silver chain with a heart on it, a special decorative hair slide – meant that one day he might want to be with her for ever. (She only found out later about the wife and two children.)

The last time she saw Sidney was a week ago, before the raids really got going. He didn't even bother to take her anywhere – didn't want her to unbutton his fly or let him fumble about inside her clothes. All he did was park up in Sydenham Street just past the Queen's Gravy Salts factory. He didn't even look at her.

'Well, I'm afraid this is goodbye, Jen.'

'June,' she said.

'Time to knuckle down.' She had no idea what this meant.

'You joining up then or summat?'

'Me?' he said. 'Oh, no! But I won't be seeing you any more.' He added briskly, 'Been fun though, hasn't it, old girl?'

She didn't like the way he was talking, as if she was something he wanted over with, like an unwanted dog he was about to dump at the side of the road.

Thinking about it, she kicked at the wall. A lump of dry, soot-encrusted moss dropped off. Sod Sidney and his puffing and panting. She'd learned her lesson with him all right. Cowing blokes – she was going to make sure she was the one in charge now, if any more came along.

In combative mood, she marched into the yard, where a couple of younger kids were playing with a go-kart.

'Out me way!' she roared, shoving past them and into the house.

Grandad was in his usual chair, seemingly asleep though it was hard to tell. Despite being in his seventies he still had a head of dark hair and a long, saggy face. His mouth was drooping open. The room stank of him – unwashed clothes, wee, his tobacco. June scowled in disgust. Otherwise though, it was surprisingly quiet, the other kids all out.

'That you, June?' Edith Perry came out from the scullery, squinting. She was a worn little woman with straggly grey-brown hair, yanked back by a couple of Kirby grips and only a few remaining teeth, resulting in the prematurely sunken look of her face. And she was so shortsighted she often couldn't tell her own children apart.

June was about to give her lip about why didn't she find someone else to do all the work, when her mother took her completely aback. Drying her hands on her pinner, she fished about on the shelf that held the family's crocks and lifted down a couple of cups.

'Fancy a cuppa tea? It'll be a weak'un, mind.'

June looked at her mother in astonishment. Not only was tea now on the ration, but even more extraordinary was Mom addressing her as a person who might want to sit and drink a cup of tea with her, *just* with her, like a grown-up. Her sisters, maybe, now they'd left home – but her, never. As kids they'd eaten perched round one pot on the staircase. There was never enough room round the table.

Mom stood there, resting her work-worn hands on the chair. June could see the blue veins on the inner sides of her arms where they poked out of the baggy sleeves of her frock. In a rare moment of noticing, June saw, sadly, what a wreck of a woman her mother looked.

34

'Go on then,' she said. 'If you're having one.'

Mom filled the pot and laid out the saucerless cups. They sat at the table.

'Who's that?' Grandad piped up suddenly. He sat up, looking bleary. 'Is that our Hilda?'

'No, Dad,' Mom said. 'It's June.'

'Oh,' Grandad said dismissively. 'Her.' And sank back in the chair, coughing, lungs bubbling.

'Want a cuppa tea, Dad?' Edith poured him one anyway, her face close up to the pot so she could see not to spill tea all over the table.

'Mom?' Jean wrestled to get back this rare thing she had hardly ever had in her life before: her mother's undivided attention.

'What?' Mom peered at her over her cup.

June took a breath for her big announcement.

'They've said I've gotta do summat – for the war. First Aid, I reckon.'

Her mother looked at her. 'Oh, ar,' she said. She looked away, fingering the chip in the teapot spout.

June stared at her. Her little triumph was wasted, like pouring water straight down the drain, and for a moment she felt like crying. But when had that ever done her any good?

Staring at her mother's indifferent face, she was filled with an enraged determination. She'd find a better bloke – there must be one somewhere. *And* she'd go and volunteer for First Aid – she'd cowing well show them all!

Five

Grace Templeton sashayed along Archibald Street on her way home, singing to herself in between drags on her cigarette. She was practising a walk that she thought would look seductive, feet lined up as if she was parading along a narrow wall – the catwalk gait she'd read about in a magazine. Turning into the entry to the back of number sixty-eight, she imagined her parish priest, Father hellfire O'Riordan's, face if he could see her now and stifled a giggle. A wanton woman! God, she thought, it didn't take much to get accused of that when you were a Catholic. Even the thought brought out devilment in her.

She stubbed out her cigarette on the entry wall and pushed open the back door, still singing away and swinging her hips.

'Oh, Grace, darlin', thank the Lord you're home!' Her mother, with her hair hanging dishevelled about her face, was kneeling on the bodged rug next to the range, changing Gordon's napkin. 'Go and give the pot a stir, will you? The stew's starting to catch!'

Cath Templeton's red-haired, Irish looks had faded over the years. Her face was thin and lined, though her smile still lit it into the sweet expression that long ago had charmed Bill, her English husband, into falling madly in love with her. Grace was very like her, a more curvaceous and robust version of her mother, her long hair a striking strawberry blonde and her face made up, lips a cheerful rosy pout.

'Marie's just sitting there doing sod all – why can't she do summat for once?' Grace said. 'I've been on my feet all day.' It was busy enough normally, working at the Co-op on the Coventry Road. But what with them losing staff to the army, and shortages and ration books to deal with, they were rushed off their feet.

Fourteen-year-old Marie, studiously pretending she couldn't hear any of this, was sitting on the fray-topped piano stool, picking out bits of tune with one hand, and holding a book with the other, making a show of reading it at the same time. The room – a table, a few chairs but not enough for all the family, a sideboard with shelves above it – was cosy but had the battered, overwhelmed look of anywhere inhabited by the whirlwind of seven growing boys. A few of the yellowed piano keys had subsided below the others, refusing to rouse themselves now to make a sound. Amid the crocks looked down statues of Our Lady and St Anthony.

'Oh, just *do* it, will you, before it's spoilt?' her mother retorted. She fastened the final pin in Gordon's nappy and took him on to her lap to suckle him. 'I've got my hands full enough, with this one and all that's going on . . .'

At the moment no one else was in apart from Marie, who skived off everything because she had a 'weak chest' – and my God, did she play on that one, Grace thought – and liked reading books so must be 'brainy'. All the lads were either still at work or out running the streets. And in any case, when did they ever raise a finger to do anything? They were little princes in Mom's eyes.

She went moodily into the back kitchen from whence drifted the smell of potatoes and singeing Irish stew. She lifted the lid of the enormous pan and moved the greyish concoction of scrag-end and carrots around with the metal spoon. Steam drifted from the potato pan. Her mouth watered – she was hungry enough to eat the whole lot right now!

'Did you hear, Theresa couldn't go to work today – there's that much damage to the factory?'

'I know,' Grace called back. 'Terrible.' It was all the customers had been talking about all day – damage to the BSA and the Queen's Gravy Salts factory in Sydenham Road where Mom's friend Theresa worked, and the firms on each side had been badly smashed up.

She gave the pot a good stir. 'I'm going to get changed,' she said, hurrying to the stairs, not wanting to stick around down there. She couldn't stand the sight of Mom with her tit out. Gordon, at nearly thirteen months, was an idle little so-and-so who was barely even attempting to stand let alone walk. Mom was still feeding him and Grace loathed the whole business. Every time there was a new baby, the sight of those swollen-up bosoms with blue veins showing under the skin repelled her. Would that have to be her one day? And if she married Jimmy – well, it could be in a year or less! She didn't want to stick around to see Gordon grabbing at his mother, latching on as if it was his divine right.

All Grace's life her mother had either been carrying a child, suckling one or – on two heart-rending occasions – burying one. Grace shuddered. She had seen too much of it: Mom with her head over a bucket in the scullery when a baby had started and all the exhaustion and blood and endless nappies that came after.

Mary and the angels help me, she thought, filled with dread. Never let me end up like that! She felt truly sinful even thinking like that. This was the one thing every woman was supposed to want – to get married and have babies. And she did want it, didn't she? One day – one distant day, maybe . . . But pray God, not yet!

But just as she opened the door to the staircase, she heard Marie say in gleeful tones, 'What about the letter?'

'Oh, Grace!' Mom called to her as she got to the bottom of the stairs. 'Sweet Jesus, how could I have forgotten!'

Grace went reluctantly back. Cath stood up, adjusting her clothing. Birthing eleven children and raising nine had shrunk her thin and wispy, her face aged for a woman of forty-one. She pushed her hair out of her face and their eyes met, each vivid and light blue.

'You don't know when you're well off, that's your trouble, Gracie. How could you do any better than Jimmy Oval? He's a lovely lad, from a good family – Mildred his mother's a saint, so she is.'

'I do know, Mom. Jimmy's a lovely feller. And I . . .' She couldn't put all her fears into words, her sense of being trapped by the thought of marrying Jimmy. And she certainly wasn't going to try within reach of Marie's flapping ears.

'Snap him up and marry him while you've got the chance,' Cath said. 'Or someone else will. A lad like Jimmy's not going to wait about for long.'

Marie, now blatantly listening, was smirking over the top of her book. It would have been hard to tell that Grace and she were sisters, except, perhaps, for the challenging look each of them had in their eyes at that moment. Marie favoured their father in colouring, having gravy-brown hair and grey-blue eyes. Grace tried to ignore her, until Marie started humming the wedding march, conducting with one finger.

Grace rolled her eyes. 'I write back, don't I? I'll take this one out of your way,' she said. With Gordon on one hip and the letter in her hand she went out to the back.

'Right, you lazy so-and-so – you can go down for a bit.' She plonked Gordon on the small remaining patch of grass where he sat on his bottom, looking at her with a quivering lip. 'No – I mean it. You stay there for a minute.'

She perched on the back step, lit another cigarette and opened the letter.

Dearest Grace,

Thanks for your letter. Sounds as if you've all been going through it up there though we don't get much proper news down here so it's hard to tell. I'm glad to hear you're all right.

We're all right over here. The worst of it's down London but a couple of days ago a plane came down about a mile from where we're posted. The pilot never got out – I didn't see it but it's been the main talk for a day or two I can tell you.

There's some queer people in this lot – you'd laugh if you saw some of them. Some say the Pioneer Corp's where they put all the ones they don't know what to do with but as I'm one of them I can't really grumble, can I?

Main thing is you're all right. I miss you, Grace. I don't know what more to say. I don't know when we'll get any leave. I know you said what you said but however many times you say it I love you and I'll wait and that's all really. I suppose I can't help myself.

Love to everyone – go and see our Mom now and then, won't you? She's ever so fond of you. I hope they're all right, her and Dad, doing ARP work – but I suppose it's no worse than sitting there down the garden waiting for Herr Hitler to drop something on them.

*Funny this letter writing. I love getting yours, they
make my week. Write soon, won't you, Grace? All my
love, as always,*
  Jimmy.

She read the letter twice, smiling in spite of herself, and
put it back in the envelope. Gordon had decided that a bit
of freedom was no bad thing and was crawling slowly
along the edge of the grass, staring with deep fascination
at the last of the potato plants.

The letter touched her. She did miss Jimmy a bit, didn't
she? She sat imagining his boyish, smiling face, sunny and
open, the way he was always so pleased to see her. She
found herself wishing he would just walk into the garden
now. He had always been there – Jimmy was just part of
her world. She knew she could wrap him round her little
finger without even trying. But that felt like the problem.
She'd never walked out with other boys. Might there not
be someone else, someone better for her, a more exciting
man who she had not yet met? These thoughts made her
feel guilty and restless at the same time.

There was a moment's peace and then Gordon let out
a squeak, having stuffed a handful of earth into his mouth
and discovered the taste not to be as good as he had
hoped. He screwed up his face, spitting and dribbling soil
and saliva down his chin.

'C'm'ere, you daft little so-and-so.' She picked him up
and cuddled him on her lap, leaning her head against the
doorpost, and lingered there, finishing her cigarette. The
air was still balmy, though the summer was slowly dying,
and a warm, milky-smelling cuddle with her plump bun
of a little brother was rather comforting.

*

The Templetons ate their tea in two shifts. First, the four younger lads, Dennis, Joseph, Michael and Adrian: 'Feeding time at the zoo,' Dad called it. Afterwards the rest of them had usually squeezed round the table – Cath and Bill, Grace and the older boys Patrick and Tony, and Marie. But now that Dad was working nights he ate with the younger ones, who were like a heap of wrangling puppies, all desperate to get outside and play again.

'Sit still now, Joseph – have you ants in your drawers?' Mom said. 'Will you have the last spoonful, Bill?' She put it on his plate before he could reply.

'Looks as if I will,' he said as Cath also slipped him another potato. He winked at Grace, who was leaning against the crock cupboard as the others ate and she smiled back. But she felt a pang of worry. His long, gentle face seemed to sag with tiredness even before he had begun the night shift and he pushed his hand back through his dark hair for a moment and rubbed the top of his head as if trying to clear it.

'Will you have your cup of tea now, Bill?' Cath fussed about him, apron on.

'Yes, but sit down for a bit, love, for heaven's sake! Adie – let your mother have your chair. You're nearly finished.'

Grace could hardly ever remember her mother sitting still – or often sitting down at all, for that matter. It was Dad who had somehow managed to find time for her as a little one.

'They're talking about sending more of the children away,' Mom said, standing by the stove in a cloud of steam. 'God knows, Bill, I wish we had some idea what was going to happen.' Tutting, she brought the teapot to the table.

'Not now, love . . .' Dad said, not wanting the young ones to hear.

When all the children were leaving Birmingham at the outbreak of war, Cath had been on the brink of sending her four youngest away as the government had advised. Small Heath, near the middle of Birmingham, was in the evacuation area. But she had changed her mind at the last moment.

'I can't be doing this,' she wept. 'If we're going to be bombed, we'll be bombed together. I'm not sending my little ones away to strangers heaven only knows where!'

Even though Dad had been saying the government were right in sending all the kids off on trains out to Herefordshire, Worcestershire and other countries around where they'd surely be safe, they could all see he was just as relieved when Mom put her foot down.

When Dad left for work that night, Grace saw them hold each other for a moment – a quiet, loving embrace which had not been normal before the war – not just for going to work. And it moved her, because she saw, for certain, that her mother and father loved each other, saw something of what love meant – and she knew that somewhere in her, she wanted it too.

Six

Jimmy joined up in the spring, from his job in one of the LNER railway yards, along with other lads in non-reserved jobs who had disappeared from the city into the forces.

He got leave after his basic training and turned up back in Archibald Street one evening during tea. When he knocked and put his head round the back door, Marie giggled, hand over her mouth.

'Ooh, look who's here.'

'Shut it, you,' Grace hissed, as everyone else exclaimed in greeting.

Jimmy's people lived across the street at number sixty-five and the families had known each other for years. Everyone loved Mildred Oval, Jimmy's mom, a solid, loving matron who would do anything for anyone. Jimmy, like Grace, was the eldest in his family, and now aged twenty-two, was a year older than Grace.

He was a strong-looking lad, compact in build like his father, Arthur Oval, very upstanding with an open, friendly face, square-jawed, with curly hair of a honey blond and brown eyes which could switch in seconds between innocence, mischief and a loving, longing gaze – a look which for some time now he had been fastening on Grace.

'Evenin', Mrs Templeton, Mr Templeton – Grace,' he added. Blushing, he stood awkwardly just inside the door, holding his army cap with both hands. His curls had been cropped and he looked taller and more serious in his khaki uniform, the sleeves rolled down even in this warm evening. Grace could sense that he wanted her to see him in uniform. And the sight affected her. She felt suddenly as if Jimmy had moved on to a new stage in life, leaving her behind, when she was the one used to leading the way. He was no longer just the kid from over the road, sweet on her.

'How's the lad then?' Grace's father smiled at Jimmy from his place at the end of the table.

'All right, ta, Mr T,' Jimmy said, very polite.

'Nice to see you, Jimmy,' Cath said warmly. 'When did you get back?'

'Oh – just a few hours ago, like, Mrs Templeton,' Jimmy said.

'How are your mother and father?'

Grace knew they were already perfectly well aware of how Mr and Mrs Oval were, but Jimmy coming back from the army like this made things strange and formal with them as well.

'They're doing all right, ta.' As he spoke, he kept casting quick glances at Grace, then away again, suddenly shy, and she felt shy as well. 'Busy – you know, with all the ARP work – well, our Dad, that is.'

'Marvellous, they are, both of them,' Cath said. 'Will you sit and have a cup of tea with us, Jimmy, before you both go out? I suppose the two of you will be going out?'

Ignoring her sister's wide, teasing eyes and her mother's seemingly innocent expression, Grace got up from the table.

'Yes – we'll go now, won't we, Jimmy?' she said firmly. 'Ta, Mom – Marie, you'll do the washing-up, won't you? See yer later!'

'Oh, *Mom*!' she heard from Marie as she led Jimmy quickly out to the street.

'God, it's a relief to get out!' Grace went striding off along the road. She felt a need to assert herself again.

'Hey – slow down a bit!' Jimmy laughed, almost running to catch up.

'Sorry.' Grace slowed her pace. It was mid-May, the weather beginning to warm. She had changed into an old frock, sage green – only a few shades different from Jimmy's uniform – its belt tight round the waist. Over the top she wore a cardigan but no coat and had let her hair down so that it lay in thick waves over her shoulders.

'God, I've missed you,' Jimmy said, his eyes moving over her. She could see all his admiration for her and immediately she felt the mixture of feelings he brought out in her: affection, of course – how could anyone not like Jimmy? – but also a prickly irritation, a sense of being hemmed in by him, as if just being with Jimmy was giving up on life somehow.

She and Jimmy had been pals for years. Only last summer things had really started to change, Jimmy getting serious, starting to talk like a lover, someone who was courting her, instead of the lad from up the street who she'd known all her life. And it was nice to go out to the pictures with him or the odd dance. Grace had gone out with him for fun, not realizing at first how serious he was.

Before he went away there had been a lot of evenings ending in long sessions of kissing and cuddling, wherever they could find a quiet spot. Grace had enjoyed all this, the attention, having someone adore her. But while Jimmy seemed to get more and more keen on her, she had found herself panicking. She liked him, of course – always had – but there was a pressure coming from him these days, the way he was talking more and more as if they'd be together for ever . . .

And now, after six weeks with Jimmy away, it felt as if they had gone back to being strangers for the moment, both of them shy and uncertain. Except for what she could see in Jimmy's suddenly serious eyes – longing, expectations, which made her panic even more.

'You're so fine, Grace.' His voice was soft, as he caught up with her. He sounded awed by the sight of her. 'You're just so pretty – I love looking at yer.'

She smiled, looking away from that brown-eyed gaze of his, not sure what to say. He never used to talk like this. Things felt as if they were moving far too fast. If only he'd talk about something else! Before, he would have been on about trains or football.

'Where d'you want to go?' she asked, not meeting his eye. 'The park?'

They strolled along to Victoria Park, the lung of Small Heath. Like most of the parks now it had signs of war written across it. To one side a cluster of men stood round the winch of the barrage balloon, its cables trailing, sand-bags dangling from others to keep it from blowing about too much. They steered away from it and walked the path round the little lake among a number of other couples, watching the ducks, smelling the oily water. Jimmy took her arm, nervously, she thought.

'Mr Edwards has joined up,' she said, for something to say. Mr Edwards was one of the managers she worked for at the Co-op on the Coventry Road. He was unmarried and in his mid-thirties and he said he really thought he ought to do his bit. 'Mrs Hodgson's in a right tizzy because they've put her in charge now.' She asked Jimmy questions about his training, about the other lads, tried to

47

keep him talking. She didn't get much out of him, except that they would be posting him on somewhere soon, but he didn't know where. He was unusually quiet though and the air between them soon felt heavy.

They were almost at the bandstand in the middle of the park. Another couple came towards them, side by side, not touching. For a second Grace found her eyes meeting those of the lad coming towards her. He had big blue eyes which locked on to hers. He looked nice, she thought. She felt his gaze sweep over her and she liked it, the way he was admiring her. It was like being stroked. She found the lad's clear attraction to her exciting. So many men out there, so many possibilities . . . Was she really just to take the first comer and settle for Jimmy?

'Lovely, that is,' Jimmy was saying. Grace dragged her attention back to him. He was staring at the elegant wrought-iron bandstand. 'You don't notice – not in the normal run of things.' He turned to her, his face solemn. She could see a nervous, trembling emotion in him just under the surface. 'I've got summat to say to yer, Grace.'

He paused for a few seconds until another couple had passed, walking arm in arm. Every so often he stroked a hand over his cropped hair, as if he couldn't get used to the feel of it. Grace waited, wondering and half-dreading what he might come out with.

'Thing is . . .' he began. He looked terribly nervous.

'Jimmy – there's no need to—'

But he held up a hand to stop her. 'I've just got summat I need to get off my chest, Grace.' He swallowed, as if trying to get up courage.

Grace felt her own heart start to pound.

'When I joined up, it weren't that I wanted to be away from yer – that was the last thing . . . But I did want you to think better of me – as a man, like.'

48

Grace was moved by this. She had never thought badly of him as a man. She was the one who was a problem, she thought, aching inside. For a moment his eyes met hers, those dark, sincere eyes, and he pulled her close to him in such a passionate embrace that she had the breath knocked out of her.

'Jimmy!' she managed to say. She had never known him like this before and it was exciting, Jimmy being forceful like that. But he drew back and held up a hand to stop her.

'Let me just have my say or I'll never get it out.' He looked down, struggling with his emotions. 'I've had a bit of time to think, see. I just don't even know how you feel about me, Grace. I know I love you. I *do*. Like – well, like a good'un, as a man should . . .'

She saw the Adam's apple move in his strong neck.

'When I've talked about us getting wed and that, you never seem keen. So I'm not sure what to think.'

He glanced up at her for a second and then away as if he could not face her reaction. Grace felt herself gripped by a terrible tension. Jimmy looked deep into her eyes, then, holding her gaze, to her horror, he sank down on to one knee.

'I've no ring or nothing to offer you, Grace, but I want to ask you if you'll promise to marry me, whenever we can. Gracie – will you promise to be my wife?'

Grace could almost hear the thudding of her own heart. She couldn't seem to speak. Did she love Jimmy? Her pal, Jimmy Oval – familiar as the skin on her own arm. They had played out along Archibald Street from the earliest she could remember – marbles and jackstones on the blue-brick pavements of home, tearing along the entries in games of tag, skinning their knees . . . They had grown up together.

But *marriage* and all that meant? Already? And yet . . . Who did she think she was – superior in some way to sweet, loving Jimmy Oval from across the street? Could there ever be any better man?

She was full of such a confusion of feelings that the word that first popped out was, 'No!' She instantly felt terrible, seeing his injured expression. 'What I mean is . . . I can't marry you, Jimmy – not you or anyone. I don't mean there's anyone else, I just . . . You know, not now – with the war and everything . . .'

'All right.' She could see he felt terribly rejected and hurt. He got to his feet, deflated. 'I s'pose that's . . . Yeah. All right. But could we be promised – engaged, like? I want to know you're my girl.'

'I – I am, Jimmy,' she said carefully. 'But let's leave it at that, eh? No big announcements?'

Grace felt terrible. He looked so upset that she almost let a 'Yes' slip out just to make him happy, while she was filled with crazed panic at the very idea of being married.

What's the matter with me? she thought desperately. Every girl was supposed to want to get married, for it to be the main thing on their mind. What else was there? She could be like Mom – or be a nun, or an old maid, a bit queer in the head like Nelly Flaherty in the parish, God love her?

Jimmy was almost the only man she had ever known closely; Jimmy, son of Mildred and Arthur Oval, people as familiar as her own limbs, kindly and good. But wasn't love supposed to be more of a thrill – of finding someone, in an exciting way instead of something that would feel more like marrying a familiar pair of old shoes?

She pushed those unkind thoughts away and tried to be as nice to him as she could, because no one deserved it more. And, now they were in the middle of a war, what if something terrible were to happen and she had sent him away rejected?

'You're my hero, Jimmy. I think it's really brave, you joining up and everything. So, let's not rush things – eh?'

He looked down tenderly at her, trying to get over his disappointment. 'God, I love you, Grace. You always was the sensible one. If I know you're mine, I can wait for – well, for ages, like.'

He put his arms round her again, in a passionate embrace. 'Give us a kiss, Grace,' he murmured. 'I've missed you summat terrible.'

'Not here, Jimmy!' she giggled.

'Why not? No one's taking any notice – they'm all doing the same!'

They kissed and cuddled for a few moments and it was nice being held and wrapping her arms round him, this boy, his cheeks smelling of Lifebuoy. Grace felt a pang. Jimmy going away had been like losing part of her childhood. Nothing felt the same any more. But the thing she had found hardest to admit was that it had also been a relief.

And now – now these terrible raids had started, she knew she was going to do something instead of sitting there night after night – she had to get out and join up, be part of it like so many other people of her age.

Seven

Violet had been telling fibs to her mother for so long that she hardly thought of it as lying. It was just something she had to do to get by.

When she first told a lie, she was four. One bright summer afternoon, with nothing to do, she had drifted up the stairs, putting her hands as well as her feet on each narrow, splintery tread. Instead of going to her own room she went into her mother's bedroom and pulled open the bottom drawer of her mother's chest of drawers, looking for something to entertain her. Among Mom's few bits of clothes – two much-darned cardigans, an old blouse, some lisle stockings – she saw a cardboard box.

The box looked old, its corners beginning to cleave apart, but it was covered in paper with a pattern of faded pink roses with a scrolling gold ribbon across it. To Violet it looked so beautiful – as if she had stumbled upon a treasure trove!

Sitting cross-legged and contented with the box beside her, she took out all the bits and pieces. As well as the papers and certificates with grown-up print and swirly handwriting which she left in a messy pile beside her on the floor, she found a gold ring with a string of green beads twined round it. There was a tobacco tin that rattled when she shook it, but her little fingers could not prise it open.

Best of all, there were a few photographs. She found a picture of a baby which she knew must be her. The others were pictures of a man and a woman getting married. They were standing outside a church. In one, she saw her mother, so small and pretty, with little curls of hair peeping out from under a white veil and a lacy dress like a princess. She was arm in arm with a man with a narrow face and dark, shiny hair. In the other picture, there was the church but this time the little woman – her face looked pinched and different – wore a long, straight coat. The man was tall, with a thick beard. That must be my father, Violet thought, peering at the pictures, although the beard made him look very different and she could not make out anyone's features clearly.

'What d'you think you're doing?'

She nearly jumped out of her skin as Mom's voice slithered, snake-like, across the floor. A chill took hold of her, her heart pounding painfully hard. She knew she had done something unforgivably wrong. There was nothing she could do to cover up her wicked trespass, so she just sat, staring at Mom's terrifying expression.

May walked slowly across to Violet and squatted down. Violet saw her mother's face suddenly alter, as if she had calculated something. Her tone changed completely.

'I don't like you going through my things, Violet.' Her voice was sweet, sickly. 'You're never to do that again, d'you understand?'

Violet nodded dumbly, frightened by the emotions that seemed to be coiled up tight in her mother.

'So – you found the pictures, did you?'

Carefully she tugged them from Violet's hands.

'See . . .' She pointed to the one of the princess dress and the small, clean-shaven man. 'That's me and your father, the day we got married. That was your daddy – you see?'

53

Violet stared at the faded face of the man with his clipped hair. The picture was small and hard to make out. But she could see that the pretty woman was Mom.

'And this one's of my friend Olive with her man friend. Olive and me used to work together. She was my best friend – everyone said we looked like sisters.'

She looked into Violet's eyes very intently. And Violet knew she must nod. But she also knew, somehow, that something about this was wrong and that in nodding she was telling an untruth. Because surely Mom had been in both pictures? And was Mom telling a fib as well? But almost immediately she could not remember properly: she must have made a mistake. And Mom had snatched everything away and was putting it all back in the box.

Sometimes, when she thought about this later, she could not decide what she remembered. None of the images had stayed clearly in her head and maybe it had been the same man and two different women, or perhaps they were in fact two different couples and she had got it wrong. One day when Mom was in the shop, she sneaked up to have another look.

Creeping up the stairs she found her heart pounding with a strange kind of terror. But when she opened the drawer, the box had gone and was nowhere to be found.

They had lived at number three Archibald Street, back of twenty-four, for as long as she could remember.

May Simms got along well enough with the neighbours back then. Mr and Mrs Baker across the yard had always been kind to her and had given her a lot of support when she turned up, a desperate young widow with a baby girl in her arms. Mrs Baker was a naturally kind lady and seemed able to see past May's awkwardness and sense of superiority which could rub other people up the wrong way.

But when she at last took over the business from Mr Quinn, it was in May's interest to be civil to all the people who came into the shop, even if she would have liked to turn her nose up at them and their humble, malodorous bundles of belongings. Even at her poorest she had tried to look her best. She would stand at the scullery mirror, putting on bright red lipstick and rubbing her lips together.

'It's my one extravagance,' she'd say, turning her head this way and that. 'I deserve a few good things in my life. Not that I care tuppence what you think anyway, you rotten old sod.' Violet never knew for years who she was talking to when she said that. But she realized later it was Mom's own father she must be addressing.

'He was a miserable, cruel man,' she told Violet. 'Ground my poor mother into an early grave. He'd fall out with his own shadow, my father would.'

Both grandparents had died some time back and Violet never met them.

In front of everyone else she was sweet as pie to Violet, and a good mother when it came to feeding and clothing. It was just behind closed doors that she came out in her true colours, always fearful, taking out her frustrations in rages, or just sitting for hours staring at nothing, smoking, sometimes having mysterious, fierce and one-sided conversations with other people who weren't there.

Every so often, she would sink into a bout of crying and complaining – about how terrible men were, about how hard her life was, how she'd never wanted a girl clinging round her ankles.

'You'd at least be some use if you were a boy – why did I have to get saddled with you?'

Most of the time Violet just closed her mind to it all. She was used to it. So Mom had wanted a boy, not her – what was she supposed to do about it?

And Mom had been all over Mrs Baker's youngest boy, Don, who was three years older than Violet. She always made a fuss of him, even gave him little gifts on his birthday. Violet could never understand all this because Mom was forever saying that men were 'wicked, filthy deceivers' and such like and she couldn't stand them. And if one thing was certain it was that that was what little Don Baker was going to turn into, however angelic he might look now.

Violet really started telling fibs when she went to school, because that was when the questions began. It was just before Mrs Quinn fell ill and Mom went to work for Mr Quinn. At that time, she had been forced into doing factory work because the money was better, starting early in the morning. Violet walked to and from school in Little Green Lane on her own.

She would get home before Mom, but as soon as May set foot through the door, it would start.

'Who did you speak to? Did you come straight home?'

'No one. Yes.' Which was the truth then anyway. Where did Mom think she was going to go? Even as she grew older, Mom didn't like her having friends – 'rough children' – or going out anywhere. She didn't go out herself – no clubs or church or anything, even though Mrs Baker tried to get her to go to chapel with her. So when Violet made some pals at school and wanted to play with them, she had to invent stories about what she'd done since she got home, hide the fact that she played out with anyone else, except here in the yard, where none of the other children were her age.

'Why d'you keep asking me?' Violet asked her once. Mom was at the table, a cigarette in one hand.

'It's a wicked world out there,' she said, flicking ash into a saucer. 'I want you where I can see you.'

One afternoon in the classroom when she was seven, Miss Holt, her teacher, loomed over the cramped double desk where she and a little lad sat side by side.

Violet started to tremble. It would have been impossible to say how old Miss Holt was. She was tall and stiff-looking. She wore very long coats when she was outside and swept along like some almost mythical figure. Surely it must be Michael who had done something wrong?

'You will stay behind after class this afternoon, Violet.'

It wasn't as if you could argue. Miss Holt never needed to dish out punishment like many teachers did, in the form of stinging strokes of a ruler on your soft, baby palms. She managed to scare the wits out of you without it. Violet spent the rest of the afternoon queasy with dread. What had she done? Whatever it was, why didn't Miss Holt say so there and then?

When everyone else had gone and Violet was left, sitting like a deserted island in a sea of empty desks, Miss Holt beckoned her to the front. She managed to scramble down off the little bench, legs shaking as she walked to the front to stand looking up at Miss Holt.

'I wanted to show you this book,' Miss Holt said, turning her grey, drill-like eyes upon Violet.

It was still not clear if this was a punishment or a treat. Miss Holt sounded equally severe whatever she was talking about. Violet's eyes flickered nervously towards the hands of the classroom clock. She was going to be late home.

'Your reading is quite advanced for a child of your age,' Miss Holt said. 'Now, I have this special book – it's a collection of fairy tales. I know you have no brothers and sisters so it should be easy to keep it safe. I wondered if you would like to borrow it? You may bring it back to me in, let's say, a week.'

Violet saw that the book had a lovely picture on the front – she could just make out a maiden with long, flowing hair standing by some blue water. There was gold in the curling lettering as well. It looked a beautiful book and she wanted it desperately. But what would Mom say?

'I don't know.' She could hardly get the words out.

Miss Holt gave a dry laugh. 'What do you mean, you don't know?'

Violet stared desperately at her. How could she explain that anything that happened at home, any change, anything even a bit different, might cause her trouble?

'I think I'll have to ask my mother.' Tears came into her eyes because she wanted to hold the book so badly, but she knew better than to take it home.

Miss Holt looked closely at her. Though appearing such an unbending sort, she seemed to understand something.

'All right,' she said. 'In that case, you may tell me tomorrow.'

As soon as she got to Quinn's, Violet saw the look in her mother's eye, even though she was barely ten minutes late. Once they were alone in the house her mother turned on her, delivering stinging slaps on her bare legs. It was one of those times when Mom went a bit mad and she looked terrifying.

'Where've you been?'

'Nowhere,' Violet said. 'Miss Holt kept me in after school.'

'So – you've been playing up at school!' Her mother's face hardened even further. 'What did you do?'

'No . . .' Violet swallowed down tears, her cheeks stinging. 'She wanted to borrow me a book – about fairies. She said I could bring it home and I said I'd ask you. Can I . . . ?'

May stood back, hands on hips, a sneer on her face. 'Your teacher decided to give you a book! What, that dried-up old bitch Miss Holt? Why the hell would she ask *you*, eh, you skinny little rat?'

She pounced, grabbing Violet's hair and twisting her round by it. 'Don't you lie to me. Where've yer been? What was you doing?'

Violet cried out, her scalp burning with pain. 'She did – she's gorra book!'

Her mother twisted her hair even further. Staring up at the scabby ceiling, scalp burning and her neck jerked back, Violet thought, But I'm telling the truth. And she saw it made no difference.

When she dared to take the book home, Mom never even looked at it. Violet spent a week keeping it pushed right under her bed. The moment she could, she would sit drinking in all the stories about fairies and wicked stepmothers and fantastical kingdoms under the sea.

There was an inscription in the front in a curling, ornate hand: 'For dear Jocelyn, Christmas 1886, with love from Auntie Sarah.' Jocelyn, Violet found out later, was the name of Miss Holt's older sister, another Miss Holt; they lived together further along Archibald Street, the very same street that she lived in. Jocelyn was not as tall as Miss Holt and she was a plumper, softer-looking person. And the book was magical.

When she handed it back to Miss Holt, her teacher told her she was allowed to go and get a ticket to borrow a book at the library. Small Heath Library, an ornate brick building with a round tower jutting into the junction between two streets almost like the prow of a ship, was on her way home from school. And Mom couldn't argue with where she had been when she saw the stamp in the front of the books.

Violet found other worlds to live in. Worlds where there were fairy godmothers to take over from wicked stepmothers and make everything all right.

And when it came to it, after two nights of having to sit with Mom during those raids, her own lie about the ARP slipped from her tongue with hardly a thought.

Eight

Tuesday 15 October

'Vi! Hang on – wait for me!'

Violet, a bag of nerves, was standing outside their ARP Post F, at number sixty-one Archibald Street. Seeing Grace tearing down the road towards her, her bright hair flying out behind, she felt a rush of excitement. Grace Templeton, who she had met on the training course, who was so pretty, so outgoing that she got along with everyone – and, most astonishingly of all, seemed to be happy to be her friend!

She waited, a grin spreading across her face. Volunteering for the ARP already felt like the best thing she'd ever done, but now she was terrified at the thought of meeting the other wardens. They were surely mostly older people and would think she was just a kid, wet behind the ears, who couldn't do anything. She looked in awe at Miss Holt's house, shored up with sandbags along the front and the two miskin lids hung from hooks on the wall for dealing with incendiary bombs. A large sign, screwed to the brickwork, read:

YOUR LOCAL WARDENS' POST
INFORMATION CONCERNING
ARP

This was really it now!

'God,' Grace panted, charging up to number sixty-one, her pink-faced fluster apparent even in the dying light. 'I thought I'd never flaming get away today – it's been non-stop! I've not had time to change – d'you think they've got uniforms for us yet?'

'I hope so!' Violet looked down at her little skirt and blouse and laughed. 'I can't see anyone taking any notice of me in this!'

'Our very own tin hats!' Grace said.

'The height of fashion!'

'Well – it is, in the middle of a raid,' Grace pointed out as they both giggled out of nerves.

In fact, since they'd begun their training, there had not been any raids as heavy as those at the end of August, but of course you never knew when it was all going to start again.

'Especially with you in your lipstick.' Violet could see that however much of a rush Grace had been in, her lips were still painted a cherry red. In a pretend affected voice, she said, 'Latest style in Small Heath, Birmingham!'

'You're a good mimic you are,' Grace said. 'We've got to wear gum boots an' all. God, I've never felt so glamorous . . . Anyway, kid – this is it.'

Sobering up they looked at the little two-up, two-down house. On a post, fixed in front of the sandbags, a black sign was painted with a white clock-face with move-able hands and lettering on it: 'BLACKOUT TIME TONIGHT IS AT . . .' The clock hands had been moved to 6.20.

'You ready?'

'As I'll ever be,' Violet said. Thank heavens she had Grace to walk in with. She really didn't think she could have managed it on her own. 'Can't be late the first day, can we? Miss Holt'll have our guts for garters!'

Violet had recognized Grace when they arrived for training in King's Norton, though she was not sure where from. They were in a group all starting their training and they had a whole lot of paraphernalia to learn about – stirrup pumps and buckets of sand and gas rattles. They were shown protective suits and masks in case of gas attacks, and how to cut someone's clothing off to be burned if they had suffered in such an attack. Thinking about it all was truly frightening.

She was really intimidated by Grace at first. She was a year older and seemed so pretty and sure of herself, where Violet felt like hiding away in the corner, not knowing what to say to people. Amid all the crowd that were there in the echoing, musty-smelling school hall, she was surprised when Grace came up to her on the first night, a smile on her face.

'You're from up our end somewhere, aren't yer? I've seen you before.'

Fancy her remembering me! Violet thought. She had recognized Grace by sight, but she felt such a mousey little four-eyes herself that she didn't expect anyone ever to notice her. She was encouraged by the fact that Grace seemed so friendly, not stuck up or superior just because she was pretty, like some girls were.

'You from Archibald Street? Or Herbert? Round there somewhere?'

'Yes,' Violet said, going pink. 'Top of Archibald. I've seen you around.' She was still trying to place the girl. It was a long street, so you saw all sorts going up and down. 'I don't remember you from school, though.'

'Ah, no – we went to the Holy Family,' Grace said. 'All nine of us!'

Catholics, Violet thought. Best not tell Mom that – she didn't like anyone who was different.

'Nine!' she said. 'I can't imagine it. I grew up on my own.'

'A bed all to yourself! Sounds like bliss to me.' Grace laughed so infectiously that Violet found herself grinning. She started to relax. 'I'd miss the little sods if they weren't around, though – they're all younger than me. I thought about joining the ATS but I didn't feel I could just go off and leave our mom to it.'

Despite Grace's friendliness, Violet had been shy of her for a long time. She seemed so glamorous with her make-up and her gorgeous head of hair. Even without any slap on she was just so lovely-looking, with those cornflower-blue eyes, her strong cheekbones and curvaceous figure. Violet found it hard to believe that someone like Grace would ever really want to make friends with her.

But they saw each other on every training night, learning about patrolling their sector, enforcing blackout regulations, about First Aid in the form of bandaging and tourniquets and dressings, about snuffing out incendiary bombs with sand and stirrup pumps to tackle fires. And then there was all the paperwork – labels to be written out, reports made. There was so much to learn and so many leaflets containing information from so many government departments that sometimes she felt as if her head was going to burst.

The two of them would travel home together. Even on the tram along the Bristol Road, Grace would sometimes start humming something, not caring who heard. She was full of chat and they shared a lot of laughs about things that had happened in their training. She was lively and infectious and Violet felt like a little brown bird next to something colourful and exotic. But it gradually dawned on Violet as the weeks went by, that Grace did not see her as the inferior person she felt in comparison. Grace was a truly nice and friendly girl and that was all there was to it.

'Come in and say hello to our mom,' she would say sometimes when they finally got back to Archibald Street. 'I've told her all about you.'

Have you? Violet thought, startled. After all, what was there to tell? So far, she had made excuses. If she was late, she'd have Mom's resentment to deal with. And she couldn't ask Grace home in return. Asking people to her house was just not something she ever did.

But she and Grace knew that sooner or later they would likely be working together back at home. And by the time they met again for their first proper night on duty, they were already beginning to feel like friends.

'It feels really peculiar going in here,' Violet said, eyeing the door of number sixty-one. Miss Holt's house felt like forbidden territory. She'd already told Grace that Miss Holt had been her teacher at Green Lane School.

'Rather you than me,' Grace said. 'I know who you mean – she looks a bit of a tartar!'

'She's not all bad,' Violet said. She thought of that day, the lovely book. 'She used to live with her sister, but she died a couple of years ago.'

The door was ajar so they tapped on it and stepped into Miss Holt's front room. To Violet's relief it seemed to be quiet inside. The light was on and looking round, Violet saw a place of brown linoleum, shabby but service-able furniture, and some limp nets at the window. Miss

Holt was not a woman for frills, though there was one elegant piece in the room: a well-polished little sideboard with mirrors in its doors, and a white, embroidered runner laid carefully along the top. There was a small vase of dried lavender standing on it and Violet could smell its faint mustiness.

'Ah, Violet!' Miss Holt appeared from the back. 'I see you are one of us now. Splendid! How are you?'

'I'm all right, thank you, Miss Holt,' she said. She felt immediately like a small child again. Since leaving that school she had scarcely had anything to do with Miss Holt until the raids started and she had come to their house. Her old teacher looked even more severe these days; her face was thinner, the lines more deeply etched, and her gaze was still just as piercing. Violet was filled with a momentary urge to turn and run, and had to remind herself that Miss Holt was, in her stiff way, quite kindly.

'Glad to hear it,' Miss Holt said. She looked at Grace. 'And you must be Grace Templeton? Well, at least you two have made good time – the others will be along with their own rather unpredictable timing, I imagine. Even Mr Powell has not arrived yet – he has further to come, of course. Come on, dears – I've got the kettle on.'

Dears? Violet thought. But it was nice. Stiff old Miss Holt was trying her best. She wondered, with another nervous plunge of her innards, about the other wardens. She knew who Mr Oval was, of course, but what would the rest of them be like?

'So,' Miss Holt explained, after rattling about with cups, 'the back of the house is assigned to the wardens, as you can see.'

Violet looked around her. The floor was covered in worn, grey linoleum. There was a table which had been moved to one side with some tidily ranked papers and a large black telephone, beside which lay a wooden gas rattle. On the wall behind had been stuck typed pages of lists. The shelves on the opposite wall held Miss Holt's humble crocks and what seemed to be a collection of games, packs of cards and little wooden boxes. And in one corner, on a row of nails, was a collection of steel helmets. Her eyes met Grace's for a moment and they each suppressed a smile. Beneath the helmets was a cupboard and, leaning up against that, a stirrup pump and bucket.

'Our post for watching the street is in my bedroom at the front, upstairs,' Miss Holt was saying. 'For the purpose of the war effort I have moved my bed into the box room at the back. After all, there's not a lot of point in a warden's post if we do not have a view of the street. There are several camp beds. Depending on how things are going, we take turns in spending the night here. We have to shift as best we can.'

She was pouring more water into the teapot.

'We'll have some tea and once the others deign to arrive, we will check all our equipment and take turns patrolling our sector until midnight.' She looked Violet and Grace up and down. 'We must make sure you are supplied with uniforms – we do at least have a spare "tin hat" for each of you.'

'Can we try them on?' Grace said, to Violet's astonishment. She was smiling at Miss Holt and who could resist Grace?

'I don't see why not – here, try these for size.'

Miss Holt lifted two steel helmets from the hooks and handed them one each. Violet took the black helmet with its white W painted on the front, feeling suddenly honoured. She pressed it on to her head.

'Ouch! The top's really hard!' The helmet seemed to be made for someone twice her size and it slipped about.

Grace pressed hers on to her thick hair. Miss Holt helped them adjust the chin straps and the two of them stood grinning at each other.

'You look like the real thing, Vi!' Grace laughed.

'So do you!'

'These are for the raids,' Miss Holt said. 'I know they're not very comfortable but given what comes raining down, they are necessary. The rest of the time you can wear these when in uniform.'

She held up a peaked hat made of cloth.

'Are there uniforms for us?' Grace asked.

'Yes – we should be able to kit you out.' She looked them up and down again. Violet was in the old skirt and blouse she wore to work, but Grace had a dress on in a deep shade of blue which hugged her curves. 'And boots – depending on your size. I may not have everything for you today . . . I'll get the rest as soon as I can.' Opening the cupboard where the helmets had been hanging she brought out several pairs of dark blue trousers. 'You can slip these on over your clothes for now.'

Violet and Grace both got the giggles seeing each other, Grace with her frock stuffed down inside the trousers and Violet with her blouse tucked into a pair so voluminous that she had to pin the waist and roll the legs up.

'Oh, my word, look at you!' Grace laughed so hard that tears rolled down her cheeks. Even Miss Holt joined it. 'You look like a clown! I bet that Herr Hitler'd be terrified if he saw us!'

'You will have learned what to look out for as you patrol the sector,' Miss Holt said as they sipped their tea. 'Breaches of the blackout, people wandering about, anyone in need of assistance. Of course, if there's a raid on, get everyone under cover, check the shelters as well as the blackout. Mr Powell has the lists of who is where, whether anyone's away for the night . . . After midnight if there's no raid, we can all get some sleep – with turns being taken to watch the street.'

Sitting very upright on her chair, she sipped her tea and said reflectively, 'They have been giving the poor Londoners a bad time lately – and Merseyside, of course. We've had what you might call a bit of a lull.' After another sip of tea, she added, 'We can only hope it lasts.'

Nine

A few houses away across the street, Mildred Oval swooped down on the table around which her family were tightly packed, to lay upon it a huge pie which was met with 'ooh's and 'aah's of appreciation.

'What's in there, Mother?' her husband Arthur asked.

Mildred laughed. 'Don't ask and I won't tell,' she said, her pink face, beaded with perspiration, beaming round at her family.

Mildred, in her mid-forties, was solidly built, with a wide girth, thick legs and ankles in brown lisle stockings. Her greying-brown hair was smoothed back over her ears into a bun and she wore an apron tied over her frock and stout, brown shoes. She was a big-hearted soul, never idle, and the back room where the family were eating was brightened by the presence of blankets and antimacassars on the two armchairs in bright colours, all crocheted by Mildred's busy fingers.

'Well, it won't be bacon, I suppose,' Arthur said pessimistically. Bacon, butter and cheese were now on the ration and they had had to get used to using ration books with vouchers in to get their weekly shares, along with all the other changes.

'There's a bit of mince and a lot of veg,' Mildred said. She plunged her big knife through the golden crust.

'Which means potatoes,' Sylvie said sceptically. 'Yum. Potato pie.'

'There's a lot more in there than just spud,' her mother corrected her. 'Look at the dog!'

Ginger, their old reddish-brown mongrel, was sitting to attention, her nose questing meat scents in the air.

'Now,' Mildred lowered herself on to her chair. 'Let's set to – your father's got to go out.' Importantly, she added, 'He's on duty tonight.'

The pie – veins of mince, potatoes, carrot and onion well laced with gravy browning and herbs – was soon distributed with cabbage. Mildred squeezed into her place at the table. Beside her was Mark, a fireman. It still felt odd without his twin brother Luke, who, like Jimmy the eldest, had gone into the army. All through their boyhood the twins had been like the two handles of a cup, but they were standing on their own two feet more now, going their own ways. Next to Mark was Sylvie, seventeen, then Charlie fifteen, both out at work, and twelve-year-old Dolly, a sweet-faced girl with wide eyes and long brown hair like her mother's. She was the only one who might have been evacuated, being of school age, and Mildred had flatly refused.

'Sending the wench off away from everyone she knows or's dear to her! I'd never dream of such a thing. Our Dolly's stopping here with the rest of us, whatever the government says!'

And then there was little John, seven, who Mildred cosseted and guarded with a tiger's passion. John was born with twisted legs and never thrived very well. He could say a few words with effort, and everyone made a fuss of him. All his days were spent in the house with Mildred. His was the only blond hair in the family, since all the others were some shade of middling brown like each of their parents. He was the worry of his mother's life.

'How will he manage when we're gone, Arthur?'

Mildred had said, over and over, all his young life. 'I can't stand to think of our little lad without us to look out for him.'

And there was no easy answer.

With Jimmy and Luke gone there was a bit more elbow room at the table. Jimmy's brief letters, like Luke's, were propped on the mantelpiece behind Mildred's favourite china jug and she fretted about them constantly.

'I gather it's our Grace's first night on?' she said to her husband. They had been pleased and proud to hear that Grace had decided to volunteer and would be joining Arthur and the others at ARP Post F in Archibald Street. They had known her since she was a child and already thought of her more or less as a daughter-in-law.

'Oh, ar . . .' Arthur attempted, any more expansive opinions he might have offered being impeded by the ingestion of pie.

'I don't know,' Mildred sighed, staring into her plate. 'I wish Grace and Jimmy had got on and got wed, the way things are. He said she wanted to wait, and . . . Well, I don't know . . .'

'Maybe she thinks he might get killed?' Sylvie suggested, with callous matter-of-factness.

'Sylvie!' Mildred said.

'For pity's sake, Sylv,' Mark admonished her.

'Poor Jimmy . . .' Dolly looked stricken. She was already a pale child and she'd been suffering with her nerves since the raids started.

'I dain't mean . . .' Sylvie slumped sorrowfully in her seat. But thinking about it, that *was* what she had meant and there was no way out of it. 'Sorry, Mom.'

'Well, I hope our Grace'll be all right with all that crew they've got there,' Mildred persevered, seizing the opportunity as Arthur swallowed.

72

'Oh – 'er's a good'un,' Arthur said. 'You know our Grace – 'er's got a lot of common sense, like . . . Won't take any nonsense. She's headstrong, though, I'll say that. And there's that other little wench coming an' all.'

'May Simms's girl?' Mildred said. 'About time that woman let her out on her own account.'

'Violet?' Sylvie was very interested in all these goings-on and wanted to be old enough to join in – though this would not be the case for some months yet.

'Funny little thing. Nice kid but quiet as a mouse,' Arthur said. 'That mother's a tartar from what I gather. Not that you'd think so to look at her, tiny little thing.' He looked puzzled for a moment. 'According to some, 'er rules that wench with a rod of iron. But knowing our Grace, 'er'll sort of take 'er under 'er wing. Just as well with all the blokes we've got – not all with the best of manners, I must say.'

He scooped the last of his cabbage and gravy on to his fork as if it was a challenge to be met.

'There's a roly-poly,' Mildred said, warningly.

'Ooh, smashing!' Charlie said. At fifteen, he could eat for England.

'Oh, dear – not sure I can manage that as well,' Arthur said. 'I'm s'posed to be fit for this job. Mind you, I feel quite spry next to one of the old fellers they've got at Post D –'e can hardly get hisself along the road. Sounds like a pair of busted bellows every time he moves . . .'

'There's a bit of jam in it,' Mildred said. This was always the clincher.

'Custard?' Arthur dared to venture.

'Custard.'

He looked at the clock, its pendulum swinging noisily on the mantel. An inner struggle appeared to take place.

'Well – I've got ten minutes. Just a crumb or two, wench.'

At one minute to six – since the walk to the post was a matter of about thirty seconds – Arthur picked up his steel ARP helmet, which he insisted on bringing home with him, pulled his coat on and turned to the family. John waved an arm, grinning. Arthur went over and put his hand on the little boy's head.

'You'll be asleep when I get back, son. Night all – see you in the morning.' As one of the daytime factory workers, he was allowed to come home by midnight.

Mildred got up and kissed Arthur as if he was setting off on a long journey. 'Bye, love. Quiet night.'

'May there be many,' Arthur said solemnly. 'See yer later, my wench.'

Ten

'So this is tonight's motley crew, is it?' Arthur Oval said, looking round at them all as he walked in.

Violet knew Arthur by sight, of course. You couldn't not like Arthur and she found him reassuring. He must have been in his late fifties, Violet guessed, with thinning, steel-grey hair slicked across his head, a fleshy face and barrel-like body in his blue warden's uniform, the red ARP badge sewn above his heart.

'Dear God,' he declared, looking Grace and Violet up and down. 'What hope've we got against the might of the Hun?'

He grinned then. 'All right, Gracie – got here at last, I see!'

Grace blushed and Violet smiled. Mr Oval was known by just about everybody in Archibald Street – he and his wife Mildred. They were kind, neighbourly people and Mildred was often seen pushing their little crippled lad, John, out in his wheelchair. Violet had soon picked up that Grace was very close with their son Jimmy, who was away in the army.

'And who's this then?' Arthur Oval said. 'I know that face, don't I? Young Miss Simms, i'n't it?'

'Violet,' she said shyly. 'I live up the top – at Quinn's.'

'Oh, ar – I know, bab,' Mr Oval said. 'Course I do.'

It was not Arthur who was in charge of this section post, but Mr Powell, a tall, reserved, softly spoken man who used to work at Lloyds Bank. He was already installed behind the 'desk', Miss Holt's table, pushed over to one side of the room. His almost bald head with the grey, straggling remains of hair – he had an equally straggly moustache – was already bent conscientiously over his lists: who was on duty and who lived where in their part of the sector; who was away; the telephone numbers for the control centre; the First Aid posts; the Ambulance and Fire Service . . .

A moment later they heard footsteps and Violet saw a young man stride in with swaggering energy, slightly bandy-legged, a cigarette dangling at one side of his mouth. He had black hair, glossy with Brylcreem, and dark, darting eyes in a thin, almost foxy face. Violet felt immediately uncomfortable. She wasn't used to men – not men like this one, anyway. Mom would have a fit if she thought Violet was hanging about with someone like this. The thought almost made her giggle.

'All right?' he said jauntily, half-closing his eyes as he dragged on his cigarette.

'All right, Reggie,' Arthur said.

'Ah.' Mr Powell looked up, then leaned to tick off his roster. 'Reggie . . .' Tick! 'Meakins.'

'All right, Mr Powell?' Reggie said. Violet couldn't decide whether he was mocking the man or being respectful. 'Oooh.' His eyes swept over the new recruits and settled, inevitably, and with intense interest, on Grace. 'Who've we got 'ere then?'

Introductions were made. Reggie nodded at Violet, but she saw how his eyes slid quickly over her to fasten back on to Grace. And while this was a relief because she found Reggie alarming, she shrank into the background and watched with some envy as Grace dealt with him.

'Grace, is it?' he said. 'Where've you sprung from then?'

Grace eyed him coyly. 'Under the gooseberry bush – where d'yer think?'

Reggie grinned, obviously enjoying being flirted with. 'And where exactly would that little bush be, eh?'

'Wouldn't you like to know?' Grace said.

Violet could see how much Grace was enjoying being pert and mysterious and Reggie was lapping it all up. She felt a pang of despair. How was she ever going to learn to deal with men? Because she *did* want to meet someone nice and fall in love and get married . . . She just had no idea how to go about any of it. What were you supposed to say? How did Grace do it all so easily? Sitting there with her hands clenched in her lap, she felt silly and dull. And she had a sad feeling that, much as she liked Grace, she was forever going to be in her shadow.

Reggie seemed set to launch into more questions when a scrawny, ghostly-pale young man arrived who was announced as Francis Paine. Violet knew him by sight as well. He worked for his father, who was an undertaker with premises at the top of the street. It was immediately obvious why Francis Paine had not been called up. He looked like an old man in a young man's body and suffered badly with asthma. He was also chronically shy and couldn't look at Grace or Violet at all as they were introduced. He had come in a black trilby which looked too big for his skinny neck and he hugged it to his chest and gave a little bow, almost as if greeting a hearse.

'Who's not 'ere yet then?' Mr Oval said.

'Mr Molyneaux?' Reggie piped up, stirring sugar into his tea. He pronounced it 'Molly-noo' and with such a look of mischief that they couldn't help smiling. Violet heard the whispery noise of Francis Paine's lungs as he stood close to her. She felt prickly with shyness at

77

meeting all these people, but Grace was already holding her own with everyone.

'Now, now,' Mr Oval rebuked fondly. To Grace and Violet, he said, with a touch of irony, 'Mr Molly-noo is an *actor*!'

'Or so he would wish us to think,' Miss Holt said, vigorously tipping grouts out of the teapot on to a scrap of newspaper. 'He is an enthusiastic amateur – rather more of his time is in fact spent at S. U. Carburettors on the Warwick Road.'

And as if entering from a cue on stage, another young man came charging in, his hair collar-length, top button undone with a little red scarf tied in the neck of it, wearing trousers of some sort of murky tweed.

'Hail, this blessed eve, fellow survivors of the fray!' he announced (no dramatic opportunity, it appeared, ever wasted). He stood at the centre of the room, moving his hands expressively in front of him. 'Never – *never*, have I had such a day of it . . .'

'Well, now yer gunna 'ave a night of it an' all,' Mr Oval remarked, unimpressed. 'Get yourself ready, lad.'

Violet and Grace exchanged glances. Violet could see the twinkle of laughter in her friend's eyes.

'Ah – now who do we have here?' the latest arrival asked. The presence of two young women was obviously a pleasant novelty for them.

There were more hurried introductions and then Mr Oval said, 'And you want to get yerself 'ere on time, lad. This ain't a rehearsal any more. It's like Mr Churchill said – we don't require no continental tyrants coming over 'ere and taking over. So – get yerself together, lad, punctual like the rest of us.'

'Now – first patrol,' Miss Holt was saying, when the

telephone started ringing. Everyone's eyes fixed on it immediately, as Mr Powell answered it in his solemn way.

'All right,' he said. 'Thank you.'

He looked at them over his half-moon glasses, seeming frozen for a second. 'Purple alert.'

'Really?' Miss Holt said. 'Did we have a yellow . . . ?'

Violet's mind was racing back over her training. The different-coloured alerts – white, no prospect of enemy action; yellow, precautionary; purple, prospect of enemy aircraft . . .

'All right, everyone – get ready,' Miss Holt said.

'Does this mean . . . ?' Grace said, her eyes wide.

'Yes, it flaming does!' Reggie said excitedly. 'Dain't they teach you anything over there?'

They all scrambled to get ready, Violet and Grace straining to remember their training rehearsals. They might have had only half a uniform but everything else necessary was there: shoulder bag with first-aid kit, gas masks, sturdy rubber boots, a stirrup pump and gas rattle, notebook – and the steel helmets.

Violet sat hers on her head again and Grace did the same.

'We will now model the modish ARP tin hats!' Grace said, giving a twirl.

Violet's stomach was churning. 'I s'pose this means we have to actually do it now! I've forgotten everything!'

'Me too!' Grace said.

The telephone rang again.

'Right. Yes,' Mr Powell said. He looked up, replacing the receiver. 'Red alert.'

The air-raid siren's chilling yowl rose into the night. Everyone seemed frozen for a second. The unearthly howl of it made Violet's body go into thumping overdrive so that she felt suddenly sick.

'In pairs – off we go,' Mr Oval instructed.

'Grace – let's go together,' Violet said quickly.

'No,' Miss Holt said. 'You need to go with people who know the sector.' The others were already heading out of the door.

'They'll be all right,' Arthur Oval said. 'They know this street like the back of their hands.'

'All right,' Miss Holt said reluctantly. 'You both stay in Archibald Street. Off you go!'

Eleven

'Talk about in at the deep end,' Violet said, following Grace out into the wailing racket. 'Oh, dear – my mom! I hope she's gone to the shelter this time.'

May, despite much complaint about being left alone and about Violet's general selfishness, had felt forced to agree to going into the shelter.

'My lot'll be running down the garden,' Grace said.

For a moment they stood out in the dark street, paralysed. Doing things when you were in training was one thing. What the hell do we do now? Violet thought. Fingers of light jittered overhead as the searchlights raked the sky. A cold dread filled her as they heard the first planes approaching. Then a voice close to her ear nearly made her jump out of her skin.

'Put yer 'ead in on my old lady, will yer?' It was Arthur Oval. He was really talking to Grace and his face wore a grave expression, more frightening than the scream of the siren.

'Yes, Mr Oval,' Grace said. 'Course we will.' Arthur Oval hurried away.

'Oh, my . . .' Violet turned her face up as the sound built, and she saw the first of a wave of dark, arrow-like shadows approaching across the sky. 'Look!'

'Quick,' Grace started off along the street. 'We're s'posed to be making sure everyone's inside!'

'My legs feel like jelly!' Both of them were having almost to shout to hear one another. Although the sirens

81

had stopped, the ack-ack guns were hammering out from all around.

There were a good number of courts of back-to-back houses at the top end of the street, people they needed to check on who had no cellar or garden in which to put up a shelter.

They had just got up to that end when the first wave of planes came over. Incendiary bombs came clattering down from the roofs and Violet felt one roll away from her foot in the darkness. She was supposed to do something about putting it out, wasn't she? But then she heard its dying sputter. Soon the first explosions of high explosive bombs were audible in the distance.

She was about to ask what they should do when Grace grabbed her arm. 'Look, there's someone – over there . . .'

The street was otherwise clear of people, but at the shadowy edge of the opposite pavement, Violet also caught sight of a movement.

'Come on.' Grace pulled Violet by her coat sleeve.

They hurried across to find the tiny form of an elderly lady feeling her way along the street, a hand on the wall. Close up, Violet recognized her. She was a bent, kindly-faced little person who must be over eighty.

'Mrs Bright?' she called out, but the lady didn't seem to hear. There was nothing for it but to shout. 'MRS BRIGHT!'

'Yes, dear?' The lady turned, very calmly, as if this was an ordinary conversation in full daylight with nothing going on whatsoever.

Violet steeled herself. What was she supposed to say? It didn't seem right, giving orders to older people, but now that was her job and Grace did not seem to recognize old Mrs Bright.

'You really must get indoors,' she shouted. The first

wave was passing into the distance now, although the hammering guns made communication no less difficult.

'Are you going to a shelter somewhere?' Grace yelled. 'We can help you, if you like?'

'Oh, no.' Mrs Bright's tone implied that the two of them were suggesting something quite ridiculous. They strained to hear her well-spoken voice. 'I'm going to sit with Lucy.'

Violet and Grace exchanged looks in the gloom.

'I always sit with Lucy – she lives in there.' She pointed to the entry into a back court a short distance along the street. 'She can't leave her bed now, you see. And I shan't leave *her*.'

'But there's a raid on!' Grace protested.

They dithered, unsure what to do.

'You really should be in a shelter,' Violet tried again.

'Oh, Lucy and I will be all right.' Miss Bright had a little bag over her arm. 'I've got my knitting. Don't you worry – Lucy and I've known each other for fifty years. We'll be quite all right.'

And off she went. They really didn't feel they could argue and were left feeling rather foolish. This ARP business was tricky!

'Here's another lot,' Grace yelled as they reached the street once more.

As the whine of falling bombs alerted them to just how close the danger was, they flung themselves to the ground as a shuddering crash came from somewhere terrifyingly close.

Violet screwed her eyes tightly shut. Moments later she became aware that her nostrils were clogged and she pushed up from the ground, sitting up choking and gasping for breath. The smell was horrible – musty brick dust and plaster.

'Jesus, Mary and Joseph,' Grace spluttered.

Struggling to their feet, they saw how the light had changed. Flames were starting to reach above the buildings further along the street. From a distance they heard the tinkle of fire-engine bells.

Grace was up and running in a second. Violet knew immediately what was going through her mind. Our house! But the fire was further down, at the junction with Jenkins Street. Violet thought of her own mother. Had she made it to the shelter? But this came first. They had to go and help. She tore after Grace, eyes stinging and coughing from the smoke and dust in the air, glass from blasted windows crunching underfoot.

What looked like two houses had been demolished and in the light from the fires, a half-circle of people stood helplessly round, trying to approach the burning house but being forced back by the flames.

'Get under cover!' Grace bawled as the planes drew overhead. 'It's not over yet!'

'Get inside!' Violet joined in.

'Bugger that!' a man's voice said, frantic. 'That's the Warings' house – there's people in 'ere.'

A fire engine hurtled round the corner. As it braked and the men jumped out, Violet spotted Miss Holt's face in the crowd, stern as a statue, then Reggie Meakins, goggle-eyed under his helmet. She pulled Grace over towards them.

'Shall we check on the rest of the street, Miss Holt?' She had never shouted so much before in her life.

'Go and report to Mr Powell!' Miss Holt replied. 'Mr Meakins and I will do what we can here. He'll be incident officer on this one.'

They hurried back to Post F to give details to Mr Powell, then out on to the street again. They turned along an entry which Grace seemed to know well, and she pushed open the gate of the Ovals' little strip of garden. In the weird orange-tinged light they could make out the curved shaped of the shelter a few yards away.

'Mind you don't trip,' Grace said.

Violet followed her down a brick path next to a vegetable patch.

'Mrs Oval? It's Grace. Can you hear me?'

The makeshift door of the shelter swung open and they saw the round face and shawl-shrouded shoulders of Mrs Oval appear, a Tilley lamp in her hand.

'Grace?'

'Just leave the lamp inside,' Grace had the presence of mind to say.

'Oh, ar, I forgot.' Mildred Oval's voice was tremulous, as she turned to put the lamp down. When she stepped outside her voice was strong again. 'We're all right in 'ere, bab. What about my Arthur?'

'I think he's all right, Mrs Oval,' Grace said. 'We just came to check on all of you.'

Violet realized, with a pang, that in fact they had no idea whether Mr Oval was safe or not – they hadn't seen him since the raid began. As they spoke there came another huge bang somewhere quite close and she and Grace found themselves with their faces pressed into the side of Mr Oval's vegetable patch.

'Lord in heaven – are you girls all right?' Mrs Oval's muffled voice came to them after a few moments.

'We're all right.' Scrambling to her feet, Violet realized she really was all right even though it had sounded as if the sky itself was falling in and she had soil up her nostrils.

'That was close, that time,' Mrs Oval said tremulously. 'I wish Arthur was here – and our Jimmy.'

'Oh, I s'pect Jimmy's safer than we are,' Grace said, trying to be reassuring.

'Can't you come in and shelter with us?' Mildred Oval said. 'I can't stand to think of you girls out in all that.' She stood aside as if to usher them into the shelter. In the meagre lamplight, Violet caught sight of the benches on each side, lined with Oval children. Ovaltinies, she thought and had a hysterical urge to giggle.

'We can't – we're on duty,' Grace told her fondly. 'You stay safe inside, Mrs Oval – we'll see you soon.'

'Bye-bye then, Grace, love,' Mildred said bravely. 'Thanks for coming to see us.'

There was a lull as they hurried, coughing, up the street to Grace's house at number sixty-eight. Struggling to see in the weird, smoky gloom, Violet reminded herself to check that no one was showing a light or anything else that needed dealing with. She felt, constantly, that she didn't know what she was doing. Grace led her along the entry to their strip of garden, similar to that of the Ovals.

'Mom?' She pulled open the door of the shelter. It seemed to be full of boys. 'Are you all OK?'

'Grace, darlin'!' Her mother was holding Gordon, who was asleep despite everything. 'Oh, you're all right, thank the Lord! What about next door?'

'Yes, they're fine. The fire's down at the bottom end. Gotta go . . .' As they hurried back to the street she said, 'What about your mom?'

They turned into court six and crossed the yard to the low brick shelter, a cheerless bunker of a place. Nervously Violet pushed the door open and was assailed by the stench of stale bodies and the grating cry of a baby. A Tilley lamp burned in the middle. People were crammed inside, some on chairs, some on the floor. A mattress had been brought in up the far end and there were children lying on it asleep in rows.

'Shut the door, bab,' the man sitting closest to it said. He added sceptically, 'Oh – are you wardens?'

Violet suddenly realized they were all looking at her. Even in her odd outfit, with just a yellow band round the arm of her ordinary coat and a tin hat – thank heaven they couldn't see the state of her trousers! – she had taken on a sort of authority. Grace was standing behind her and she realized she needed to say something.

'Yes, we are. Everyone all right in here?' she asked loudly. As she spoke, she caught sight of her mother on a chair at one side, next to Mrs Baker.

And then something astonishing happened. May looked across at her and raising her voice, said, 'That's my daughter, you know – that one – the warden.'

Violet wasn't sure whether to be embarrassed or feel gratified that Mom wanted anyone who didn't already know, to be sure that she was her daughter. Well, that was certainly something new!

'We're all right, bab,' voices piped up.

'As we'll ever be!'

'We know you're looking after us, bab,' Mrs Baker called out. Violet was warmed by their faith in her, people in their yard who had known her all her life and been kind to her. Violet felt suddenly as if she had grown up, all on one night.

She leaned down to the elderly man by the door. 'Do you know a Mrs Bright, from across the way?'

'Ooh ar – little old Maud Bright! Known 'er for years. 'Er's a good sort.'

'Only, we met her outside and she wouldn't go into the shelter – said she'd sit with her friend . . .'

'That'll be old Lucy Snell. Go back years they do.

Maud had her grandson living with her – he's in the Air Force, I believe. And Lucy's on 'er own of course.'

'Should I try and get them to a shelter, d'you think?' This had been weighing on Violet's conscience.

The man shook his head. 'You wouldn't get Lucy Snell out –'er's past it, bab.' He considered for a second and added, 'I don't s'pose there's much to be done. Just leave the old girls be, like – they'll either be all right or they won't.'

Engines could be heard droning in the distance.

'Oh-oh,' someone said. ''Ere we go again.'

Twelve

Friday 18 October

'All I want is to get into my bed and sleep, not stand in the Co-op all day!' Grace said.

It was three days later. Once again, they had been out during a bad night of raids; they were heading home in a chill dawn. Now the raid was over they had their helmets swinging round their shoulders and put on the blue service caps they wore the rest of the time when there was no shrapnel dropping on their heads.

'God,' Grace said, grinning suddenly. 'Have you seen the state of your face?'

'Well, yours is no better,' Violet retorted.

The air was full of the stink of the raids – wet plaster, scorched masonry and horrible whiffs of gas.

'We might get an hour's kip in first,' Grace said.

Violet felt so wound up that she thought she would never sleep anyway.

After several nights of bombardment, it seemed astonishing any of the street was left standing. The All Clear had not sounded until well into the small hours. Wave after wave of planes had come over and they had heard their bomb loads exploding from all directions across the city. Small Heath had suffered its share of it.

There was a direct hit on three houses close to the junction with Butler Street. That section of the street was still cordoned off and blocked by rubble and hosepipes. 'By the grace of God,' as Miss Holt would say, they were all houses which had shelters and no one was killed, but the shocked occupants had to be taken in by neighbours or relatives.

Already, after these harrowing nights of bombing, this terrifying, sleep-deprived life was beginning to seem like the only one they had known. At least their proper uniforms had now arrived and Violet and Grace were kitted out in blue trousers that more or less fitted and the brass-buttoned coats of proper air-raid wardens.

Violet felt rather something in her new outfit. She wished she might have been one of the wardens who had met Mrs Churchill – Clementine, what a romantic name! – when she came to Birmingham a few days ago. Miss Holt had shown them the picture in the paper.

'Anyway,' Grace was saying, 'at least we kept together. I wouldn't fancy going out on patrol with that Reggie bloke – he looks the sort who couldn't keep his hands to himself.'

Violet laughed uneasily. She knew what Grace was implying. But she wasn't quite sure if Grace really meant what she said and secretly quite fancied a walk-out with Reggie Meakins!

'What about Mr Paine? He looks like a little ghost!'

Grace did a brief imitation of his stiff, almost corpse-like manner, pressing his hat to his chest.

'He's just like that!' Violet giggled.

They were quickly getting to know the characteristics of their fellow wardens. Violet had been startled by the to-the-death competitiveness with which Miss Holt played board games, for example. She was very shy of Reggie, who made her uneasy with his jokes, and the way he kept staring lustfully at Grace.

'And that Mr Molly-noo,' Grace mocked. 'Hey –
d'you know what Reggie told me? He came in with a
book one day, was sat reading it and it had his real name
in the front – you'll never guess what it is.'

'Go on – what?'

'He's called Percy Froggat!'

'He's not!' Violet started giggling.

'He is – and he was furious when Reggie found out.
"Quentin *Molly-noo*" is his made-up name for when he
acts in plays.' She burst out laughing as well.

'I don't even feel tired any more,' Violet said. 'I feel a
bit mad in the head, to tell you the truth.'

Grace gave her a sideways glance. 'Nothing new there
then.'

'Oh! You . . .' Violet nudged her and they both laughed
again about nothing very much. 'Oh, look, the Church
Army – let's have a cuppa before we go home, shall we?'

A number of familiar faces from the street were there
as well as an ambulance crew and a couple of police.
Violet caught sight of Reggie Meakins with a cup in his
hand, talking to someone. The cheerful Church Army
ladies were handing out cups of tea and thick, folded
slices of bread and marge.

'Come on,' Violet said. She was starving suddenly.
'Might as well.'

A lady was standing nearby with a blanket round her
shoulders and two little girls huddled close to her. She
looked shocked and miserable.

'At least we're all alive,' she kept saying, over and over.
She had a strange, wild look in her eyes. 'We're alive – at
least we're alive. My 'usband's working nights . . . I don't
know where we're gunna go . . .'

'I thought we'd got everyone sorted out?' Grace murmured to Violet.

They went over to the woman.

'Which house is yours?' Violet asked her. She didn't even recognize her.

'Oh – Chapman Road,' the woman said, in a floaty voice as if she hardly knew. Suddenly she began to weep hysterically. 'My house – it's gone – it's all gone!'

Violet and Grace looked at each other. The poor woman must have been just wandering about, not knowing what to do. Her children started crying as well, seeing the state she was in.

'Look, come along with me.' Grace turned to Violet. 'I'll take them to Mrs Oval's for now – at least they can get warm and have a sit-down.'

Mildred Oval, after some nights crouching in the Anderson shelter, declared she had had enough.

'I can't go out and volunteer for any other jobs,' she had told Grace. 'What with our John and the others. But at least I can do summat for people. I've told Arthur, if there's anyone in trouble, bring 'em here if you don't know where else to put them. I'd rather be doing that than be out in the shelter trembling in my boots!'

So far, they hadn't troubled Mildred, but now she seemed just the right comforting person to look after this poor woman.

Violet watched as Grace guided the bewildered mother and her children away down the street, the little girls clinging to each other's hands. One of them had a little rag doll cuddled to her under one arm.

'Here we are, dear – nice hot cup of tea. I bet you could do with it!'

The Church Army lady handed her a thick white cup and Violet cradled it between her hands.

'And you?' She spoke to someone over Violet's shoulder.

'Oh – yes, please, missus,' a male voice said. After a second, having evidently sampled the beverage, he followed up with a groan of pleasure, 'This is the best cup of tea I've ever had – and the best bit of bread!'

The Church Army lady laughed. 'Well, I'm glad to hear it!' she said.

Violet, moving away, glanced back to see a lad in a policeman's uniform, cradling his cup in his hands as if it was precious treasure. He was a solid-looking boy with a round, cheerful face. He saw her looking, held up his cup and said, 'Cheers!'

She couldn't help smiling, he looked so jolly and friendly. Without thinking she raised her cup back. He grinned and came over to her so that for a moment of rising panic she wished she hadn't caught his eye. As he approached, she saw he had a pronounced limp.

'That were a night, weren't it?' he said.

Violet nodded, suddenly tongue-tied. To her annoyance she felt a blush seep through her cheeks.

'How's life in the ARP then?'

'All right.'

'All right?' He seemed to find this funny. 'Well, I'm glad it's all right! You working in the day an' all?'

'Yes,' she said. 'Hughes's Biscuits.'

'Oh, ar, I know. I'm in the Post Office – can't join up 'cause of my dodgy hip.'

'Aren't you a policeman?' she said.

'Me?' He laughed uproariously. 'Nah – I'm just a bit of a tit, really, I am. But they was so desperate they put me in the Specials.'

He showed her the band on his arm. 'SPECIAL CONSTABLE 332' – a volunteer policeman, not a regular.

'My job's to look out for chancers pilfering stuff from bombed houses, that sort of thing. Well – apart from

93

about the umpteen other little jobs they 'ave lined up for us.'

Violet couldn't help laughing. She knew the feeling.

'Any road,' he said, handing the cup back with a nod to the lady. 'Best be off. No rest for the wicked. Ta-ra – see yer round!'

'T'ra,' Violet said.

He gave a little wave and limped away through the smoky air. Violet watched him, warmed by his cheerfulness after their long, gruelling night.

'Mother of God, you poor girls, what a night!' Mrs Templeton greeted them at the door with Gordon clamped to her hip.

Grace had said, 'Come in and say hello to our mom on your way home, eh?'

'It was bad,' she said now, sinking down at the table. 'I've never put so many incendiaries out in one night.'

'I'd best not stop,' Violet said. 'I need to let Mom know I'm all right.'

'Of course you must,' Grace's mother said, 'but just have a quick cuppa – it'll see you along the road.'

Violet couldn't resist sitting down for a bit. The tiredness seemed to fall on her suddenly like a weight, but it was nice to be with other people and have a chat. Mrs Templeton's kindness and another cup of sweet tea were both very welcome.

The room seethed with Templeton lads as well as Marie, who smiled at her, what a pretty girl she was! Violet was suddenly amid the bustle of large-family life and, overwhelming as it was, she felt the warmness of the welcome and that this kind of chaos was something to be envied. It made her smile, seeing all those boys milling about in the cramped room, one cramming a heel of bread into his mouth, another two squabbling over whose shoes were whose, cuffing each other . . . And little Gordon on his mother's lap, chewing his own fist and gurgling.

'He's a lovely little boy,' she said to Mrs Templeton, looking at Gordon's happy, currant-bun face.

'Oh – he's happy enough if you carry him about all day long,' Cath said wearily. 'He's too idle to do a thing for himself – aren't you, you little devil?' She snuggled her nose into the boy's cheek and he chuckled with delight.

'Proper bloke, aren't you, Gordon?' Grace said drily, but Violet could see her fondness as she said it.

'I hope your father'll be home soon,' Cath said, plonking Gordon down on the floor – to his annoyance – to bring them cups of tea. Even her freckles looked pale with exhaustion.

Violet had met Mr Templeton once now and thought how lucky Grace was. She liked Mrs Templeton with her warm Irish ways and tall, gentle Mr Templeton with his crinkly face and dry sense of humour. So this was what it was like to have a father – a *nice* father and a mother who wanted you! I want this, she thought, every time she came here. Family – a proper family.

'I wish to God he wasn't working nights,' Mrs Templeton went on, sinking down at the table as the girls drank their tea. Gordon immediately pulled himself up and stood with his chubby hands clutching her skirt. 'I'm scared to death every moment he's at the BSA in these raids . . . And I don't know how you girls are supposed to get by on no sleep at all . . . Are you off to work now, Violet?'

'Yes.' She yawned. In this warm house, the worst tension now over, she felt ready to sleep for hours. 'I'd better get going or I'll drop off here. Thanks, Mrs Templeton.'

Violet walked down the entry and stood in the yard for a moment. It wasn't yet seven in the morning.

Mrs Baker came out of her house, heading for the lavs at the end of the yard. Her fair hair stood out in a chaotic cloud round her head.

'Ooh, I'm glad to see you're all right, Vi,' she called.

'Morning, Mrs Baker,' Violet said. 'Yes – we're all all right, ta.' Quietly she added, 'Thanks for getting Mom to go to the shelter.'

'Oh – yer all right, bab.' Mrs Baker smiled. She understood, Violet knew. Mom and Eileen Baker went back years. 'We were all right – don't you fret.'

Pushing open the door of number three, she ached for the room to be full of warmth and laughter and family squabbles like in Grace's house instead of Mom sat there endlessly smoking. How nice Grace's evenings must be. Her dad could even play the piano.

May was by the stove, the kettle clouding the cold room with steam.

'I see you've decided to come home at last.' She turned, a stony look on her face.

Violet looked wearily at her, peeling off her coat. Who was that woman who had looked so proud of her in the shelter the other night? Was that her just showing off in front of the neighbours? You never knew with Mom.

'The All Clear went hours ago – so where have you been?'

'Doing my job,' Violet said. 'There's a lot to do – not just when the raid is on. We have to check on everyone, help people.' She was too tired to speak any more. Why did she have to explain? She was the one who had been up all night.

Her mother stood staring at her.

'If I ever hear anything . . . That you've been

misbehaving . . . There are all sorts out in this, under cover of darkness. You just mark my words, my girl. Being out at night leads to nothing but trouble.'

Here we go again, Violet thought bitterly. The warmth of Grace's family was still on her and for a moment she had almost forgotten. Did Mom care that she was even still alive?

May went to the range and plucked off a pair of bloomers that had been hanging drying.

'Here – you'll want clean clothes.'

'Thanks.' Violet kept her tone even. Doing the practical things – food, clothes – Mom did all that, it was true. It seemed to be all she was up to in the way of love.

'I suppose you want a cup of tea?'

'Yes, please,' she felt obliged to say, even though she was now awash with two previous cups. Her mother slammed one on the table in front of her.

'Can't even look me in the eye now, is that it?'

'I'm just tired, Mom.' She looked at her then. 'I've told you . . .' She spoke softly. 'I'm not interested in men . . . Boys . . . Why would I be after everything you've warned me about?'

Her mother's eyes bored into her for a long, silent moment. 'Men are not to be trusted at the best of times. They're only ever out for themselves. And this war is a recipe for chaos and disaster,' she said. 'Everything's falling apart.'

She walked off, her back rigid.

Violet worked all day on the line at Hughes's, packing biscuits as if she was a machine herself. She was jumpy with exhaustion. Her head ached and she felt as if she was in a dream, the rows and rows of biscuits blurring in front of her eyes. Everyone was talking about the raids, praying for a quiet night.

June Perry, however, seemed to be full of beans on the way home, despite having been up all night at the Baths, the area's main First Aid post. Violet, tired as she was, was beginning to realize that June's conversation was changing – for the better. It was a good while since there had been any mention of the dreaded Sidney. Instead, June was importantly full of the goings-on at the Baths.

'I bandaged up this feller last night,' she said. 'A right one 'e was – I mean 'e had a great lump of metal stuck in the side of his head and d'you know, even with that and me sorting him out, he pinched my backside!'

Violet laughed suddenly, taking even herself by surprise. June looked gratified.

'There're some terrible things,' June went on in her doomy voice. 'There was a lady went back inside to get 'er budgie . . . 'Er lad come into us all covered in blood. 'E was standing at the back door when it happened – flattened, the house was. He saw 'is mother disappear inside . . .'

'Oh God, how awful,' Violet breathed.

'You oughta do yerself up a bit,' June said, the conversation swerving so fast that Violet hardly kept up. 'You're quite nice-looking really, even with the specs. Only you could do with a bit of slap on – I can give yer a lipstick of mine if you like?'

Violet didn't say anything.

'You want to look more feminine,' June said. Her hair was pinned back in black waves and rolls each side of her fleshy face, which was powdered and rouged, her lashes thick with mascara. 'The lads love to see a well made-up woman.'

'Good for them,' Violet muttered. She thought of

Grace, who always managed to put a bit of eyeshadow and lipstick on. But Violet didn't know where to begin and she didn't feel it was her somehow.

The only blokes she came across most days were at the ARP post and she certainly wasn't making her face up for the likes of Reggie Meakins. For a moment she thought of the lad she had met this morning. He'd been different – a breath of fresh air.

Thirteen

Friday 25 October

'Here he comes,' Quentin Molyneaux said, peering through to the front of Miss Holt's house as the door opened again. 'Large as life and twice as natural!'

'What – old Ache and Pain, is it?' Reggie said. He sat leaning forward, knees splayed, blowing smoke at Miss Holt's ceiling.

'Hello, my dear.' Quentin ushered him jovially through to the back room. 'Filled a goodly number of coffins today, have we?'

'Mr Molyneaux!' Miss Holt objected. 'What a dreadful remark to make! After last night as well.'

As Francis came into the back room, Violet suddenly realized he was younger than she had thought – barely thirty, perhaps. The constant strain from his weak lungs seemed to hollow out his body and aged him terribly.

'My humble apologies.' Quentin directed one of his stagey bows at all of them. 'Utterly tasteless. Especially in our present, unfortunate circumstances.'

'What would those be then?' Reggie said.

'War, Reggie?' Grace said, rolling her eyes. 'Remember?'

Reggie pulled a silly face at her and Mr Powell leapt to his feet, knocking the collection box for War Weapons Week off the table. It fell with a tinny crash.

'You flippant little sod!' he erupted. 'Half the city was ablaze last night, people killed all over Birmingham and you . . . You make your . . .' He flapped his arm towards Reggie. 'Your childish, *mindless* jokes . . .' He ran out of words and sat down, fuming.

Reggie held out his hands as if to protest: *What did I say?*

'I was there, pal – remember?' He spoke quietly. 'I was out in it all with the rest of yer!'

'A whole shelter was wiped out in Hockley last night,' Miss Holt said. She was at the table with a crossword puzzle. 'Twenty-five or more people killed . . .'

'And they smashed up the Empire Theatre, burned it to the ground!' Quentin Molyneaux announced tragically.

'So shut it, Reggie,' Grace said, picking up the collection box and feeding the spilled coppers back into it.

'All right, all right – *bloomin' 'ell*!' Reggie slumped back into his chair. Any further comment he might have made was choked off by the telephone's loud ring. Purple alert. Enemy planes were on their way.

'Flamin' 'eck – not again!' Reggie said. 'They're cowing early tonight. Drink up – you might not get another chance.' He pulled out his whistle. 'Come on – toot-toot.'

'Shall we go in and see Mrs Bright and Miss Snell?' Violet shouted above the racket. She had had a tender spot for the two elderly ladies, but nothing she ever said could persuade them to move during a raid.

They hurried along the entry and tapped on the door. Seconds later an upstairs window opened and a quavering voice said, 'Yes?'

'Wardens here,' Grace called up. 'Are you both all right?'

'Oh – yes, thank you.' They heard Maud Bright's calm

101

tones. 'Lucy and I are quite all right.' There was a pause while she said something inside the room, then her voice came through the window again. 'Can I make you a cup of tea, dear?'

'I'm afraid there's another raid,' Grace told her.

'They surely must have heard the sirens?' Violet said.

'Yes, I know,' Maud Bright said, as if this was of no relevance whatsoever.

'Thank you, anyway,' Grace said. 'Are you sure we can't get you both to come to the shelter?' They felt they had to keep trying.

'Quite sure, dear, thank you,' Maud Bright assured them. 'We'll be all right here.'

There was nothing to be done.

'God bless them,' Grace said as they walked off. It made Violet feel quite emotional. What lovely friends those two elderly ladies were!

The German bombers hammered Birmingham for hours. Mr Powell was on the phone on and off all night to HQ in the basement of the Council House, to the head of the wider sector, to the First Aid post, the fire station. All the other wardens were out on the streets.

By three in the morning, two houses in the street had been hit. One of them was usually occupied by the Sullivan family, who emerged, shocked but alive, from their Anderson shelter with their four young children.

Grace knew the family from the parish and she and Violet ushered them along the street to the Ovals' house. Mildred immediately sprang into action and settled them all into her little front room. Sylvie, who was seventeen, and young Dolly got busy with tea and blankets and trying to give the best comfort they could.

'The poor, poor souls,' Grace said as they headed back

to the wreckage to see what else needed doing, stepping over the hoses and the lumps of rubble. 'Oh, God – that other house – that's Mr and Mrs Strong's, isn't it?'

It started to drizzle as they stood, watching. The blue incident light shed a ghostly pallor into the street. Mr Oval stood beside it, acting as incident officer, gathering information about the raid, who had been in, who might be missing, what help was needed. Mr Powell was also there in his white Head Warden's helmet. Violet saw he was talking to a good-looking lad in a fireman's uniform.

'Oh!' Grace said. 'That's Mark – Jimmy's brother!'

She dashed over to say a quick hello, then joined Violet as they went to speak to Mr Powell.

'The fires seem to be dealt with,' he said. His voice sounded very strained. 'But that house had no shelter at the back.' Mr Powell pointed. 'There's only a little yard. I think Mr and Mrs Strong must still be inside.'

'Oh, no,' Grace breathed.

The Strongs' house was across the street from their ironmonger's shop. No one had seen them.

Suddenly, emerging from a nearby ambulance, a solid-looking figure moved towards them.

'Vi?'

Violet squinted into the darkness.

'June!' She was surprised at how pleased she was to see her. 'What're you doing here?'

'They sent me out with the ambulance tonight.' She sounded very serious, different, Violet thought. They were all changing, fast, over these weeks. 'They found anyone?'

'No,' Violet said. 'Grace – this is June. We both work at Hughes's.'

'D'you 'ear about the Carlton?' June said. Her love of bad news was evidently unchanged. 'Cinema in Balsall

Heath? Got hit earlier on – they say there's a terrible lot been killed.'

As they were both taking this in, a shout went up.

'There's someone in here – quiet, everyone!'

Just as he said it, the siren lifted into a long, unbroken wail again over the city, to pronounce the All Clear.

'Oh, thank God,' Grace said.

'We've still got our work cut out,' Mr Powell said. 'This could take hours.'

A miraculous quiet came down on the dark street. The men shifting lumps of mortar, the voices and crunch of boots on the rubble, all stilled.

'I can hear someone!' one of the rescue workers called. 'A woman, I think.'

'That'll be Mrs Strong!' one of the neighbours called out. 'It's all right, Nance – hold on! We're coming for yer!' she shrieked into the rubble. People were emerging all along the street now, looking dazed and horrified.

There was a pause and then the shout went up. 'We need someone small – who's the smallest person?'

Violet suddenly found herself pushed forward by June and Grace. 'Here – Vi – 'er's tiny!'

'She'll 'ave to do. Send 'er over 'ere!'

Violet put most of her bits of equipment down by Mr Oval's incident lamp and went nervously forward. She could just make out a dark, sloping shape ahead of her. Up close, she saw that one of the men in charge of the rescue was a strong, solid fellow with well-defined cheek-bones. He beckoned her to climb deeper into the wreckage.

'Mind!' He grabbed her arm after a moment. 'That's far enough.' He shone his torch and she saw a kind of gap in the angled remains of the wall. 'Think you could get under there? She's in there somewhere.'

Violet's stomach curdled with fear. No! her mind was screaming. Please, no! But how could she refuse?

Then, from under the rubble she heard, quite distinctly, a woman moaning.

'I'll try,' she said. She handed him her first-aid kit. 'I don't think I'll get through there wearing this – you'd better pass it me if I get in.'

She had not noticed what a lot of people had gathered behind them until she glanced back to see an expectant crowd, all now watching her. As she scrambled over to begin this horrific task, her legs shaking so that they were almost giving way under her, she was faced with the narrow black hole into which it was now evidently her job to disappear.

I can't, she thought, shivering. She looked up at the rescue man, wanting to say, *No, I can't, don't make me.*

And then, from behind her, came a low cheer.

'Go on, wench – he'll help you!' someone shouted.

And suddenly that group of people watching, all pinning their hopes on her, made her feel strong and determined. She had to do it!

'Go in feet first,' the man said. His voice was deep and reassuring. He spoke calmly, as if this was the sort of thing you might do any day of the week. 'You're on a slope here so you should be able to reach the ground inside without any trouble.'

'I'll try,' she said faintly.

Turning, she squatted down and posted her feet through the gap. As she did so she heard another sound from below and this, too, gave her courage.

'I'm coming,' she called. 'Just hold on.' She was not aware of anything else now – just herself and the man and the poor trapped woman below.

'You'll have to turn a bit,' the man said. 'Give us your hands.'

Bracing herself and holding his hands, she managed to twist about and squeeze her hips through the gap. Her right foot connected with something and, still holding on to the man's hands, she yelped and quickly pulled her foot up again. Was that a body? Was she stepping on someone?

'All right?' He was bending over, his face close to hers. She liked his deep voice and she felt he was with her.

'Yes,' she gasped. She lowered her toe again. 'OK – that's it. I can reach the ground.' She gave a small sound of distress as her body tugged her down. 'Oh – it's so narrow . . .'

The tight space squeezed the air out of her lungs and for a moment she was overcome by panic. She would be stuck here, halfway into this hole, unable to breathe . . . She forced the rest of her breath out and pushed down frantically, raising her arms and twisting her shoulders until she was squatting down. Now the hole was above her head and she was in the dark.

'That's a girl!' the man's voice came down to her.

Panting, she felt about her. There was space around her that she could move into.

'Pass me the torch – my first-aid bag . . .'

He passed them down and suddenly, she was kneeling on what she realized was linoleum, wet and covered in grit and hard lumps. The stink of sodden masonry was overpowering. Flashing the torch, she found herself in a weird space, everything slanting above her, a mess of wood and brick. It felt as if what must once have been the back kitchen was now this cramped, musty underworld. What if it all fell in on top of her? Water dripped down the back of her neck and she sobbed in a breath, shuddering, trying to still her panic.

'Hello?' Her voice came out weak and trembling.

'Who's that? Is someone there?' The voice was faint, husky. It came from somewhere to Violet's right. And then the voice cracked. 'Get me out – help me . . . Please . . .'

Fourteen

'It's all right, Mrs Strong,' Violet called out to her. 'I'm one of the wardens. We're all here to help you. Just hold on.'

'Oh,' she heard faintly in reply. 'Help me! Where's my Harold?"

Violet pushed herself up again so that the top of her head reached just over the edge of the hole. 'She's alive – I'll see if I can get to her.'

'Violet?' She heard Grace's voice and she sounded really worried. 'Oh, I don't like this . . . Be careful, Vi!'

'I will,' she said, trying to sound strong. She could just hear people murmuring to each other outside.

'We'll do all we can out here,' the rescue worker said. 'But we'll have to be very careful – don't want this lot coming down on yer.'

'Right,' she said, steeling herself so that she didn't start demanding to be pulled out of this death trap straight away. 'I'll go now . . .'

Kneeling, she held the torch with one hand and crawled along, sharp things digging into her knees, her trousers becoming heavy with water. All she could see ahead was rubble and darkness, but immediately in front of her there was a space and she made quite fast progress.

'Mrs Strong?' Her voice sounded thin down here, as if she had no substance.

There was a pause so long that for a moment she feared the worst.

'Here. Over here . . .' came at last. 'Please . . .' The voice was more slurred than before. Violet felt her heart speed up. Mrs Strong sounded in a bad way.

'Try and stay awake, Mrs Strong,' she said. 'I'm close to you . . . Just guide me, will you?'

Further along she began to see what the problem was. Ahead of her, the way forward abruptly ended in a soot-coated section of brick. The chimney breast, she guessed. There was a small space above it, wide enough to fit her arm through, no more.

Oh, God, she thought. I can't get past here. I can't even get near her, never mind help her.

'Are you there, Mrs Strong?'

She heard a thin moan in reply.

'I'm going to go and get some other people to help. You hang on there, won't you, dear? We're all doing our best to get you out.'

The space was not wide enough to turn round so she backed up as fast as she could, calling encouragingly to Mrs Strong as she went. To her surprise it took no time at all whereas she felt she had been crawling along there for ages.

When she put her head through the hole again, the rescue worker, Grace and several others were all clustered round. Even June Perry was still there. There was a greyness to the chill air now: daybreak was coming, the blue incident light still glowing to one side of the street. A mobile canteen had parked nearby and people were gathered round. It felt like another world out here.

'I can't get to her,' she said softly. She didn't want Mrs Strong hearing how far they still were from her. She explained about the obstacle.

'Right, lads,' the head of the rescue team detailed the

others. 'Keep shifting this stuff. That lifting gear's on the way – hope they won't be long.'

'Should I go back in and stay with her?' Violet said. It seemed so terrible to be entombed down there without a human voice. 'I think . . .'

'What?' the good-looking man said.

'Well, I think she's fading.'

He stood thinking for a moment. 'No – you'd best stay up here. We don't want to lose you as well. We'll keep calling to her – she should be able to hear us.'

'Come here – we'll get you out.' Grace and June took her hands and hauled her out of the hole.

Violet took in great gulping breaths – never had filthy old Brum air, full of smoke and dust, felt so clean and merciful.

Just as she was out, Mr Powell appeared, Mr Oval with him.

'Vi's been down in there,' Grace said. She sounded proud. 'We're still trying to get Mrs Strong out.'

'Any sign of Mr Strong?' Mr Powell asked quietly. They both shook their heads. He accepted this with quiet resignation. 'What a night.'

A lorry appeared and had to be manoeuvred into place to winch the masonry out of the way. It seemed to take forever. All the time they kept calling out to Mrs Strong, saying they were coming, that she should hold on. It wasn't possible to hear if she was replying. On and off Violet could hear a woman sobbing somewhere nearby. Violet found she was shivering. It was cold and she felt shocked and suddenly utterly exhausted.

'You all right?' Grace turned to her and put an arm round her shoulders.

'I'm afraid it'll be too late,' Violet said, feeling tears rise in her. The grey morning light, the mess and stink and misery of it all began to overwhelm her.

Finally, accompanied by a muted cheer from everyone around, the workmen managed to get a hold on the heavy lump of charred masonry and lift it away and to one side.

'Oh,' Violet gasped. 'Oh, I hope she's all right.' She didn't know Mrs Strong very well, but she felt bound to her after being with her in that terrible black place under there.

Everyone was working frantically now. June and another stretcher bearer waited nearby. Violet watched June, full of wonder. She looked grown up, suddenly, and capable. Eventually a shout went up. 'Here – she's here!'

Quiet descended. A crowd of men were still scrabbling in the rubble. After more bits had been cleared away Violet caught a glimpse of an arm, the cuff of a marrowfat-pea green cardigan, filthy and dripping with water. Carefully, tenderly, the woman was gathered on to the stretcher, one man pulling her skirt down. The medic went to her and squatted down, feeling for a pulse. Everyone waited. Violet forgot to breathe.

Then she saw Mrs Strong raise her head, just slightly. Violet's breath seemed to come back to her. She hurried over.

'Mrs Strong?'

'Hello, bab.' She lay back on the stretcher.

'I was just down there with you – I'm Violet Simms. How're you feeling?'

'Oh, I'm all right, thanks. Yes – glad to be out of there, I can tell yer.' She gave a joyous smile. 'I heard your voice, bab – made all the difference, that did, having someone there.' She seemed cheerful, quite perky even. 'Has anyone seen my Harold?'

Violet swallowed. 'Not yet, I don't think. But we're all looking for him.'

June came closer then. 'We're going to put you in the ambulance now, Mrs Strong,' she said loudly.

'All right then,' Mrs Strong said, lying back. 'I'm not deaf, bab. No need to shout.' She seemed content, lying on the stretcher, her brown hair all wet and stringy. 'Ta-ra-a-bit.' She gave Violet a little wave.

They carried Mrs Strong to the ambulance and slid her inside. Violet saw June's back as she leaned over to speak to her. But within a moment there was something wrong. June's stance changed from leaning in to say something, to leaping up beside Mrs Strong. She shouted to the man on the ambulance crew, who was walking round to get in.

Violet started to walk towards the ambulance, dread clutching at her throat. She and the man reached the back doors at the same time. Inside, June was squatting next to Mrs Strong.

'Gone,' she said. Her eyes were wide with shock. 'Just . . . Just like that. A second ago.'

'No.' Violet's mind couldn't take it in. 'She can't be. She was talking . . . She was all right! She was going to be all right!'

Grace came up beside her. June was still looking stunned.

'I'll write out the label,' Grace said, fishing in her bag.

'Internal injuries, I expect,' the man on the ambulance crew said. He shook his head. 'I've seen it before. Dear, oh, dear. Come on – we'd best get going.'

Violet felt as if her legs were giving way under her. 'She can't be dead,' she kept saying as Grace wrote out the label, then handed it to June to identify Mrs Strong. 'She can't be . . .'

'After all that,' Grace said tearfully. Violet felt Grace's

arm round her, holding her up. 'Come away, Vi, you've done the best you could.'

Violet cupped the warm mug of tea the woman in the Sally Army van had handed to her. She was still standing near the bombed-out houses, waiting for Grace, who had nipped home to check her family were all right. Violet drank the sweet brew. Now that she was alone she started to shake, her body reacting as the shocks of the night began to take hold of her. She didn't want to be alone. To her surprise, she found herself wishing Miss Holt was there. She would have something sensible to say – she always did. Feeling as if her legs might give way, she leaned her back against the nearest wall, trying to hold her cup steady.

In the dawn light, the damage was starkly clear: the smoky air, the jagged gaps and stinking mess of bricks and plaster, the scattered remains of furniture and crushed belongings. A slew of sodden paper lay near her feet – someone's personal papers by the look of them. Perhaps they had belonged to the Strongs. She looked away, taking a sip of tea.

Subdued conversations went on around her. The man leading the rescue team walked over to the canteen as if to get a drink. Violet saw Grace, on her way back, stop for a word with him. Even from a distance his eyes seemed vividly bright, looking out of a face coated in grime. At his neck was a blue scarf. She saw Grace smile and wondered what they were talking about.

''Ello again.'

For a second, she was too dazed to realize anyone was talking to her, but then she saw the young Special had appeared at her side.

'Oh – hello!'

'I s'pose you've got a name?'

'Violet.' She managed a slight smile. She still felt shocked and wobbly and tried to hide the fact that her hands were trembling by gripping her cup. It was nice to be distracted from her thoughts. 'What about you, Special Constable 332?'

She was surprised how easy she was with him, not like with most men.

'Oh – I'm George,' he said. 'It's nice to see yer again.' He seemed to have a naturally cheerful disposition, but after last night even he was rather quiet.

''Ere,' he went on, eyeing her with concern. 'You must be all in. Want to come and sit down for a tick?'

Nearby was another lump of masonry and they took their cups and perched on it, slightly away from the crowd grouped round the van. They sat side by side in silence for a moment, sipping their tea.

'It was you went down under the building then?' George said. She heard the admiration in his voice.

Violet nodded. Now, in the gathering light, it felt unreal to her.

'That was brave. Seems like they got her out all right.'

'Yes,' she agreed, suddenly feeling almost too exhausted to speak. 'But then . . . She didn't make it.'

'No!' He looked very shocked and she could feel that he was wondering, in a kindly way, what to say. 'That's terrible, that is.' After another pause, he said, 'What was it like – under there?'

'Horrible.' She felt her throat ache and swallowed hard, clenching the cup in her hands, trying to keep control of herself. 'I feel a bit . . . I dunno . . .'

'I'm not surprised, after that.' George took another mouthful of tea. He seemed different himself, she realized now; tense, not like when she met him before. He kept

114

looking round him, restlessly. After a few moments he turned to her and started talking all in a rush.

'I . . . I had to . . .' He stumbled. 'Last night, there was this shop, on the Cov Road – hardware shop from the look. This bloke was . . . I mean, I went to see what the damage was. He was lying half out the front, half in half out, like. I thought 'e'd just been knocked over by the blast – the roof was caved in and everything . . . And when I went to . . . I tried to take him by his arms and . . . I pulled on his top half and – his legs just came away from the rest of his body . . . I ended up just pulling half of him out . . .'

His shoulders started to shake then and he put his head down to hide his emotion.

'God,' he said. 'It were horrible . . .'

'Oh, how . . .' Violet couldn't finish, she was so choked with tears, but George nodded as if just these words had been enough. He wiped his face quickly, ashamed of having broken down, and when he turned to her, she felt him realize that she was crying as well, feeling hot tears adding to the drizzle soaking away the crust of filth on her face.

'You can't stop seeing it, can yer?' George said. 'Eh.' He reached out and touched her hand for a moment and it felt so comforting. 'You gunna be all right?'

She nodded, wiping her sleeve across her face. 'Yeah. Course. Have to be, don't we?'

George nodded. He drained his teacup and sat up straighter. 'You won't say nothing to anyone, will yer – about me . . . I mean . . .'

'No,' she said, touched. 'Course not.'

George turned to her and gave her a watery smile. 'Ta. I never meant to . . . Only it were 'orrible. Nice of yer to . . . A right pair, aren't we – and me keeping on like, when you're upset.'

'Don't be silly,' she said. 'It's been a bad night.'

'D'you 'ear about the Carlton?'

Violet nodded.

'They was all there in the front rows, just sat there, stone dead – hardly a scratch on 'em, apparently.'

He shook himself and put the cup down, as if trying to change his mood.

'D'you know – I never talk to anyone like this as a rule.'

She glanced at him, smiling, then away. 'It wasn't a regular sort of night,' she said.

'True. You got a point there.' He looked shyly at her. 'D'you fancy . . . Sorry if I'm speaking out of turn, but I don't know when I'll see you again. Would you meet up with me, sometime, like? I'm a clumsy idiot I am – I'm trying to ask you out, Violet. Violet what?'

'Simms,' she said, her mind racing. What was she going to do? She'd never walked out with anyone before. Was this what he meant? George was so nice, so sweet, it didn't exactly feel like being asked out. But what on earth could she say to Mom? Damn it – she'd have to just get round it, as usual. She was twenty, for heaven's sake!

'Yes,' she said shyly. 'I'd like that. Sometime.'

George punched the air, his still-smeary cheeks lifting into a grin. He seemed the sort of lad who would not remain downcast for long. 'You just made my day, you did!'

Fifteen

Grace hurried along the entry and through the garden
gate, to find her mother ushering the rest of the family
out of the shelter. In the wet, murky morning, they
looked like little ghosts, draped in coats and blankets. She
could hear Gordon grizzling.

'Grace!' Her brother Dennis caught sight of her, ran
along the garden and threw his arms round her waist.
Grace hugged his skinny body, really touched. She found
tears in her eyes.

'Hey, Den – that's nice! You all right?'

He nodded his head against her body and she ruffled
his hair. Den had always been a softy.

'Oh, thank the Lord you're here,' her mother said. She
was laden with blankets, a flask, a bag swinging from one
arm, as well as the howling Gordon. 'Jesus, Mary and
Joseph,' she exclaimed over the racket Gordon was
making. 'The state of you – have you seen yourself?'
Grace could see all the strain of worry in her eyes as she
added, 'Any news of the BSA?' Dad should be due home
soon, after the night shift.

'No,' Grace said, thinking, surely she would she have
heard about it if anything had happened over there? They
had heard about the bomb that hit the Carlton cinema –
but she decided not to say anything about that. Why
spread bad news?

'I've seen out there . . .' Mom nodded towards the
street, her face grim. 'Everyone all right? Arthur?'

117

'Yes.' She had passed Arthur Oval on the way home. 'Violet's all right too – she's had a hell of a night of it, though.'

But her mother was distracted by Gordon's persistent complaints. 'I need to get this one fed . . .'

As they all shuffled into the house, the rest of the family emerged from the Roses' shelter next door. To Grace's amazement Marie flung her arms round her as well.

'You all right?' Grace said. 'You must've been really scared.'

'Mr Rose held my hand,' Marie said. She didn't seem to know whether to be pleased about this or not.

'Bless him –'e's a kind old feller,' her mother said.

'I need to go and see how Vi's getting on,' Grace said. 'It's been a bad night. I just came in to check you're all all right.'

'We're grand,' her mother said, though she was obviously exhausted. 'Go on – off you go then.'

She couldn't see Violet straight away so she headed to the Sally Army van finally to get a cup of tea.

'You look as if you could use that, dear,' the lady said.

Grace nodded and smiled her thanks, too drained of energy for conversation. She sipped the fast-cooling tea as the light grew stronger, seeing the outlines of destruction at each end of Archibald Street. It was like a dream. Surely she'd wake up soon and this terrible night would fade, their street be back to normal, how it had always been? Everyone around her seemed different, their faces grey with dust. She could feel it like a mask on her own skin. She wondered if she looked like everyone else, their features stern with shock and exhaustion, changed, with a sudden awe at being alive.

She caught sight of Violet a short distance away, sitting

118

on a broken section of wall with someone who seemed to be a policeman. She was about to hurry over, thinking something was wrong. But she suddenly saw that it was not like that: she would be interrupting. The lad was looking at Violet as if she was the best thing he'd ever seen in his life and Violet was all lit up. Grace had never seen her like that before. She turned away, suddenly full of wistful longing. That was just how Jimmy looked at her. For a second, she felt terribly alone and longed for Jimmy to be there, for him to take her in his arms, the way he did just before he left – sturdy, faithful Jimmy.

The sight of a familiar face coming towards her through the scattering of people broke into her thoughts – Francis Paine's pale, solemn features – and she quickly turned away.

'Hey, watch it!'

'Oh! Sorry!' She had almost knocked the tea out of the hand of a man standing behind her and some of it spilled down his front. 'I'm ever so sorry,' she repeated. 'I'll get you another one . . .'

'You're all right – no harm done,' he said, wiping at it. There was an unusual scarf tucked into his overalls at the neck – a woolly sky blue with some kind of red edging. His face was covered with dark swirls of dirt and that, along with the blue scarf, seemed to make his already striking blue eyes stand out even more. Grace realized it was the man from the rescue team who had brought Mrs Strong out from her house. Something about him made her pulse pick up its pace.

'That was a bad'un,' he said.

'Yes. I'll say.' The sadness of it seeped further into her. 'Poor Mrs Strong.'

'D'you know 'er?'

119

'Yes – well, only by sight. Mom knew her, though. Being stuck down there . . .' She shuddered. 'I can't stand to think about it.'

'That little pal of yours did a good job.' He jerked his head in Violet's direction. 'Shame how it ended – but it was brave, that.'

'Vi? Yeah – quiet little thing but she's stronger than you'd think.'

The man laughed. 'Oh – you an' all, I'm sure. Still can't get used to you wenches being out in all this.' He drained his cup. She felt him looking at her then, cradling the cup between both hands. Their eyes met. It was not a passing look – more as if he was studying her – and Grace felt herself blush. There was a power to him that affected her.

'Best be off,' she said, giving a brief smile.

He nodded and they went to take back their cups.

'Ta – that was just what I needed,' Grace said to the Salvation Army lady, feeling she'd been a bit short with her before.

'Bless you, dear,' the woman said. 'It's the least we can do.'

'I'd best get on.' Grace found herself suddenly reluctant to leave. The man lingered as well. 'Got to get to work.' She rolled her eyes. 'We've got to get through the day somehow, eh?'

'Where is it you work then?' he said.

'Co-op – on the Cov.'

'Oh, ar – I know. I'm at Whitworth's.'

'Garrison Lane?' Whitworth's Motor Accessories was one of the big firms in the area. 'Reserved job then?'

He nodded, holding out a hand, withdrew it and wryly inspected it before offering it to her again. 'Not too bad, considering! Harry Cobb.'

Grace laughed, shaking his hand. 'I'm Grace Templeton. I live just up there.' She nodded along the street. 'This is our patch – ARP, I mean.'

'You can keep an eye on your folks then?'

'Yeah – they were out in the shelter all night.'

He seemed to want to keep her talking. And she did not mind being kept. It was hard to see exactly what his face was like under all the muck, but it made him look even more tough and rugged. He was an attractive man, a manly man. Beside him, Jimmy seemed like a schoolboy. Her fond longings for Jimmy a few moments ago faded as she looked into this fascinating face.

Harry Cobb pushed his hands into his pockets and stood looking round for a moment.

'Well, I'd best be off and get cleaned up.' Turning, he gave her a smile so broad she could only smile back and he did not hurry to look away. 'No rest for the wicked, eh. I 'spect I'll see you around somewhere.'

'Yeah – the way things are going!' She made herself start walking away, towards the ARP post to report in. As she got to the door she couldn't resist looking back and saw Harry Cobb just moving out of sight along the street.

'My goodness, Grace, do look where you're going,' Miss Holt said tetchily as they collided in the doorway. 'We'll never get the war won with you going about facing the wrong way.'

Grace stood in the back room of the Co-op, bagging up flour. The shop was one of several in the Co-op family among the shops along the busy Coventry Road, one of the main arteries bringing all the commerce and traffic in and out of the heart of Birmingham. Trucks roared back and forth along the road snorting out black clouds of filth, and there was a constant hurry of feet along the pavement, women rushing from queue to queue with their ration books, delivery cycles and vans and scurrying messenger boys.

It was almost dinner time. All morning, Grace had felt waves of exhaustion passing through her.

I need summat to eat, she thought. She'd managed to get a couple of cobs from the bakery on the way in, with cheese and onion, and the thought made her mouth water.

Her apron was heavily dusted with flour and she beat at it with her hand, managing to flick floury dust into her eye as she did so.

'Ow – damn it!' She clasped her hand to her stinging left eye, trying to sort out the watering irritation of it when she heard her manager calling from the front.

'Yes, Mrs Hodgson?'

A hand over her one streaming eye, she went out to the shop. The main ration-book rush had already passed that day. The shop's glass cabinets and shelves contained much less food than before the war and what there was of the rationed foods such as bacon and butter had already gone to the morning queues of housewives. Apart from Mrs Hodgson, there was only one person in the shop. And Mrs Hodgson was standing behind the counter with her arms folded and an air of not being at all sure about all this. The other person was Harry Cobb.

'Oh!' Grace said, feeling idiotic. 'Hello! Er . . . Sorry – got summat in my eye.'

Harry Cobb laughed. 'Oh – hello again.' To Mrs Hodgson he added, 'We were out last night – on duty I mean. This young lady's a warden.'

'I'm aware of that,' Mrs Hodgson said tightly. Her feet planted wide apart, she gave off an air of someone who was not shifting herself to go anywhere.

'I just come in to get some, er . . . You got a tin of . . .' He looked round for inspiration. 'Soup?'

'Did you want me, Mrs Hodgson?' Grace said. Her eye was smarting horribly and she felt very silly standing there with her hand clamped over it.

'Fetch Mr Cobb a tin of soup,' Mrs Hodgson said, stern-faced. 'There's pea or Scotch broth.'

'I'll have pea then,' Harry Cobb said.

Grace went along the shelves, pulling at her eye in the attempt to get tears to wash the flour out of it. She was aware of Harry Cobb watching her all the while. It was startling to see him cleaned up; his face was swarthy as if he had been outside a lot, there was that muscular body, those piercing eyes.

'Here you are.' She still wasn't quite sure why she had been called out to the front, other than that Harry Cobb must have asked for her. The thought made her blush. Her eye was at last beginning to settle down. She removed her hand and blinked several times.

His gaze had a dizzying effect on her, in particular because it was obvious he had come especially to find her. But neither of them could say anything with Mrs Hodgson standing there like a sentry on duty.

Harry Cobb paid for the soup, touched his cap, said, 'T'ra then,' with an amused little smile and went out. He turned for a second as if to see if Mrs Hodgson had gone, but she had not. They saw him pass in front of the window.

Mrs Hodgson gave Grace a very straight look. 'You want to watch that one.'

'I don't really know him, Mrs Hodgson,' she said.

'Well,' Mrs Hodgson said, 'if I was you, I'd keep it that way. He looks like trouble to me.'

As she turned to go out into the storeroom, Grace made a face at her back.

Sixteen

Violet's mind was crowded with all the events of the night as she walked home along Archibald Street in the dismal wet. It had been the worst night she could remember, but chatting with George, the policeman, had pulled her out of her own thoughts and given her something else to think about. And – oh, my goodness – she had promised to meet him! She was tingling with nervous excitement. She wouldn't say a word to Mom about it – but she knew nothing was going to stop her.

Just as she was about to go into her own back court, she saw someone passing into the entry across the road. It made her wonder about old Mrs Bright. Crossing over, she went along the entry into a yard similar to the one where she lived herself. A few young children were out, splashing in an oily puddle that had gathered, their mothers, some in aprons and headscarves in a huddle by the yard tap, chewing over the events of the night before. It was only when they stopped talking and looked warily at her that Violet remembered she still had her warden's uniform on. Some people loved the wardens, others saw them as interfering busybodies. A few weeks ago – though it seemed like a different life altogether now – she would have wanted to turn and run away. But she was getting used to this warden business. It was her *job* to check on things and she felt bolder, taller even.

'Morning!' She kept her voice friendly, but firm. 'Everyone all right in here?'

'Yes, ta.' But the eldest of the group of women, a tough-looking body with a cap on, took a drag on a cigarette and stood with narrowed eyes, as if to say, *And what do you want?*

'Is this where Miss Snell lives?' Violet asked. 'I've just come to see if she's all right.'

'That's 'ers,' another, curly-haired, woman said, nodding towards one of the houses at the side of the yard. Violet looked up at it. The roof appeared undamaged. 'You won't get much out of 'er though – 'er's bedridden – never answers the door.'

'Yes, I know . . .' Violet went to the door and tapped on it. There was no reply. Feeling the women's eyes on her back, she tried the door and went in. It opened into a plain little room that she could see had once been kept spick and span and cosy. There were pretty curtains, now dusty and tired, some nice sticks of furniture and an armchair with a patchwork cover draped over the back. But the fire seemed long unlit. The room smelt of coal dust and had a chill feeling, as if it had not been sat in in a good while. Someone had taped the windows against blast, though.

'Hello?' she called up the stairs. There was no reply. Concerned, she closed the front door and tiptoed up the bare treads of the winding staircase.

Like most of these little houses, its upstairs consisted simply of two little bedrooms side by side. Creeping to the first, the boards creaking under her, she looked inside.

In the bed was an old lady, fragile as a bird, her grey hair parted in the middle and smoothed neatly back from a thin face with pale, almost translucent skin. It was a sweet, rather noble face. The bed was very tidy and well made with a sheet turned over neatly at the top.

And beside her, in an armchair, was Maud Bright. She had her knitting in her lap and her veined hands were clasped together on it, a rug draped over her knees. Her head was tilted to one side, pushing her straggly waves of grey up at the side. Her mouth was slightly open.

For a second, Violet had a terrible feeling at the sight of the two old ladies, both so completely still. Her heart started to pound. Were they . . . ? What had happened in this house? But then Maud Bright let out a little breathy noise through her mouth as she slept. Violet breathed out again herself. The poor old dears must be exhausted.

Looking round the room she saw a pretty china po' half-pushed under the bed, a tiny vase of dried flowers on the chest of drawers and the reflection of light in a tilted mirror behind it. There were also cups and saucers, as if the two ladies had had a cup of tea after the raid was over and then drifted off to sleep. The atmosphere of calm order felt like a miracle and her throat ached as she stood looking at them.

Bless you both, she thought, wiping her eyes. She crept out of the room and down to the yard again.

'She all right?' The women were still standing where they had been before, near the tap. 'She's got 'er friend with her, I s'pose?'

'They're all right,' Violet said. She smiled, suddenly filled with a sense of elation. 'All safe and sound.'

Walking into her own yard, she felt a sense of wonder that it was still the same as ever: the uneven lines of blue bricks which paved it, tin baths hanging from nails, doors of some of the houses flung open to let the air in. Steam was already curling out into the air from the copper of water heating in there. From somewhere she could hear the sound of sweeping, and a baby was crying. Mrs Baker came out of the brewhouse at the far end of the yard, hauling on the mangle.

'Oh, Violet!' She came hurrying over. 'Are you all right, bab? We was worried to death about you last night.'

'Yes, ta, Mrs Baker, I'm all right.'

Lucy and Maud had driven her experiences of the night out of her mind for a time. But now Mrs Baker's kindly, worried face brought a lump to her throat. She wanted to pour out what had happened, about Mrs Strong and her having to go down into that awful, dark, cramped, dripping place. As she thought of it now the terror went through her more than it had at the time and she swayed on her feet.

'Oh – oh, dear!' Mrs Baker caught her by the shoulder to steady her. 'You look all in – what a terrible night. Your mother was worried to death.' She glanced towards the shelter at the end of the yard and lowered her voice. ''Er's sweeping out the shelter.'

Violet gaped. 'What – Mom?'

Mrs Baker winked and touched her arm. 'I know. Life's full of surprises, eh?' She turned back towards the mangle.

'Here you are at last,' her mother said, coming in a moment after her. 'You've been a long time.' She sounded neutral for once – neither pleased nor angry. That was what being worn out did for you, Violet supposed.

'There's always more to do even after the All Clear,' Violet said, pulling her cap off and unbuttoning her coat. It felt like days since she'd last been home, not just hours. She sank down on to a chair feeling she might never get up again.

Her mother bustled about, making tea and some bread and marge with a scraping of plum jam.

'Ta. I could do with that.' Violet ate ravenously. May,

128

apron over her frock, sat down opposite her. For a moment, things felt calm.

'Mrs Baker said you were cleaning out the shelter.'

'Well,' May said, sitting up straighter, somehow important. She lit a cigarette and sat back, eyes narrowed against the smoke. 'Someone's got to – the state of it.'

'Good for you,' Violet said carefully. But she was glad her mother seemed to be finding things to do – she was always good at practical things. She went to switch on the wireless.

'Don't!' May snapped. 'It's nothing but gloom and doom. I don't want to hear it.' After a few moments, she said, 'So you ain't going to ask after yer mother then? How she got on after this terrible, terrible night? I haven't had a wink of sleep. I thought we were going to die in that shelter. And you come home and . . . Not a word.'

Violet looked across at her. Words were certainly forming in her mind. Not as bad as the night poor Mrs Strong had, she thought furiously. For a moment the horror of the blackness under that house shuddered through her. Then George's face swam into her mind, that cheerful, kindly face. The sweet, miraculous conversation they had had. A boy who seemed to like her, who had arranged to meet her later! She drew strength from this amazing development.

'Sorry, Mom,' she said quietly. 'I'm just starving hungry, that's all. Thanks for the breakfast. Was it bad?'

'Well, what do you think?' May started working herself up. 'Sat there on a hard chair all night in that stinking shelter with the most . . .' Her face contorted. 'Disgusting things going on. There's only a bit of curtain and a bucket in one corner and . . . And all the argy-bargy – they never cowing stop . . . Arguing about this, then keeping on about that . . .'

129

'Better to be there, though, than under the stairs on your own,' Violet reasoned.

'Well, I wouldn't be on my own if my only daughter wasn't so selfish – going off, leaving me . . .'

'Mom . . .' She was too tired even to lose her temper. Just as she had thought things were improving! 'You could be doing summat else – not just sweeping out. You could volunteer, be a warden, the Women's Voluntary thing, First Aid . . . Then you wouldn't have to sit there.'

'Don't talk silly, I've already got a business to run – and you're no help these days, gadding about the way you are . . .'

'Gadding about?' Violet sat up, on the brink of exploding – something she had never, ever dared do in all her life. It had taken the war to make her see just how self-pitying her mother was, how wrapped up in herself. Selfish – talk about the pot calling the kettle black!

But then the old reflex came into play – Mom had had a hard life being widowed so young. It had been a grinding struggle for her bringing up a child – her, that burdensome child – on her own and she should be grateful. She bit back the sharp words that were fighting to leap from her throat.

'I'm going to put the kettle on and have a wash,' she said, getting up. 'My feet are like blocks of ice.'

Her mother sniffed. 'Some of us have got to get to work. I'm going to the shop and I'll expect you in later.'

It was Saturday. Violet spent a luxurious hour heating up two pans of water, having a good scrub-down and washing her hair. She sat on afterwards, by the range in the one easy chair, with her feet in the basin of warm, soapy water.

'Ah,' she murmured, lolling back in the chair. 'Bliss.'

130

A pulse of excitement went through her. She was meeting George later. She wasn't used to lads. She'd had very little to do with men, and what with the way Mom carried on about them, it hadn't seemed worth the trouble. But George was different. With him she had hardly thought about him being a boy as such – she just felt comfortable and happy with him, with his nice, jokey ways and round face that lit up when he smiled.

They were going to meet at six o'clock – outside the library, Violet had suggested. And they'd have to hope to God there was no raid tonight. *Please*, she prayed. Please just for once.

When she was dry and dressed, she made another cup of maid's-water tea, reusing the grouts, and sank down into the chair again, covering her knees with a wool jersey. Exhaustion took hold and she closed her eyes. Jagged images of the night spiked at her mind. She tried to force them away and imagine George's face, his grin, the way he looked at her. Smiling, she finally drifted off to sleep.

'Oi – I said I wanted you in the shop!' Mom's voice hauled her out of a deep sleep so suddenly that she felt sick. 'You're not the only one dain't get any sleep last night, yer know.'

'Oh, Mom – I'm on tonight as well.' Why couldn't she just be allowed to sleep for a bit?

'What?' May's hands went to her hips. 'I thought you said you wasn't?'

'Well, I am.' The lies slid from her practised lips. She looked up, wide-eyed, at her mother. 'Mr Powell changed the rota.'

She knew there was nothing Mom could say in the face of Mr Powell.

'Well, that's too bad then, in't it?' Her voice was harsh. 'You come and take over while I get to the shops. I'm late as it is. Fetch me the ration books – there'll be nothing left, else.'

Come ten to six, she put on her coat and ARP cap as usual as if she was going over for her shift.

'Let's hope it's a quiet night,' she said brightly to her mother. 'And I can get back early.'

She walked along towards Miss Holt's house and then, glancing back as if her mother might still be watching, held tight to her bag and the string of her gas-mask box and half-ran along to the Coventry Road.

The day had brightened, the sky clearing, and this evening the light was lovely, but she knew that the clear sky boded no good. The lack of cloud was a gift to the bombers.

The corner of Green Lane and her beloved library were almost like a lighthouse on a promontory looking out to sea. Before she had even crossed the road, she could see a figure standing by the wall in the glowing autumn evening. He caught sight of her and pushed himself off the wall. He was in his dark Special Constable's uniform and he made a smart, compact-looking figure.

Violet was smiling before she had reached the opposite, white-painted kerb.

'I never thought you'd come,' he said, beaming back at her.

'Why?' She was indignant. 'I said I would, dain't I?'

George looked abashed. 'Well, yeah, I s'pose, but still . . .'

'Well, I'm here now. Should've brought my library book back while I was at it.' She was chattering out of nerves. 'It's overdue – there's not been time for reading lately.'

'You like a read then, do yer?'

'Yes,' she said. 'Nothing like it. Do you?'

'Nah, not really. Used to read comics but I ain't much of a reader.' He looked round. 'Where d'yer want to go?'

'Go?' She realized she had no idea whatsoever, not being someone who ever went out with boys, or with anyone for that matter.

'We could go to a pub for a quick one, but that might be a bit . . . Or we could just have a wander.'

'All right,' she said, relieved. All she wanted was to be with him.

As dusk fell, they headed instinctively along the Cov, the main road lined with shops and always busy with traffic, towards the park and it wasn't many minutes before they were chatting easily. George told her he lived in Cattell Road, that his dad worked in a factory making gear boxes, that he had three elder sisters. When Violet said it was just her and her mom at home, George looked at her sorrowfully.

'You ain't got much family then? That's a shame. Your mom's a widow?'

'Yes – my father died when I was a baby,' she said. 'I don't remember him at all.'

'That's sad, that is,' George said. He added jovially, 'You'll have to come and meet our lot – my sisters're all right – most of the time, anyway!'

She laughed. That sounded nice. She loved seeing other people's families, like Grace's, with all the goings-on there. She was just about to say so when the sound of the first air-raid siren gave out its rising crescendo, soon to be joined by others. Violet felt the hairs rise on the back of her neck.

'Oh, my Lord,' George said. 'You'd think those buggers'd give us a bit of peace for once.'

'I'll have to get back,' Violet said, every nerve in her body jangled by the sound.

'Me too. Come on.' He reached for her hand and together, they started to run. Later, Violet thought, We held hands! But then there was no time to do anything but steady her gas mask and dash along.

Seventeen

Sunday 27 October

It had been a night of heavy bombing, though none fell in Archibald Street. The city was alight, the sky a sick, ominous red and, as the news came in gradually the next day, they heard of many deaths.

By the following morning after the All Clear, Violet, who had spent the night working alongside Grace, felt as if they had been through another long, hellish journey. As the morning light seeped through the smoke-filled air of the city to reveal the destruction, she felt not one day older, but several years.

Just as she walked exhaustedly back to Post F, Miss Holt was coming out with a big jug in her hands. Seeing Violet, she stopped, and to Violet's tired surprise, she saw her old teacher's face soften.

'Ah, Violet! You're back – I'm glad to see you're all right.'

She spoke in her usual stiff way, but Violet could feel how great was her relief at seeing her appear, unharmed. And when Miss Holt smiled at her, the sweet warmth of her expression brought tears to Violet's eyes. Dear old Miss Holt. She had been worried, she could see.

'Yes, I'm all right, thanks, Miss Holt. What a night.'

'Well now, let's get ourselves warmed up.' Miss Holt

became suddenly brisk again and started pouring cups of tea.

Everyone was subdued with exhaustion and the horror of seeing so many familiar places – houses, factories, churches – reduced to broken heaps of wreckage. Only Mr Powell stayed inside, writing up his reports, while the rest of the ARP volunteers lingered in the street with some of the neighbours, somehow needing to be together. It was a comfort to see Arthur Oval and Mildred, who had come out to join them. She still had her hairpins in, head wrapped in a scarf, and she'd brought little John, a blanket over him, in his chair. Everyone made a fuss of him.

'All right, mate?' Reggie Meakins bumped his fist gently against the little boy's shoulder. 'You're not scared, are yer?'

'He's not too bad, considering,' Muriel said fondly. 'Dolly gets in far more of a state than our John.'

'You're a good little soldier, ain't yer?' Reggie said. John was beaming up into Reggie's grimy face and Violet watched, thinking, That's nice. Reggie was annoying but he wasn't all bad.

'All right?' Reggie came up to Violet and Grace, smirking.

'I don't know what you've got that grin on yer face for,' Grace said crossly.

Violet noticed that she was looking about her as if in search of someone. She wondered what was going on. But the thought was wiped from her mind when she caught sight of a dark-clad figure limping along the street. George! She wanted to cry with happiness. As she began to slip quietly away, she heard Reggie say, 'Ooh – where's 'er off to, then?'

George saw her coming and waved happily. As he drew close, she saw his mucky face crinkle into a grin and her heart lifted. He was all right! And how lovely it was having someone who was just so honestly pleased to see you!

'All right, Violet?'

'Yeah,' she said. She felt the dried grime on her own face crack as she smiled. 'Survived another night.'

His face sobered. 'That were a bad'un, weren't it? There was a shelter bombed over in Summer Hill – quite a few in there . . .' He tried to look cheerier. 'Listen – I'll come and meet you out of work if I can. Or I'll come to yours, if you like . . .'

'No!' Violet said. She had to keep him away from Mom, at least for a while longer. Seeing how startled George looked at the way she'd almost jumped down his throat, she added, 'I mean – there's no need for you to traipse all the way down here.'

'Even if they're at us again tonight –' He rolled his eyes. 'We might manage a half-hour . . . ?'

'All right.' She smiled. Mom would be expecting her home but she'd find some excuse. 'See you later.'

George turned to go. 'Fingers crossed!'

Grace had seen Harry Cobb earlier in the night. They had both been to assist at the wreckage of a bombed house in a nearby street. Mr Powell's list said that there ought to be a Miss Jenkins and her lodger inside and the rescue team were hauling at the pile of destruction which had once been their house, calling out to whoever might be underneath. Every so often Harry Cobb held up a hand for silence as they listened. But there was nothing. Eventually, after hours of work, two bodies were brought out.

It was still dark when the job seemed to be finished. The ambulance left with the remains of Miss Jenkins and her factory-worker lodger. Groups of people stood huddled, shocked, between the long worms of hosepipe. The recue team were needed elsewhere and started to pack up. Grace saw Harry Cobb looking round and within a moment his eyes fastened on her. He strode over.

'All right?' she said softly. In the gloom he was only an impression, the power of those eyes muted by the dust and darkness.

Harry nodded. 'You?'

'Think so, yeah.'

'I've got to go.' He was speaking very quietly but there was a force of emotion in his voice which filled her with excitement. 'But – I want to see you, Grace. D'you get a dinner break? See if you can get out at one – just for a few minutes, eh?'

'All right.' She knew she would – whatever Mrs Hodgson might say.

As Harry Cobb disappeared into the murk, Grace put her hand in her coat pocket to touch the latest letter she had from Jimmy. *My dear Grace . . .* Always the same. Jimmy really wasn't the writing sort. Not much to say. A few bits about the lads in the camp. *I love you . . .*

Should she feel guilty, for the way Harry Cobb made her feel? For that look of hunger she saw in his eyes every time he looked at her? Of course she should! But it was as if Jimmy Oval and Harry Cobb were part of two different worlds with nothing to do with each other.

She drew her hand out of her pocket again and went over to find Violet. She was trying not to think about the fact that she knew nothing about Harry Cobb and that she found she didn't want to – about the possibility that she was playing with fire.

All Monday morning, the prospect of seeing Harry filled her with such jittery excitement that she didn't even feel tired. She joked with the delivery boys as usual, rushed about cleaning and dusting, taking tins off shelves at the back and tidying everything.

'You've got ants in your pants today,' Mrs Hodgson remarked, standing behind the counter in her flat, bunion-distorted shoes. She was in her fifties, a neat lady with tightly curled greying hair – and a good sort, even though almost everything she said seemed tinged with disapproval.

'I think it's because of last night,' Grace said. 'It was non-stop and I've not had time to unwind at all.' This, at least, was true.

'You poor girls,' Mrs Hodgson said, with sudden warmth that took Grace by surprise. 'I was in the cellar all night and I thought about you all out there. Terrible.'

'I'm not sure I'd want to be in the cellar either, though,' Grace said. 'My mom's out in the shelter with all the family and it seems worse just sitting there under it.'

'Your mother and father all right, are they?' Mrs Hodgson said. She knew Cath Templeton slightly – she came into the shop now and then.

'They've got shelters at the BSA,' Grace said, rubbing a duster over the already clean counter. She eyed the clock. It was a quarter to one. Mrs Hodgson seemed in such a good mood today that Grace said quickly, 'Is it all right if I pop out for a few minutes at one o'clock today? Our mom asked me to get a few things if I had time.'

'All right,' Mrs Hodgson said. 'Just let me have a quick ciggy and you can take your break then.'

Grace could hardly believe it had been so easy. Mrs Hodgson was a complete cigarette addict so she soon went out for her smoke. As soon as one o'clock came, Grace took off her overall and hurried outside. Immediately she heard a 'psst' – and there he was, waiting on the

139

opposite corner. Afraid that Mrs Hodgson could still see her – though why she was so afraid of this she did not ask herself – Grace tilted her head to indicate that they should move further along.

As they walked, she knew he must be watching her from behind. She knew her hair looked nice, curling under and rolled back from her forehead. She had her close-fitting blue dress on again and set off with her most hip-swinging walk. Further down by the police station, Harry crossed over and joined her. She watched as his powerful body came striding across the street.

'Come along 'ere.' He kept walking until they reached a narrow side street with warehouses on each side. Grace glanced round as she followed him along it. There were a few blokes about and she felt horribly self-conscious. What am I doing wrong? she asked herself. Nothing: and yet, in truth, everything.

Harry stopped a little way along by a wall and turned to her. Looking up at him, seeing that powerful blue-eyed gaze boring into her again, she felt her cheeks pinking. Every other thought left her mind and simple, basic desire coursed through her, of a kind she had never known before.

'I can't stop thinking about you, Grace.' He spoke in a low voice, leaning close to her. 'Ever since the first time I saw yer – you're all I can think about.' He sounded bewildered and everything he was saying made her blood rush, her breathing turn shallow. The feeling of being noticed, desired – well, that was a thing! 'I don't know what you've done to me, sort of thing.'

She knew she ought to say something to break the spell she already felt caught up in. She should ask him questions about himself, to bring things back to reality. At that moment it felt as if there was nothing else but the two of them, standing in this scruffy street, his eyes fixed hungrily on hers. Every nerve in her body felt alive to him. But she couldn't seem to begin.

'Can we meet?' he went on in a low voice. 'Later. I dunno . . .' He made a frustrated sound. 'There's not much time, is there, for anything these days?'

Grace thought, desperately. What with work and the ARP and Mom needing her home to help, when could she fit it in?

'What about after work?' she said. 'If you're out? About six, say – here, by the pub?'

Harry thought for a second. 'I should be able to – just for a bit, any road, as long as there's no raid by then. All right. I'll see yer then.'

He reached out and, for a second, dared to caress her cheek. Their eyes locked together. Grace felt as if her body was on the point of exploding – it was so strange and electric and she wanted more and more of the feeling.

'See yer later,' he said softly.

She watched him walk away, suddenly feeling as if she was another Grace standing beside her real self: a dangerous stranger.

Eighteen

Violet spent the day at work in a dream. At the end of the shift she ran into June.

'Terrible that, the other day,' June said.

'What – Mrs Strong?' Violet hitched her bag on to her shoulder. She had not seen June to talk to since that dreadful night. 'I know.' Her eyes filled. It still felt very raw. 'I thought she was going to be all right.'

'Well, you can't always tell from the outside,' June said. She seemed to be full of information these days – Violet couldn't help admiring her even though she was annoying. 'You did what you could. You have to just put it behind yer. Come on –' She took Violet's arm and it was strangely comforting. 'Let's get out of 'ere.'

When they got outside, June nudged her.

'Eh – who's that?' She was all agog at the sight of a young man in a police uniform waiting outside Hughes's Biscuits, an irrepressible smile already breaking over his face. 'He's looking over 'ere!'

Violet cheered up immediately. 'That's my friend George.'

'Ooh,' June said. 'You never said. You walking out with him?'

'I dunno really,' Violet said. She certainly wasn't telling June everything even if she was a bit more bearable nowadays. 'There's never time, is there?'

June gave a raucous laugh. 'Oh, there's always time if you make it, bab!'

George stood very upright, legs astride and hands clasped behind his back like a soldier on 'stand-easy'. The uniform flattered his round, friendly face and sturdy frame. To Violet's irritation, she realized she was going to have to introduce him to June.

'All right, George?' she said, as all the other women hurried on past. 'This is June – we work together.'

'We're pals, me and Vi,' June said importantly. 'I work in the First Aid station at the Baths.'

'Thought I'd seen you before somewhere,' George said. June softened at this, pleased with the recognition. Her size and her strong, dark features meant she was a once-seen-never-forgotten sort of girl.

'I can't walk back with you today, I'm going with George,' Violet said firmly, marvelling at herself. How things had changed in just a few weeks!

'All right.' June seemed caught between huffiness and making eyes at George. 'T'ra then, Vi.'

It was already getting dark and there was a sharp chill in the air.

'She looks a bit of a one,' George said as June took herself off. He sounded amused.

'She's all right,' Violet said. 'Just always wants attention.'

'Fancy coming back to mine for a cuppa?' George said. 'You can meet our mom and whoever else is in.'

Violet was torn. Her own mother would be expecting her home. And she did feel badly about the amount she was out these days, leaving Mom to go the shelter. But she knew she was not going to say no. Amid all the other terrors, May's anger didn't seem such a fearsome thing these days.

'All right – I mustn't be long, though,' she said.

'Come on then,' George said happily. 'It ain't far. We live up this end – opposite the Sentinel Works.'

As they started walking, George turned to her bashfully and said, 'I hope this is all right. Me introducing you to the family. I don't want you to think I'm getting above myself.'

'I like meeting other people's families.'

George smiled. 'Only – I'd like to think we was walking out together, like.'

Violet felt a thrill go through her but to cover her blushes, she said, 'Before flaming Hitler puts paid to every evening, you mean?'

George looked startled, as he sometimes did, at the sharpness of the response in her gentle voice.

'Well – yeah!' A noisy truck passed, pumping out filth into the already smoky air. Violet coughed. By the time it had passed, George still seemed to be waiting for her to say something.

'So, is that all right?' he prompted.

'Us walking out?' Excitement tingled through her. A boy – a nice lad – was asking her to walk out with him! She had never really believed this would ever happen, what with her own bespectacled shyness and Mom watching her like a hawk. 'Oh, yes – yes, please!'

George laughed then. 'Well, in that case, Miss er . . . ?'

'Simms.'

'May I be so bold as to take your arm?'

'You may.' She found herself grinning. George always made her feel better about life, within a few moments of being with him.

They linked arms and walked down along to Cattell Road. Violet realized that despite the bombing and blackout and sadness of everything, she suddenly felt happier than she ever had in her life before.

Where George lived was a little corner terrace.

'Mom!' he called out as they pushed in through the front door. He led Violet through a dark front room to where there was a light on at the back.

Immediately Violet could smell the mix of damp fustiness, Vim and boiling vegetables common to a lot of houses in the area. But laid over it was the mouthwatering aroma of fried onions.

'That you, George?' a woman's voice called.

The back room was much warmer than the front. A plump, pink-cheeked little woman turned to greet them at the stove. Violet realized immediately that George was the spit of his mother: she had the same round face and jolly smile. She turned the gas down and came forward, wiping her hands.

'Hello, son,' she said. 'Who's this?'

'Mom – this is Violet who I told yer about,' George announced, looking fit to burst with pride.

'Hello, Mrs . . .' Violet stopped, mortified. What on earth was his name?

'Cherry,' she said. Even the name was cheerful.

'Pleased to meet you,' Violet almost curtsied in her embarrassment.

'You too, bab, at last,' Mrs Cherry said, smiling broadly. She had a yellow flowery apron on over her clothes and her hair was thin and mouse brown, chopped to shoulder length and held back from her face with a couple of kirby grips. 'We've heard a lot about you from George,' she said. 'In fact 'e hardly ever talks about anything else.'

It was George's turn to blush now.

'Where're the wenches?' he asked. Turning to Violet he said, 'Vera – 'er's the eldest, lives up the road, couple of kids. Husband's in the army. But the others still live here.'

'Nance's taken Pilot out down the road – should be back any minute,' Mrs Cherry said. 'Alice's gone off with *him* again.' This was spoken with a roll of her eyes.

'Mom don't like our Alice's boyfriend,' George said, as if this was not entirely obvious.

'No, I don't,' Mrs Cherry said vehemently. 'I wouldn't trust that one as far as I could throw him. But there's nowt I can say'll make 'er listen to me.'

'Alice is going on twenty-six, Mom,' George said quietly.

'Old enough to mek 'er own bed and lie on it – I know,' Mrs Cherry said. 'But I don't like to watch it happen, that I don't.'

Violet was beginning to feel rather plunged in at the deep end of family business and Mrs Cherry, seeing her awkwardness, said, 'What am I thinking? Sit down, Violet – there's tea in the pot. I'll pour us all one.'

'Mom?' A shout came from the front, along with a sudden general commotion. Violet heard an animal leaping about and a moment later a large, muscular dog with a brindled coat, squashed-up nose and slobbery jowls came rushing into the room and leapt at her.

'Pilot, c'm'ere!' Nancy shouted, of which the dog took no notice whatsoever.

Mrs Cherry immediately tried to get him off but the dog was so heavy and in such a state of excited delight, paws up on Violet's legs, licking and sniffing, that it proved a struggle. Violet got the giggles and squirmed as he stuck his wet, snuffling nose in her ear.

''E's gone mad,' Nancy announced. 'I could hardly hold him. I'm sure there's gunna be a raid any minute – he knows, I know he does.'

She came and joined in the wrestling with the over-enthusiastic dog. When he had been brought to the ground, whimpering and still gazing adoringly at Violet, introductions were made. Nancy was blonde and pretty with blue eyes and high cheekbones, and – as Cherrys went – surprisingly slender. Violet knew she was George's younger sister and was nineteen.

'Sorry about that,' she said. 'He's gone off 'is 'ead. It's the raids done it.'

''E's not the only one,' Mrs Cherry said dolefully. 'I've not felt myself since it started. My nerves are in rags.'

Violet smiled at Nancy. 'It's all right. He's nice.' She liked dogs though it would have been hard to say what sort this one was.

'It's hard on animals, all this,' Mrs Cherry said, bringing the teapot over. 'I'd never've got him if I'd known what was coming. Tain't right. 'E don't like it neither.' She nodded her head towards the corner where Violet saw, for the first time, a lone green budgerigar sitting with a depressed air on the perch of a little cage.

'Not much fun for any of us, come to that,' George said.

'So you're in the ARP?' Nancy said. She held the dog close to her by the collar, stroking him and gradually calming him down. 'I'm thinking I might join as well.'

'Oh, no, you're not,' Mrs Cherry said, pouring tea with a slightly threatening air.

'Mom – I've got to do summat!' Nancy said.

As they wrangled over this, though affectionately, Violet sat back, enjoying just being there. It was a room like so many other back rooms she had ever been in: the old black-leaded range with knick-knacks on the mantel, a gas stove on the back wall now, brown linoleum, a table and chairs and white food store with a fold-down front. She felt at home both in the house and with the warm welcome from George's family.

After they had chatted for a while and drunk their tea, Violet got up to go. To her amazement, Mrs Cherry said, 'Won't you stay for a bite to eat with us? We can spin it out for a little'un like you.' Violet was really touched – it was a generous offer when food was so short.

'That's nice of you, she said, 'but Mom'll be wondering where I've got to. I'm late enough already.'

'I'll walk yer home.' George got up straight away.

'Oh, no, you're all right – there's no need,' Violet said.

'Don't talk daft – course I will. It's dark. Any road, I can come and say hello to your mom.'

Violet felt herself freeze inside. But she didn't argue. At least, not until they were walking along, arm in arm outside.

'I must be the happiest man in all of Birmingham!' George announced, beaming into the darkness.

Violet laughed, but she felt very uneasy. She was struggling with herself all the way. She had become used to telling fibs to people – Mom especially – so much, that it came as second nature now. It would be so much easier to keep making excuses to George about her mother. But she knew she didn't want to start off with him on that footing.

'Look,' she made herself say when they were getting close to home. 'You'd best not come in and see my mom.'

'Why?' George sounded uncertain suddenly. 'Don't you think I'm good enough for you?'

'No, George.' She stopped and spoke earnestly. 'It's not that. Not in the least bit. I just need to sort of prepare her. She's a bit funny about men and she's none too keen on me going out. It's not you as such – she's just not easy. Sometimes I think she'd bite off her nose to spite her own face, as they say! It's difficult to explain . . . I don't want her spoiling things.'

She looked down, ashamed. 'She mustn't know we're meeting – not yet, anyway. Can you live with that?'

George frowned. 'Well, that's a bit rum, I must say. Don't she want you to be happy?'

'Not that I've noticed,' Violet said drily. She tried to sound kinder. She could see this was truly outside George's experience. 'Maybe she does – in her way. But as I say, I'd just rather we kept things to ourselves for a while. If things were to get . . .' She looked down, shyly. 'You know . . .'

George moved his face closer to hers in the dark. 'What? Serious? *I'm* serious, Vi – I don't know about you.'

She was moved by him, by the way he was able to be so true and straightforward in his feelings.

'Yes,' she said. 'I am. Course I am. Meeting you has been the best thing ever. It's just, when it comes to Mom – I don't want her spoiling things when it's early days, that's all.'

'All right,' George said. 'Well, you know best, Vi. Come on – I'll walk you 'til we're close anyhow. It'll give me longer to be with you.'

They turned into Archibald Street and soon reached the entry into the yard.

'This is me – best stop here,' she said.

'All right.' George paused, looking at her. 'You're lovely, you are.' Seeming full of wonder, he leaned forward and gently kissed her cheek. 'Might see yer tomorrer.'

Violet watched him walk away before going inside to face her mother's wrath at how late she was. At that moment, the old guilt she had felt all her life, her dancing round Mom's moods and being kept under her thumb – all of her tolerance of that was hanging by a slim thread.

Nineteen

Grace stood waiting on the corner where she had said goodbye to Harry Cobb in her dinner break.

She had her coat collar turned up and her air-force blue hat with a brim pulled down low over her eyes. Lighting a cigarette to calm her nerves, she stood, bewildered, in the acrid-smelling darkness, wondering to herself what she was doing there. The Grace who everyone assumed, as night followed day, would settle down with Jimmy Oval, the Grace who had told Mom she was just popping out for a while to check something with Mr Powell at the ARP post . . . And now this new Grace, full of an unfamiliar, fizzing excitement, who had refused to answer Marie's nosey questions, had dared herself to come and stand on a street corner like a woman of the night, waiting for a man she hardly knew.

It was another bitterly cold, cloudless night. Come on, she thought frantically. Or the siren'll go off again! She finished her cigarette and trod the butt under her heel, pushing her hands into her pockets and keeping her head down, terrified of being recognized. People picked their way past her. A lorry with its lights masked rumbled slowly along. Thank heaven there was only a shred of moon. It would be awkward if she met anyone she knew – they were not far from the Co-op after all and the area was full of her customers.

'Grace?' She heard him before she could even make

him out in the blackness of the street. His voice was low. There was a husky roughness to it.

Her whole being lurched with excitement. What am I doing? She had never before had feelings like this towards any man. Her body felt electric.

'Yes – here.' She spoke very softly.

She could only make out the outline of him, broad-shouldered in a coat, a cap, taller than she remembered and suddenly right beside her.

'You came then.'

She felt ashamed when he said this – as if she had done wrong. Who was this man really? She knew nothing of him: his past, his present, whether he was – God forbid – already married. But at that moment she didn't want to know. It was as if they were in a dream place, here in the black of night, separate from the people and obligations of the daytime.

'I know where we can go,' he said.

She was frightened suddenly. A chill like cold water. Go?

What had she expected? A romantic setting, sitting opposite Harry in some softly lit room while they chatted and flirted? All they had were this cold night and the dark, dirty streets.

'Where're we going?' Her voice came out small and young-sounding. What did he think she was here for? She had not been out with anyone but Jimmy, but she was certainly no innocent by now as to where babies came from. But she was used to younger men who she felt more in charge of. She didn't know how she was supposed to behave when she felt like this, when his very voice raised goose pimples on her skin making her *want*, want him with a power that seemed stronger than her usual will.

'Well, there ain't many places we can go.' He stopped

and took her arm. 'You all right, Grace?' She was reassured by his kindly tone.

'Yes. I'm just not . . . I mean, I don't usually do this sort of thing.' Whatever this sort of thing was, exactly.

'You don't need to worry.' He squeezed her arm. 'It's just nice to see yer.'

Feeling she had slipped somehow into another life, Grace walked beside him.

'How was last night?' she asked. Their Civil Defence work gave them a common footing.

'Pretty grim – as usual.' He sounded wretched and she was even more moved by him. He turned to her. 'D'you get frightened – being out in it?'

'Sometimes,' she admitted. 'If you've got summat to do it's easier just to get on with it. But sometimes – yeah, it's been horrible and I'll be shaking all over.'

'Seems wrong to me, you ladies doing that sort of work.'

'We're all getting used to it,' she said. 'And I don't envy my mom, sat out there in the shelter just waiting to be hit. It seems better to . . .' She was about to mention Mrs Oval taking people into her house, but that almost seemed to bring Jimmy into the conversation and she stopped. The thought of Jimmy gave her terrible pangs of guilt. Steady, familiar Jimmy – her known quantity. Jimmy who now seemed from another time.

'You girls do a fine job,' he said. He was speaking softly, wooingly. 'Here – come 'ere a minute, Grace . . .'

Harry guided her into a side street. It was so dark, they had to fumble their way along. He stopped her and turned her so that they were facing each other, laying his hands on her shoulders.

'I can't stop thinking about you, Grace.'

The words thrilled her. At the same time she knew she

ought to put a stop to this – yet she was full of excitement and desire, as if the two Graces were fighting each other as his deep voice went on close to her ear.

'You're a fine woman, Grace – so beautiful. I just wish there was somewhere nice I could take you for this – somewhere refined . . .'

For this? she thought, panic rising in her. What was he expecting?

But what had *she* been expecting, overcome by romantic excitement? And here she was in a dark alley on her own with a man she hardly knew. A big, strong man.

'You're so fine, such a looker . . .' He inclined his head suddenly and she felt his lips on the side of her neck, gentle, seductive. The feel of it flowed through her whole body and she took in a sharp breath.

'Like that, do yer?' His voice was a soft murmur. 'Oh, Grace, Grace . . .'

His lips met hers. For a moment, in some watching part of herself, even as she kissed him back, responding to the force of him, the old Grace who could still pass judgement, stood shocked. But finally that Grace slipped away and she was just with Harry, with the smells of him – hints of plaster and dust, of sweat and soap – with the hungry press of his lips and his arms pulling her closer and closer to him.

After a time, he stopped his kissing, tilted his head back and drew in a fierce breath. In that instant he seemed to decide something. He started tugging at the buttons of her coat, clumsy with need, struggling with her clothing, pulling her blouse out from the waist of her skirt. The air was a cold shock on her skin and the roughness of his hands against her flesh brought her abruptly back to reality.

'Don't!' she said sharply. 'What're you doing?'

She pushed at him, tugging her blouse back down and buttoning her coat.

'Sorry.' He backed away. He too sounded as if he had woken from a dream. 'I never meant . . . Only I thought you . . .' He stopped, sounding worried, ashamed even. 'I'm sorry, Grace – I got carried away. Only you're just so . . . God, I've never met anyone like you.'

'I hardly know you,' she said. She desired him, it was true, could hardly stop thinking about him hour after hour, but she had not imagined this. She wanted sweet words, and kisses, maybe even promises . . . 'You can't just . . . Not like that!'

'I got carried away.' He stood without touching her now. 'That's all. Don't hold it against me. You girls – you don't know what it's like to be a bloke. When we see a beautiful woman it's just . . . It's as if your brain just runs out the door . . .'

He was so boyish and so crestfallen than she laughed, forgiving him.

'Well, no harm done,' she said. 'I just think things should go a bit more slowly, that's all. I don't want you thinking I'm that kind of girl, do I?'

'I know you're not, Grace,' he said earnestly. 'You're quality, you are – as well as damn pretty. I could see that the first time I met yer.'

He took out a packet of cigarettes and offered her one. She saw the orange tips glow as they lit up and they stood smoking side by side.

'I hope those ruddy Germans can't see that,' he said. 'They'll be along any time now if they're coming tonight.'

'Some of our wardens won't even use a torch,' she said. 'They're superstitious.'

She heard him laugh, slightly, then there was a silence between them.

'Harry,' she said seriously. 'I don't know what to think. I don't know you. I've even got someone – you know, away in the forces . . .' She was on the verge of asking him about himself, but somehow the words wouldn't come out of her mouth.

There was a silence, then he said, 'Any night now – tonight – we could die, that's all.'

She felt the force of this. It was true. It was his way of saying, *Don't ask, don't think – we're here and that's all we know.*

'And if we have other nights,' he went on, 'I'd like to spend some of them with you.'

Moved by this, she felt her feelings turn towards him again. Now was now and he was right – they might all be dead soon. Without saying anything she put her arms round him and they held each other, kissing and caressing in the darkness. Here was this moment. That was all she had and all she could know.

II

1940

Twenty

Thursday 14 November

'D'you think they'd let you in then?' Arthur Oval said. 'After all, it's the cathedral – it's all just for the nobs, I 'spect.'

He and Mildred were having breakfast, some of the kids at the table with them. Both their faces were heavy with exhaustion – Arthur's especially looked almost as saggy as that of the family's old dog Ginger, who lay patiently by the fire, head on her paws but vigilant in case of scraps.

'Well, you'd hope so – it's a house of God,' Mildred said, pushing herself to her feet to refill the teapot. 'But I dain't mean *I* was going in person – I've got far too much to do. I'm sure there'll be a good turn-out, though.'

'What?' Sylvie said, appearing at the bottom of the stairs. 'What're you on about?'

'Mr Chamberlain's memorial service,' Mildred said reverently. She had been truly upset to hear about the death of Neville Chamberlain, who had been MP for Ladywood and, as Prime Minister, had to announce the outbreak of war. The service was to be at St Philip's Cathedral the next day. She took a mouthful of tea and went on, 'He did a great deal for this city, Mr Chamberlain – whatever some may say about him. He was only trying to stop all this that we've got into now.'

'Oh, ar . . .' Arthur gave a huge yawn. 'You're right about that, my lady – that you are.'

'This is all getting too much for you, Arthur,' Mildred said solicitously. 'Man of your age up all hours like this. It ain't right.'

'None of it's right, though, is it?' Arthur said, pushing up on the table and shaking as if to get himself on the move. 'But what can we do, eh? Mind you – they was daylight raids yesterday.'

Over the past weeks the sirens had gone off almost every night, sending them fleeing to the shelters, but often for nothing as the planes passed over. It still meant nights of worry, cramped and cold, never being sure when the bombs would be meant for them again. But yesterday there had been a daylight raid causing damage at the Austin Aero-Engine factory at Longbridge.

'I don't know if I could bear to go into town, nowadays,' Mildred said. 'What with all the destruction – even the cathedral. It's wicked, that's what it is.'

St Philip's Cathedral had been damaged by fire, and there was damage to the town hall and art gallery, as well as so many other familiar buildings.

'I'd best get to work,' Arthur said. 'See you later, bab.' Mildred got up and he went to peck her on the cheek. As if thinking again, he turned back and took her well-upholstered form in his arms. 'That's my wench.'

'Ooh, Arthur!' Mildred chuckled, kissing him back. 'What's come over you?'

'Dad!' fifteen-year-old Charlie protested. Sylvie and Dolly both giggled.

Arthur clipped Charlie affectionately round the ear before patting John's head. Little John squirmed with pleasure.

'Enough from you lot. Your mother,' he announced

160

solemnly, 'is a magnificent woman and the queen of my heart – and don't you go forgetting it.'

'Oh, *Dad*,' Sylvie said, a lopsided grin on her face. She was seventeen and walking out with a lad herself. 'That's lovely, that is.'

'Any road – you lot'd best be off to work as well,' Arthur said. 'See yer later.' He picked up his hat and headed for the door. Turning, he said, 'You're marvellous, all of yer – you know that, don't yer?'

Grace looked up as the door of the shop opened. Mrs Hodgson had just gone out for her break and she was holding the fort alone.

'Oh!' she cried, her pulse picking up speed. 'What're you doing here? Don't let Mrs H catch you!'

Harry had not been into the shop since that first time, as Grace had told him how suspicious Mrs Hodgson was of him. She felt glad she'd just touched up her lipstick, almost as if she had known he was coming.

Harry grinned. 'I was just thinking about what I needed to buy.' He made a face. 'But I don't need to bother now, do I?'

He glanced around, checking they were really alone, and leaned on the counter, edging across so that he was as close to her as possible. Grace leaned her elbows on the other side so that they were almost nose to nose. Their lips met.

'It's the first time I've seen you in daylight for a long time,' she said. 'I'd almost forgotten what you look like.'

There were the vivid blue eyes, the strong-boned face. But in truth, he looked older than she remembered.

'I ain't forgotten you,' he said gallantly. 'It's carved on my memory, your face.'

'Oh, you.' She pecked a kiss on his nose. 'You've got

161

a smooth tongue, you have. Here – where d'you get that funny scarf from?'

In daylight she could see that the scarf was a baggy blue home-knit, its edges roughly decorated with red blanket-stitch. Harry glanced down at it and grinned sheepishly.

'Oh, my sister. Years back when we was kids. It's a bit rough but it keeps the cold out.' He reached for her hand. 'Meet me tonight? If nothing goes off?'

For a moment she wanted to ask, *So are we courting, or what?* But somehow questions never felt the right thing with this mysterious man.

'Same place, same time?' They could usually snatch a bit of time early evening.

'Yeah.' He lingered, his eyes fixed on hers. He took a strand of her hair between his fingers for a second and stared at it in wonder, then into her eyes. She could see the frank desire in them and it made her look down, blushing. 'I wish it was now. God, you're a looker, Grace.' He released her hair and pushed himself off from the counter. 'I'd better tear myself away. See you later, gorgeous.'

It was lucky he did as the door opened as soon as he had left and a lady came in asking for a bag of flour and some Andrews Liver Salts.

The excitement of meeting Harry was what was keeping Grace going through all the dark nights, the raids and horror of it all. There were very few times when they could ever meet, because there had been so many raids. When they did there was nowhere to go. Harry said he didn't want to take her into one of the pubs.

'I want you all to myself,' he said. 'Not with other blokes all gawping at you.'

So, dark streets and even darker corners where they could exist for a while and have a kiss and a cuddle was what it amounted to. But having that to look forward to lit up Grace's days. In the shop as she stacked tins and packets on shelves, weighed out rations of tea or bacon for customers or swept up at the end of the day, she dreamt about her meetings with Harry, remembering the feel of his body close to hers, taut with desire, the sweet things he said to her.

'One of these days I'll make you mine,' he had said last time.

Grace's heart began to race. Harry always seemed to live in the present – what was the use of looking forward, was his attitude, when they none of them knew how things would be next week, never mind next year? And he knew about Jimmy – she had felt bound to tell him that, almost as a way of protecting herself. She no longer knew what she felt about anything. Was she in love with Harry? It felt as if she was. He was all she could think about.

When she received a letter from Jimmy, she tried to direct all her feelings on to him. She wrote chatty letters back and tried to pretend things were all as they had been. But the truth was, in all her fantasies, day and night, and in the burning of her body, all she could think of was Harry Cobb – a man who made her feel like no one else ever had. And now what was he saying? Was he trying to say that one day they would be one – that he would make her his wife?

She dashed home after work and her mother had tea ready for all of them. She held Gordon while Mom dished up, a stew heavily padded with turnip, too distracted to pay her too much attention. Michael was gabbling excitedly about how they'd seen a Spitfire chasing off a Messerschmitt over the park.

'God, you know all the names already, don't you?' Grace said.

Her mother came to the table with plates. 'For goodness' sake, where's Dennis got to? Anyone seen him? And Joseph?'

'They're out doing something with that little gang of theirs,' Marie said scornfully.

'D'you want me to go and find them?' Michael said, scrambling up from the table.

'No, no – just sit down and have your tea,' Cath instructed impatiently. 'At least some of you can be eating it while it's hot.'

'It's full moon tonight,' Marie said. They all looked at each other. Everyone knew what that was likely to mean: a clear view for the enemy bombers.

'Are you on tonight, Grace?' their father asked.

'Yes. I'd best be off in a tick.' How easily the fib slid off her tongue. She sent up a silent prayer. Forgive me just this once, sweet Lord . . .

'Heaven be praised you've got those shelters over at the works, Bill,' Cath said. 'I never have a moment's peace when you're over there.'

'It's a nuisance,' Grace's dad said, shovelling his meal down as fast as he could. 'You're trying to get the job done and off they go, flaming sirens again . . . We don't always bother to go out – there's cellars in the factory do just as well.'

'You go over to that shelter, Bill, and make sure you look after yourself.' Cath brandished the serving spoon in his direction. 'I don't want you taking any chances.'

'All right,' he said, in a voice which Grace knew, meant that he would do whatever he was going to do anyway.

She smiled at him, and she saw him give her a wink in return.

'You keep safe, Dad,' she said. She handed Gordon back to her mother. 'See you all later.'

Putting on her warden's coat and cap, she hurried out as if she had urgent ARP duties to fulfil. In fact, she was not on the duty rota that night. Her breath shallow with anticipation, she hurried out into the darkness of the streets, where she knew Harry Cobb would be waiting.

Twenty-One

Violet reported to the post at six o'clock to find Miss Holt and Mr Powell already ensconced in the back room. Miss Holt was sitting on a chair close to Mr Powell's desk and everything seemed so cosy that Violet almost felt she was interrupting something. For the first time, she couldn't help wondering whether there was a Mrs Powell, or whether . . . But she was pretty sure Mr Powell had mentioned his wife.

'Ah, Miss Simms,' Mr Powell said, ticking off her name. His careful lists, written out in tidy copperplate, were arranged neatly close to the telephone.

'Bang on time as ever,' Miss Holt said warmly. 'Good girl.'

Violet had realized over the months that she was in the ARP that Miss Holt, in her stiff, formal way, was growing very fond of her.

'There's a drop left in the pot if you'd like it,' she offered. 'I'd better boil the kettle again.'

'Thank you, Miss Holt,' Violet said. She went to hang up her coat. 'I'll do it.' As she put the kettle on to boil, she remarked, 'It feels quite peculiar outside – the moon's so bright.'

'Yes,' Mr Powell said quietly. There was a tone of foreboding in his voice.

Violet had a bad feeling about the night herself, but it wouldn't do to say so. Mr Powell and Miss Holt would not approve of anyone expressing unnecessary doom in the face of that ominous, glittering, bombers' moon. *Sufficient unto the day is the evil thereof*, was one of Miss Holt's favourite sayings.

'Oi, oi – do I see a nice full teapot?' Reggie Meakins said as he came breezing in.

'No, as a matter of fact, you don't,' Miss Holt said. 'But fortunately for you, Violet's making a fresh one.'

'Ah – good wench.' Reggie gave her one of his winks. Violet looked away.

Reggie had obviously come straight from the factory and he looked rumpled and tired.

'There's a slice of bread and butter if you like,' Miss Holt said, more sympathetically. 'The "butter" is fanciful, of course, but you get my meaning.'

'Thanks, Miss Holt,' Reggie said, ramming the bread with its scraping of marge into his mouth. With his spare hand he aimed an imaginary dart at the wall. 'I could eat a horse.'

Francis Paine came in then, carefully unbuttoning his coat and, as ever, standing about looking pale and awkward. He brought his own smell with him: sweat and mothballs and a strange, chemical whiff.

'No Grace tonight?' Reggie said.

'Grace is off duty.' Mr Powell spoke without looking up. 'As is Mr Oval – unless, of course, more is required of us . . .'

'You come on patrol with me tonight, Violet,' Miss Holt decreed.

'Yes, Miss Holt.'

Quentin Molyneaux launched himself into the room next with a flourish, held out one skinny arm and pronounced:

'*It is the very error of the moon:*
She comes more nearer earth than she was wont,
And makes men mad!'

'Ah,' Miss Holt, holding up a finger:

'*Do not swear by the moon, for she changes*
constantly!'

'Oh, pack it *in*,' Reggie snapped. They liked to play what Quentin called 'Shakespeare Snap'. It drove Reggie mad with irritation. 'There's no need for all that claptrap.'

'A little culture never hurt anyone,' Miss Holt argued reasonably.

Whatever smart-alec reply Reggie might have given to that was cut off by a cry.

'Grace! Grace? You gotta come!'

Boots came clumping at top speed through the front room and one of Grace's freckle-faced brothers – Violet thought it was Joseph though she was not quite sure – stood in the doorway, chest heaving. There seemed news of something terrible in his eyes.

'She's not here, dear,' Miss Holt told him kindly. 'She's not on duty tonight.'

'But Mom said . . .' The boy looked round desperately as if he couldn't believe his sister was not there. His eyes fixed on Violet a moment and she saw him recognize her.

'What's up, pal?' Reggie went to ruffle his hair, but he was having none of it. He turned and went tearing back out to the street.

'Wait!' Violet ran after him, but he was as fast as a rat up a drain and she had almost to sprint to catch up. 'Joseph, isn't it?'

He slowed. She caught his arm and spun him round and he crumpled and started to shake.

'I'm Vi – Grace's friend, remember? Whatever's the matter?'

He started sobbing then, a really distressed little boy. He was only about ten, Violet realized.

'It's me brother Den. We was playing, down in there like, and . . .' He spoke in jerks between the sobs. 'One of them houses . . . And it come down on him . . .'

'Oh, good heavens!' Violet said. 'Is anyone there – have you told anyone?'

'Yeah – our mom, but Dad's at work and she wanted Grace, but we don't know where she is and we don't know what to do! We gotta get him out!'

'Just wait there a minute.'

Violet dashed back to number sixty-one.

'Miss Holt! Mr Powell! He says there's been an accident – those houses down the end. They were playing and, from what he says, it must've collapsed on his brother!'

Mr Powell grabbed the receiver and dialled immediately. Miss Holt dashed out with Violet, firing questions as they hurried back to Joseph. The street had an odd feel in the weirdly bright moonlight. They could hear the boy's sniffling sobs before they reached him.

'Come on, young man – you show us,' Miss Holt said.

They found Cath Templeton, Grace's mother, standing helplessly with Gordon in her arms and a crowd of neighbours, all digging in the rubble of the bombed-out house. She was sobbing and calling out desperately to the people to help him.

'Oh, hurry up – please – please, get him out!'

Someone had brought a Tilley lamp and stood it nearby and Violet hurried over to her in the dim light.

'Mrs Templeton?' She touched the frantic woman's arm.

'Oh!' Cath jumped violently. She looked so strained and different from usual that she was almost like another person. 'Oh – it's you, Violet. It's my Dennis – Joseph came home and said . . . The number of times I've told them and told them not to play in these places but the little devils . . .' She was overcome for a moment. Gordon was snivelling as well. 'We haven't heard a sound out of him. They can see his boots . . .' She sobbed. 'He's dead, my poor little lad – I know 'e is!'

'They're all doing the best they can.' Violet couldn't think what else to say. She was close to tears herself. It looked bad. She remembered Mrs Strong for a second and a shudder went through her. The thought that Dennis, Grace's sweet little brother, was under all that weight of brick, was too horrible to think about. 'Would you like me to hold the baby?' she offered.

Wordlessly, Mrs Templeton handed Gordon over and he sank heavily, damply, into Violet's arms, quietening for a moment as he stared into her face.

'Hello,' Violet said. 'You're a little lump, aren't you?' She felt like crying herself, seeing the state Grace's mom was in. And where the hell had Grace got to? Everyone had seemed to be expecting her to be at the ARP post, whereas she had assumed Grace was at home . . . It wasn't as if there was anywhere else much to go at this time of night.

Mrs Templeton had gone over and was frantically trying to help clear the weight from her son, sobbing helplessly as she did so. Just then they heard an engine stop abruptly nearby and a rescue team arrived. Violet looked round to find Miss Holt standing beside her.

'I'm afraid there's nothing we can do here really, Violet,' she said in a low voice. 'We'd better get back on patrol.'

'Here we are, Mrs Templeton.' Violet went to her and handed Gordon back. She knew Miss Holt was right, really. 'I've got to go. I hope . . .' She was about to say, *I hope he's all right,* but she could not get the words out of her mouth.

She and Miss Holt had just set off along the street when the blood-chilling rise-and-fall wail of the sirens began once again, across Birmingham.

Grace, wrapped in Harry's arms, had lost track of time completely. How the minutes flew by when they were together! She loved the full force of Harry's attention, his desire and her own body alive with wanting him. She felt like a real, grown woman, in the arms of a strong, manly man.

She knew she was playing with fire but she tried not to think about any of it too much. Live for the moment! That was the thing to do these days. Being with Harry Cobb felt as if they were in a world of their own in the darkness, away from the day-to-day realities. All she wanted was to feel his lips on hers, his body pressing insistently against her.

But tonight Harry was being more insistent in every way. Each time they met, he pushed a little further and Grace was finding it harder to keep limits on how far things went. She found his desire exciting while feeling constantly that she ought to tell him to stop.

Tonight, his lips fastened on hers, he had both his hands under her blouse and camisole and was fiddling awkwardly with the fastening of her brassiere. Her flesh was up in goose pimples from the freezing night air. No good girl would allow this sort of thing – especially a good Catholic girl! She imagined the face of Sister Veronica, one of her teachers, for a moment and froze with horror at herself.

'No – Harry, don't . . .' she tried.

But, after a tussle, Harry suddenly managed to tug the hooks and eyes apart. With a groan of pleasure he pulled her bra up and cupped his palms over her breasts. His hands were surprisingly warm and the sensation of their rough flesh stroking her nipples was enough to stop her asking him not to. It was so wrong and embarrassing – thank goodness for the dark – but so exciting . . .

'Oh, God, Grace, you're something you are,' he whispered. 'Just let me once, will yer? It won't hurt, will it – just the once? He pulled the sides of her blouse apart, tugged the lacy front of her camisole down and nuzzled at her breasts.

The lower half of her body was full of melting, wanting sensations so that she was finding it harder to resist. In the battle between her mind and body, her body was starting to win. Within seconds, Harry was pulling at her skirt, starting to slide it upwards. Once again it was the chill of nakedness on the flesh above her suspenders that acted like a cold shower.

'No – Harry, stop, no!' she was saying, when the howl of the air-raid siren cut through everything.

Harry cursed even more. He seemed to come back to himself and pushed Grace away, almost angrily.

'We'll have to go,' Grace said, hurriedly readjusting her clothes. Harry was doing the same.

'Right.' He sounded stunned, frustrated. 'Sorry . . .'

They were almost shouting. 'Right – come on. Give us your hand.'

They started to run, parting hurriedly at the end of the Coventry Road. Grace dashed as fast as she could to the Archibald Street ARP post, to find that everyone was out on the streets except for Mr Powell and Francis Paine. Francis also seemed to be getting ready to leave.

'Grace,' Mr Powell said gravely. 'You'd best go home . . . Actually, your mother won't be in . . . Look, my dear, there's been an accident – to do with one of your brothers. They're down at the houses at the end. Go now, quickly, and find your mother.'

By the bright light of the moon and the searchlights raking the sky, she saw a cluster of people further down the street. The cold, gritty air burned her nostrils and her lungs ached from running and from dread. What had happened while she had been out, behaving in a way she never ever should have . . . ? Was this God punishing her for her sinful acts?

Running up close, she could see that all attention was fixed on a spot inside the first of the bombed houses where someone had set out one of the blue incident lights.

'Here we go!' a man was shouting. 'We got him!'

Just as he called out, the sirens stopped, and there was a sudden quiet in which everything seemed to be waiting. There were no planes overhead, she registered – or at least not yet.

Grace heard Gordon making his little noises and it helped her locate her mother in the knot of people. She stumbled over through the wreckage. Who was it under there? What had happened? A terrible feeling came over her when she saw Joseph, crying uncontrollably. She went to him and put her arm round his skinny little shoulders. He leaned into her.

'What happened, Joey?' she said. 'What's going on?'

But just as she said it, the silence deepened. The men who had lifted all the debris off were kneeling. Someone shone a torch for a moment and Grace saw a dark figure on the ground. And then she heard her mother's voice.

'Oh, my boy – my little Dennis!' Cath Templeton sank to her knees, still holding Gordon, beside the crumpled little body.

The man kneeling over Dennis straightened up and shook his head. 'I'm sorry, missus.'

Twenty-Two

Marie's face was a white oval in the gloom as she met them at the front door. She had stayed in to look after Michael and Adrian. Seeing the expressions on her mother's face and those of Grace and Joseph, she let out a terrible wail.

'Go and put the kettle on,' Grace ordered her gently. She couldn't think about how she felt herself. She had to look after Mom and the others.

She steered them into the back room. Joseph was still hiccoughing and sobbing. She led her mother to a chair and lifted a grizzling Gordon from her arms. His nappy was soaked through and she set about changing him and settling him down to sleep upstairs. Meanwhile Marie made tea and when Grace came back down, she found her mother sitting rocking back and forth, a stunned expression on her face.

Grace sat down and reached for Joseph, who was still standing there, lost. She pulled him gently on to her lap and he sobbed, leaning up close to her. She and Marie tried to explain to Michael and Adrian, who were eight and five, that Dennis would not be coming home again. This seemed to bring their mother back to herself. She held out her arms to her weeping young sons.

'I wish Bill was here,' Cath sobbed, clasping the little boys to her while Marie hugged Joseph. 'Oh, sweet Jesus, he doesn't know – I'm going to have to tell him when he gets in! Oh, our poor little Dennis – he was such a sweet-natured boy!'

It was true – they all knew it.

They sat close together round the fire, drinking their tea, all in shock. Mom talked in fragments, her mind going over and over what had happened that evening, about where they'd taken Dennis's body, about needing to see Father to arrange a funeral . . .

'I should never've let him out – you run wild, all of you! – and I was about to go and call them all in and then Joseph came running . . . Oh, my Lord. And then . . . Grace. Where were you? Grace?'

Grace's blood thudded round her body and she was sure Mom must be able to see the flush go through her cheeks. How could she even begin to tell Mom the truth!

'Oh – I'd just popped in to see Jimmy's mom.' The lies tumbled out, sounding improbable even to her. 'I hadn't seen her in a good while, and then just when I was about to come home the siren went off, so I thought . . .'

But her mother had drifted again and Grace realized she was not listening.

'But –' Marie sat up, suddenly realizing. 'The sirens went off – but there hasn't been a raid, has there?'

Those who were actually on duty at sixty-one Archibald Street returned to the post for a time after they had checked on all the houses in the street. It was as if they needed to be together and they sat round, talking about what had happened to Grace's brother. Mildred Oval came across the road, having heard somehow, and stood in the doorway between the two rooms in her big coat as she often did, as if always on the point of leaving, shifting her weight from one plump ankle to the other. Sometimes she spent an hour or so there, one arm braced against the door frame.

'What a terrible thing,' she kept saying. Her plump face looked weighed down with one woman's sorrow for another. 'Fancy . . . Terrible.'

Violet felt the sadness of it as a pain all across her chest.

'I sent Grace home with her mother,' Mr Powell said. 'Poor soul. What an awful thing.'

'Lads will be lads,' Reggie said, lighting up a cigarette.

'But so unnecessary a death,' Miss Holt said sorrowfully.

'One more for your lot, eh?' Reggie baited Francis Paine.

'I'm afraid that's part of the job,' Francis said stiffly. Violet heard the faint rustle of his lungs as he spoke. He looked such a fragile man. In fact, she realized, she hardly thought of him as a man at all – just an odd, somehow sexless, presence. He seemed strange and old before his time that she felt sad for him, but he was so stiff and starchy that it was hard to like him.

The clock on the mantelpiece ticked loudly into the silence. It was almost nine o'clock.

Violet sat wishing powerfully that George was here. How lovely it would be to see his friendly, cheerful face!

'It's quiet tonight after all,' Miss Holt said, frowning.

'Best get out and have another look.' Mr Powell stood up behind the table and put his white Head Warden's helmet on. He had just taken off his spectacles and was giving them a polish on the edge of his jersey when they heard a shout outside.

'Oh, dear – what now?' Miss Holt said wearily.

Since they were all going anyway, they went out to the street. There was something different about the light now, Violet noticed. An odd, copper tinge to the moonlight that had not been there before. It was not like the glow from fires over Birmingham, but fainter and strange.

There was a man outside who Violet recognized from further down the street.

'See that?' He was pointing at the sky, shouting to anyone who would listen, which at this moment was just the local ARP. 'That's *Coventry*! The whole ruddy place's gone up!'

Mr Powell stopped him. 'Tell me – what d'you mean, my man?'

The man explained, over-excited with shock.

'Me brother's on fire watch on the roof of Patterson's. I went up to take him a bite to eat and a cup of— Anyway, it's unbelievable! You can see Cov from here if yer get up high. Never seen anything like it – the whole cowing place is ablaze!'

Violet listened, chilled.

'They're smashing it to smithereens – and it'll be us next!' Apparently bound to tell everyone he could find what he had seen, the man hurried feverishly away.

'Seems like they're the poor sods getting it tonight, not us,' Reggie observed.

'My God,' Miss Holt said, with unguarded emotion. 'Is there no limit to this depravity?'

It was a long, distressing night in the Templetons' house. Grace and Marie helped get all the distraught little boys to bed.

'I'll never be able to sleep,' their mother said. 'I'll sit up a vigil for poor little Dennis – go and fetch my beads, Marie. I'll begin a novena for him.'

'Mom – you should go to bed,' Grace argued. The thought of having to offer to say the rosary with her half the night, was too much. 'You'll be exhausted in the morning.'

'You go to bed, if you like,' Cath said mournfully. 'I'll sit up for my boy.'

With tears in her eyes, Marie brought her mother's pearly rosary beads from the top drawer of the chest of drawers.

'I'll pray with you, Mom,' she said, looking at Grace and it was meant kindly. *Go to bed*, her eyes said, *I'll stay with her.*

'I'll stay for a bit,' Grace whispered, grateful.

The three of them started with the best of intentions. Grace joined in the rosary. *Hail Mary, full of Grace . . .* The prayer circled round and round. *Holy Mary, Mother of God, pray for us sinners, now and at the hour of our death, Amen . . .* God forgive me! Her thoughts plagued her, heavy with a guilt that telling the rosary only seemed to make worse. The thought of having to do this for another eight days was terrible. And in the end her mother's own prayers ran into silence. Cath lay back in the chair, completely exhausted, her eyes closed and the beads still looped round her fingers. Marie's eyelids were so heavy she could not keep them open either.

'Go on up, sis,' Grace whispered. 'I'll put some covers over Mom – we needn't disturb her.' She felt an overwhelming tenderness towards them both – towards all her family. 'I'll be up in a tick.'

'Thanks, Gracie,' Marie said muzzily. She suddenly leaned down and kissed Grace's cheek as she went past and disappeared upstairs. Grace put her hands over her face and her whole body started to shake.

After a few moments she dried her tears and went to get covers from her parents' bed to lay over her mother, tucking the blankets as warmly as she could round her

179

feet. Upstairs, she lay on her own cold side of the bed, reliving the horror of the evening, of realizing that her brother had been entombed under the rubble. Little Dennis – the most sweet-natured of the lot of them. And all the while she was with Harry . . . She pulled the covers over her head and let herself weep properly, quietly, so as not to disturb Marie beside her, pouring out her own shame and loss.

At work the next day, all she could think of was Dennis and of her poor father when he came home from the BSA's night shift to be greeted by this news. He knew something was wrong as soon as he came in. The sight of his wife's face and the fact that never before had he walked into a room containing all his young lads and found the ominous silence which met him today, immediately signalled something bad.

'Oh, Bill!' Mom cried, seeing him. She went over to him.

'What's happened?' He seized her by the shoulders. Grace saw his tired face stiffen with dread.

Their mother broke into weeping again. 'I hardly know how to tell you.'

But she did, she had to tell him. Their father raked his hand through his salt-and-pepper hair, his face distraught.

'No – not little Dennis?' He said it several times and then sank down in the chair and just sat staring ahead of him. Eventually he asked more about how and why and what time? And Grace had never seen him with a look on him like that before, her dear dad, his long face pale and lined, his whole body sagging as if someone had kicked him.

All day, Grace felt tormented by guilt and sorrow. She could see Mom had not taken in anything she said, that she would not be going to check with Mrs Oval to see if Grace had called round. Mom was too caught up in her grief for Dennis. And what difference would it have made anyway? Even if she had been at home, it would not have changed anything.

But the guilt of it ate away at her all the same. If she had not been out carrying on with Harry Cobb, she would have been at home to support her mother at the right time. It would not have saved Dennis, but she would not feel like a scarlet woman in the way she did now.

As she went about her work, she kept fighting back tears and eventually Mrs Hodgson noticed and she had to explain what had happened.

'Oh, my word,' Mrs Hodgson said kindly. 'I am sorry, bab. What a terrible loss for your family.'

She went very easy on Grace that day and Grace was grateful to her. Otherwise, everyone was talking about Coventry. No one had ever imagined anything like it: people were saying there was hardly any of the city left standing – not even the cathedral. It was hard to take in or believe the extent of such destruction.

But worst of all was the fact that, even surrounded by all this tragedy, Grace still could not stop her mind drifting, with a kind of excited relief, to the thought of standing, once again, in Harry Cobb's arms.

After work, Grace really did go to see Mildred Oval.

There was a little balance in her mind that said, *Well, it wasn't true that I saw her last night, but if I go and call on her today maybe that will make it a little bit better . . .* She was really fond of Jimmy's mom and it was true that though Mildred popped in to chat to the ARP wardens,

Grace hadn't been in especially to see her for ages, which only added to her guilt.

When she tapped on the door of number fifty-six, there was a long pause and then Jimmy's sister Dolly, whose thirteenth birthday had just been swallowed up by all the tragedy, peeped out of the door. She looked very solemn but she managed a smile when she saw Grace.

'All right, Dolly?' Grace said fondly. 'Haven't seen you in a while – I thought I'd pop in and see your mother.'

Dolly Oval led her through to the back room, where Grace came upon all the family, except the older brothers away in the forces, all standing or sitting round the room. Seated on a chair in the middle, looking shocked and different, so much so that it took her a moment to recognize him, was Mark Oval, Jimmy's younger brother. He somehow looked years older than when she had last seen him.

'Oh, Grace!' Mildred came over to her straight away and wrapped Grace in her arms, something she had never once done before. Startled, Grace yielded to her embrace, guilty as Judas. 'We heard all about poor little Dennis. Your poor mother – I am so sorry, bab.' She sounded close to tears. 'I'd've gone over to see her but then Mark came home and . . .'

'I know,' Grace said, trying to hold back her emotion in front of everyone. 'Those little so-and-so's – you try telling them not to play in them places and what do they do?' But her own tears started to come anyway and everyone made kindly noises.

'Have a cup of tea with us, bab – I'm ever so pleased you've come to see us,' Mildred said. 'Have you heard from our Jimmy?'

'Yes.' Grace dried her eyes. Suddenly it felt very warm and comforting to be back in the heart of Jimmy's family.

It was all so familiar. She had had a letter from Jimmy a few days ago. 'He seems all right.'

'Better than here, I reckon,' Mildred said. 'We was just hearing all about last night from Mark – they sent them over to Coventry to help out.'

Grace turned to look at Mark. He had obviously given his face a quick wash, but there was still a grey griminess about his ears and neck and he looked completely wrung out. He sat with his arms resting on his thighs, seeming lost in his sense of shock. Ginger the dog was lying at his feet, eyes turned up to him as if to offer succour.

'So it was bad, was it?' she said. They had been so caught up in things over Dennis that they had not heard anything much.

'It were just . . .' Mark struggled to find the words. 'It's gone – almost all of it. There's just . . . Destruction.' She could see he had been crying and this shocked her to the core. Mark – tough, joking Mark who never let anything much bother him.

He rubbed his hand over and over the top of his head. 'Nothing but destruction, everywhere.' After a moment he said, 'The worst of it was, they hit the water main and we was left standing there . . .' He held his hands out as if still clutching a dry, useless hosepipe. 'The Cov blokes who were from there . . . They was just stood there, crying, some of 'em – couldn't do a thing.'

He looked into up Grace's eyes and his were grey pools of shock and horror. 'I ain't never seen anything as bad as that before – nothing like.' He looked down and stroked the dog. Quietly he added, 'Those bastards. They just went back and to, each way across the place as if they were weaving – until they'd smashed just about every-thing.'

Grace listened. It was hard to take in this complete scene of devastation, so much of it all in one moonlit night. She stayed chatting a while and just as she announced she had to go, Mildred said to her, 'Oh – Grace. Our Jimmy must've said to yer that he's due some leave soon? Before Christmas, any road – he'll be coming home for a couple of days at least.' She beamed at her prospective daughter-in-law. 'Now that'll be summat to cheer us all up, won't it?'

Twenty-Three

Tuesday 19 November

'Arthur, love – wakey-wakey!'

Mildred Oval stroked her husband's shoulder as he lay in bed, as if trying to massage some sign of life back into him. She was in her nightdress, a woolly cardi over the top, a few rollers pinned waywardly into her hair. Her fleshy face smiled down at him tenderly.

'Seems a shame to wake yer,' she said as Arthur, who had been blissfully deep in slumber, started to stir. 'But time's getting on. I've brought yer up a cup of tea, lovey.'

Arthur had crawled into bed at some point in the small hours after the raid of the night before finished. He turned on his back looking dazed, hands rasping over his stubbly face, trying to bring himself round. Mildred kicked her shoes off and the bed shook earthquake-wise as she clambered back in beside him. The bed was a cosy place, with a top layer of blanket crocheted by Mildred in a host of colours.

'Your tea's on the side – don't let it get cold,' she said.

Arthur sat up, groaning, and reached for the cup and saucer. 'Ta bab. I 'spect this'll bring me round. Summat's got to.'

'At least we had a few hours in bed together.' Mildred snuggled up to him, her cup held close to her chin. 'You poor old devil, having to be out there like that.'

'No one come in 'ere last night, then?'

Mildred was still on standby now, every time there was a raid, to take people in, though she insisted on the rest of the family staying in the shelter – except little John, who always wanted to be with her.

'No. Not this time.' She sipped her tea. 'We was out in the shelter the whole time.'

'Is it dry?' Arthur stretched, then pushed himself up in the bed. 'I never checked yesterday.'

'I wouldn't say dry . . .'

Arthur looked at her. 'You should've said, old girl – I'll 'ave a go at it before I head off this morning. Give it a quick bail-out.'

'Ta, love – I never 'ad time last night.'

She leaned her head on his shoulder and let out a heavy sigh. 'This has been a terrible week. When's it all going to end, Arthur?'

She felt his shrug under her ear. They sat quiet, leaning against each other, warm and cosy. It was the one snatched time of the day they had to themselves. Eventually Arthur reached across and laid his hand on his wife's broad thigh.

'I s'pose everything ends – in the end,' he said profoundly. They sat quiet after this. There seemed nothing else to say.

'I'll get up in a tick – cook you a good breakfast,' Mildred said. She kissed his stubbly cheek, sniffing him. 'You smell of . . .'

Arthur frowned. 'What?'

'I dunno. The war. It's that sort of . . .' She sniffed him again. 'Nasty, burned smell.'

Arthur rubbed at his face. 'Not surprising.'

Just then they heard a shuffling sort of noise outside the bedroom door.

'Hark!' Mildred said. 'Is that the dog – or John?'

'Mo – om.'

'Oh, it's our John!' Mildred got nimbly out of bed.

She went to the door and found the little lad on his hands and knees outside, looking up at her with his sweet, trusting smile.

'Hello, our John – you coming in with us a tick?' She let him crawl into the room and they hoicked him up so that he was between them in the bed. Mildred put her arm round the little fellow, full of protective feelings. He smelt warm, of sleep and boy.

'All right, mate?' Arthur said. 'Come to keep us company, 'ave yer?'

John made his happy noises, laughing and squeaking, and the three of them cuddled up together in a warm, brief refuge before the grind of the day had to begin all over again.

Violet worked all day at Hughes's, exhaustion passing through her in waves, her stomach acid and unsettled. There had been a raid last night, but for the previous week things had been more patchy. The sirens would go off most nights, but the prayer of every person waiting under the searchlights and ack-ack guns, *Keep going, please, just keep going*, seemed to have been answered.

Last night she had been out, patrolling with Miss Holt as Grace was off duty. She had finally managed to snatch a few hours' sleep once the All Clear had gone off. The days at work could feel even longer than usual, though, after all that.

Her eyes followed the lines of ginger biscuits she was packing, blurring sometimes with fatigue.

'Have these biscuits got any sugar in them at all?' Her neighbour peered at them.

Violet shrugged. 'I s'pose they put in whatever they

can get hold of.' They were no longer making anything really sweet – all the biscuits were plain and dry. The ginger biscuits felt more like little rounds of cardboard these days.

'Come on, you lot!' red-haired Bett, two up the line, called out. 'Let's liven this place up a bit!'

Someone started singing at the other end, 'Somewhere Over the Rainbow' . . .

'Oh, no, not that one – it brings a great big lump up in my throat!' a woman down the line complained.

But they sang along, Violet with a smile on her lips, thinking of George. She had seen him a couple of days ago and her body felt warm and tingling at the thought of his kisses. She looked up and one of the other girls caught her eye and winked.

'Who've *you* got on your mind, Vi?' she called, bursting out laughing. 'Look at 'er face!'

Violet blushed furiously and looked down, but her smile got bigger as they all launched into 'Ma! He's Making Eyes at Me'.

This was by far the best way of getting through the day and she joined in. Singing songs seemed to send a bolt of life through your head, woke you up, lifted you out of all the gloom and sorrow. It gave you something else to think about other than all the sadness and destruction – and her innards struggling to digest a stale corned-beef sandwich!

And she also had George to think about – the miracle of George. That the two of them were now snatching every possible moment together. It was all so giddying, so astonishing! He was so lovely and sweet to her. He seemed to adore her and Violet's hungry heart had found itself falling very quickly in love with this cheerful, kindly lad.

All this was something she had barely ever dared to hope for. It lit life up with a golden glow, even amid all these fearful days and nights. Even if she did have to keep George a secret from Mom, even if there were only precious, brief times when they could manage to see each other, George – and his warm, welcoming family – were like a song which played constantly in her heart, and chimed with the voices all around her as they sang, building a stairway to the stars.

June fell into step beside her as they all poured out of the factory. She didn't hide from June any more. But she did get tired of her trying to talk about George.

'How was last night?' she asked quickly before June could start on her.

'We've 'ad worse,' June said. 'It was bad over Sparkhill and we had a few in . . . Tell yer what, though – I met this bloke – ever so good-looking.' She nudged Violet, who did not especially appreciate being nudged. 'Never got 'is name but I hope I bump into *'im* again!'

There seemed to be a trail of 'blokes' that June went on about during the walk home, but Violet had never really heard of any of them sticking around for long.

'T'ra then, June,' she said firmly, when they got to the top of the road. 'Gotta run.'

The Templeton household was a fragile, tender and unusually quiet place that week. Cath had organized a funeral for Dennis with the parish priest. All the young ones kept getting upset, especially Joseph, who had been there when the house caved in. He kept waking in the night, screaming his head off. Grace, though full of her own mourning for her little brother, did her best to comfort them. She let Joseph come into bed with her and Marie and they cuddled him close.

She was at home every moment she could be during those days, out of sorrow, but also out of shame for not having been there that night.

On top of all that, she was full of the pain of her own feelings. Despite everything, when she tried to turn her thoughts and feeling back to Jimmy, she was still full of confusion. She wrote and told him about Dennis. Jimmy had played with her brother when Dennis was very small and she knew Jimmy would be really upset to hear what had happened. He wrote straight back, sending all love to her and the family. And she found herself wishing he was here to talk to. Yet, when Harry Cobb came to mind, despite her remorse for what had happened, it was with a bolt of excitement and longing to stand in his arms and be held and comforted. She felt as if she was hooked on him and could not get him out of her head.

Yesterday afternoon, on her way home from work, she had slipped inside the Church of the Holy Family. She knelt, gazing at the flickering red sanctuary lamp and the shrouded presence of the Blessed Sacrament. The musty, incense-tinged air was comforting and familiar. But it did not give her peace.

'Dear Lord Jesus,' she prayed inwardly. 'I know I'm a terrible, sinful person. I've offended against you . . . I feel so badly and I don't know what to do. With myself, I mean . . . Forgive me for talking to you directly – I can't go and tell Father O'Riordan about all this, I really can't . . .' She closed her eyes and breathed in deeply, hearing faint sounds from the road outside, the tiny noises of the building, the door shifting in the wind. 'I don't know what I'm doing. I don't really know myself any more. Just help me, dear Lord – please.'

The funeral was on Friday and tomorrow they would bring Dennis, in his coffin, in here for the vigil beforehand. Imagining all of it, them all gathered together and poor little Den up there at the front, cold and still . . . She lowered her head on to the back of the pew in front and allowed her tears to flow for a few moments.

But soon, she hauled herself up again.

'Come on,' she muttered, wiping her eyes. 'Pull yourself together.'

There was no time to indulge in her emotions. She had to get home, get some tea down her and go out again. She was on duty.

Twenty-Four

'So, d'you think those buggers'll come over tonight?' George said.

It was just gone six o'clock and Violet and George were standing in a quiet spot near McGauley's bike shop on the Coventry Road, where they sometimes arranged to meet for a quick chat and a cuddle. She could just make out George's outline in the gloom, half a head taller than her, could feel his warm breath on her cheek as they held each other.

'Hope not.' Pulling him closer, loving the feel of his solid shape, she rested her head on his shoulder. 'Let's not think about it, eh? Let's just pretend . . . I could stand here for ever, just like this.'

She couldn't quite put it into words. *Let's just live now as if there's nothing else and no one else*, was what she might have said. It doesn't matter that we're standing in this dank, smelly entry in the pitch black, that horrible things are happening and any minute now the bombs might start to fall again. At least we have this now, here. Just us together.

'I feel a bit funny about your mother, though,' he said, cuddling her close. 'It's not right, Vi, the way things are.'

'I know,' she said into his chest. A helpless feeling overcame her.

George kept bringing this up. There was Violet, visiting the Cherry household as often as she could. She loved that almost as much as she loved George himself. Mrs

Cherry was always in the back room, usually busy cooking something by the gas stove. Violet had realized that Mrs Cherry was more fragile than she first appeared. It was the war, she said, the bombing. It had made her all nerves. But she was always warm and welcoming.

And she liked his sisters, Alice and Nancy, who were both friendly as well (she still hadn't met Vera, the eldest, though she had met Alice's bloke, who had shifty eyes, and Violet could see what Mrs Cherry meant). And there was Pilot the dog. Mr Cherry, who worked at a rolling mills nearby somewhere, was a small, very quiet man, which was probably for the best in that very female household. He just rolled his eyes a lot, but he also seemed nice when he said anything at all.

Yet all the while, she had been spinning yarns to Mom about where she was going and had not told her anything about George. It was true, Mom had been pulled out of herself a bit these days, which was a relief. She and Mrs Baker seemed to have taken charge of the shelter, trying to keep it clean and lay the law down. As she spent so many nights sitting out there now, she said someone had to make it as bearable as possible and none of those other idle so-and-so's would lift a finger to do it . . . All the same, Mom was so rigid, needing to control everything. Violet still wanted to keep George away from her.

'Is it me?' George asked – as he had already asked, several times. He just couldn't understand it.

'No – it isn't you at all.' She reached up and stroked his cheek. 'Honest. I dunno. Maybe I'm being stupid. It's just – she gets all in a tizzy if I . . . I mean, the ARP duty is the only time I've really managed to go out, apart from school and work. She never wants me to leave or go anywhere or see anyone.'

'I see,' George said. Though she could hear that he

didn't, at all. There was always so much going on in the Cherry household that it was probably a relief if anyone went out.

'What was your father like?' George said. 'Can you remember?'

'No, I told you – I was only a few months old when he died. I've seen a picture . . . At least, I think so.'

She immediately wished she'd never said that. How peculiar it sounded! How could she explain the strange memory of that day when Mom came up and found her sitting on her bedroom floor and the box and those photographs. Two photographs – and still her mind was all confusion as to which picture was of her father – or her mother for that matter. Raising the subject with Mom felt completely unthinkable.

'The thing is, George . . . In May, on my next birthday, I'll be twenty-one. So I'll be free to . . .' She stumbled. It seemed such a brutal thing to say. 'I mean, I can do what I want then, can't I?'

George was silent for a moment. 'You don't mean I can't meet her until after that?'

'No. You're right,' she said. 'I'm being daft. I'll have a think. You ought to come and meet her. I know she'd like you. She can just be a bit funny – with me, I mean.'

George squeezed her. 'Well, when you think it's right, love. I don't want to force it – but I'd like to meet your family, is all.'

'Well, she's it,' Vi said. 'I don't seem to have anyone else. They're all dead.' She frowned. 'Oh, except for an auntie somewhere, on my father's side, I think. All I know is her name is Elsie, but we never see her.'

'Don't fret,' George said. 'If that's how it is, well, that's that. We'll have to get going in a minute. Give us a kiss – eh?'

His lips searched for hers in the dark and in those moments, they truly forgot everything else and lost themselves in each other.

'Well, it's not too bad,' Bill Templeton said.

Grace was standing outside the air-raid shelter with her father as he bent his lanky body to get his head in through the door. He held up the hurricane lamp, inspecting the inside. All the earth-floored shelters were prone to developing puddles – or flooding completely in heavy weather – and there had been quite a bit of changeable weather lately.

'I should've remembered earlier.' He sounded tense. 'I'm going to have to be off soon.'

'Look, I'll do it, Dad – you go,' Grace said. She felt anxious to help, to do good for her family as much as she possibly could. Everyone was so tired and sad – and she had things to make up for.

'You not on duty now?'

'Not unless there's a raid, no. You go, Pop . . .' This was her old, child's name for him. 'I'll do it.'

'That's a girl. Ta, Gracie.' He emerged from the shelter and they stood together for a moment in sad, companionable silence, breathing in the smoky evening air and looking back at the house.

'I can see the light in the back from here,' Grace said. 'Mom's forgotten the blackouts.'

'You'll have her for that,' her father said.

'I'll be down on her like a ton of bricks.'

They both laughed a little. There was another silence and her father sighed.

'It's been an awful week.'

'Yeah, you can say that again.'

Suddenly, unusually, he put his arm round her

shoulders and hugged her close, the lamp held down at his other side. Grace felt all her tears rise up, but she swallowed them down.

After a while, he said, 'I'd best be off. You be careful, wench. Keep an eye out, won't you?'

'Course,' she said. She knew he meant for all the family. 'I always do.'

He seemed reluctant to leave.

'And you look out for yourself now, Gracie.'

After Dennis, it felt as if anything could happen.

'I will, Dad. You too. Give us the lamp. You have a good night.'

Full of love for him, she watched his tall but slightly stooped form disappear along the side of the veggie patch to the house. She turned and started scooping water out of the shelter with an old tin mug. As she slung the water out, she heard the drops land on the remaining cabbages, their leaves arched over like little umbrellas.

'You're looking very chipper,' Reggie said to Violet when she got to number sixty-one. 'Been 'aving a good time, 'ave yer?'

Reggie's hair was Brylcreemed back as usual and his dark eyes twinkled with fun. He was all right really, Violet thought, but she was still not used to all this kind of teasing and turned away, blushing.

'Oi, oi,' Reggie said. 'Someone's looking coy!'

Violet had arrived all in a rush after spending the last possible moments with George. And yes, she had been having a good time, but she was embarrassed by the suggestive way that Reggie said everything. She hoped her blushes did not show in the dim lighting of Miss Holt's house. Miss Holt had lit a fire in the back room and the warmth made her cheeks flame even more.

'Your mind is a sewer, Reggie,' Quentin said. 'Leave the poor girl alone. Can't you see she's made of finer stuff than you?'

'I only asked . . .' Reggie began indignantly, but then Grace walked in and he decided to shut up and light a fag instead.

'Ah,' Miss Holt said. She was the sort of teacher who would say, 'Good *evening*, Grace,' to a child who might be late for a class. Since now it was evening already she was having to find substitutes for this particular brand of sarcasm. 'I see you've finally managed to struggle over here, Grace?' she said instead.

'Sorry, Miss Holt,' Grace said.

She seemed different, Violet thought. Before she would have made a face or said something cheeky back. Now she was subdued. 'I was just bailing out the shelter for Mom before I come out.'

'Good wench,' Arthur Oval said. He was sitting with a mug of tea in his hand. 'That's Civil Defence work in itself. Go easy on 'er, Miss Holt.'

Miss Holt, who had evidently momentarily forgotten about little Dennis, looked chastened. 'It's all right, dear,' she said more gently. 'It's only a few minutes past six.'

Mr Powell sat at his table, squinting down at his lists. A newspaper a few days old lay beside him. 'COVENTRY – OUR GUERNICA' the banner headline read. Quietly, he ticked off their names.

'I see they've put that it was Cov in the paper,' Reggie said resentfully, taking a look at it as he sat down. 'When it comes to Brum, they never tell anyone about what we've had chucked at us, do they? I mean, I can stand those bloody Jerrys bombing us – but what sticks in my throat is, no one seems to *know* they're bombing us.'

'They're protecting our industries,' Miss Holt pointed out.

'Well,' Reggie said frowning. 'That's all very well . . .'

'So,' Mr Powell said quietly, looking up from his lists. 'This is it then, for now. No Francis tonight. Ah – have we filled the sand buckets?'

'I'll do it,' Quentin said, with a martyred air. 'As I'm up. My night to be the skivvy.'

'It should be one of the first things we do,' Mr Powell said reproachfully, though as much to himself as anyone else. Miss Holt had a supply of sand heaped in her back-yard.

At seven-fifteen, when the telephone rang again, everyone in the room swivelled round to look.

Mr Powell's face didn't change. He put the receiver down and looked up.

'Red.'

Twenty-Five

'Oh, my giddy uncle!' Reggie cried, as they all hurried out into the chaos of sirens, ack-ack guns and sweeping searchlights.

'Aunt!' Quentin shouted.

'*What?*' Reggie bawled.

'Giddy aunt. *Aunt!*'

'Just shut *up*, you two eejits,' Grace snapped, her face turned up to the sky. The planes were almost overhead and already they could see the flare of light in the distance. Violet's heart was pumping, her whole body filled with urgent energy.

'Grab one of the bin-lids, Vi!' Grace called to her.

'Off you go now, everyone!' Miss Holt's voice rose shrilly amid the racket. 'Spread out – cover the sector!'

As Violet and Grace made their way up one side of the road, then down the other, the raid moved closer. The whistle of falling bombs sounded horribly close. They had to throw themselves to the ground several times, lying curled up together as the ground shook under them and they could hear the crumble and splinter and crash of masonry in the neighbouring streets.

Violet kept her eyes clenched shut, lying next to Grace, just waiting for something to fall on them, for the next bomb to come and hit the street where they were lying, for each moment to be her last . . . Keep going, just please keep going . . . Please let George be all right . . .

And then they could get up and move on until the next time, looking round desperately to see if there were houses hit nearby, for the telltale flames and clouds of dust.

They spent a long time checking the shelters, seeing that everyone was under cover, the blackout still in place. Violet even ran into the yard and knocked at Lucy Snell's door. Stepping inside she called up the stairs.

'Hello – this is your warden. Are you all right up there?'

She heard a floorboard creak and then Maud Bright's voice came clearly down the stairs. 'Yes, thank you, dear. We're quite all right.'

'Well – goodnight then,' she called up. It seemed such a silly thing to say but she couldn't think of anything else.

Arriving back at the wardens' post, they went in to report to Mr Powell. Violet saw with surprise that it was nearly ten o'clock. Hours seemed to have melted past. They were speaking to Mr Powell when Reggie Meakins came hurtling in, his face stretched with urgency.

'They've hit the BSA!' he yelled. 'It's bad – direct hit. There's a whole lot of the night shift inside . . .'

For a moment Violet could not make sense of this. Then she saw Grace's face had gone white as a sheet.

'Dad,' she whispered.

'Grace – you go over there with Reggie and see what you can do to help,' Mr Powell said, seeing that, in the circumstances, getting over to the BSA was simply what Grace must do. 'All the off-duty wardens have come in now – we'll manage. I'd better stay by the telephone. You two –' He looked at Violet and Francis Paine. 'Get back out there.'

Violet's heart sank, but there was nothing to be done.

She felt sick. Poor, poor Grace. What on earth was she going to find over there in Armoury Road?

Violet made her way down Archibald Street beside Francis Paine's bowed, skinny figure. She had been on patrol with him a couple of times before and found him very awkward. He was not an easy person to be with and she could never think of anything to say to him. But tonight it was far too noisy to be making conversation and the smoke made him cough badly. She started to feel sorry for him.

They did all the usual checks. Reaching Grace's house, they hurried along the entry. As Violet went to knock on the makeshift door of the shelter, she found Francis standing uncomfortably close to her. A shiver went through her.

'D'you mind?' she shouted – communication had to be at the top of her voice with all the pandemonium going on.

Francis stepped back, though he still seemed to be staring at her. What a queer bloke, Violet thought.

'Hello? Mrs Templeton?'

The door cranked open and Cath Templeton's face appeared looking haggard and anxious.

'Oh, hello, Violet.' She tried to give a little smile. 'It's nice of you to come and see us, darlin'. Yes – we're all right as we'll ever be in in this.'

They exchanged a few words before Violet said she had to go.

'Just stay safe in there,' she added. 'You're doing the best thing.' Even as she said it she was amazed at these grown-up-sounding words that seemed to come out of her mouth these days.

'God bless you, darlin'.'

'She seems a nice lady,' Francis remarked, to Violet's surprise.

'Yes, she is,' Violet said. 'I'll check on my mother and the neighbours next, I think.' As they squeezed back along the entry it suddenly occurred to her to ask, 'What about your family? Should we go and see?' Paine's Undertakers was right at the top of the street, behind the tramway depot.

'I might look in on my father when we are passing.' He sounded reluctant.

'Does he . . . I mean, do you have to . . .' She stopped in the mouth of the entry where it was a bit easier to hear. 'You know, all the people who die in the raids?' She didn't like to say quite what she was thinking.

'Oh, yes,' he said, without emotion. 'They bring the remains – in sacks.'

The reality of this hit Violet like a blow. This young man beside her, who everyone made fun of – she realized, shamed, that she had no real idea who he was.

'It must be . . . horrible . . .' She could barely even imagine.

'It makes it very difficult to identify people,' Francis said.

She wanted to say something – the right thing. But she had no idea what that might be. And Francis's odd, dispassionate manner made it hard. As they carried on towards her own entry, another wave of planes could be heard.

'I think we should get under cover,' he said. The street was deserted so there was no one else to usher into safety.

'Come along here,' Violet said, hurrying into the entry. 'We can check on the shelter – kill two birds with one stone!'

But as she turned, she felt Francis Paine's hand on her back almost as if he was steering her. She turned, startled.

'What're you doing?'

'Nothing.' Sounding sulky, he drew his hand back.

As he followed her, the hairs stood up on the back of her neck. She shrugged her shoulders to try and shake it off. Don't be daft, she thought. He's just awkward and shy. But in those few seconds she suddenly felt really unnerved by him and it was a relief to step into the yard, even though the planes were now right above them.

Glass crunched underfoot as they dashed to the shelter and the first bombs came down. Violet pulled open the door and they flung themselves into the stinking fug and crowd of the shelter as the first impacts began outside. The self-appointed warden of the shelter, an older man called Mr Scott, was sitting near the door.

It was no quieter inside, but Violet immediately realized that the noise going on was something quite different. Most people were sitting tensely quiet, but from the back were coming desperate moans and cries.

'Is everything all right?' she asked Mr Scott.

'It's that Mrs Crosby,' he said, with distaste. 'Someone's gone out to get the midwife, but it don't sound like they're going to make it in time.'

Oh, good God, Violet thought. She pushed her way through the throng. By the light of a hurricane lamp hanging from a hook on the wall, she saw a ring of women around the birthing Mrs Crosby, who was on the floor on her hands and knees. Susan Crosby was a friendly blonde woman, who Violet knew slightly. She already had several children. At present she was kneeling with her head down, groaning, and seemed far too caught up in her own pain to worry about anything else.

'Yer all right, bab.' Violet realized it was Mrs Baker

speaking. 'You can do it – you've done it before and we're all here to help.'

'We've all been through it!' another woman encouraged her.

'Violet!' Turning, she caught sight of her mother, close by, seated on a chair with her hands tensely clasped together. 'Can't you do summat for her – find the midwife?'

'Someone's already gone,' she said. 'I don't know as I could do any better – there's a full-blown raid going on out there!'

As if to remind them, a mighty crash sent everything shuddering and a few people screamed. Violet could hear someone sobbing with fear not far behind her.

The groaning and screaming started up again and Violet felt really quite peculiar. She had to get a hold of herself. She was on duty – she had to set an example!

'Is she all right?' Violet asked Mrs Baker, who had got down on her hands and knees beside the labouring woman.

Eileen Baker raised her flustered-looking face.

'It's going quick now – 'er's very close to having it. I do wish the midwife'd hurry up and get 'ere.'

Mrs Crosby lowered her head, panting like a worn-out horse between each bout of pain and the next. She moved her hips from side to side, trying to ease her discomfort.

'Oh,' she moaned. 'It's coming . . .'

'It's 'er fourth,' someone said. 'So 'er' d know.'

The moaning intensified. Everyone realized that the baby was indeed coming.

A quiet came over the place.

'It's all right, bab,' Mrs Baker was saying. 'I'll help you . . . Come on – we've got to get your bloomers off.'

'Oh, good God,' Violet heard Mr Scott say. 'Is this what they've reduced us to?'

She stood helplessly as Mrs Crosby tensed herself on all fours. Others were removing some of her clothes as she groaned and cried out. Within moments she was straining so that the ligaments in her neck stood out like cords. Her screams reached a high-pitched stream of sound. The other women were all encouraging her, keeping her company in the birthing. Everything suddenly happened very fast. Someone cried, 'The head's out! Come on, Susan – you can do it. You're nearly there!'

After the final, agonized scream, another silence fell on the entire space of the shelter. Through the noise going on outside came the sound everyone was waiting for: a little cough, a cracked yowl. The baby was letting them all know that he had arrived.

'Oh – a little lad!'

And everyone was breathing again and talking and people were offering whatever they had – a scrap of material, a cardigan to wrap him in, a drink of tea for Mrs Crosby. Mr Scott had had a kettle boiling all the while in preparation.

Violet saw the wonder of childbirth for the first time. The woman who a moment before had been racked with pain, her face stretched into screams, was seated on the floor holding her little boy, her face now soft with joy. And however grim and foul-smelling the place, however unkempt and sweaty, her expression was that of a young, pretty, happy woman looking into the face of her child for the first time.

And suddenly, in the midst of all this, Violet glanced round at her mother and saw that she had her head in her hands, quietly sobbing as if her heart was breaking.

*

A bit later, when there was a lull in the raid, Violet said to Susan Crosby, 'It would be better for you not to stay here, wouldn't it? Come with me and I'll take you to Mrs Oval's house – she'll look after you.'

The poor woman was sitting on a newspaper on the hard floor, having delivered the afterbirth, and she was now starting to look cold and uncomfortable and exhausted.

'Go on, Susan – go with the warden. You can leave the other little'uns here with us – we'll look out for 'em,' someone said. Mrs Crosby's other children were fast asleep on a mattress in the corner with some of the other infants.

They all helped her. She needed to dress again, padding her bloomers to stem the blood, and to wrap the little boy to carry him warmly along the street.

Only then, Violet became aware of Francis Paine again. He had propped himself well out of the way of all this by the wall, close to Mr Scott.

'You stay here,' she said. He wasn't going to be much help in any of this. 'I'll take Mrs Crosby down the road and come back for you.'

It was quiet outside for now. Violet helped Susan Crosby out of the shelter. She carried her baby on one arm and seemed to be wrestling with her clothing with the other.

'Are you all right?' Violet said shyly.

'Oh, yes, ta,' she said cheerfully. 'Just don't want me drawers falling down in the middle of the street!'

Violet was amazed how recovered she seemed after all that. If anything, she felt she was more shaken up by it all than Susan Crosby was herself!

'He's lovely,' Violet said, though in truth she could see

very little in the smoky blackness. 'What'll you call him, d'you think?'

'Oh, this'll be Eddie, after 'is dad. 'E's my first boy, see – ain't yer, yer little devil?' she asked the wrapped bundle fondly.

Violet smiled. Susan wasn't that much older than she was herself, but she already had four children and it made her seem years advanced.

'You wait here a minute,' Violet said. She ran down to the air-raid shelter and Mildred came out fully dressed and ready as if it were the middle of the day.

'We need you, Mrs Oval,' she said. She hurried back round and waited with Susan until Mildred opened the front door.

'Mrs Crosby's just had her baby,' Violet told her.

'In the cowing air shelter!' Susan Crosby informed her. 'Just my luck, in't it?'

'Oh, my word – you come in here, bab,' Mildred said. 'I'll get the kettle on straight away. We'll make you comfy.' Violet became aware of the sound of more planes approaching.

'I must go,' she said.

As Susan Crosby carried little Eddie into the house, Mildred said, 'That's all right, bab – I'll look after her.' She leaned closer. 'Have you heard about the BSA?'

Twenty-Six

By the time the All Clear sounded sometime before dawn, Violet felt as if she had lived the longest night of her life. They had been on the go non-stop. From the destruction in their own area she knew it had been the worst raid yet. When dawn came, what had happened across the rest of the city would soon be all too evident.

Back at the post, Miss Holt brewed tea, refilling her big metal jug several times and taking it outside to offer the wardens and anyone else who might be in need. Violet and the others drank it in a drained, exhausted silence. All of them were covered in dust and muck, their noses clogged with it, their feet and bodies aching. Mr Oval had a cut across his cheek which he kept swabbing with a hanky Miss Holt had given him.

'You'd best go and get that stitched, Mr Oval,' she said, watching him. 'It's deep.'

'I'll come with you,' Violet offered. The sweet tea had revived her a little. 'It's on my way – I'm going over to find Grace.'

'There's a dear,' Miss Holt said wearily.

Violet and Arthur walked through the cold darkness, the air a fug of mist and smoke. Looking along streets on their way to the Baths, they saw the devastation of the raid – shops and houses down, the streets half-blocked with rubble, fire hoses, people standing numbly looking, the sound of women crying.

'You go on and find Grace, bab,' Mr Oval said. 'I know you're worried. I'll be all right – long as I know my missus is safe.' Violet had told him about Susan Crosby and the baby.

'Let me just see you're all right first,' she said.

As they went into the post at the Baths, they were met by an atmosphere of barely controlled mayhem. Several bodies covered in bloodstained sheets had been placed, for want of anywhere else, along the corridor close to the walls. Violet and Mr Oval looked at each other in silence. Inside, the main First Aid area was abuzz with sounds and there were more terrible sights. All sorts of people with injuries waiting to be seen were sitting on benches, wrapped in old blankets or coats. Most were shocked, trembling and silent, though some were weeping quietly. Somewhere a child was screaming in pain. Violet saw an elderly man with a bloodstained rag pressed to his head, rocking and muttering. And all of them were coated in plaster dust.

The nurses and first aiders were working frantically hard. Violet thought she saw Bett from work over the corner and then she spotted June, bending over a little girl whose face was a mass of blood. She realized it was this child's cries she could hear. She was howling with pain and terror as June was trying to clean her wounds. June had a white scarf tied over her hair and wore a white apron over her clothes, bloodstains and other marks all down it. Violet watched her talking softly to the little girl. June, she realized, looked rather magnificent.

'June,' she called softly. June looked up, said something else to the little girl and hurried over, her face solemn. Close up, she looked strained and exhausted, but she was calm.

209

'Oh – Mr Oval!' she exclaimed, seeing him with Violet. 'You sit down here – I'll see to 'im, Vi.'

Arthur Oval sank down gratefully on one of the narrow wooden benches. 'Ta, bab. I'll wait my turn with the rest. You go, Vi – go and find our Grace.'

'They hit the BSA,' Violet explained. 'Grace's dad – night shift . . .'

'I know,' June said, for once not in a know-it-all sort of way, and for a second their eyes met.

Violet hurried away. 'See you later, Mr Oval.'

Exhausted as she was, she hurried over to the Birmingham Small Arms works in Armoury Road, all the time keeping an eye out in case she should see George. Worry gnawed at her. Was he all right? She could not rest happy until she knew, but at this moment she had to get to Grace.

When she came in sight of the devastation at the BSA, she stopped, appalled. It was light enough now to see that one of the main buildings had had a direct hit. Around the broken mass of destruction, the rescue teams were working hard, others joining in or standing in quiet desperation. There was the usual foul, acrid stench that filled the air when the body of any building was smashed apart.

She could see no sign of Grace anywhere. Shyly, she approached a group of men all standing at the edge of the mass of wreckage.

''Scuse me . . . ?'

They all turned to her, seeming stunned. She saw that they must be workers from other sections of the factory. For a moment they seemed to be looking to her, as if she might be going to tell them something, and she realized it was her ARP uniform.

'My friend's here somewhere – she's in the ARP,' she said quickly. 'Her dad was on the night shift. Can you tell me . . . ?' She gestured.

A man whose eyes seemed to shine glassily out of the dirt all over his face, pointed.

'That's . . . Well, it was . . . The New Building. There was a direct hit . . .' He seemed to be in shock. 'There's a whole lot of 'em didn't make it out to the shelters, see. They stayed in the cellar underneath.' He shook his head. 'I dunno how many's in there. The whole lot come down – all the machinery fell through the floors, like . . .'

The others joined in, seeming to want to explain. The high-explosive bomb had landed on one of the works' tallest buildings, having four storeys, each floor a workshop containing heavy machinery, now all collapsed inwards and lying with its tangled weight entombing the people below.

'How many . . . ?' she asked faintly.

'Must be at least fifty.' The others nodded in agreement.

'They've got about half a dozen out,' a younger man in the group said. 'But they can't even reach most of 'em. We've moved everything we possibly can by hand . . . Sorry . . .' Abruptly, his shoulders started to shake and he put his hands over his face, turning away.

'Hey, pal,' the third man said. He led him away a little, talking to him quietly, an arm across his shoulders. It was so upsetting to see that Violet felt like crying too.

'They've had to pump water out of the Cut to put the fires out,' the first man said. He looked across towards the canal. 'It's risky, this bit of the site. Anything they might do trying to dig them out – there's a risk of flooding the whole place.'

Violet stood looking round bleakly. It seemed an impossible task. Was there anyone still alive under there, waiting, hoping? It was a terrible thought. She stood, helpless like the rest of them.

A few minutes later, she spotted Grace. She was moving about frantically between groups of people, speaking to them, moving on, seeming to be beside herself. Violet hurried over, trying to avoid tripping over anything.

'Grace! Grace, wait!'

She saw her friend's head turn and, in her eyes, something she had never seen before, a wild, almost crazed look. Grace came running up to her.

'My dad! Have you seen him?'

'No. Grace, I've only just got here . . .' She seized her friend's hands. They were icy cold. It was terrible to see Grace like this, her usually cheerful, joking friend, close to the brink of hysteria. She held her gently and tried to sound calm.

'Come here, Gracie . . . Come over here with me.' She led her, gently, a little distance from the huddles of people standing in the ashen, terrible morning. She realized that quite a few of them must have had someone on nights in the building and she could hear heartbroken sobbing and crying.

An arm round Grace's shoulders, she said, 'Just tell me.'

'He's down there! I know he is!' The grief and worry she had been holding on to all these hours came bursting out in sobs. 'He was on nights – and I've been here for hours and not found him. He'd've . . . I dunno, come and found me if he was able, I know he would!'

'Grace, he would have had no way of knowing you were here,' Violet pointed out, her arm pulling her friend close. Carefully, she asked, 'Did he work in the New Building – that's the one, isn't it?'

'Yes! . . . No! I'm not sure – and I dunno who those people are under there, why they weren't in the shelters . . . I've been here hours and hours and there's no sign of him! How can I go home and face our mom?'

'Could he have gone home already?' Violet asked.

Grace stared at her for a moment, then shook her head. 'He'd never do that – just go home when there's all this and people needing help . . .' She started to give way even more then, crying her heart out.

'There's a whole load of people under there,' she sobbed. 'They're trapped – how're they ever going to get them out? And it's all been such pandemonium . . . Our dad must be down there – because he isn't anywhere else!'

'Well, maybe he's not,' Violet said, though inside she couldn't help the awful feeling that Grace was probably right. The atmosphere of the morning was so desolate, especially after the force of the bombardment last night, that it felt as if no good news could possibly come out of it. 'Maybe he's . . .' But she couldn't think what to say. Where else could Grace's father be?

Grace sagged against her, suddenly overtaken by exhaustion. As they stood there together one of the rescue workers moved towards them. Neither of them took much notice until he was right up close. He seemed vaguely familiar to Violet.

'Grace?' he said.

To Violet's amazement, Grace's face lit with a terrible hope and she flung herself into the man's arms.

'Oh, Harry! Oh, thank God you're here!'

Violet realized who the man was. His face, with those bright blue eyes, was engraved in her memory from the morning after she had had to go in under the bombed-out house to find poor Mrs Strong. But how was it that Grace seemed to know him so well? They had walked into each other's arms like people who were very closely acquainted indeed.

'Help me – please help me find my dad!' she begged. 'He was working last night – I don't know where he is!'

'I'll do what I can,' he said. Violet saw the hopeless look in his eyes as he glanced back towards the bombed factory. 'But there's nothing else you can do here. Haven't you got to get to work?'

'Yes,' Violet said. 'In a couple of hours.'

'Best go home then.' His voice was kind.

'I don't want to go and leave him,' Grace cried helplessly. She let go of the man, seeming to remember herself. 'But I'll have to go home. What am I going to say to Mom?'

They walked in silence. Violet was not going to ask anything. But as they were turning the corner into Archibald Street, Grace looked at her suddenly.

'That man – on the rescue team. It's just . . . He and I – we had a bit of a . . .'

'You don't have to explain to me,' Violet said. She found she was too worn out to care. Grace was supposedly engaged to Jimmy Oval. But it wasn't any of her business and at this time in the morning, after the night they had had, none of it seemed to matter. Grace's dad was missing and she was worried about George. Where was he and was he all right? And now, too, they had to face Mrs Templeton and break the news to her that her husband was missing.

'Shall I come in with you?' she asked Grace.

'No, it's all right,' Grace said. She stopped at the end of the entry, obviously in utter dread of going in. Reaching out, she touched Violet's arm. 'Thanks, Vi. You're a pal. See yer later.'

Twenty-Seven

From outside the back door Grace could hear the familiar noises of her family as they began the day. It felt like the most terrible moment of her life, knowing that there were these last seconds when they were all there, not knowing, before she had to step inside and tell them . . .

'Ah, Grace – thank the Lord!' Her mother's tired face lifted into a smile as she spoke above the hubbub of the other children. She immediately poured Grace a cup of tea. 'What a night we had. At least you're here – I wish your father would hurry up and get home too.'

She hasn't heard, Grace thought. Her face felt set, stony, as if she couldn't move it.

'Mom.' She tried to sound casual, as if it was nothing. 'Can you come here a tick?' She gestured towards the front room. 'I just need a quick word.'

Her mother's face tensed immediately and following Grace she pulled the door between the front and back room closed and held on to it.

'What is it? Oh, Grace . . . What've you got to tell me? Let me sit down for it.' She lurched over and sank on to one of the chairs.

Grace's right hand went to her heart, which felt as if it was racing so fast it might give out. She opened her mouth and the words just wouldn't come.

'Holy Mother of God, what is it?' White-faced, Cath perched on the tatty leather chair.

'Mom . . .' she said hoarsely. Her tears came then and

made speech even more difficult. 'We don't know anything for sure, but . . . They hit the BSA last night. And I've been there for hours and I can't find Dad anywhere.' She sank to her knees on the floor then, sobs breaking out of her.

Her mother was silent for a long minute, but then Grace felt herself being pulled firmly to her feet. Her mother was strangely calm.

'Get yourself up – and tell me, *quietly* . . .'

Grace quickly whispered the horror of the night. She didn't mention the people trapped, or exactly what had happened. It seemed too terrible, all at once.

'They just think they might not have got everyone out,' she said. 'And I couldn't find him – I've been looking for hours.'

Cath Templeton sank on to the chair again. Her face was very grave but she was fully in control. Grace was strengthened by the steely look of her.

'All right,' she said. 'Now, Grace, dry your eyes and get yourself together. This is what we are going to do. We go in there and get everyone off to work and to school. And we don't say a word until we know something for sure. And then . . .' She seemed to drift for a moment. After that was unthinkable. 'Then we'll see.'

Violet stood at Mrs Oval's door, waves of tiredness passing through her. She felt as though she might collapse if she didn't sit down soon.

Mildred Oval came to the door looking surprisingly fresh, all things considered.

'Oh, hello, Violet!' She spoke very quietly, glancing behind her. 'Oh, you poor lamb, you're fit to drop. What a *night*!'

Violet nodded wearily. 'I just thought I'd pop in, see how you got on with Mrs Crosby?'

Mildred Oval smiled and put her finger to her lips. 'Come on in, bab.'

Violet tiptoed into the Ovals' front room. There was not much furniture in it but there were a couple of armchairs by the hearth. In one, fast asleep, with the little baby snoozing at her breast, was Susan Crosby. She looked pink-cheeked and settled.

Mildred and Violet exchanged smiles.

'She's a tough one,' Violet whispered. 'Is someone looking after her other children?'

'One of the neighbours, I think. Her house is all right so she can pop off home as soon as she's ready. Says 'er husband's on nights. I've given her a cup of tea and a bite to eat.'

'Thanks ever so much, Mrs Oval,' Violet said, warmed by the sight. Susan Crosby's baby seemed the one good thing to have come out of that night of hell. She thought of Grace and her heart ached.

'And thank you for helping my Arthur,' Mrs Oval said. 'He said you was ever so good to 'im. They've patched him up and he's upstairs having a rest.'

'He deserves it,' Violet said.

At least we've all come through the night in one piece,' Mildred said wearily. 'That's summat to be thankful for.'

'I'd better get going,' Violet said. 'Mom'll be mithering about me. T'ra for now.'

On the line at Hughes's, her exhausted, overwrought mind kept flashing images at her from the night. The girl at the First Aid post, the terrible screams; the sight of Susan Crosby birthing her baby which, looking back, she felt disturbed by. And Grace's face, the white shock on hearing what had happened at the BSA.

She let these memories play through her mind. Others joined them. Grace running into the arms of that man.

And all the time, forcing through all these shocks to the system, was the endless worry. George. It had been the worst of nights. Where was he – was he all right?

She was so tired and preoccupied by the time the shift ended that she took in hardly a word of June's burblings as they came out of Hughes's. Something about this feller she'd been on about before – things seemed to be developing in carnal ways that Violet didn't necessarily think anyone else needed to hear about. She wanted to tell June to shut it, but was rescued by the sight of a face in the street just outside the factory. A face that was smiling straight at her.

'George!' All the grinding exhaustion fell away and she dashed over to him, throwing her arms around him. Who cared who else saw or made comments?

'Oh, you're all right!' she cried, tearful suddenly. 'Oh, thank God!'

'Yeah, I'm all right. Hey – what's all this? No tears!' He looked tenderly into her face.

'Sorry. I'm all right. It's just been so . . .' She shrugged.

'I know. I had to come and find yer – I've been worried sick. Mom had an incendiary come in upstairs – in the front bedroom. It was before they went down the cellar and Alice smelt it – they was damn lucky the whole house dain't go up.'

'Oh, my Lord!' Violet gasped. 'Was there much damage?'

'Put it this way –' George took her hand and they started to walk amid the emerging crowd of factory workers. June was long gone. 'Mom and Dad won't be sleeping on that mattress again, that's for sure. And there's a blooming great hole in the roof. But it's all right – Dad'll fix it up for the moment.'

'Poor things.' Violet smiled with relief. 'Oh, my – I'm so pleased to see you!'

George squeezed her hand.

'You heard about the BSA?' she said. 'Grace doesn't know if her dad's down in there.'

George looked at her. 'Oh, good God,' he said.

Grace passed the worst day at work she could ever remember. It was impossible to think about anything other than Dad and the BSA and what was happening. All morning she kept bursting into tears, even when there were customers in the shop. In the end, Mrs Hodgson took her into the back to ask what had got into her, and it all came spilling out.

'Oh, my Lord,' Mrs Hodgson said. Her face took on a gentler look than usual. 'There was me thinking this was going to be a lot of nonsense about some man. You poor thing. Look – I can't send you home, there's too much to do. But if I can let you get off early, I will do.'

As Grace tearfully thanked her, swabbing her face, Mrs Hodgson added, 'This terrible war. Wicked, that's what it is. Just wicked. I don't know where it'll all end.'

It was nearly four o'clock before Grace managed to get away. She practically ran home, even though she knew really that if there had been any news of any sort Mom would surely have come to tell her.

She found her mother in the back room as usual with little Gordon sitting placidly on the floor nearby. The other lads were playing outside. As Grace hurried in, their eyes met and Grace saw that there was no news, that her mother was holding on so tightly to herself that she was like a taut piece of wire. But she also knew that Mom did not want her to say anything, for them to put into words the possibility – even just between the two of them – that Dad was one of the people trapped under the New Building at the BSA, that he was not coming home.

'Pass me that pan, will you, darlin',' was all Mom said. 'And can you start on the taters?'

They stood together, making food. Little Adrian ran in, howling, with a cut finger and Grace bound it up with a strip of rag. Marie came home from work and looked from one to the other of them.

'Dad still asleep?' she said.

Grace's head darted round as her mother said, 'Yes – don't you go disturbing him. It was a bad night.'

Grace, in her exhaustion, began to doubt her own sanity – was Dad in fact upstairs and asleep in bed all this time? She almost felt she must go and look, before she saw her mother give her a stern glance. She realized that Mom just couldn't take any of it in herself, could neither accept nor find the strength to force this new reality on the rest of her children.

'Marie,' Mom said, 'run down to Mrs Turner's and get a box of matches, will you?'

When Marie had gone out, Mom did not look round. She just kept stirring the saucepan.

Marie had not been back long and it was nearly six o'clock. She was having a moan about someone in the factory where she worked, still not seeming to notice that her mother and sister were strangely quiet.

'Marie, go and call the others in for tea,' Cath was saying, when they heard a loud rapping at the front door.

Grace and her mother both froze, looking at each other.

'Shall I go?' Marie said impatiently.

'No!' Cath pushed past her so forcibly that Marie cried, 'Ow – Mom!'

Grace and Marie stood looking into the front room. It seemed to Grace that it took an age for the front door to open, as if several weeks passed between her mother walking to it and the door swinging back to reveal a policeman on the doorstep.

'Oh, my!' Cath's hand went to her throat. She grasped the edge of the door frame. 'What?' she whispered. 'What is it?'

'Mrs Templeton?' he asked. He was a middle-aged man with a deep baritone voice.

Their mother nodded. Grace could see that she was quivering all over and Grace felt as if her own legs were going to give way.

'I've come to give you a message,' he said. 'It's been passed along, sort of Chinese whispers-like. It's about your husband – Mr Bill Templeton?'

Grace saw Mom nod dumbly.

'He's in the Queen Elizabeth Hospital – was taken in during the night.'

Marie turned to Grace, utterly bewildered. 'What? But she said he was upstairs!'

Twenty-Eight

Sunday 8 December

'Oh, I do wish your father was back home! I don't know what to do! Gracie, what am I to do?'

Cath Templeton sat sobbing at the table in the back room. They had just come in from church. Grace was making breakfast, hoping that would raise their spirits after fasting through the early Mass.

Gordon stood by Cath's chair, whimpering and pulling at her sleeve. He was sixteen months old and these days he was experiencing something new in his little life: his mother weeping. He did not like it.

Grace sat down opposite her mother. All through Mass, she had been aching inside as well. More children were being evacuated from the city. Families who had decided to take their chance with the bombs before the German *blitzkrieg* began, were now seeing the reality of what it could do. So many had been killed, so many families devastated, that there was another attempt to move them out.

'Things are different now, aren't they? Our dad might think differently about it too. You could ask him, Mom – he's well enough now . . . And what did Father Lawler say?' Grace thought her mother might have sought counsel from the parish's younger priest instead of grim old Father O'Riordan.

'Oh, I don't want to trouble your daddy – not with him lying there. And Father Lawler's a nice enough young man, but how would he know, with him not having any children of his own?' This surprised Grace – her mother usually set a lot of store by the priests. Cath looked desperately across at her. 'What do you think I should do?'

Warmed by having her own opinion sought at last, Grace reached out and took her mother's hand across the table. 'You're talking about sending the little'uns – Joseph, Michael and Adie?'

'D'you think they'd keep three little brothers together?' Grace could feel her mother's fingers twitching in agitation. 'That would make it better for them, wouldn't it now?'

Grace felt a great weight of sorrow on her. Her pesky brothers drove her mad a lot of the time, but the thought of sending them away – especially little Adie, who was only five – broke her heart. She felt exhausted and wrung out.

'I think they do, if they can,' Grace said. She had no idea really, but the thought made her feel better as well.

It seemed the only way. But it also felt unbearable, especially with the loss of Dennis still so raw in them.

'I think . . .' Her mother sat staring ahead of her, a desolate expression in her face. 'I'll have to let them go. I mean, imagine if . . .'

But neither of them wanted to imagine anything worse than had already happened.

Her father was still in hospital. When she and Mom had first gone over to see him, after finding out the amazing, miraculous news that he was not one of the poor souls

224

trapped under the BSA's New Building, neither of them had been able to hold back their tears.

Grace walked on to the ward arm in arm with her mother and there he was, lying there on one side in a row of men who all seemed to have suffered awful injuries. Dad had a cage under the bedclothes to lift them off his legs and a pulley arrangement holding up one of his arms. It was such a shock seeing that. But, under all the paraphernalia, there was Dad, alive. Alive!

'Bill!' Grace watched, her eyes filling as her mother hurried over to him and kissed and kissed his face. 'Oh, my darling – oh, you're here.' She poured her love over him. Eventually she stood back so that Grace could give him a kiss. Seeing her father's face, shaved and remarkably unmarked, smiling up at her, she burst into tears.

His neck was braced as well and all he could do was turn his eyes to them and whisper, 'Hello, my girls.'

He was only just able to speak then. It was one of the nurses who had to tell them that he had been trapped under fallen masonry outside the building and not found until sometime in the small hours of the morning, from where he was taken away in the ambulance. It was going to take him some time to recover.

A large number of people had been injured in the BSA bombing. Many were now presumed dead. Only a handful had been brought out alive, though the desperate attempts to find some way to get through and rescue more, had gone on for as long as possible.

Everyone in the area was haunted by the thought of it. The idea of blowing up the wall on one side of the factory was rejected: it was so close to the Cut that it would likely have flooded the whole place, drowning everyone inside. The horror of it gripped people's minds. Rumours circulated that people going into the BSA works heard voices calling out from under the wreckage of the New Building. Fifty-three people were missing, presumed dead, and production of rifles had come to a standstill.

And three nights later, another bomb hit the BSA, though much less damage was done.

It was a long way to the Queen Elizabeth and visiting their father was only really possible at the weekend. Mom went with Marie or Tony, or less often, with Grace.

After several days of rocking painfully between one decision and another – I'll have to let them go! – I'm never letting them go to strangers! – Cath, with Gordon in her arms, took her other three little lads to New Street station one wintry morning to join the new wave of children being taken away, it was hoped, to a safer billet.

Grace knew they were going that morning, before they knew it themselves. She said a special goodbye to each of them before she set off for work, desperately trying to hold back her tears.

'Bye, Joseph . . .' She kissed his cheek and he squirmed. 'Bye now, Michael . . .'

'Oi, Gracie – what're yer doing? Gerroff!' He wiped her lipstick from his cheek vigorously with his sleeve and it made her smile, while bringing a lump to her throat.

Adrian accepted her sudden affection with bewilderment. She gave Adie a special little squeeze. He smelt of milk slops and he put his arms round her neck. She just managed to get out of the front door before bursting into tears.

'This one was waving to them as the train went out,' Cath told Grace later, sitting with Gordon in her arms, crying her eyes out. 'We could see Joseph's face through the window as he went and this one kept waving away . . .'

226

She sobbed, pressing a hand to her chest. 'Oh, Gracie – I think my heart is actually cracking part.'

Grace wept again along with her mother. The house felt so quiet and strange without Den and her three other young brothers wrangling around causing havoc. And no Dad either. The war was emptying the house, breaking up the family bit by bit. Those who were left treated each other with a new tenderness. Her brothers Patrick and Tony, who were nineteen and eighteen, had become suddenly more grown up. Grace was even getting on better with Marie these days, especially now Marie was out at work. Nor did any of them need to go into Mr and Mrs Rose's Anderson shelter either – there was room for everyone who was left.

But through all the family's suffering, there was a secret part of herself that Grace could not tell anyone about. It filled her with shame, but she could not seem to help herself.

Even in her sad, shocked state, she still could not rid herself of her overpowering desire to see Harry Cobb.

Nothing in her life felt quite real. There were the terrifying nights out in the air raids, the damage and horrific injuries she had seen, and even when there was no bombing the night-time streets felt more sinister to her these days. She was nervous, jumpy in the darkness full of alleys and black corners, of criminal deeds and the tap of footsteps of people around you who you could not see.

She even started to imagine there was someone following her as she went home from a shift. It was not too far along the street, but always, somewhere, there seemed to be that quiet, almost furtive rhythm of shoes stepping along the pavement behind her. She told herself she was getting silly and nervy and must be imagining it.

Life before the war had faded into unreality. Jimmy

was part of that. It was so long since she had seen him that despite their brief letters to each other, he felt like part of another life when she had been a different person.

She knew she was betraying him with Harry, but Harry now seemed the only thing that was real. They did not see much of each other – a stolen hour perhaps once or twice a week at most, depending on the intensity of the raids. And there had been a succession of quieter nights lately.

Every now and again he would come and meet her out of work. The longing expression she saw on his face thrilled her, filling her with desire in her turn. The snatched times they had together felt like a break from the exhausting awfulness of the days and nights. A dreamtime of passion, of holding and longing to lie with Harry and to take things further, which also filled her with a burning shame. But all the time, that desire was growing stronger.

'My God, Grace, I want you,' Harry would sigh into her ear in his gruff voice. 'You're a woman, all right – I've never known anyone else who makes me feel like this. It's a lonely life without you, I can tell you.'

He would put his head back in the darkness and let out a sharp breath, as if trying to keep his desire under control, which only made her own flare up all the more.

Her swirling thoughts were a confused mix of desire and all the dark guilt and prohibitions of her Catholic upbringing. When she went to Mass now, in her shame, she thought about abstaining from communion, but realized this would only attract attention. But her cheeks flamed as she approached the altar. How many of her thoughts were those of a sinful, fallen woman! Supposing she went all the way with Harry and fell pregnant? What on earth would become of her then?

And, niggling in her mind in a place she never visited for fear of what she might find, was the question, why did Harry not insist on making an honest woman of her? This was a question to which, in the flame of her desire for him, she never truly wanted an answer.

And what does it matter anyway? she thought, when her fantasies about Harry reached boiling point. Any night, I might die! I don't want to die never knowing what it's like to be with a man . . . If only things were different and they were not standing together in some smelly entry but able to lie together, for her to see Harry's naked body and he hers . . .

In the midst of all this, Jimmy had written to say that in a few days he was due to be home on leave, that he was longing to see her. Though it was only a few months since she had seen him, it felt like years. All she could think of these days was Harry Cobb. She was full of sin, full of longing for him. The very last person she felt like seeing at the moment was Jimmy Oval.

June Perry was meeting her feller in a place off another entry in Small Heath, in the storage shed of a small firm where she had once worked. She knew her away around this dark, kissing corner – all the more so in the blackout – where they would not be disturbed. June was certainly making the most of it.

She had curled the ends of her hair and pinned it back, made up her face and applied a good coat of powder and a deep red lipstick. Looking in the cracked mirror of the scullery at home she had turned her head this way and that, viewing her fleshy, handsome face with its big eyes, strong, dark brows and full lips. She looked pretty hot stuff these days and she knew it.

And this man made creatures like that Sidney bloke

and some of the others she'd knocked about with seem right prissy pieces of work. Most of them were like silly little boys in comparison.

But this feller . . . Oh, my! He was by far the best-looking man she had ever been with – and he was flaming hot stuff himself! She'd go anywhere with him – give him anything, the way he made her feel. Well – almost anything.

'I've never met a woman like you,' he'd mutter, running his hands over her hungrily. 'Just the feel of yer – you're magnificent!'

And June, with all the splendour of her body and the aching need between her legs, pressed herself against him, feeling that at last someone truly appreciated her.

Twenty-Nine

Wednesday 11 December

'What about the Sunday after next?' Violet said.

George had met her out of Hughes's and they were now walking along, blissfully, arm in arm. They hardly ever went in for entertainments – dancing or the pictures. Just being together, walking, nattering, even in the dark, was such a pleasure, they didn't seem to need any more than that.

'Blimey,' George said. 'You're making a right meal of this. I'm scared out of my wits of meeting your mom now. Why not this Sunday?'

Violet sighed. 'Sorry. I s'pose I'm putting off telling her. She can be . . .'

'Difficult – yeah, you said.' He sounded fed up. 'I mean, you're a grown-up woman, Vi. What can she say?'

'It's not just what she *says*.' Violet sighed. How to explain? 'It's just how she *is* a lot of the time. She has a way of making you feel bad . . . Look,' she appealed to him, squeezing his arm. It wasn't like George to be grumpy. 'I will tell her, I promise! It's not you, love, honest – you're the best thing that's ever happened to me. I just don't want her to spoil things.'

She could tell he really didn't understand what Mom was like, the way just one look of that doll-like face could make Violet feel terribly guilty, even now. It was something she had to battle against.

'Have you got the steam to come to ours for a cuppa?' George said when they reached the end of Cattell Road. He never stayed out of sorts for long. 'We can go out again after if Jerry keeps quiet.'

'Ooh, yes, please!'

There was nothing Violet liked better than going to the Cherrys' house, feeling almost part of a proper family. As well as the warm welcome from his mom and sisters, there was Pilot resting his jowls on her knee and gazing at her, alert for any stray crumbs dropping into her lap. She had always loved going to Grace's house for the same reason. But she seemed to be so busy these days – maybe with the mysterious man friend she would never open up about. And the one time she had called at the Templetons' house, number sixty-eight had felt a sad, silent place after Den's death, with the little boys evacuated and no Mr Templeton to give them all a tune on the old rackety piano.

'C'mon then,' George said, recovering his temper quickly as he usually did. 'Eh – before we get there, how about a kiss?'

They stood back by the wall and in the smoky winter darkness, cuddled up in each other's arms.

'I love you, George,' Violet said, feeling she still needed to make amends. 'You're the best.'

George made a happy sound, close to her ear, then kissed her cheek.

'And you're my wench – the girl of my dreams, you are, Vi! Come on – let's go and get you that cuppa tea.'

They had just loosed each other and turned along Cattell Road when the air-raid siren moaned into life, provoking George into a range of curses so ripe but so unusual coming from him, that they brought a blush to Violet's cheeks.

She had no sooner got to the ARP post in Archibald Street than the All Clear went off. Mr Powell rolled his eyes.

'Oh, for goodness' sake,' Violet said furiously.

Grace looked at her. 'What's up with you?'

'Nothing. Well . . .' She lowered her voice. 'I was with George, that's all. Could've stayed where I was.'

'Well,' Miss Holt said as they all took off their bags, put down their equipment and settled down again. 'Put the kettle on, Arthur, will you? Better not to have a raid than to have one, wouldn't you agree? Who's for a game of—'

She never got to the end of the sentence because the air-raid warning went off again.

'Oh, flippin' 'eck!' It was Grace's turn this time.

It went on like this all night – exhausted people in and out of air-raid shelters. The wardens decided to go out anyway, much of the time. At one point Mildred Oval, coat thrown on, pink-faced and agitated, appeared at the ARP post.

'Are they gunna make up their flaming minds whether there's a raid on or not? My kids are up and down the garden and I've had the dinner on and off . . .' She disappeared again, not apparently expecting an actual answer.

However, she was back the next evening. Miss Holt was in full debate with Mr Powell about all the criticisms being levelled against Civil Defence preparations – the shortage of water since some of the mains had been hit, the fact that people were not being fed and sheltered fast enough.

The others sat about – Reggie smoking and Quentin joining in the discussion off and on. Grace looked very tired and strained, Violet thought, and she wondered if this was because of the mysterious man she was seeing, but now did not seem the moment to ask about it.

'No one was quite expecting all this . . .' Mr Powell was saying mildly.

'And no one expected the common man – and woman for that matter – to be so brave and upstanding!' Miss Holt interrupted him. 'Our houses may be down, but our spirits are up – that's what the ordinary British housewife is saying!'

And then Mildred Oval came steaming in. Sometimes when she visited she brought her crochet with her, but she was quite wool-less tonight.

'As Arthur's off tonight, I thought I'd come and tell you.' She seemed about to burst with emotion. 'The King was here – in Birmingham!'

They all knew this, of course, because word had gone swiftly round and even though it had been a surprise visit, His Majesty was greeted and cheered wherever he went and people started singing, 'God Save the King'.

'And what's more – he shook hands with my Mark! He was inspecting some of the fire service people and he took Mark's hand in his . . .' She paused dramatically. 'And shook it!'

'How splendid,' Miss Holt said.

'Yes – and d'you know what he said?' Mildred beamed round at them all.

They waited.

'He said, "Good work, my man." The King. George the Sixth of England. He said, "Good work, my man" – *to my son!*'

'That really is rather something, Mrs Oval,' Mr Powell said.

'Oh, he's a nice gentleman,' Mildred said. 'I've always

thought so – and him having all that problem with speaking and being shy. But Mark said what a nice man he was.'

'Good for you, Mrs Oval,' Miss Holt said.

'Yes, well . . .' Mildred said. 'I'd better get home. Arthur'll want his tea. But I thought you'd all like to know. Oh! All this excitement and I'm forgetting why I came. Grace, Jimmy's coming home on Sunday!' Her face was radiant. 'I thought you'd want to know straight away – we got a telegram!'

Violet watched Grace, expecting her to light up at the news. She would have done if it had been George coming home after months away! Grace did smile – but to Violet she didn't seem exactly over the moon. She wondered if she was imagining it.

'Oh, that's the best news!' Grace said. 'Thanks for coming and telling me, Mrs Oval!'

Mildred beamed at her and hurried away again. Grace's smile faded. There was a silence.

'Well,' Mr Powell said. 'That's nice.' He pulled out his pocket watch. 'Six-thirty, and no raid yet.'

'How splendid,' Miss Holt said again.

Thirty

Sunday 15 December

Grace hurried down Archibald Street after work, her hat pulled low over her eyes. It was already almost dark. A hand in her coat pocket, she fingered the sheet of paper folded in there, feeling the blood hammer through her veins. She glanced at the Ovals' house across the road and hurried in along the entry to her own house.

'Oh, Grace!' Cath said as soon as she stepped inside. 'Jimmy's just after having called in! He's been home no more than an hour – I said you'd be over straight away!'

Grace hadn't seen her mother looking so lit up for a long time. Mom was very fond of Jimmy – and even more of the idea of her and Jimmy being married.

'All right,' Grace said. 'Just let me get through the door.'

'Why aren't you excited?' Marie demanded. She was stirring something at the stove. 'The love of your life has just arrived! You've got no heart, Grace!'

Shut up! Grace wanted to scream. *Just shut up – don't say a single word to me!* Her nerves were on a knife edge, every inch of her body tense.

Saying nothing, she ran up to the bedroom still in her coat and sat on the edge of the bed she shared with Marie. Marie had better not follow her, being nosey, butting in!

She felt that if she heard Marie's footsteps on the stairs now, saw her coming into the room, she might hit her.

She drew in a deep breath, trying to calm herself. The Ovals would be waiting for her. Jimmy would be there, the family all making much of her as they always had: Mildred now talking about her almost as if she was a daughter-in-law. There'd be Dolly, slipping an arm round her waist, Jimmy looking at her as if she was the eighth wonder of the world, the way he did . . . How could she face them? She was wicked, terrible. But she did have to – there was no way out of it.

Pulling the scrap of paper out of her pocket she read it once more, then slid it well in under her side of the mattress.

'Here she is!'

Mildred beamed at her as she tapped on the back door and put her head round it. Grace forced her lips into a smile.

'All right, Mrs O – Mr O?' She nodded at Mark, Sylvie and Charlie, who were round the table. The wireless was on, smooth music streaming out in the background.

'Grace!' Dolly got up and flung her arms round her.

'Hello, Dolly.' Grace gave her an affectionate squeeze and looked down at her. 'I swear you're getting taller every day!'

Little John, in his special chair with a bar across to stop him toppling off, squirmed with excitement at seeing her and reached his hand out.

'Hello, sweetheart.' She squeezed his hand.

And lastly, finally, she could not avoid looking at him any longer.

'All right, Jimmy?'

'Grace.' He smiled, but she could see a reserve in his

smile. Was he shy after all this time or could he see her guilt, smell it on her like a fishmonger's whiff?

'Come and sit with us, bab,' Arthur Oval said. He was leaning back, smoking. 'You'll shove over and let Grace have a seat, won't you, Dolly?'

Dolly reached for a stool from by the stove and Grace settled in her seat.

'Nice to see you off duty for once,' Arthur said, as Mildred poured her a cup of tea. 'Like old times.'

'Sort of,' Grace said. She looked at Jimmy. 'Must be a shock, coming back. The state of the place?'

Jimmy shook his head, his eyes solemn. 'It is. Terrible. Mom and Dad've been telling me. I can't hardly take it in.'

There was an awkward silence suddenly, as if everyone could feel the tension between them. Jimmy had been away for so long it was hard to know where to start.

'Our Grace has been doing a grand job in the ARP,' Arthur said. 'Out there in all of it with just a tin hat between her and the bombs.'

'Well – you too, Mr O,' Grace said, blushing. But she was pleased by the compliment.

'Not a thing I ever thought I'd see,' Mildred said sadly. 'Wenches like you having to do all that sort of thing.'

'No. Well – a lot of things have changed.' Grace glanced at Jimmy, and away again. She could feel his eyes on her but she found it hard to look back.

She lingered round the table with the family in the cosy room, Sylvie helping John to eat his bread and marge, everyone chatting. It was nice to be with them, felt easy, and above all, it put off the time when she knew she would have to be alone with Jimmy.

Because all the time she still had the feeling of being split in half. There was the Grace who belonged here, knew every inch of this room as well as she knew her own house and who loved this family who had, for a long time, seemed her destiny. And there was the Grace whose body was restless with desire, whose mind was leashed to the scrap of paper which Harry had managed to thrust into her hand over the counter at work yesterday.

He had come in and bought something – she could not even remember what – and, when giving her the money, slipped the little screw of paper into her hand before going out again. Grace pushed it into her pocket until later when she had a moment alone in the store-room at the back when she reached for it, trembling with eagerness.

Monday night. H.

Nothing more. Just those two words tied her to him, to her own desire, to the thought of running into his arms.

'D'you want to go for a drink?' she asked Jimmy, when the moment came. 'It's so cold out.'

They had already stepped out into the dark and she was shivering in her coat. The air was bitter with smoke.

Jimmy stopped her, just inside the entry.

'I don't care where we go, Grace. I just want to talk to yer.' He put his hands on her shoulders. She could only just make him out in the gloom, his eyes two dark pools. But his voice was clear enough: solemn, reproachful.

'All right,' she said cautiously. 'What – here?'

'Why not? I dunno where else we're gunna go. Look . . .' He hesitated, turning his head away, then back. 'Look, Grace – what's going on?'

'How d'you mean?' she said. In the darkness, for a moment, she thought, Harry. They had stood close like this so many times. Her body tingled at the thought.

'You're just . . .' He reached for the words. As he did

so he released her shoulders, lowering his hands. 'I dunno if it's the war – everything that's going on, or what . . .'

'It's been bad,' she put in, trying to find reasons because she already knew what he was trying to say and she needed something to say to him because of the string of desire that was tugging at her all the time, even as she stood with him. The desire that kept whispering *Harry* in her mind.

And then she could think of no way of explaining, no way of finding any honesty. Because in all this, what was real and lasting and what was really her and what she felt was so impossible to tell. So instead she held her arms out.

'Come here,' she said.

Jimmy hesitated for a moment, then wrapped his arms round her. Grace turned her face up and Jimmy's lips fastened hungrily on hers. His kisses were so hard and passionate that her desire for him lit and she was soon forcefully kissing him back. Never before had things between them been as fierce as this, their bodies pressed close, both of them breathing hard.

'My God, Grace!' Jimmy pulled away. 'I've never known you like this!' He put his head back and blew out hard through his mouth. 'You'll have to be careful or I won't be able to help myself.' She could just make out his grin as he looked down at her. 'So you've missed me then?'

'Course I have,' she said. What else should she say? She was confused and spinning between worlds old and new – life with Jimmy before the war and the way things were with Harry now. Was Harry real – now that she was standing here with Jimmy?

'I'm not complaining,' Jimmy said, as his lips reached for hers again.

*

Later, when they could no longer feel their feet, they went back inside, chatted with the family. Grace realized that Jimmy was now quite reassured that all was well. So far as he was concerned, nothing had changed. And since she did not know what else to do, she acted as if nothing had either.

'I've got to go back Wednesday morning,' he said as he finally walked her across the road, each holding the other's hand, at close to midnight. 'Don't s'pose you can get off work in the daytime?'

'No, I don't think so. We're short-staffed as it is,' she said.

'Never mind. We'll have tomorrow night – and Tuesday.'

Tomorrow night. *Monday night.* Her mind raced.

'I think I'm on duty,' she said. 'In fact, I'm sure I am.'

'Oh, come off it!' Jimmy said, frustrated. 'Can't you change it? Dad'd change shifts with you if you're not on together.'

Grace thought quickly. How could she manage this? It was a curse that Jimmy's dad was a warden at the same post.

'I'll check,' she said. 'If I am and there's no raid, I can get off early, OK?'

The next morning, on the way to work, she hurried over to Post F to check the roster, apologizing to Miss Holt for disturbing her so early in the morning.

'Quite all right, dear,' Miss Holt said.

To Grace's relief she was sitting in her night clothes drinking a cup of tea and seemed too tired to take much notice. Monday the 16th . . . Grace's eyes ran down the list. Damn and blast it! She was on duty and so was Arthur Oval! Her mind raced.

'Thanks, Miss Holt!'

She went tearing up to the top of the street. 'R. D. Paine, Undertaker' it said on a tarnished little plaque. Francis opened the door to her knock. In the bright morning light, she saw that his eyes were an unusually pale blue and red-rimmed. He reminded her of a white rabbit. Seeing Grace, he seemed almost to flinch and she saw him having to collect himself to speak to her. It made her feel impatient.

'Sorry . . . Only, I need to swap with someone for duty tonight. You're not on – would you mind taking mine and I'll do yours Thursday?'

Francis Paine stared at her for an uncomfortably long time until she almost asked if he had heard what she said. His gaze seemed to go through her and something about him made her shiver. What was it about him? she wondered. He never did anything much, yet he seemed so unlikeable, and made himself so uncomfortable to be with. She tapped her foot impatiently.

'Yes,' he said eventually. 'Yes. All right.'

'Ta – thanks!' And off she went again, rushing to work. Monday . . . And now tonight she was free!

She took the little note she had prepared out of her coat pocket and as she passed the Ovals' house, she slipped it through the letterbox.

Thirty-One

Grace walked along the blacked-out street, head down and hands in her pockets in the bitterly cold darkness. The tapping of her heels on the pavement rang loud, each step taking her closer and closer to him . . . It was like being at the end of a piece of elastic, pulling, stretching, daring herself to keep straining on further.

Tonight, she would decide. It had to be tonight.

'So – there you are.'

Harry must have heard her coming and suddenly he was standing in front of her in the street so that she almost collided with him.

'Oh!' She jumped. 'Oh – it's you?'

'Who else was you expecting?' He laughed.

'No one. I didn't see you. It spooks me standing about in the dark.'

He took her hand to pull her closer.

'Grace.' His lips were close to her ear. 'Grace, Grace. Come on – I know somewhere else we can go.'

He seemed to know the way and all she could do was follow as he walked a little ahead, holding her hand and feeling his way along. Her heart was beating terribly fast, with a combination of excitement and dread. They passed along the entry into a yard and she found him handing her in through the door of some building.

'Where are we?' she whispered. There was a musty smell with a hint of tar. She did not dare move for fear of what she might tread on.

'Oh, just somewhere I found,' he said. He took her in his arms. 'It's all right, no one'll hear us and there's nothing much in here – you don't need to worry.' He moved his lips close to her ear. 'Not about anything.'

Holding each other close, they started kissing passionately. Soon, their hands were tugging each other's clothes, reaching underneath to feel each other's warm flesh. It was all feeling – Harry's lips, his arms, his breath. She could see precisely nothing. It was very easy in the all-enveloping darkness to forget anything except their bodies and the hungry desire she felt for him, him pressing urgently against her, their lips, the feel of his muscular back under her palms.

Tonight I'll do it – I'll let him, she thought, as Harry's hand found its way to her breasts, tugging her brassiere out of the way, lifting and stroking her so that she gasped. It had to be, she thought. Just this once – she had to let him . . .

'Like that, do yer?' he said.

But there was something in his tone that chilled her and brought her back to herself. Something smug and calculating, as if she was a machine he was tuning.

'Yes, course I do, but . . .' She pressed her hand over his, where it was touching her breasts. 'But . . . Harry. Stop. I need to ask you something.'

'What?' He was angry at being frustrated.

'Look – I've never asked you and I've got to. I hardly know a thing about you, Harry. I mean, for a start . . . Are you married?'

She felt him move his head, as if taken aback.

'No! Course not!' His voice, suddenly loud and angry, rang round the inside of the little building. 'What d'you think I am?'

'I don't know. I'm not saying . . . But you never tell

244

me anything. Why couldn't we go to wherever it is you live?'

'Because it's not . . . It's a dump. I share it with other blokes and we couldn't . . . It wouldn't be private. Look, come on, Grace, I dain't come here to talk . . .' He leaned in to kiss her again, his hands beginning to stroke gently at her bare sides.

'So if you're not married,' she persisted, 'why don't we . . . I mean, you never ask me anything about the future, or tell me you want to be with me.' She felt her throat tighten then. To her annoyance she was close to tears.

'Oh, Gracie.' His hand stroked one side of her head, caressing her hair. 'I'm sorry. I'm not much of a one for words. Of course I want to be with you. You're the most amazing girl I've ever known. It's just – the way things are, all this meeting up like this, we never really get a chance, do we?'

'Well, let's try and get out – for a day, shall we?' She was fizzing with happiness suddenly. 'A Sunday? I can get away after the early Mass.'

'All right. Yeah – let's do that,' he said. 'Only now – let's enjoy what we have here, eh? Before it's time to go or the Hun starts on us again.'

He began making love to her again, fiercely. Grace's mind was racing, a great weight lifting from it. If he was free, she could be with Harry, this could be real!

His hand stroked up her thigh, under her skirt, pushing down inside her knickers and again she gasped, feeling his fingers prodding at her. It felt so wrong, so dirty!

'No!' She flinched, pulling away. 'We can't, Harry – not like this. It's wrong – I don't want it to be like this, not my first time. We can be together – get married, do things properly, can't we?'

Slowly he withdrew his hand, giving a sharp sigh.

'I'm sorry,' she said, kissing his cheek. 'But it's better that way, isn't it?'

'If you say so,' Harry said. He sounded angry and cheated. 'But we could name a date – and then it wouldn't matter either way, would it?'

'What – really?' She strained to see him in the darkness. 'Oh, Harry – are you asking me to marry you?'

'Yeah.' He laughed suddenly. 'Yeah – I suppose I am.'

As soon as she knocked at the Ovals' back door, later on, Jimmy stepped outside.

'All right, Gracie!' Jimmy bounced out and immediately took hold of her, hugging her tightly in the entry. 'Finally let you out, did they? Nice of Mr Hitler to let us off tonight!'

She did not respond to his embrace but stood stiffly. She could feel Harry still on her body. She had managed to hold him off until they had set a wedding date, parting with the promise of more soon to come. She felt tense and dishonest, her mind still tied elsewhere.

'Hello, Jimmy.'

He backed off, sensing how distant she was.

'What's up?' He sounded hurt.

'I need to tell you something, Jimmy.'

He waited, and suddenly she was really scared. She opened her mouth, trying to say the words that would change everything. All these years they had known each other, and all this time she had known Jimmy loved her and wanted to marry her.

'Well – spit it out then.' He tried to joke, as if sure it could not be anything serious.

'I don't know if . . .' she started, then trailed off. 'Last time . . . When you were home, what you said – about us?'

'Getting wed? Yeah. I've been waiting, Grace. Nothing's changed for me, I can tell you that.' Looking suddenly worried, he went on, 'What're you trying to say to me?'

'I'm so sorry, Jimmy.' She was glad she could not see his face to know the pain that would appear on it when she spoke. Because she meant him no harm, her old friend. Her chest ached. 'But I'm promised to someone else.'

Jimmy's hands dropped to his sides.

'What?' he said. He stood stunned. 'What d'you mean? Who? Do I know him?'

'No, you don't.'

'Well, what's his name?'

'Why – what does it matter?' She felt impatient of him asking the wrong questions. Wasn't he supposed to say, *But I love you, don't you love me*, not keep harping on who the other man was?

He stood there for a moment.

'I was never good enough for you, was I?' His voice was bitter and sad.

'Course you were – it's not that.' She felt terrible now. Was this all wrong? Was she making a terrible mistake? It was as if Harry had cast a spell on her, of longing and desire that she could not break free from, as if she was addicted to him. She could see nothing else straight. And now here she was, saying these things to Jimmy, hurting him, closing a door she had wanted to keep open to their future. She could not fathom herself, but this felt like the only thing she could do.

'All right.' Jimmy drew back. 'Well – that's it then, I s'pose. I'm not going to beg you, Grace. You know what

I've felt and I've been hoping all this time. But if your mind's made up, what can I do?'

She was shocked. She had expected him to be angrier, or to beg and try and get her to change her mind. Jimmy was prouder than she had realized. Or was it that she had held off for so long, messed him about – that he was already prepared for this? And because he was not getting angry, putting pressure on her, she felt more regret.

'Did you want to go out tomorrow?' she said. 'Like we said? Go to the pictures or summat?'

Jimmy was by the door of the house.

'Not much point now, is there?' he said coldly. 'So long, Grace. Nice knowing you.'

She heard the door open and close and she was left alone in the dark entry. She rested her head against the filthy wall and burst into tears.

Thirty-Two

Saturday 21 December

Violet stood behind the counter in Quinn's. It was Saturday afternoon and the main rush had died down. The morning had been busy with everyone reclaiming pawned bundles of clothes and other items after pay day yesterday. Sunday-best coats, suits and frocks, the odd come-in-handy vase or fob watch or other ornament pawned for end-of-the-week change, were back with their owners, until Sunday was over and the week's pay packet ran thin again.

By four o'clock, the light was dying. A heavy grey sky sank low over all the rooftops so that it was difficult to distinguish cloud from the smoke trickling out of the chimneys along Archibald Street.

After the last harried housewife had left with her bundle, Violet took out her latest read from under the counter. It was called *The Murder at the Vicarage* by Agatha Christie and normally she would have been lost in its world almost instantly, walking beside Miss Marple in her quest to solve all the mysteries.

But today butterflies turned somersaults in her belly and she could not distract herself. Tomorrow. George was coming to tea. And as yet, Mom didn't know this because Violet still hadn't dared say anything to her, despite giving George to believe she had.

Even with George, she found herself bending the truth, burning with shame as she did so. It felt terrible because George was straight as a die, always honest and truthful. He had had no reason not to be and she knew he would have found all the fibs she had had to tell impossible to understand.

Why're you being so silly? she tried to reason with herself. You're twenty years of age – you could be married with a couple of kids by now and you're scared to tell Mom you're even walking out with a boy!

I'll tell her tonight, she vowed, staring across the dark shop. At tea time. And I'll try and bake something – not just have broken biscuits from Hughes's . . .

Unable to concentrate on Miss Marple's goings-on, she tidied the already well-ordered shop, fussing with the few things left on the shelves, some of which had been there from time immemorial. There was a brass telescope with no case round it, long tarnished black and usually rolled to the back of the shelf. It had been there since before Mr Quinn left and whoever once owned it must have long died.

Violet took it down and looked at it. It was rather a beautiful thing – or could be if she got some Brasso on to it and lots of elbow grease. She wondered if Mom knew it was still there. Maybe she could give it to George – he'd like it, surely?

She was standing in the fading light, the telescope weighty in her hands, when there was a 'ting' from the door. She turned and shoved the telescope to the back of the shelf before facing the new customer.

To her surprise, it was not one of the well-known faces from the street – crazy Miss Glover on one of her odd errands, or a housewife running late. Instead, there stood in front of her a young man in naval uniform.

What on earth? Violet thought. She had never seen the young man before – he was not a local, she was quite sure of that. Yet at the same time there seemed something vaguely familiar about him, even in this light, that she could not put her finger on. He stood smart and upright, the navy-blue cap at a slight angle. As Violet looked at it, he put his hand up and dragged it from his head as if she had reproached him in some way for keeping it on.

'Yes?' she said. 'Can I help you?'

'I, er . . .' He ground to a halt, seeming lost for words. He moved closer. Violet realized how dark it had become – he could hardly see her.

'Hang on a tick.' She went across and switched on the light, which dangled baldly above them. By its meagre illumination, she saw a lad with a round, pleasant face and cropped brown hair.

'Are you lost?' she asked, trying to be helpful.

'I . . . I don't think so. This is Quinn's, in't it?'

'Yes . . .' She walked back round the counter. Her heart was beating harder now as if in warning of something though she had no conscious idea what.

'I was looking for a Mrs, er . . . Actually, I'm not sure of the name . . .' His voice was beginning to tremble. 'Could be Simms?'

Violet frowned. 'Yes – Mrs Simms. That's my mother. I'm Violet Simms, her daughter. Is it . . . ?'

She was about to say, *Is it bad news?* But she could think of no bad news it could possibly be unless it was about this Aunt Elsie who was supposed to be out there somewhere but who she had never met. She knew of no other surviving relatives.

'Look,' she said, rather brutally. 'I can go round the back and get her – but why d'you want her? You might as well spit it out.'

'I think she's the one . . .' He lowered his head, seeming emotional, then looked up at her with a desperate, shy need. 'My name's Tom Smith. And I think Mrs Simms must be my mother.'

There was the moment when Violet stared in utter bewilderment at this stranger, with his oddly familiar features. The moment when, not able to speak above a whisper, she said, '*What*? What d'you mean?' while sensing deep in her somewhere, despite everything she had ever known or been told, that this young, scared-looking man was not lying, that somewhere along the line – perhaps before she was born? – goodness knew what had happened.

There were the moments while she led Tom Smith – and who was he? Her brother? Half-brother? – round along the entry and she saw their doorway, number three, getting closer and closer across the yard, with Mom inside it . . .

And then she and this Tom Smith were walking in through the door. The wireless was on, a man's solemn voice coming from it. Her mother was in the scullery. Violet immediately closed the door out of habit to keep the light in, but now they were all shut in together in this strange dream of an afternoon. And Violet, into this peculiar new world she was entering, said quietly, 'Mom.'

Her mother came out of the scullery, trying her pinner at the back. Raising her head, she stopped as if she had been turned to stone, with elbows still jutting out. Violet would never forget the sight of her face. On it dawned the hungry, longing realization of who was standing before her even when he had not said a word. Violet reached over and clicked off the wireless. There was a second of complete silence.

'Oh!' Mom's hands whipped up to her mouth. She

stared, her eyes stretching. 'Oh . . . Oh, my Lord . . .' She seemed to sag then and grasped the back of a chair as if her legs were giving way. But she kept slowly moving forwards, towards him, her eyes never leaving this stranger's face.

'Is that you? Is that my little Tommy?'

Violet saw a terrible look of distress pass over the lad's face.

'I . . . I think so,' he said. And then he was sobbing, just like a little boy, and Violet watched as her mother went to him and gently stroked the tears from his face.

'My boy,' she said, in tones so gentle and loving that Violet felt her own throat tighten and tears come as well. Never, in her whole life, had she heard quite that tone from her mother, not to her, not sincerely – not to anyone. Except, she realized, something close to it to little blond Donald Baker from across the yard.

'My little boy,' Mom was crooning. 'Oh, my word, look at you! You lovely, lovely boy. *My* boy. You've come back to me – I always knew you would.'

Then, all Violet could feel was emotion – the emotion in the room from her mother, from this nice-looking, bewildered young man, from her own confused and hungry heart. And at that moment it felt as if Mom and Tom were the only ones in the room – as if she did not exist. She had no idea what was going on and she said the only thing there seemed to be to say at that moment.

'Shall I make us all a cup of tea?'

Even then, they didn't get to the bottom of it, not really. The three of them sat at the table with the teapot. Violet found herself feeling sick, as if something terrible had happened which might somehow turn out to have been her fault, even if she really couldn't see how.

'Did Elsie tell you where I was?' Mom asked.

'Yeah,' Tom said. He paused, swallowed. ''Er told me a while back, that if I ever wanted to see you, like, you'd told 'er this was where to come. Only I never . . .' His voice hardened. 'I thought you never wanted me. So I weren't going to come and find you.'

Violet watched her mother, her face a wide-eyed mask of dismayed emotion.

'Any road, all this happened.' He swept his arm round, seeming to be indicating the whole of the war, the bombing and havoc. 'And I joined up and the long and short is, I'm being posted overseas. Dunno where. So, I thought, Well, this might be it. If I'm ever gunna find 'er, I'd best do it now, just in case, like.'

Violet saw her mother reach over and clasp his hands in hers. There was such a pathetic hunger in her face.

'I'm so glad you did, son. I never meant to leave you . . . It wasn't you, it were him!'

Tom's face changed and Violet saw a hurt fury in it. He pulled his hands back out of May's reach.

''E's not that bad, the old man. 'E brung me up on his own – never 'ad no choice, did 'e? And you never 'ad to leave, you ran off because you *wanted* to, everyone said so!'

'No – it weren't like that . . . I had no choice, Tom! You don't know, only what he told you. You were too young to know anything that was going on.'

'Not too young to know that one day I had a mom and the next day I dain't! That my mother was a selfish whore!'

Tom got abruptly to his feet, almost knocking over the half-drunk tea.

'I should never've come. I wanted to see what sort of mother I had.' He sounded disgusted, let down. Violet

254

saw that in his dreams he had harboured something that could never be – something quite different from this childlike little woman he had found who could only ever blame other people. 'Someone who might be sorry for what she did. But now I know, don't I?'

'Tom – don't go, my love, not so soon! I *am* sorry – but give me time to explain . . .'

'There's nowt *to* explain, is there?' He rammed his cap proudly on his head. 'I dunno why I come 'ere – I'm a fool to myself thinking it'd be any different. I can see how it is – you went off and got yerself a new family.' To Violet, in a different, gentler tone, he said, 'I know it ain't your fault, none of it.'

He marched to the door. Stopping for a moment he turned and looked at Violet again, somehow apologetically, as if there was something he felt he should say but could not find the words.

'No! Tom – don't go!' Their mother flung herself across the room towards him, but he wrenched the door open and strode off, disappearing along the entry.

Her mother stood with the door open, as if frozen, staring out into the darkness.

Violet stayed sitting at the table for a moment, numb with the unreality of what had just happened. Then she leapt up, pushed past May through the door and ran out across the yard. A brother – she had a brother! He could not disappear again like that, the brother she had always wanted.

'Tom!' She tore along the entry and at the other end, shouted his name again, frantic. He'd left no address, had not told them anything about where to find him. He had come into their lives for less than an hour, turned everything upside down and now, somewhere, he was out there vanishing into the night.

'Tom! Tom Smith!' She shouted louder than she ever had before, even during a raid, and her voice bounced off the walls. But she did not know which way he had gone and in the darkness, she could see nothing of him.

Weighed down by a terrible sense of loss, of something that when this day had begun she never knew she had, she went back to the house, to find her mother still in the doorway.

'You're showing a light.' She could hear the coldness in her voice as she said it.

They went in and Mom closed the door reluctantly behind them, her shoulders sagging, as if the fact of moving the wood of the door into place was shutting out the possibility of ever seeing her son again. She walked across the room, ignoring Violet as if she was not even there, and sank down at the table where her cold cup of tea awaited her.

Violet looked at her mother, sitting staring across the room, lost in thought. And it was this, the feeling of being shut out again, obliterated almost, on top of all Mom's lifelong self-pity, her feeling of the right to control all Violet's movements, that began to fuel the pilot light of rage that was already burning inside her.

'So,' she dared to say.

May reacted immediately, with an angry, dismissive gesture, still not looking at her. As if to say, *I'm upset – you keep out of it and leave me alone. What do you matter in all this?* She reached in her pocket for her cigarettes and lit up, an elbow on the table, the other arm hugged round her waist.

Violet's mind started to race. A brother – half-brother? Was that what Tom Smith was to her? Either way, there were all sorts of things about her mother's life of which she clearly knew nothing. Things that must have happened before she was born – surely it had to have been before? Relatives, people she had never heard of . . . And those photographs she had seen all those years ago, photographs of . . . Who? Mom – or someone else? What did any of it mean?

My God, she thought to herself. Her blood began to bang in her ears. All this time I've felt so bad about telling a few fibs just to be able to get out from under her; me, feeling like a terrible sinner! When all this time . . .

The scale upon which she had been lied to was so enormous she could still not take it in.

'Mom.' Her voice came out low, and with a force that she could see startled her mother.

May turned slowly towards her, a stony expression on her face. 'Don't speak to me,' she almost growled. 'Don't you ever ask me anything.'

Violet stared at her. '*What?*'

'You heard,' Mom said. 'Just get out – leave me alone for a bit.'

The rage swelled until she was beginning to shake.

'Oh – it's leave you alone now suddenly, is it? Well, *no* – I'm not going anywhere. I'm staying here and you're going to explain to me what the hell has been going on all these years. It's no good trying to cover up again, thinking you can hide all the lies you've told me! But first I've got summat to say to *you*.'

Her mother tightened the grip of her arm around herself, her face contemptuous, as if to say, *What could you have to say to me?* 'Spit it out then.'

'I've been walking out with a lad. His name is George Cherry. He's the nicest person I've ever met and I've invited him round to have tea with us tomorrow afternoon.

His mom's ever so nice – she's really good to me. They're a lovely family – he's got three sisters.'

She watched her mother's face, the realization dawning that something – everything – had changed. There was shock in it – and a touch of fear.

'I expect we'll get married,' she finished. 'Soon as I'm twenty-one. It'll be up to me then. Because I love him and he loves me.'

Her mother lowered her head, not saying anything, almost as if she was bored.

'And he's coming tomorrow and we're going to give him a nice tea and a nice welcome. Aren't we?'

She didn't give her mother a chance to answer. Getting to her feet, she tidied away the cups. Pouring Tom's undrunk tea into the sink in the scullery, she found tears running down her cheeks. She was standing watching the orange-brown liquid disappear down the hole when the air-raid siren went off.

Thirty-Three

Sunday 22 December

Grace stepped out of the Church of the Holy Family on the Coventry Road, into the cold, grey morning, incense and cigarette smoke on the freezing air making her nostrils sting.

All through the Mass, in the plain, modern church, her thoughts had wandered. She tried to keep her mind on her prayers. For Dad to be home by Christmas. And for all her little brothers, somewhere in Worcestershire. At least Michael and Adie had been taken to live together and Joseph was somewhere nearby.

'God, I wish I could go and see them,' her mother kept saying. 'D'you think we should bring them back now, Grace? It all seems to be settling down. God, now I wish I'd never sent them away.'

Just as the boys had left the city, the raids had tailed off. Mom kept lurching from one position to another. Nothing felt right – Dad away, the boys with strangers. And now, Grace kept reminding herself, she was promised to Harry Cobb. She and Harry Cobb were going to get married.

And yet so far, it had not felt right to tell a single soul about any of it, even though Jimmy had evidently announced to his family that their engagement was off. Arthur Oval had said a few sorrowful words to her about it when they were next on duty together. But he ended by saying, 'Just give it time, wench. No good being hasty at times like this.' And patted her on the shoulder. She could see that he thought she would change her mind.

At the edge of her attention she was aware of her mother and friends talking outside the church, sympathizing with each other. Mrs Riley had a husband in the forces, Mrs O'Shea had sent two of her children away as well. All was worry and misery, the air full of 'God love her's and 'pray God's. The chapel of the school next to the parish church had been wrecked by a bomb in the past few weeks. What next? Was nothing sacred?

Grace stood next to Marie, waiting for their mother. She had the collar of her navy coat pulled up and it smelt faintly of incense. She felt a sudden craving for a cigarette. Marie was having a laugh with a girl from Wexford who'd come over to do factory work.

Throughout the solemn, swirling Latin of the Mass, all Grace had been able to think of – God forgive me, she thought, her cheeks blazing – was Harry and what had happened last night . . .

Something had changed over the past couple of weeks. Harry seemed less intent on seeing her. And Grace had decided it was her own fault for putting so much pressure on him. But how could he be losing interest in her when they were supposed to be engaged to be married?

He had used to plead with her, with that force of his that so excited her, for them to meet. And when they did meet, his pressure on her to . . . Well, to go further, was the only way she could put it to herself, blushes rising in her cheeks at the very thought . . . That had become pretty forceful as well.

What did it matter now anyway? she was starting to

think. They were promised to each other. If she were to give in to him, to let him go the whole way – well, that would make him want to see her, wouldn't it? And if she caught for a baby – well then, couldn't they just get married quickly so that no one would be any the wiser? His desire swept her along and she knew that next time she saw him, she really might give in to him, however much it was a sin.

So last night, when she met him, she was almost trembling at the thought of what she might be about to let happen. But when Harry arrived, in the dark of the Coventry Road, he was in a bad mood. She had never seen him like that before. Usually he was all charm, wooing her. Something had changed.

They went to the dark alley where they usually went and with no more ado, he latched his mouth on to hers and started tugging at her blouse. Grace, who had been primed, ready for love, for giving all of herself, felt herself withdraw, hurt by his hard, distant manner.

'Harry,' she said. 'Hold on – stop . . .' She wanted to ask him to be more loving, to be nice to her. Instead of which he made a frustrated, angry noise and grabbed her hand. Tugging at his fly buttons with his spare hand, he guided hers down to his . . . Dear God, the feel of the thing, thick and hot against her fingers!

'That's how much I want yer!' he growled at her. He was like someone else, as if he had turned on her. 'I've said I'll marry you, ain't I? So what's up with you now? If you won't do the thing proper at least let me get off myself. I can't stand any more of this!'

And as she fumbled, not having much clue but feeling she must do as she was told, he took both her hands, showed her how to hold him and he pumped his body, his thing moving between her hands until he finally gasped and shuddered to a stop. Her hands were covered by warm, sticky stuff. He subsided then, and half-turned away from her to button himself up, seeming no less cross with her.

'Don't think I want it to be like this,' he said. 'That's what you've reduced me to.'

Grace stepped away, hurt, disgusted. She felt too embarrassed now to say, *But I was going to, if you'd been nicer to me* . . . She wiped her hands on the filthy brick wall, having nothing else. He didn't even seem to want to kiss her again after that. She had just not known what to say and they parted and went home. She lay in bed last night, upset and burning with shame.

Jimmy had never behaved in such a way to her. Every time she thought about Harry now, she felt sick with shame. And now she had gone and said that she would meet him later this afternoon.

After what had happened, she'd managed, without bursting into tears, to say, 'Do we always have to meet like this? We're engaged, aren't we? We don't have to meet in this hole-in-the-corner way all the time. Why can't we just go out – do summat nice? And we can talk about what we're going to do – set a date for our wedding?'

She wanted him to relent and be loving and excited about it.

'All right,' was all he said, pulling his clothes straight. 'Yeah. You got a point.'

They had arranged to meet in Victoria Park. Being Sunday, there was nowhere much else to go. And now Grace thought about it, she felt more nervous than ever, as if she was still pushing too far out, stretching at that piece of elastic because she couldn't seem to help herself.

But she had no idea what she was going to do if it snapped back on her.

'What're you doing?'

May Simms came into the kitchen as Violet stood, peeling and slicing a cooking apple into little chunks, the tangy smell of the fruit in her nostrils. She felt her mother watching her and she didn't look round. It gave her a powerful, yet also shameful, feeling that she was doing something Mom could not control. All the same, her hands shook as she sliced off the green apple skin. She was so used to being scared of her mother, of her bitterness and judgement.

'Making a cake – for this afternoon. For when George comes.'

She had made sure she got hold of her own egg and ration of sugar for the week. There was not really enough of either but she padded out the cake mix with apple, sprinkling a tiny pinch of allspice on top as that was all they had.

'You haven't managed to poison me against all men, you know. I've found someone to love me.' There was a silence behind her. Violet felt the hairs rise on the back of her neck, as if Mom might attack her, and she couldn't stand it so she turned to face her. 'Were you ever going to tell me the truth – about any of it?'

The usual, bitter expression came over her mother's face.

'I don't s'pose so.' She made a sour, dismissive gesture and looked away, fiddling with something on the table. 'Just leave it. It's all in the past.'

Violet stared at May, hurt and anger rising to choke her. The nonsense and lies she had put up with all her life, all that self-pity and the way Mom had played her to get her own way! She was damned if she was going to just let her carry on hiding the whole history of her own family from her. She struggled not to give in to her temper, to find something reasonable to say.

'It may be for you – but what about poor Tom? And what if I was to have a child?'

Her mother's gaze snapped back to her. 'What're you saying? You're not . . . ?'

'No, course not! But later – if I get married. What do I tell my child? I don't even know where my own name comes from! Do I just lie, the way you've lied to me?'

May sank down at the table.

'I only did it to protect you . . .'

'Protect *you*, you mean!' Violet was astonished at what was coming out of her mouth – at what was even in her thoughts.

'Life's been cruel hard,' her mother said, with her lips turning down in the self-pitying way she had. She sat down by the table. 'What do you know? You were just a child. You don't know what I've been through to bring you up.'

'I was there,' Violet said. 'Remember? Let's stop talking about you for a change and talk about Tom. Who is Tom? Who's his father? Who's *my* father, for that matter?' Her bewilderment took over as the questions poured out. 'What about those wedding pictures? You told me one of them wasn't you – but it *was* you, in both of them, wasn't it? You lied to me about that – I know you did.'

She had been thinking about this ever since last night, wrestling with her memory. But she had known even when she was three and she knew now – that face was Mom's in both of the pictures.

Her mother was looking down at the table, spinning

264

an old bone-handled knife round and round as if waiting for it to point out her fortune.

'What kind of woman are you? All my life you've told me this *tale* about being a widow and I believed you. Course I did! Mothers don't lie to their children, do they? And now it turns out you're a mother who does. And everything's just . . .' She trailed off with a gesture of her hand, noticing as she did, that she still had cake mix daubed on the back of it. She licked it, tasting the bland sweetness of it.

'So, is Tom my brother – or what? Do we have the same father?'

Her mother's face tightened and she looked up. For a second Violet saw something in her eyes, a depth of – what? Fear? Shame?

'Pour me a cup of tea, Vi.'

The pot was almost cold but Violet poured out the stewed dregs.

Her mother took a sip which made her grimace, and lit a cigarette.

'I told you – he's your half-brother.' The words came out reluctantly. It felt to Violet as if she was trying to squeeze juice from a dried-up fruit.

'So who's his father? Mr Smith?'

There was a pause. Mom gulped her drink, took a drag on the cigarette. Violet saw the cracked lipstick on her lips and it left a red ring on the end of the cigarette.

'All right,' she said harshly. 'I'll tell you. Then no more questions – I don't ever want to talk about it again.' She glanced at the door to make sure it was tightly shut.

'No,' Violet said, the anger flaring in her. 'If I want to ask you questions, I'll ask them! I'll flaming well decide, not you! It's about time you were straight with me – about all of it.'

Even as she spoke, she was amazed at herself. Fancy speaking to Mom like that! How had she become so changed and bold? She thought of her brother – half-brother – his face, just a little like her own and something else fell into place with a jarring pain.

'All that fawning and fuss you made of Don Baker when he was a kid! That was all about Tom, wasn't it? I always felt as if you really wanted him, not me!'

'Oh, don't talk so silly – he was just a nice little lad . . .'

Violet stared at her, could feel the force of her own emotion needing to pour out.

'So. Those pictures for a start. Of your weddings. Where are they? I want to see them.'

'I burned them. Years ago. I never married your father anyway.' She gave a laugh. 'How could I? I was still married to Bob. Terence and I just had it taken for the look of it, you know – church in the background.'

Their eyes locked on to each other's. Violet was trembling, her emotions a mixture of hurt and rage.

'You tell me. Everything. *Now*. My George is coming here this afternoon – someone who I really love . . .'

'*Love!*' Her mother almost spat the word out. 'Huh – roses round the door, is it? Well, we'll see, won't we.'

'Don't you talk to me about it like that – not about him and me!' Violet leaned, enraged, across the table. 'George's never been anything but good and kind and truthful to me. I want all the lies and dirty secrets out of the way before he gets here. And I don't want there to be any more – ever again.'

May, looking utterly startled by this new Violet, sat stunned for a moment. Her mouth twisted down sulkily.

'All right.' She sat up straighter. She could see she had no choice. In an almost indifferent tone, she said, 'Sit down then. I'll tell you.'

Slowly, Violet obeyed.

'I married Tom's father in 1916. His name was Robert Smith.' As she said his name, her mouth tightened with disgust. 'We never got on. It was an unhappy marriage from the word go . . .'

'Well, why did you marry him?' Violet said.

'He seemed all right – before. Turned on the charm, how they do. Then Tom came along.' Her face softened. 'Beautiful baby he was . . . But Bob was . . . Well, he was just . . . I couldn't abide him near me.' Again she grimaced. 'A while after, I met another man – fell for him . . . Really fell, not like the first time.'

'What – and all the time you had a little baby?' Violet said, utterly shocked.

'You don't stop wanting . . . I mean, Tom was two – he wasn't a tiny baby by then . . .' May looked down, her own shame and embarrassment taking over. 'Any road, to cut a long story short, Terence gave me an ultimatum – he made me go off with him. I couldn't take Tom – that was the condition. Terence wouldn't have it.' She stopped, a terrible look on her face. 'I've looked back countless times and thought, how did I do it? How did I walk out like that, leaving Tom, turning my back on everything? But I *had* to do it – he made me. I'd've lost him otherwise and I was in love with him. I became a fallen woman overnight. I wasn't myself, I don't think. It was a kind of madness came over me.'

'Was he . . . my father?'

May nodded. 'If it's any use for you to know, he was called Terence Hemmings. We went to London – so I'd no hope of seeing Tom. He was with his father in Erdington, that was where we lived . . . I dain't think I'd ever see him again. It was terrible. And of course, in the eyes of the law I was still married to Bob . . . But then I found I was expecting again . . .'

There was a silence. May stared ahead of her, her expression hard.

'We were living in this horrible place in the east of London. I hated it there. Like here but worse. And I dain't know anyone. Soon as he knew I had a baby on the way, Terence did a bunk. I should've known he never loved me when he wouldn't let me bring my Tom . . . All he was out for was himself . . .'

She stopped. The warm smell of baking cake began to curl round the room. May sat silent, remembering. She looked young, just for that moment. Young and terrified.

'I came back up here. At least I knew Birmingham. It was where I come from. I dain't go anywhere near Erdington, though. Never dared. I went back to my maiden name, Simms – didn't want anything to do with either of them. Eileen Baker was kind – and it was Mr and Mrs Quinn saved me. They let me work in the shop even before Ma Quinn fell ill. And we had that room over the shop back in them days. Kindly people they were. I'll never forget Mrs Quinn's goodness to me – more than I deserved.'

'Taking in a poor widow,' Violet said.

Her mother gave her a bitter look. 'You never know what you're gunna do 'til you have to do it,' she said harshly. 'What would you know?'

Thirty-Four

Harry Cobb had told Grace he could come and meet her in the park by half-past four that afternoon.

She had not been to Victoria Park for a long time and as soon as she walked in, she remembered being there with Jimmy.

I'm sorry, Jimmy, she whispered. First she walked all of the diagonal paths across the park, one after another, thinking, each time she reached the middle of the park where they cross, Now he'll come. She felt like a stranger, a shameful person, as if she was standing outside herself. And she felt silly because the men tending to the barrage balloon were there and she felt as if they must know what she was about. It felt as if the Grace who had come here arm in arm with Jimmy Oval was someone else altogether. And yet the Grace who was here in the freezing cold, in red lipstick, waiting for an older man called Harry Cobb – her fiancé! – now seemed just as strange to her. But he had promised to marry her so she could do away with all the painful, embarrassing feelings that had plagued her. She had been truly obsessed with Harry Cobb. She had almost allowed herself to become one of *those* sort of girls. Girls talked about in whispers; loose and sinful. Girls who spread their legs, who had no shame and must be cast out. She had heard it many times, and how close to it she had been. But now she was engaged, what did it really matter?

Full of shame and longing, she walked round the lake

in the cold. Defiance flared in her. It was all very well, these old biddies gossiping, but what if she was killed next week? What would it matter then whether she was a virgin or not?

It would matter to God . . . Priests, nuns, teachers rose up before her. *The shame would fall on your family and above all, upon your mortal soul . . .*

But I'm getting married, she retorted to all of them. *So there. Harry and I are going to set a date today.*

Half-past four came and went and she kept walking up and down in the cold. If only there was some warm place where they could go – a house, a bed, where no one else would see . . . Her thoughts kept turning to that. Just to give herself to him once, to learn the feel of lying with a strong, masculine man . . . Soon she would give Harry what he wanted so badly. The longing and excitement of it overwhelmed her as she walked up and down in the dying light.

It was only when she heard a distant clock striking five that she faced the fact that Harry Cobb was not going to come. The cold seeped into her, misery and disappointment darkening every thought. The world of desire and fantasy she had been living in burst open, letting in the cold truth: Harry didn't really love her. Not at all – and he never had. If he had, why would they have had to creep about like this? He wasn't coming, he wasn't going to marry her either, he had just said it to get what he wanted. Harry didn't care about her. Someone who truly loved her would never have left her standing here all alone. What a fool she was! All her fixation on him, all the questions she had chosen not to ask him, and all her desire now felt dirty and humiliating.

It was almost dark. Near the bandstand, where she had walked with Jimmy before he left, she let her tears flow.

How sad and awful and miserable everything was! The bubble she had been living in had protected her from her feelings about the devastation and death all around her. But now that seemed to invade her and she felt close to despair. So many terrible things had happened since the war started. Brutal, tragic things. What was the point of anything? All that life seemed to be was struggle and death and no meaning in any of it.

In a storage hut at the back of a yard, off the Coventry Road, on a layer of sacks and old newspapers, June Perry sat astride her man. The ghostly light through a cobwebby little window fell on her massive white thighs as she bunched her frock up round her waist and rode hard on the broad, strong body beneath her.

'Let me see yer,' he panted, tugging at her blouse. June unfastened her clothing, freeing the generous swell of her bosom. Soon, both of them were in a state of high excitement, she writhing on him, he with his hands on her breasts, crying out as he plunged into her.

'Oh, no, you don't!' she said, as his excitement reached its peak.

Deftly she lifted herself off him and held him as he came, giving her low, gurgling laugh. 'Still got more for me? You're a proper one, ain't yer?'

'And you're a proper woman!' he groaned, hips flexing until finally he was spent.

After a moment, she climbed on to his thighs, still rocking gently on him. She shivered.

'It's flipping cold in 'ere!'

He felt around the floor nearby and picked up the nearest thing that came to hand – a wool scarf.

'Here –' He reached up and wrapped it round her neck. June snuggled its scratchy wool against her chest.

'Ta – that's better'n nothing I s'pose!' She started to button up her clothes as well, wrapping the scarf round her neck.

The light had almost died and she could just see the brightness of his eyes. This was a man, all right. What a man! But she knew. She could sense it – all the signs were there, the way he evaded her questions. Her gaze had grown cool.

'You're married, ain't yer?'

He was quiet for a moment, then he laid a hand over his eyes, letting out a defeated little groan, as if to say, *You got me there.*

'This always happens to me,' she said. She felt cold and sad, but she wasn't letting him see that. 'What's up with your missus, then? There's always summat. *Oh, my missus won't do this. Won't do that . . .'*

Harry removed his hand. He seemed shamefaced. She heard the rasp of stubble as he rubbed his cheeks.

'We've got six kiddies – had 'em quick as shelling peas. She don't want no more.'

'Don't blame 'er, poor cow,' June said. She managed to keep her voice light, mocking, as if she had not a care in the world. 'My mom had thirteen – living, that is. Like a sow. I ain't having any – never, not if I can help it.'

The man let out a long sigh. Too late for you, she thought. You should've thought about that, shouldn't you, not let her catch for six of 'em?

'What's your other name?' she said. 'Demon lover!'

He laughed, released, pleased with himself. 'Cobb.'

'Harry Cobb,' she said. 'That's nice.'

She clambered off him, wiping her hands on a piece of sacking nearby. She might go with him again, she thought, looking down at him. He wasn't bad. But the bugger was married – course he was. Just for once, she'd thought she might be on to something she could really have for herself.

'T'ra then.' She walked out, leaving him still with his fly undone. She coiled the wool scarf round her neck. It was nice and warm. Might as well get summat out of all that, she thought.

After having a weep, by which time her feet were so cold she could scarcely feel them, Grace made her way home. She wanted to slink inside, go upstairs to bed without anyone seeing her and lie there with all her sad, humiliated thoughts.

She was so wrapped up in misery walking up Archibald Street that it was only as she drew closer to number sixty-eight that it dawned on her that there had been footsteps behind her, steady, almost stealthy, for some time. She looked round. It was dark now, the air smoky, and she could not see anything. The footsteps had stopped.

Maybe whoever it was went into their house, she thought. She walked on, but a second later she heard it again. Someone had stopped, waited when she did – hadn't they? The hairs on her flesh stood up and she began to panic.

She was almost home, so she strode faster and plunged into the darkness of the entry. Walking to the end, she waited, ears straining. She was only steps from the back door but even so, her heart was pounding like mad in the darkness. Was that somebody coming closer, reaching the entry?

The roots of her hair tingled, as if every pore of her was on alert. In the pocket of her coat was her little torch. She thought about getting it out and shining it along the entry, but any move she made, her beating heart and the swish of the fabric of her coat, seemed deafening. Was that someone at the end of the entry, coming closer? All she could do was hold her breath, paralysed.

Someone else came rapidly along the street, their shoes tapping the pavement, and it seemed to break the spell. Grace dashed to the back door and rushed inside, pushing it shut violently.

'What's up with you?' Marie asked, laughing. 'Got the bogeyman after you?'

Something felt different. Grace took in who was in front of her, in the back room, and gasped with joy.

'Dad!' There he was, in his chair, his leg still in plaster, stretched out in front of him, a few cuts still healing on his face, but her dad – alive and here at last! Gordon was by his chair, standing looking at him, awed. Her mother's face was wreathed in delight. Tony, Patrick and Marie were all there too, grinning with happiness.

'Oh, Dad! They never said you were coming!' She went and flung her arms round him and he laughed joyfully.

''Ello, Gracie, love – where've yer been? Your face is cold as ice!'

'They brought him in an ambulance!' her mother said, buzzing about with the teapot.

'Are you all right, Dad?' Grace asked, sitting in front of him as Mom passed round more cups of tea. Grace warmed her hands on hers gratefully. Oh, it was so wonderful to have him here!

'Bars of iron,' he said, twinkling at her. 'Never better love – for seeing all of you and being home. And look –' He held his scarred hands out and waggled his fingers. 'Least my hands are all right!'

'So we can have a tune,' Mom said.

Grace smiled, feeling the warmth of the room, the joy

of seeing him. All her woes in the park seemed to shrink back to something small and silly. She beamed up at him.

'And I tell you another thing,' Cath said. 'Tomorrow, I'm going to find out how to get our little lads back – I'll go down there myself if I have to. That Jerry's not bombing us at the moment and if it's the last thing I do, we're all going to be together for Christmas!'

'Well, that was all right,' George said as he and Violet set out from Archibald Street. 'I don't know what you was making all that fuss about!'

She had said she would walk him to the corner – both of them knew this was an excuse to get outside together and snatch a kiss and cuddle before the week's relentless routine began again. For this momentous occasion she had put on her best dress – in a soft purple wool – and pinned her hair back, making the most of what wave there was in it. Her face had smiled back at her from the scullery mirror and she could see that she looked prettier and happier than she had ever imagined possible.

Even the cake hadn't turned out badly. It was a thin thing, a bit on the tart side, but moist with the apples and George had had three slices and praised it to the skies.

'If our mom makes a cake, it's gone again in minutes in our house,' he joked to May Simms.

'Well,' she said, smiling, her charming side on display, 'you'd better get stuck in while you have the chance. Cut him another slice, Vi!'

Because Mom could be nice, when she wanted to. She could turn on the charm all right. And she knew she had to be nice today.

'Well – we had a bit of a do this week,' Violet said as they walked along in the dark. She had decided to tell George everything – whatever Mom said. No secrets, no lies – that was how she wanted things to be. She was sick of lying. 'I'll explain it all to you, but not now, OK?'

'Why not?' He spoke lightly. 'Can't be that bad, can it?'

Violet looked round at him. How sweet he was! Innocent, in a way. What was he going to think when he heard about her suddenly finding she had an elder half-brother? She almost chickened out. For a start she had hardly recovered from the shock herself – and maybe there were things best left unsaid?

But then George added, 'Go on – tell us then.' He seemed to sense that she was really worked up. 'Nothing can make a difference to what I feel about you, Vi.'

'All right – but take my arm,' she said. 'I want to feel you close – it's not very nice, what I'm going to tell you. See, I never knew a thing about all this, but last night, I was in the shop . . .'

She told him the events of the day before, the bombshell of Tom Smith turning up. She recounted all the things she had learned, but when she got to the bit where Tom had stormed out, she found herself getting really upset.

'I don't know why I'm crying,' she sobbed. 'It's just . . . I dain't want him to go. We'd hardly had a chance . . . And before he left, he turned and said to me that it weren't my fault or anything . . . I mean, I wasn't even born. I suppose he just needed to see his mom, see what sort of person she was and whether he remembered her right. He was only a tiny boy – two, I think – when she went off with this other bloke.' She stopped to blow her nose and they stood in the dark near the corner of Cattell Road. 'My father, that was,' she added, bewildered. 'She said his name was Terence something-or-other. Hemmings, I think.'

'Blimey.' Violet could hear that George was having a job to take it all in as well. She felt as if her entire reality had changed shape overnight. But another realization came to her now that made her sob all the harder.

'He looked nice, Tom did. I've always wanted a brother or sister and he come to see us, and . . .' She stopped and wept.

'Eh, come 'ere . . .' George, in his sweet, old-fashioned way, took her in his arms and cuddled her against his chest. 'Don't get so upset, my bab . . .'

'But I don't even know where he lives or anything!' She looked up at him woefully in the dark. 'He just came and went like that and we never asked. He's in the navy and he said they're posting him overseas. I might never see him again!'

'Oh, dear,' George said. 'Oh, dear, oh, dear . . .'

'My mother's kept all this from me, all this time . . . I still can't hardly take any of it in.'

There was a silence and then George said, 'I s'pose 'er dain't 'ave much choice really, when you think about it.'

Violet looked up at him again. It was a kind thing to say about a woman who had run off leaving her husband, her child – for another man who had betrayed her. Not everyone would have said something like that.

'I do love you, George,' she said softly. 'You're the nicest person I've ever met.'

'Oh, now!' George laughed. 'That's going a bit far!'

'No,' she said seriously. 'It ain't. I *do* love you. You're the best – you really are.'

'Love you too, little Vi.' He squeezed her close. 'You're my girl, you are. Did I tell you how pretty your hair's looking today? 'Cause I should've done.'

'No, but you have now. And you don't look so bad yourself.' She cuddled him. George had arrived in what was clearly his Sunday best – with an old but respectable jacket over his shirt.

'Well,' George went on. 'I hope, one day . . .' He hesitated and she could almost feel his blushes burning the night air. 'I hope one day you might just say you'd be my wife.'

She gasped, looking up at him. '*Really?* Are you asking me?'

George let out a laugh of sheer joy. 'Yeah – reckon I am!'

'Of course I will!' she said, with not a second's hesitation. 'Yes, George – I will, I will!'

III

1941

Thirty-Five

Wednesday 12 February

'Well, aren't you the lucky one,' Grace teased as she and Violet struggled through the freezing darkness of Archibald Street, huddled up in their ARP coats. 'Oh, Lord, I can hardly talk, my teeth are chattering that much!'

It was half-past six and they were on patrol. Thick, wet snowflakes fell through the darkness and slopped on to the already sodden street. In the weeks since Christmas there had been very few raids and more time on duty nights at Post F for all of them to sit killing time. After all the hours they had spent together and the things they had experienced, the girls had long lost their shyness and opened up to each other.

'I *am* lucky,' Violet agreed. She almost felt like skipping along the road, not caring about the cold or wet. She and George were happy as could be – and they were engaged to be married! The fact that Mom kept needling her about it wasn't going to dent her happiness. She was tired of all her mother's carry-on. 'But you're engaged too, aren't you?'

'Well . . . Not exactly.'

Having checked on one side of the road, they were standing at the kerb, ready to cross over. Giggling, they linked hands and jumped over a huge puddle that had gathered in the gutter.

'Good job you put your torch on or we'd have fallen straight in that!' Grace said.

'So, that other man of yours – Harry, is it?' Violet persisted, once they'd got to the other side.

'Yeah – well,' Grace said. Violet could hear the reluctance in her voice. 'Can't really call him *my* man!'

'What d'you mean?' Violet stopped, trying to peer at Grace under the umbrella. 'I don't really get you, Grace. D'you love him, or what?'

Even over the wind she heard Grace's sigh. She looked ahead of her. 'I dunno. Sometimes I think he makes me a bit sort of mad in the head. I thought it was over before Christmas, and then when he came back – I couldn't seem to say no to him.'

'But what about Jimmy?' Violet just couldn't understand it. She only knew Jimmy Oval by sight but he'd always seemed such a nice lad.

'Jimmy's . . . Yeah. He's nice – nice enough . . .' Grace hung her head and Violet really couldn't tell what she was thinking. 'I just . . . I s'pose I wanted to sort of see who else there might be. And Harry's . . .'

'Married?' Violet suggested brutally.

Grace's head whipped round. 'Why d'you say that?'

'Well, all this creeping about. Why doesn't he just ask you to marry him? Haven't you asked him, straight out?' Things seemed quite simple to her. What she and George had was so straightforward – you loved someone and you got married.

'*Yes*,' Grace said. She was looking away and didn't seem to want to say any more. 'He said he isn't.'

'Oh, well,' Violet said as they walked on. 'A man of mystery!' She was regretting her bluntness a little and tried to laugh it off. And Grace was looking quite peaky these days – thinner and drawn in the face. But she obviously didn't want to talk about it.

'Oh, look!' Violet said as they went on, arm in arm. 'Can you believe it!'

Just ahead of them in the wet and gloom, they could just make out the tiny, shuffling figure of Maud Bright.

'Evening, Mrs Bright,' Violet said. 'Are you all right?'

'Oh!' Maud Bright peered up from under her hat brim. Close to, Violet could just make out her startled face. She was making her way along in her usual fashion, one hand on the wall to guide her.

'It's only us ARP girls again,' Violet said. 'Are you going to see Miss Snell?'

'Yes, dear – I've a little treat for us.' Maud Bright patted the bag she had over her shoulder as if it contained treasure. 'A nice bottle of sherry – or what remains anyway!'

'Well, that'll cheer her up,' Grace said. 'D'you want us to walk round with you, Mrs Bright?'

'Oh, no, no, dear. I'm quite all right.' As usual Maud Bright treated any offer of help as a quite extraordinary idea.

They said their goodnights but the two of them watched her until she melted away into the entry to Lucy Snell's yard.

'She's been walking up and down there for years,' Violet said. 'She could do it with her eyes shut – the blackout makes no odds to her!'

'Tell you what,' Grace said, nudging her. 'When we're like that, I'll bring you round a bottle of sherry, all right?'

Violet laughed, but she was truly touched. Was Grace saying they might now be friends for life? That was a lovely thought and only added to her glowing sense of happiness. The mousey, trapped little person she had felt before the war was definitely branching out!

Because there was another thing that as yet she had told no one but George. Something else which gave her a wondering sense of joy. A couple of weeks after Christmas, a letter had arrived addressed to her. Luckily she had received it while May was in the shop so that there were no questions.

She didn't recognize the handwriting, which was untidy and backward-slanting, and she took it up to her room and opened it, frowning as she wondered if it had been sent by mistake.

There was one little sheet of paper.

Dear Violet,

I'm sorry for what happened when I came that night. I feel ashamed now. I shouldn't have lost my temper like I did. As I said none of this is your fault or mine we don't choose our parents.

Maybe when all this is over we can meet up again and talk things over. That'd be nice. I felt as if I'd like you, seeing you there and when it comes to it, it'd be very nice to have a sister like you. But it's up to you of course.

Keep well in the meantime and I hope life treats you well.

Your half-brother,

Tom Smith

Thirty-Six

The girls finished off their patrol and went back to Post F.

'Oh, thank the Lord,' Grace said as they walked in. They took their coats off and shook the worst of the wet off them out through the door. Grace lit up a cigarette and said longingly, 'My idea of heaven right now is a hot bath and my bed.'

'That I can't summon up,' Miss Holt called from the back. 'All I have to offer is a cup of tea – and we do have a visitor.'

This was nothing unusual. Now there were fewer raids people often popped in, Mildred Oval especially, often bearing a few slices of cake or some biscuits for them, and some of the other neighbours or local constables would pop in for a chat. Miss Holt's house had become quite the social centre of the street.

But going through to the back, who should be installed with Miss Holt and the others again but June Parry. She too had started turning up occasionally. She liked to get settled in, holding the floor by regaling them all with stories from the First Aid post. Mr Powell didn't approve of June's gossip, but Mr Powell was off duty tonight. Arthur Oval was on the chair in the corner, seemingly fast asleep.

'All right, June?' Violet said, without much enthusiasm. She was sitting at the table laughing with Reggie and Quentin, her coat still on and a scarf muffled up round her neck.

'All right, Violet?'

'Another quiet night then so far?' Miss Holt said.

'Yes.' Violet moved gratefully closer to the crackling fire. She could hear the kettle hissing on the gas. It was only then that she noticed Grace staring at June Perry with a thunderous expression.

'Grace? You all right?'

'What?' She tore her eyes away from June, but there was such a strange, angry look in her eyes that Violet didn't like to say any more. What the hell had got into her?

She was distracted from noticing anything further by spotting the new attraction in the room. Reggie, Quentin and June were poring over a box containing old 78 records and on the table was an old-fashioned gramophone.

'Oooh!' Violet said. 'Is that yours, Miss Holt? I've never seen it before.'

'It is,' Miss Holt said with dignity. 'I saw it yesterday, in Coolidge's – on the Stratford Road. It still seemed in passable condition so I indulged. The records came with it.'

'That's a beauty, that is,' Violet said and Grace nodded, though she still looked stunned and really upset. Violet knew she couldn't ask Grace what was the matter, with all these people around.

The body of the gramophone was ornate and the big brass horn gave off a dull shine in the dim light.

'You do realize it'll have been nicked from a bombed-out house, don't you, Miss Holt?' Reggie said.

Violet thought of some of the stories George had told her about thieves pilfering from ruined houses, making the most of other people's misfortunes.

'Not necessarily,' Miss Holt said stiffly.

'Oh, I'd lay money on it – reckon you might find yourself in receipt of stolen goods!' Reggie said.

Miss Holt gave him a look. Over the months they had come to a teasing accommodation of each other. However, this particular look was lost on Reggie since he was busy staring at June, just like a dog eyeing up a juicy bone, Violet thought, amused.

'Well, if I am, Mr Meakins,' Miss Holt said, 'I'll wait for the police to appear and then hand it back like a lamb.'

'That's it – you tell 'im, Miss Holt!' June said, rather cheekily Violet thought, given that she had also been one of Miss Holt's pupils in the past.

'In the meantime,' Quentin said, 'we can have a tune. What about this one . . . Blimey, these are all out of the ark!'

'*The Bohemian Girl*,' Reggie read over his shoulder.

'Go on – put it on,' June said, making eyes at Reggie. 'Sounds romantic.'

'What about Mr Oval?' Violet was saying, but then realized he had his eyes open anyway.

'It's all right,' he said muzzily, stretching himself. 'Ooh, 'ello, girls.'

Reggie put the record on, and among breathy crackles, twiddly piano music poured out. Reggie looked unimpressed but Quentin was enchanted.

'Ah – how adorable,' he said dreamily. '*I dreamt I dwelt in marble halls . . .*'

'Let's see what else there is,' Reggie said, looking through the records again. '"Your Tiny Hand is Frozen" . . . Blimey – everything really is from before the turn of the century. Shall we have the wireless on instead?'

'No! Let's play a few of them,' Miss Holt said.

They sat through 'Your Tiny Hand is Frozen'.

'Ah – *La Bohème*,' Quentin said dreamily. But by the

end of the stirring music, everyone looked rather miserable and Violet saw that Grace's eyes were full of tears.

'You all right?' she whispered.

'It's such emotional music,' Grace said quietly. 'It just brings it all back – before the war, when Dennis was still with us, and . . . Well, all of it . . .' Tears ran down her cheeks.

'Oh, dear, oh, dear,' Mr Oval said. 'This is no good, is it?'

'Let's have summat cheerful,' June said.

'Yes,' Miss Holt added, 'and then I think you had better take yourself off, June. We are all supposed to be on duty even if you're not.'

June pouted for a moment, like a little girl who has been ticked off.

'Ah – this is more like it.' Quentin put another record on and held his arms out to Grace. 'Shall we dance?' But Grace shook her head.

'I'll dance with yer!' June said. Getting up she threw off her coat and scarf to show her very ample figure in a black calf-length skirt and a tight-fitting pea-green jumper which left nothing to the imagination. Quentin looked a bit intimidated, but gamely held out his arms.

'There's no room for that!' Miss Holt protested.

But June and Quentin managed to jig around playfully in the small space as 'Two Merrie Men A-Drinking' poured from the gramophone. Violet saw Grace watching June with a strange, stern expression on her face. June and Quentin clowned around until the crackly record ended and June's full-hearted laugh filled the room. It did cheer Violet up, but Grace looked just as furious and miserable.

'Right – I'd best be off.' June tucked the blue scarf round her neck again and put her coat on. 'Night all. TTFN.'

The kettle was now boiled and the duty roster for that night – Miss Holt and Arthur Oval, Violet and Grace and Reggie and Quentin – all settled down by the fire. Quentin was to stay and watch the street from upstairs later, in turn with Violet. Grace, stony-faced, seemed in a world of her own. Violet knew something was wrong and she felt sad and uncomfortable but she let Grace be.

'It seems as if all's going to be quiet again,' Miss Holt said. Brightly, she continued, 'How about a game of whist, Violet, dear? And you, Mr Molyneaux?'

Violet smiled. 'All right, then.'

It suddenly occurred to Violet that despite everything, her old teacher, surrounded by all this company, was probably having the time of her life. And, she thought, though this was a strange way to make friends, the truth was that the same could be said of herself.

Thirty-Seven

The evening when Grace had stood in Victoria Park, getting colder and colder as she waited for Harry Cobb and gradually realizing he was not going to come, she had truly thought it was finished and that she would get over him.

The whole of Christmas passed without her seeing him. She had put on a cheerful face and joined in with the festivities. They held a Christmas meal at Post F on Christmas Eve – even having a turkey! Violet helped Miss Holt cook the bird and some of the others chipped in – Mildred Oval brought roast spuds and joined in the meal and everyone rustled up what they could, Quentin arriving with bunches of carrots, and Francis became the hero of the hour by producing a plum pudding which he claimed had been gifted by an aunt of his and pre-dated the war.

Miss Holt had even agreed to a few decorations, so Reggie and Quentin climbed on chairs and hung some paper streamers. On Christmas Eve, all the wardens squeezed into the back room and soon the place was a fug of cooking smells and cigarette smoke and warm bodies as well as laughter and jokes. Grace had looked at Violet across the table, her cheeks very pink, eyes full of laughter behind her specs, and thought, My, how she's come on. She found herself envying Violet – she looked so pretty and happy, bless her! And she seemed to have found the one man who was right for her.

She knew Jimmy had told his family they were no

longer engaged, but apart from the comments Arthur Oval had made, no one had said anything much, though she wondered if she had imagined that Sylvie had been rather distant with her when they had met. A sharp pang of sorrow went through her thinking of it. What have I done? Her emotions were like rapids, currents of muddled feeling milling about in different directions.

Banishing her thoughts, she tried to pay attention to the joke Reggie was telling and to laugh at the right moment. It was Christmas, after all!

'Now, everyone . . .' Mr Powell waited for a lull when all the laughter had died down and suddenly sat up very straight. 'Let's have a toast.'

Most of them were drinking ale, and cups and glasses were held up.

'As we stand almost on the eve of a new year,' Mr Powell began impressively, 'let us drink to victory – to the defeat of Herr Hitler, to peace!'

They all joined in, 'To peace!' though Reggie had to spoil it by saying, 'Piece of what?' and laughing in his suggestive way. Miss Holt didn't half give him a look.

But it was a lovely evening and Grace laughed and sang 'Hark the Herald Angels' and 'While Shepherds Watched' and joked along with the rest of them. Dad was home and Mom had gone all the way out to the country to fetch her little lads back again so Joseph, Michael and Adie were all tucked up at home too. There were so many good things and she counted her blessings. She even managed to forget Harry for the moment.

And over the following days she determined to shut all that out of her mind for good. It was over, and that was that. He had only promised to marry her to get what he wanted. What kind of person did that?

*

291

But one day in early January, when she was behind the counter in the Co-op, at dinner time, in he walked. Mrs Hodgson had gone out for her break and Grace wondered if he had been watching and seen her go.

The moment she saw him, her heart started pounding. He came and stood before her, looking pained and awkward. All the hurt and anger surged up inside her.

'I waited ages for you!' she snapped. 'It was freezing – and then you don't get in touch – nothing, all this time!' To her extreme annoyance she realized she could not hold back her tears because it *did* hurt and it *did* matter, and that he had caused her more pain than she had allowed herself to admit. She wiped her eyes impatiently, but the tears kept coming.

'Sorry,' he said. Shamefaced, he stared down at the floor. 'I just couldn't. Summat came up – and then, over Christmas like, you know . . .'

'Do I know? What? That you had to be with your wife, your family?' She was shooting in the dark but it hit home.

'Yeah. Well.' He looked up then and met her eyes, looking really uncomfortable. 'Yes.'

'What?' Grace felt as if she'd been slapped. 'You *are* married then? What – with kids?'

'Six.'

Grace stared at him. Of *course* he was married. Why else would he have been so secretive? Why had she been so *stupid*?

'How could you not tell me when we first met?' Her voice had gone thick and out of her control. 'All this time . . .'

'To be honest, Grace, it took a while before you even asked, and by then we was in too deep . . .' He did look shamefaced though. 'And I was so . . . I mean, you're special, Grace. Life with the wife is . . .' His eyes darted to her and away in his embarrassment. 'Thing is – what with the kids – having them's never been easy for her, like. She don't want no more. So . . .'

'I see,' Grace said icily.

He looked very downcast. A chink opened in her feelings, seeing the vulnerability in him, and she softened her tone.

'So you wanted . . .' A blush rose in her cheeks. Talking about things like this in daylight was very different from standing in the dark in each other's arms.

'I wanted you.' He gave her a frank look. 'You're a fine woman, Grace. I know it ain't right, not really. But even just a cuddle with you makes my life worth living, I tell yer. I ain't got much else – you're what's keeping me going, to be frank with yer.'

'I see. And I'm supposed to believe all this flannel, am I? You must think I was born yesterday. You just go round telling every woman some tale so's to get your way.'

Harry shrugged, with a helpless look. 'It's just how it is,' he said sadly. 'You're the one I want – if things were different.'

Grace tried to keep her flinty expression, but his words had found a way into her emotions, the way he stood there, his blue eyes full of shame and dismay, of longing for her. She mattered to him. Even if it was all wrong, she argued with herself that maybe she was in fact doing poor Mrs Cobb with all her little children a favour.

'If you never want to see me again, I'd understand,' he said, his voice quiet and humble. Those blue eyes met hers. 'I'm not much good to you, am I?'

'Look,' Grace said. 'Mrs Hodgson'll be back any

293

minute and if she finds you here . . . I'll meet you, Harry – but go now, for heaven's sake!'

'Tomorrow?' he said, turning on his way out.

'All right – yes. Same place,' she said, desperate to get rid of him. And then he was gone. And she stood in the shop, uneasy, shamed, but excited. Harry still wanted her – he was still going to be part of her life.

And so, every few days for the last month, she had been sneaking off to meet Harry Cobb again and could tell herself that she and he had something special. It may not have been the convention, but it was nothing to do with anyone else – it was just theirs.

Thirty-Eight

'It looks like another quiet night,' Miss Holt said, when it got to ten o'clock.

It had been quite an enjoyable evening, Violet thought, even if Grace had suddenly gone off into her funny mood and sat turning over the pages of an old *Woman's Weekly* for most of the evening. Violet had spent some time talking with Quentin before he went to take his turn at the watch post upstairs. Over the months she had found that he was quite nice to talk to when he was not constantly acting. He was in fact even shyer than she was, she understood now. But he was genuinely in love with acting and with Shakespeare especially – he knew all his plays. Gradually they had all got used to and even fond of each other. Even Reggie had learned that he did not have to spend every minute trying to provoke them all. Sitting around the fire, everyone was relaxed and sleepy.

'Some of you might as well go home,' Miss Holt said. 'Reggie, Violet – I think it's your turn to stay?'

Violet nodded. She was quite happy to stay and sleep on a little camp bed upstairs.

'Mr Oval?' Miss Holt nudged Arthur, who had dozed off once more in the one armchair. He woke with a start. 'Why don't you go home and get a proper sleep in your own bed?'

He got up, muzzy with sleep. Violet thought how

exhausted he looked. He was not a young man, to be up all hours like this.

Grace stepped outside with Arthur Oval and Reggie. The sleet had stopped and the wind had abated, but the night was wet and raw. Any light from the moon was obscured by thick cloud.

'Goodnight then, bab.' Mr Oval still seemed half asleep and he and Reggie set off one way, Grace the other.

Grace stood for a moment in the relief of the darkness, her face crumpling into the lines of misery she had been trying to hide all evening. Seeing June Perry, all she had wanted to do was go over and scream at her, tear her eyes out if necessary. Her world had quietly crumbled and she knew she could not let a single thing show.

There was June, flaunting herself as usual – and round her neck, that scarf . . . Grace's eyes fastened on it the second she walked through the door. She was mistaken! No, she wasn't. There could not be any other home-knitted scarf in the world quite like that one – the shade of blue that so brought out the colour of Harry's eyes, the rough red blanket-stitching all along the edges. It was so familiar, so part of Harry – and yet there it was round the cow June's fleshy neck. And how did *that* come to be?

She kept telling herself all evening that there must be some explanation – that Harry had lost it somewhere and June had been the one to find it. It was possible – why not? And yet, somehow, without asking June, she knew. June and Harry . . . But she did not want to spell out the rest. *You're the one I want*, he'd said, full of self-pity. Grace burned with rage. Harry was such a liar! He used her and lied to her again and again and she had let it happen. Who had in fact had made the scarf that he said was knitted by his sister? His wife, most likely – or a daughter even! She felt desperate – hurt and foolish – and already she could not hold back the tears which had been waiting in her all evening. She pressed her hands over her face, her body racked with sobs.

'Oh, God,' she whispered. 'How *could* he . . .' But the much bigger, more shameful question lurked behind it. How could *I*? She just wanted to curl up and weep all night. After letting go for a moment she wiped her eyes and went to cross the street.

There were only about thirty yards between Miss Holt's house and her own. But seconds after setting off, she heard a sound that broke through all her miserable thoughts, setting every nerve of her body on high alert. Once again there were footsteps behind her, seeming to keep pace with hers. She stopped and looked round. Could it be Harry? But it was so dark, she could not see a thing. And he would call her name. All her instincts told her that it was not him behind her.

That short distance home felt suddenly endless. Her heart was pounding, the blood rushing in her body, telling her to run, while her mind was saying, Don't be silly, it's just someone walking home. But all the while she walked faster and faster, her ears straining to hear the sounds behind her. For a second, she walked on tiptoe to silence her own footsteps – and behind her, there it was again, that steady, furtive sound.

In the damp gloom she made out the white-painted front step of one of the neighbours' houses and knew she was nearly home. The thought of plunging into the darkness of the entry was too much for her and she felt in her pocket for her torch before stepping inside.

She stopped just at the entrance, listening, her eyes straining to see along the street. It had gone quiet. Grace waited, all the hairs on her body tingling. She had a most horrible feeling that whoever was behind her had also stopped and was waiting just out of sight. She even began to think she could hear someone breathing, like a tiny little rustle of wind through leaves.

After a few seconds, she couldn't stand it. Turning, she had just begun hurrying along to the back, when she heard someone come to the front end of the entry and stop.

'Who's that?' Grace switched on her torch and shone it towards the street. She tried to sound commanding, but her voice was trembling. 'What d'you want – why're you following me?'

He just stood there, eerily quiet: a man in dark clothes and a trilby hat, his head down so that she could not see his face.

'What do you want? Leave me alone!'

As she shone the torch on him, though, she began to make out that he looked familiar. He tilted his face up just slightly and she made out Francis's pale, oval face.

'For God's sake!' Her voice came out shrill. 'What the hell're you doing, creeping about like that?'

Her fear disappeared for a second, seeing it was just one of the ARP people. But it seeped back again in the face of his weird silence. What was the matter with him? He was a strange young man. He had not been on duty that night, so what was he doing lurking about here?

'Look – I don't know what the hell you're doing here, but I'm going inside to bed,' she said.

'Wait!' Her words forced him into action. His hoarse voice came to her. 'Wait a second, Grace – please.'

She stayed where she was, pointing the torch at the ground. Francis Paine took a couple of steps towards her. She could hear his laboured breathing.

'You stay there!' she ordered sharply. 'What's all this about?'

His voice burst out as a desperate plea. 'Grace, I . . . I . . .' And he was right up close to her, grabbing at her. 'Can I kiss you?'

'*What?*' She found herself laughing, pushing at him. '*No!* Get off me!'

She could hardly see him in the gloom, but he carried on standing there a slight distance away and there was something truly pathetic about him. She realized he was someone she hardly ever looked at or noticed.

'Sorry,' he babbled at her. 'Only, the way I feel about you, Grace . . . I've never met anyone like you! I love you – and I've never had a lady friend, as such . . . I've never kissed a girl. I don't know how to do any of it, how to talk to girls, like . . . And you're . . . Well, I love you, see, and I want to kiss you.'

'No!' Grace said. God, what a weird bloke. 'Francis, you can't just . . . I mean, you can only kiss someone if they want it too. And to be honest with you, I don't want to kiss you.'

She wasn't sure if she found him more pitiful or ridiculous. He thought he had these feelings so she was just supposed to fall in with his plans! She had an uncomfortable thought suddenly that she might have somehow given him the wrong idea. Had she flirted with him in some way? Surely not – she had hardly ever even spoken to him!

'How old are you?' she said more gently.

'Twenty-six.'

'And you've never walked out with a girl?'

'No – not . . . No. But you see, you . . .' He started coming towards her and suddenly he was up close again and she could hear his labouring lungs. He grabbed at her arm.

'Let me kiss you, Grace! I'll go mad if I don't!'

'Get away from me!' she shouted, trying to push him off. He was stronger than he looked and she had to tug really hard to get out of his grasp and pull away along the entry. 'Don't you take another step, you creep, or I'll get my brother out to see you off – he's a lot bigger than you are!'

Reaching the end where she was within a couple of steps of the back door, she felt safer.

'Look, this is not the way to go about any of this, all right? If you want a girlfriend you need to make sure she likes you as well – and whatever you think you feel for me, I don't feel the same. So go home and *leave me alone*.'

'But—'

'But nothing!' She lost sympathy with him and her temper flared. It had been such a terrible evening and now this. 'No wonder you've never had a girlfriend if you go on like this. Look – we've got to work together at the post. I can pretend that nothing ever happened if you promise never to do anything like it again. But if you do – anything, *ever* – I'll report you to Mr Powell and there'll be a proper stink. So you keep away from me and behave yourself. All right?'

'You stuck-up bitch.' The words hissed along the entry to her. Grace was chilled by the cold hatred she heard in them. 'Think you're summat special, don't you? Flaunting yourself all the time. Women like you, you Jezebels, you *sluts* with your foul, sulphurous holes, your vileness . . .' He turned and walked furiously away along the entry, more hateful curses coming from his mouth which chilled her with their foulness.

Grace rushed to let herself into the back kitchen,

bolting the door behind her. Everyone else had already gone to bed and she was able to recover alone, leaning on the table, breathing heavily. She realized she was shaking all over. She felt dirty, as if Francis Paine had somehow violated her, even without once touching her. And all her thoughts about Harry – how he too had used her and deceived her – flooded her mind. What was wrong with her? Was there something cursed and sinful about her that made men treat her this way?

She sank down at the table and at last let the sobs shake their way through her body.

'Time to wake up, dear – work beckons, I'm afraid!'

Violet opened her eyes on the narrow little camp bed to find Miss Holt standing over her with a cup of tea, a sight that even after all this time, she found startling.

'There we are, dear – that'll get you going,' she said, as Violet quickly pushed herself to sit up. 'I've given it a good stir.'

If Miss Holt was awake first on these mornings – and as an early riser she almost inevitably was – she often brought tea round. And she was always dressed by that time.

'Thank you, Miss Holt.' Violet was touched by her kindly tone and her smile. And no one had ever brought her cups of tea in the morning like this before!

'You're very welcome, dear,' Miss Holt said, giving her what could only be described as a fond smile as she left the room.

When she got home it was still early, but her mother was already down in the kitchen.

'Oh – I wondered when you were going to bother coming home,' she said as Violet walked in.

'Well, it was just as usual,' Violet said. 'It was my turn to stay.'

'It's always your turn, isn't it?' May said, sawing at the end of a loaf of bread. 'Anyone'd think you dain't have a home.'

Violet didn't say anything. She had had a reasonable night's sleep but the camp bed was not the most comfortable. And she thought about Miss Holt standing there with a cup and saucer, stiff but kindly. Miss Holt's house had started to feel more like home than her own.

'Can't even be bothered to speak to me now, is it?' Mom baited her. 'You seem to have plenty to say to Miss Holt. There's her with her house full and me all alone.'

'Well, Miss Holt gave up her house,' Violet pointed out, 'to help other people. So she's hardly ever *off* duty. How would you like that?'

'Oh – standing up for that dried-up old biddy now, are yer? I'll have you know I've swept out and disinfected that shelter for *other people* I don't know how many times and a lot of thanks I get for it. Miss Holt's not the only one *helping other people*, you know.'

Violet didn't reply. May turned to the stove, muttering to herself, and Violet stood looking at her tidy little figure, the attractively curling hair. What a pity you can't just be a nicer person, she thought. In the past she would have turned all the trouble on herself – it must be her fault. She was a bad girl and could never please Mom. There must be something wrong with *her* . . .

Now, though, she found herself looking at her mother almost as if at a stranger, one who had lied to her – or at least concealed from her enormous, important truths – all through her life. She just could not admire the way May had behaved – not so much her mistakes, but all the lies and cover-up that followed.

Other people would judge her harshly, she thought. But lying even to *me* . . .

And now, she realized, she's jealous of me – of me being young and having someone to love who loves me back. She can't even bring herself to be happy for me.

Speaking in a calm, even tone, she said, 'Well – I suppose you'll be used to not having me in the house, by the time George and me get married.'

May turned her head, her face twisted with scorn. 'Oh, don't be silly – he's not going to marry *you*. That's what men do. They're all talk when they want summat – don't kid yourself!'

And Violet's day, which had begun well, was suddenly cast under a pall of doubt and misery. It was only when she saw George again that evening and they went round to his mom's, that all her insecurity vanished again. There *were* kindly people in the world who meant what they said – and her George was one of them!

Thirty-Nine

Wednesday 9 April

'Goodnight, bab – mind how you go, the pair of yer.'

Mrs Cherry stood on her doorstep in her pinner to see them off – something which in itself surprised Violet. George's mother was so kind! Being used to her own mother and her mean-spirited moods, Violet had waited to see if Mrs Cherry might have sides to her. She was so used to this that she expected to find the same everywhere. But there was no sign. Mrs Cherry was as she was – straightforwardly kind.

'Oh, I s'pect it'll be quiet again,' George said. 'See yer, Mom.'

They said their goodbyes and set off arm in arm. The air was mild and it was not dark yet. The bitter winter was now over and going outside not nearly such an ordeal. It had been quiet again for a long time as well – the last main raid in early March and now it was nearly Easter time.

'I can't get over how nice your mom is,' Violet said.

'Well, yours ain't that bad,' George argued. He still found it hard to believe Violet's descriptions of how May, his future mother-in-law, could be when she was alone with her. Violet had not held back. She vowed there would be no more lies about anything, not with George. And it was a relief to confide in him. Even so, she did try to be fair and explain that Mom was the way she was because she was so terrified of people finding out about her past.

As they reached the end of the Coventry Road where they had to part, the church clocks started striking six.

'Whoops,' George said. 'We're gunna be late. Best get weaving.'

'It'll be all right,' Violet said. 'There's no raids at the moment anyway.'

'Your Miss Holt might be all right – she's got a soft spot for you – but I'll be for it!' George made a face of mock dread. 'Give us a kiss, kid! See yer tomorrow, after work?'

'Yeah – course. Meet you back here – by the bike shop.' They embraced hurriedly, exchanging kisses.

'Love yer,' George grinned. 'Gotta run!'

Violet watched fondly for a second as his limping figure lurched along the road. Filled with warm, loving feelings, she hurried along Archibald Street. It was only later she would punish herself with a dreadful anguish. How easily she had said goodbye! And I never said I loved him back . . .

Violet arrived at Post F to find the night's team all ready for work – Mr Powell and Miss Holt, Mr Oval, Reggie and Quentin were already installed. And standing in the doorway of the back room as Violet peered in, were Mildred Oval and the dog. Ginger looked up at Violet with her smiling doggie face and wagged her tail.

'Hello, girl.' Violet gave her a pat. 'Ooh, you're lovely and soft, you are.'

'Hello, bab! Sorry – I'm in your way . . .' Mildred Oval let her squeeze past. She had her big coat on, hanging

305

open over a navy frock patterned with pinhead-sized white dots.

'Your friend June has been here as well,' Miss Holt said, standing by the stove. 'On her way along to the Baths.'

Violet nodded without too much enthusiasm. She had already had a dose of June today, after work.

'We all know why she comes here, don't we?' Quentin said coyly.

Reggie looked up with boyish innocence, narrowing his eyes as he took a drag on his cigarette. 'I don't know what you mean, Perce.'

'Mrs Oval has brought us a cake,' Miss Holt said. The kettle was muttering as ever.

'There's no egg in it,' Mildred Oval said. 'It'll be like a brick, but I've done my best.'

'Course you have, love,' Arthur said loyally. He was on his way out to the back to fill up the sand buckets. 'Mildred could make a cake out of thin air if 'er put her mind to it.'

Mildred's face softened as she watched her husband.

'I worry about him sometimes,' she said, lowering her voice. ''E gets ever so weary. Can hardly get out of bed some mornings.'

'I know 'ow 'e feels,' Reggie said, yawning.

'No, lad,' Mildred said, her pink face unusually severe. 'I don't think you do.'

'Well, let's hope for another quiet night,' Miss Holt said. 'Will you have a cup with us?'

'Oh, no – yer all right. The dog needs a bit of a walk and I must get back. Dolly's minding our John. Just thought I'd say hello . . . Come on, Ginger.' She turned. 'Bye all – see you later, Arthur!' she called in his direction.

Muffled, from the back, they heard his voice, ''Ave a good night, my bab – keep safe now.'

Violet patrolled with Miss Holt that evening. They covered their part of the sector, finding everything in order, as did the others, in turn.

Miss Holt, who was given to sudden random outbursts of teaching, regaled her for much of the way with details about the disaster of English merchants selling opium to the Chinese.

'And there was the most extraordinary culture there, before the 1830s, when those disgraceful men got their filthy mitts on it,' she said vigorously. 'Such greed and destruction!'

Violet was really not sure what to say so she nodded.

'Ah – I see Miss Glover has finally mastered her black-out curtains.' Miss Holt rolled her eyes and she and Violet exchanged a smile.

Violet was quite relieved by this break from the Opium Wars.

'You'd hope so, after all this time!' she said.

'Now – let's check the shelters.'

She could see that Miss Holt rather enjoyed all this.

The two of them eventually got back to the ARP post to find Mr Powell and Reggie locked in an unusually energetic debate.

'I don't know how you can say such a thing!' Mr Powell seemed really agitated. 'Mr Churchill is our man of the hour – the way he has taken the helm – those speeches!'

'I keep telling yer, I ain't arguing with Mr Churchill 'imself,' Reggie said heatedly. 'Fight 'em on the beaches – that's what we gotta do, I know all that! Man for the job, that's Mr Churchill. What I'm saying is, in the end, the common man's gotta make a clean sweep of that lot. After the war's over things'll be different – Labour government, fair shares for all . . .'

'You need to have more respect, young man!' Mr Powell was beginning to look really agitated. His fingers trembled as he picked up his pen to wag it at Reggie.

'I think,' Miss Holt interrupted, 'it might be time for a game of Canasta – don't you? Come along, Violet.'

Several cut-throat games of Canasta took place. Violet partnered Quentin and Reggie Miss Holt. Arthur Oval snoozed and Mr Powell silently – sulkily, Violet thought, since he was not used to being challenged in any way – checked his lists and read the paper.

Just as Miss Holt was dealing for another round, the telephone rang. They all stared at it in disbelief. There had been so many quiet nights lately.

Mr Powell, forever on his dignity, never looked at any of them when he was on the telephone, as if he was trying to keep them in suspense. He nodded and put down the receiver before finally looking up.

'Purple,' he said.

'Oh, blimey, already? 'Ere we go.' Reggie fumbled in his pocket for another cigarette. 'Better get one in while I've got the chance. Want one, Vi?' he teased. She was tempted to say yes but shook her head, though she smiled at him.

'That's the spirit,' Reggie said. 'Anyone ever tell yer you've got a pretty smile?'

'Yes, they have,' Violet said, blushing.

'Oooh!' Reggie did a little wolf-whistle. 'Things are coming on!'

'That's enough,' Miss Holt said, and he subsided. He had speedily smoked halfway down one cigarette when the phone rang again.

Mr Powell picked up the receiver with an air of dread. 'Right. Thank you.' To the rest of them, 'Red.'

'Oh,' Quentin said, as the sirens began to howl outside. 'There's our friend Wailing Winnie again.'

'Mother of God – I thought it was over!' Cath Templeton cried. 'There's me after having got the little ones to sleep at last!'

'Why can't they just leave us alone?' Marie grumbled, hurrying to the stairs. 'Oh, no – I haven't put my things out! Joseph – you get Adie up.'

'Help get the boys ready!' Cath called to her, going to the kitchen. 'Michael can never get his legs into his trousers . . . I should have left them down there where they were . . . God, I haven't even boiled a kettle ready. All this again, and in Holy Week! They've no respect.'

'I'll have to go, Mom,' Grace said, quickly gathering her things. She felt really bad leaving her family in the middle of all this.

'You go on, Grace – can't be helped . . .'

Grace was about to run out of the front door but she rushed to her mother and, to Cath's surprise, planted a kiss on her cheek.

'Good luck, Mom – have the best night you can. I'll be round.'

'And you be careful now, darlin'. God bless.'

Then Grace was outside, hearing the first bombs falling as she hurried along the street. Bordesley, she guessed – not far away.

Forty

From the beginning of the raid there were high-explosive bombs falling all around the area, smashing Small Heath, Bordesley, Sparkbrook, Sparkhill and the middle of the city – as well as who knew where else.

George was sent to patrol along the Coventry Road. As the attack intensified, towards midnight, he hurried, as best as his hip would let him, back and forth from houses to the local ARP post, helping the living, reporting the dead, while the sky turned red once more with fires across Birmingham and shrapnel rained down on his steel helmet.

He had already been into a number of bombed-out houses and reported back to fetch rescue teams and ambulances to the scene. Walking out along the road, soon after midnight, he could feel that the raid was nowhere near over. The sky was alight, the air filled with smoke. The up-whistle of bombs made him cringe and press himself into the lee of the nearest wall until the crashing and shaking died down and allowed him to move on again. Fire teams were frantically putting out blazes caused by incendiaries and he could hear the bells of ambulances and fire engines.

God Almighty, this is a bad one, he thought, taking refuge in an entry for a moment as another wave of bombs landed. Everything shook so much that he was afraid the buildings would fall from the very shock of it. He waited for the wave to pass, his eyes squeezed shut.

All the time he thought about Violet, his lovely Vi. Was she all right? What was happening in her part of Small Heath?

At last, coughing, he went out to the street again. Immediately he stepped on a lump of something in the road and fell over, ricking his ankle and skinning the side of his hand as he fell.

'Sod and damn it!' he shouted at the heavens, sitting up to massage his ankle. 'You bleeding bastards!'

He got up and limped onwards, hand and ankle stinging. Looking along a side street, he could see that it was almost blocked by rubble that had not been there before. There was a fire building up at the far end. He hurried back to report it, then made his way to the street again. A number of terraced houses had received a direct hit and he could smell the sickly, frightening whiff of gas.

The first house he came to had collapsed at the front and he realized he could not easily get into it. It was almost a pile of matchwood.

'Hello!' he called. 'Anyone there?'

Though the wave of planes had passed over for the moment, it was still far too noisy outside to hear anything. The guns were pounding further north somewhere and there were sounds of creaking masonry.

I'll check the others and come back to this one, he thought. Stepping backwards, he trod on something strange and soft. Thinking it might be a child's toy or something of that nature, George shone his torch down at it. For a second, he could not make sense of what he saw. It was something coppery-coloured, hairy, though bloodied at the edges. Turning it over with his foot, horror dawned. He felt his own hair stand up on his head and his insides heaved. Turning, he retched repeatedly

311

into the gutter. He had trodden on a human scalp. He stood groaning for a second, bent over.

Come on, Georgie boy, he chastised himself. Don't think about it. Get moving.

'Anyone there?'

He heard a shout from the end of the street and saw the silhouette of one of the local ARP wardens for that area in his helmet and big boots.

He called out to him and the man, middle-aged, wiry-looking with a little moustache, joined him.

'This looks a bad'un.' They had to shout.

'I can't get in there.' George pointed to the first house.

'All right. You try that next one along, pal – I'll go next door.'

The second house still had most of the remains of the front wall, though the roof had collapsed. There was no door, but he walked in through the remaining door frame and shone his torch round. Though it was strewn with rubble, he saw the remnants of a front sitting room, chairs and a settle with splintered wood batons and plaster and muck all over them.

'Hello? Anyone home?' His voice sounded thin. There was an eerie silence. Was there a shelter – he thought not – or a cellar? Or were there still people upstairs in bed, buried by rubble? 'Is anyone here?'

Shining his torch through to the back room, he could see that there was less damage, but he couldn't see anyone there either. Kicking stuff out of his way, he was moving towards the back room, when the light of his torch fell on something. There was no door on the cupboard under the stairs – whether there had been before the raid, it was impossible to say. The light fell on a pale shape and he moved closer. The sight that met him made him jump back with a jolt of shock, his heart going like mad.

'Oh, my word,' he said. 'You made me jump!'

Shining the torch in, he saw there were three people sitting under the stairs.

'Why dain't you call out? I'm here to help, you know.'

It was then that his scalp began to prickle again. There was an older man, almost bald, and two girls, and they all just sat there, staring like mannequins in a shop window. Mannequins covered in dust. Looking more closely, George saw that the older of the two girls, who had long brown hair, had blood trickling in a line down from her nose. They were as still as statues.

'Oh, no.' He got to his knees and quickly crawled in to examine them in the tiny space, gently picking up the thin wrists of the girls, who could only have been about fifteen and seventeen or so. He felt for the man's pulse then. There was not a flicker of life in any one of them.

George's own heart felt as if it would burst out of his chest. He found himself gasping as if he had been punched in the guts. Respectfully, he replaced the man's cooling hand back on his thigh. He looked at the girls' faces, so still, like waxworks. He wanted to howl. But that wouldn't do. The planes were mustering outside and the warden was calling him at the door.

'Hello, pal? You still there?'

He emerged backwards from the understairs cubbyhole.

'There's three of them in there,' he said quietly. In the peculiar light of the torch, he shook his head.

'Oh, dear, oh, dear,' the warden said. 'That'll be Mr Garfield and his daughters . . .'

'Is there anyone else? Upstairs?'

'No – that's it. There was just the three. Wife passed on some time back. Blast got 'em, then?' The force from bomb blast could cause mortal internal injuries and hardly leave a mark on people.

'Looks like it,' George said. He was trying not to cry. This warden was the type who would be very unimpressed if you were to break down.

'What about next door?' he asked.

'Much the same story,' the warden said grimly. 'Ceiling came down on them. Only thing left alive in there is the cat.'

When Grace came on duty, Francis Paine had also just arrived, wheezing hard.

'Right,' Mr Powell said. 'Miss Holt's gone out with Miss Simms. Mr Meakins is with Mr Oval . . . Let's see, yes, Miss Templeton – you and Mr Paine – go round to the top of Herbert Road, will you? There'll be more wardens the other end of the street so far's I know. I'm sure Mr Molyneaux will be in any minute . . .'

'I could wait for him,' Grace offered.

'No, no,' Mr Powell said irritably, with a dismissive gesture. 'Go on, both of you – off you go.'

Grace's heart sank at the thought of being with Francis Paine. They had barely even looked each other in the eye since what had happened. Had the circumstances been different there was no way that Grace would have gone anywhere in the world with Francis, but this was not the moment to argue.

'You'd better not try anything,' she hissed as they set out down Archibald Street into the mayhem.

'I won't,' he said. He had a cold and his voice and general breathing seemed worse than ever. 'I told you. I love you.'

'Well, you've got a mighty odd way of showing it, is all I can say,' Grace retorted. 'Given the language you used.'

There was a long silence. The searchlights danced, guns rattled. And then she thought he said, 'Sorry.' But she wasn't quite sure that was what she heard and the next minute she couldn't have cared less. The planes were overhead and there were bombs dropping so that whatever Francis may or may not have said, and any other consideration at all, was secondary to staying alive.

'I should stay here for as long as you can,' Miss Holt said as she and Violet peered into the shelter in the Ovals' strip of garden, checking that Mildred and the family were all right. 'No – you stay inside too, Ginger.'

'It's all right –'er can go out for a tick,' Mildred said.

Ginger squeezed out through the door, gave Violet an amiable glance and ambled off along the side of the garden. Violet stood behind Miss Holt, looking at the rooftops of the houses behind in Arthur Street, dark shapes against the lit-up sky. Pray God they would all still be there by morning.

'It sounds terrible out there,' Mildred was saying. 'You let me know the minute anyone needs me, Miss Holt, and I'll be there.'

They worked their way along gradually. In the shelter in Violet's yard things seemed to be much as usual. Mom gave Miss Holt her usual rather superior look, as if to say, *Interfering Old Maid.* Violet did not meet her eyes.

'They're certainly keeping it a lot more spick and span in there lately,' Miss Holt remarked. 'It seems your mother has been very effective.'

'Hmm,' Violet said. They glanced at each other. Miss Holt did not say any more.

The raid was long and terrible. They helped a couple of people to get under cover early on in the night, but mostly the street was deserted. As the bombardment picked up force, the sounds of crashing and breaking glass, the shaking ground and banging guns, were almost ceaseless.

During one particularly heavy few moments, as bombs were raining down on Small Heath, Miss Holt pulled Violet into the shelter of one of the entries.

If there's a direct hit, we shan't stand a chance, Violet was thinking, bracing herself against the side wall next to Miss Holt. But at least under here for a few moments they could keep out of the way of flying glass and shrapnel.

Instinct told her to wrap her hands over her head as the ground shook under them. But she tried to keep control of herself and she stood with her head ducked, clenching her fists as tightly as she could. She tasted blood in her mouth and realized she had been biting down on her lip. Gradually the sounds moved away and another wave had passed.

'By the way.' Miss Holt spoke suddenly, her voice seeming very close in the dark entry. 'I want to tell you something, Violet.' Before Violet had the chance to be startled by this, she went on, 'My name is Rosamund. Everyone now calls me Miss Holt. And since Jocelyn, my dear sister, has passed from this life I have wondered if there is anyone left who knows my full name. Rosamund Joan Holt.'

'Oh,' Violet said. This was all rather strange, but she understood, sort of. 'That's . . . a nice name.'

'It is,' Miss Holt agreed. 'My mother had rather good taste in names.' She was silent for a moment and Violet thought that any second she would order them both out on to the street again.

'I've no other family,' Miss Holt said. 'There was an aunt out in Alcester, but she's long passed on . . . Of course, during these rather fraught years, the ARP has become something of a family. You might say sort of substitute brothers and . . . sons and daughters.' She glanced at Violet. 'It's come to mean a great deal to me, dear.'

Violet tried to smile in the darkness but she was not sure that Miss Holt could see, or was even looking at her. She felt suddenly very fond of her, stiff old biddy that she was.

'It's nice, that,' she said shyly. And she realized that she felt the same.

'Yes,' Miss Holt said. 'It is rather, isn't it? And I do hope when all this is over, if we're all still . . .' She trailed off.

'I'd love that,' Violet said. Tears pricked her eyes. 'You're very good to me, Miss Holt.'

'Yes,' Miss Holt said, turning brisk again. Well . . . Anyway – come along now – off we go again, dear.'

Forty-One

June Perry had not been rostered on duty that night. And when the siren went off, she was not exactly prepared for an emergency, being huddled up in an intimate position against the wall of a factory alley with Harry Cobb.

'It's too late now – I can't stop!' Harry groaned, his hands on June's breasts as she held him, lunging against her – and, as June thought later, smirking to herself as she hurried along the Coventry Road, even that racket wailing in his ears had not put him off his stride!

She had no illusions about Harry Cobb. He blew hot and cold, disappeared for days and weeks then came sniffing round again. He was married. She knew she couldn't expect anything from him. But he was an attractive man and she found him exciting. She quite liked the thrill of all this secret creeping about as well, even though it was never going to lead anywhere. And – so far as she was concerned – it was certainly not going to lead to her ending up in the family way, either. Harry had to be content with what was on offer and that was that.

As she hurried along to the Baths, she heard the first impacts of bombs not far away and she tried to move even faster.

'Oh, thank heavens you've got here,' one of the nurses said, the moment she arrived. June hurriedly tied her hair back. 'It's going to be a bad one – I can feel it. Here – get everything ready for an extra dressing station over there, will you, please? It won't be long before people start coming in.'

'Just let me wash my hands.' June hurried away to scrub them with carbolic soap, blushing to think what they had been doing only a few minutes earlier. And then she forgot all about Harry. She was so intent on her tasks that it took her mind off the raid, which was intensifying by the minute outside.

Things had to be done properly. She was surprised at how particular and orderly she could be. Even now she still felt a thrill of pride every time she put her apron on with the red cross on the front. And doing as she was bidden, she sorted out a bottle of iodine, scissors and bandages, tweezers and dressings.

I'm a nurse, she thought. This is what I'm going to do. I'm going to get trained and be a proper nurse! That'll make 'em all sit up!

Grace and Francis Paine were kept far too busy that night to have time to think about anything that might have happened between them. Grace couldn't stand Francis – despite Violet saying she felt sorry for him. But then Violet hadn't been followed home and spoken to like that by him, the pathetic, filthy little sod!

The raid was so intense, so terrifying, that all they had to think about was hurrying back and forth and trying to stay alive. The fact that Jenkins Street school had been almost destroyed in an earlier raid meant that there was one less place to take victims of the raids for shelter. There was the school at Dixon Road, but Grace sent up a quiet thank-you to Mildred Oval – at least they knew they could count on her as well.

Sometime around midnight, a bomb fell on two houses at the corner where Archibald Street abutted Jenkins

Street. The impact was enormous and both Grace and Francis, some distance away, were flung to the ground.

Grace lay on the pavement, her arms wrapped over her head. Everything shook and it felt as if the world was ending. Her head was filled with frantic, scrambled prayers . . . *Holy Mary Mother of God . . . Hail Holy Queen, Mother of Mercy . . . Oh, dear God Jesus, help us and save us . . .*

Lying there in the crazed darkness, she became suddenly aware that someone had their arm round her and was pulling her close. For some seconds, in those moments of dark, animal terror, this felt impersonal. It was a comfort knowing someone else was there. Harry, she thought. To be held close by Harry. She still saw Harry every so often. She had come to accept that he would never be reliable or be hers – but he was so attractive, so hungry to see her . . . Seconds later, as the ground stilled again, it dawned on her that the arms pulling her close were those of Francis Paine. She leapt up, shoving at him.

'Get off me! What the hell're you *doing*?'

'I'm just trying to keep you safe,' he said huffily, getting to his feet. He coughed for a long time, his lungs heaving, and Grace felt herself soften slightly. Whatever else Francis was, he was a poor specimen and she could see that doing this work must be a struggle for him.

'Well, *don't*,' she said, only less fiercely. 'If I'm gunna be hit by a bomb, that's not going to make any difference, is it? Come on – we've got to get down there.'

The devastation was terrible. Her first thought was, there can't be anyone in there alive! But seconds later she saw two small figures standing in the road near the smashed-up houses. She hurried over to find two little girls, about eight and ten, and she squatted down beside them.

'Is that your house?' she asked gently, wondering if they had come out of one of the neighbouring ones to have a look.

They both nodded dumbly. Each had dark hair cut in a pudding-basin haircut and they looked very alike. They were barefoot and wearing nothing but pale little cotton shifts. Shining her torch quickly over them, they seemed to have barely a scratch on them but they were both shivering convulsively. She had to get them inside.

'Are you both all right? Were you in there?' More nodding.

She just couldn't see how they came to be here, standing unharmed on the pavement. She stood up slowly, trying to make sense of this.

Can you tell me,' she spoke very gently, 'who else was in your house?'

For a moment she thought she was not going to get an answer. Then the older of the two said very quietly, 'Our mom. And Gina.'

Grace looked at Francis over their heads.

'I'll take them to Mrs Oval's,' she said.

'No!' the younger girl suddenly shrieked. 'I want our mom!'

Francis looked helpless and Grace saw she was the only one who could deal with this.

'We're going to get some help to find your mother,' she said. 'But you might have to stand out here for a long time and it's very cold. I'd like to take you to see a kind lady who will help you and you can sit by the fire – and she's got a lovely doggie called Ginger, and Ginger likes making new friends. Come on, girls – let me take your hands.'

After a moment Grace found herself with a trusting little hand in each of hers.

'You see what you can do here, OK Francis?' she said. 'Don't just stand there!'

'I *won't*,' he said savagely. 'What d'you take me for?'

There was no answer to that. Grace led the girls up Archibald Street. When they reached the Ovals' house, she said, 'Just wait by the door for a couple of minutes and we'll let you in, all right?' She tore along the entry.

Mildred Oval immediately launched herself into action. She ordered Charlie and Sylvie to stay in the shelter with Dolly. The dog had already shot out of the shelter, Grace was glad to see, having promised the girls that she would be here.

'Come on, our John – you come along with me,' Mildred said, climbing out of the shelter. She lifted the boy out after her. 'He's always happier with me,' Mildred said quietly. 'He'll fret if I leave him in there.'

'Here, John – we'll give you a chair lift, shall we?' Grace said. 'Save you carrying him, Mrs O.'

They linked hands and Mrs Oval reached down and hoicked John up round the waist to sit him on their linked arms.

'Like a little emperor,' Mildred said. 'Look at you!'

They hurried along, Grace uneasily aware of the sound of another lot of planes approaching. They went in at the back and she dashed through to open the front door.

'Come on, girls!' She hustled them inside. 'Now – this is Mrs Oval and she'll look after you.'

'Hello, little'uns!' Mrs Oval said, beaming at them. 'Oh, bless yer. Come on in and we'll get you settled.'

Grace watched her with great fondness. Here they were at nearly one in the morning, in the middle of a dreadful air raid, and Mildred greeted anyone who came to her house like a long-lost friend. She took everyone into the blacked-out front room and put the light on.

'This is Ginger and she likes a lot of fuss – so I expect you could give her that, couldn't you, while I get the fire lit?' Mildred said. As the girls crouched on the floor, patting the dog's silky coat, Grace saw a new, calmer light come into their eyes. 'And this is my little John. Now – what are your names, dearies?'

They whispered – Pat and Jackie.

'Well, I expect you'd like a nice cup of cocoa, wouldn't you?'

'You're marvellous, Mrs Oval,' Grace said, tears in her eyes. 'Thanks ever so much. I'd best get back.'

'Off you go, bab,' Mildred said. 'I'll go and put a drop of milk on for these two. You go careful out there.'

Grace went out to the street, mentally offering prayers of thanks for Mildred Oval being there. They were prayers she would regret for the rest of her life.

Forty-Two

The First Aid post was stretched to the limit.

The walking wounded were coming in all the time, a few finding their own way but mostly led, dazed, by the ARP wardens or police.

June was dressing wounds as fast as she could manage, trying to calm screaming children and reassure shaking mothers and old men. Some muttered or shouted in confusion. There were piles of blood-soaked clothing in growing heaps around the room and an area where people lay in rows, too badly injured to sit up. They looked strange, almost like dummies in their white coating of plaster or their faces red with brick dust. She was horrified to see how many of them were children, lying so quietly, too quietly. June longed to go over and help but she had been told where to be and that was where she had to stay. One of the nurses was trying to assess who was the most urgently in need of attention.

June looked around despairingly. Lines of people waiting, some covered in blood, a few with cloths pressed to their faces – a lady holding a small green cushion to her head and shaking all over. *Oh, my God, how many more? How're we ever going to get through this lot?*

And all the time, more bombs fell outside.

She bent over her next patient, a young woman whose face was gashed and bloody all over with glass splinters. June was trying to still her trembling hands to pick out the bits of glass with a pair of tweezers. The woman winced, trying not to make a fuss. She saw June's expression.

'It's really bad out there, ain't it?'

'Seems like it,' June said. She had to speak quite loudly over the racket. A baby was crying its head off nearby: a woman was sobbing. 'All this glass –' She eyed the woman's face. 'Was that from your house?'

'I – I dunno – it might've been.' The woman was in shock and seemed confused. 'I went out to the yard for a minute to get a bucket of water – I was stood by the tap and suddenly there was glass flying everywhere.' She let out a sob. 'Why're they doing this to us? What've we ever done to them?'

'Now, now, try not to cry – it'll only make your face smart,' June said.

There was a crash from outside, terribly close. The lights flickered, everything shook, plaster and bits tippling down from the ceiling. People screamed and some were sobbing with terror. June ducked instinctively, however much she tried not to show her fear. You couldn't help it.

There was a commotion soon after by the door. June felt panic rise in her. More people were coming in and the open door let in the bangs and whines from outside. How were they ever going to manage?

Amid the huddle of stunned or weeping people, a familiar face came into focus. He looked along the hall, caught her eye and hesitated, before moving towards her.

'All right, June?' It was the first time she had seen Reggie Meakins look like this – sober, serious, not constantly joking. He took his hat off for a moment and raked his hair back. His swarthy face was streaked with layers of filth and he already had an air of stunned exhaustion.

'Just about, yeah.' A look of understanding passed between them. 'Bad out there?'

'I'll say.' He took in the room, all the people and said, as if awed, 'My God.' Shoving the hat back on, he said, 'Gotta go. See yer, June.'

'See yer, Reggie.' It was as if, for a second, there was a pool of quiet around the two of them, as if no one else was there.

'Take care of yerself,' she said. 'Don't do anything stupid.'

He laughed wearily. For a second he reached out and touched her arm. 'Yeah. You too, June. Mind how yer go.'

She watched his departing back in the dark ARP clothes and helmet. For a moment she had seen that under all the mucking about and bluster, he was really scared.

'Oi – mate, leave that and get over 'ere! You're wanted round the corner!'

George followed the warden as ordered, along the Coventry Road, only dimly aware of the extra pain he could feel in his hip. The sky was a lit-up inferno. The night felt like an eternity. None of them could keep up with what was happening and at moments, faced with hellish sights, George felt he was about to lose his mind. The raid was so ferocious that they were being made aware of new damage and casualties all the time. He had seen firemen weeping in the street unable to keep up.

It felt as if wherever you looked were stinking piles of the rubble of collapsed houses, water seeping over everything where fires had been put out. People who were not part of the emergency teams, but who had come out of cellars and shelters to help, were pulling and scraping at the wreckage, trying to locate missing neighbours. They quickly formed teams, passing lumps of masonry and hauling timber out of the way with their bare hands. Shrapnel rained down from the sky and most of the people had no protective clothing or tin hats.

George was close to despair, seeing these sights, the burning buildings across the city, the struggle which seemed on the point of out-manning them all. When would it ever end? Was this Coventration as they had come to call it? Would there even be a city left when the dawn light seeped over it?

'Down here!' the warden yelled.

Another side street. George didn't even know quite where he was. Birmingham had become another place, not the daytime city he had known all his life. It was a cauldron of noise and flames and devastation where old streets vanished or were blocked by heaps of rubble.

'There's a whole lot down along 'ere!' the warden shouted. They reached the spot, the corner of another row of terraces, these with front walls blown off and all sorts of bits and pieces lying about the street. 'Couple of shops – I think. You take a look in there, pal – I'll go to the next one.'

By the look of it, George thought, clambering over the heap of destruction, it had been a hucksters' shop – a little corner store selling all sorts of items. His foot kicked against something metal – a galvanized bucket went clattering across the rubble. Jars of sweets and all sorts of packets and boxes were scattered about.

Climbing down into what had been the front room, he lurched forward on to his hands and knees and his hand landed on something bristly. He recoiled, heard himself give a yelp of horror. The human scalp filled his memory and for a second a panic rose in him so complete that he was paralysed. As his sense returned, he realized that what his hand had in fact landed on was an upturned scrubbing brush. He found himself laughing in a crazed way.

'Come on, yer silly bugger.' He got into a squat and tried to progress through the room, which was a tangle of broken wood shelving and stuff that had come down from the ceiling.

And then he thought he heard something, even above all the noise outside.

'Hello?' he called. 'Police here. Anyone there?'

It was so noisy outside he didn't expect to hear anything, and he jumped when, weirdly close to him, a desperate voice said, 'Help me! Please! I'm stuck.'

It was a woman's voice, though he was not certain that it had been she who had made the sound he heard before.

He called to her that he was coming, asked her to tell him where she was. He shone his torch but all he could see was angles of broken wood and the half-collapsed ceiling. After a moment he heard the plaintive little noise again and realized it was a cat.

Another wave of planes came over. George was seized with terror. Supposing there was another direct hit – he might be entombed in this house . . . He ducked, as everything shook and crashed about him. Something bashed against his helmet on the way down and curses spilled from his lips – a tin of something, he thought; heavy, whatever it was.

Coughing, he crawled onwards, calling to the woman. She must have been sheltering under the stairs and he was getting near but he still couldn't see a thing.

'Are you in pain?' he shouted.

'No-o,' she said uncertainly. 'I can't feel my legs at all . . .' For the first time her voice wavered into a sob.

'All right – now don't you worry,' George said. 'I'm coming.' He felt a right idiot. He was all this woman had between fear and darkness and some sort of hope and it didn't seem much. Not much at all.

'Thank you,' she said, strangely polite.

Edging onwards, he felt almost defeated. How the hell was he going to reach her? There was so much debris. Sneezing from the dust, he inched forwards, terrified that any move he made might bring everything down. The bangs and shudders of the raid only made him tremble all the more.

He tugged at a plank that had fallen diagonally across his path and, managing to shift it, he made out the entrance to the dark space under the stairs. He shone his torch into it and jumped back in shock as something came flying at him, yowling, scratching his face as it flew past. It landed with a small commotion and fled away somewhere.

'You met the cat then?' came the voice from within.

'Yeah – I certainly did.' He could feel blood on his cheek. 'Where are you? And what's your name?'

'I'm Mrs Gledhill. Polly. I'm under the stairs. Can't move my arms.'

Again, he shone ahead of him. The remains of the house were all a jumble. In the thin beam of light, he could just make out a woman's head, lifted from the floor to look at him, amid the debris. Apart from the fact that her face was the strange red that brick dust lent to it, she looked almost as if she was tucked up in bed because the rest of her was invisible. George felt panic seize him. What the hell was he supposed to do now?

'I s'pose my shop's all a state?' She sounded so unnaturally calm and conversational that it made George feel a bit peculiar.

'I'm gunna have to go and get help,' he said. 'I'll run to the warden's post and I'll be back. Just keep still, all right?' He felt foolish saying this.

Painfully he clambered out and tore along the road. He was back within less than fifteen minutes.

'Hello?' he called into the hole again.

'I'm still 'ere,' she said. 'I ain't wandered off if that's what you're worried about.' Her jocular tone made it sound as if there was nothing much wrong. He thought she must be in her forties. 'Can you help me get my arms out? I don't like not being able to use my arms.'

'Well – there'll be a rescue team here to help soon, I hope,' George said. 'I don't think . . .'

'Please.' She sounded desperate suddenly and vulnerable. 'I think I could stand it if I could just get my arms free.'

'All right,' George said. He thought, I'll go through the motions anyway, make her feel I'm trying. He managed to clamber through what looked like a hole but was in fact the gap between several angles of fallen bits of the building. The staircase still seemed to be in place, but the side wall had collapsed in and Mrs Gledhill was buried under chunks of masonry. It was a sobering sight. George inched closer.

'Right,' he said. 'I'm just gunna start to move some of these bits from on top of yer, all right?'

He started to work in the confined space, moving small, loose bits that he could get his hands round, atremble all the time in case he dislodged something that would make things worse. The place was such a mess it was hard to predict what might happen. With despair he knew how busy it was out there. It could be hours before any of the rescue teams arrived to start shifting the rubble.

'Right,' he said after a little while. 'I think it'd be better if I don't move too much of this stuff. I'm just going to come and sit—'

He never finished the sentence. Moving one step back, readying to sit himself down, his gammy leg gave way and he fell sideways into something hard. There was a terrible groaning and splintering and the last thing he felt was a weight cracking down on his head.

Forty-Three

The air was thick with smoke and dust, clogging their throats. Francis kept having to stop, doubled over with coughing. His frail body looked like a little tree bent by the wind.

'Are you all right?' Grace found herself forced to ask.

'Yes,' he gasped.

He really didn't sound all right, Grace thought. The night had been so long and terrible that she felt pushed to her limits. They had come to one house where they found the crushed, bloody remains of a mother and two children and there had been many people with injuries, weeping with distress at what had happened to their home, their streets.

Though Francis hardly ever said anything – he barely had the breath for one thing – Grace saw that he was gentle with people. And in his way, brave. He was a strange, creepy man and she didn't like him any more than before, but she had a fraction more regard for him. It felt almost as if what took place between them before had been some kind of dream.

The night was wearing on, the raid relentless and unceasing. All of them were exhausted and overwrought and everything was in short supply – people, water, even blue incident lamps and labels for fixing to the casualties. Grace had run home once to check on her family and they were all right. But with every hour that went by she felt more worried. Had a bomb fallen there as soon as she left? She didn't think so but that fear played like a background tune all through everything else.

'As we're up this end, I'd better look in on my father,' Francis said in his odd, mechanical way.

'All right.' Grace knew Mr Paine the elder by sight. He was quite old – his only son must have come along late in life – and always very much on his dignity, with a solemn undertaker's expression at all times. Francis's mother was dead so there were just the two of them.

She thought about this as they hurried to the top end of Archibald Street. But as they did so, they heard the droning approach of planes above them again.

'Quick,' Francis said. 'Come in here.' He went to pull her into an entry and for a moment she resisted. He felt her hesitate.

'It's all right,' he said resentfully. 'I'm not going to *do* anything. I know you don't want me.'

Well, at least that message has got through, Grace thought. Dirty little bugger.

They waited, cringing against the wall as a cluster of explosions rocked Small Heath and Grace prayed, her lips moving. Not Mom and Dad . . . Keep them all safe, please, O Lord, keep them safe . . .

'That sounded close,' she said, after hearing the crashes coming from somewhere close by. 'D'you think that was Archibald or Arthur?'

'Could've been either,' Francis said. The planes were moving further away. 'I'll just check on him quick like, then we can get back to work.'

Paine's Undertakers was in the shadow, at all times, of the Tram Depot and always looked a dark, gloomy little place.

'Where does your father shelter?' Grace asked.

'He goes under the table in the back room,' Francis

333

said. He stopped to cough and he was wheezing badly. 'It's a big table – he makes a bed under there.'

'So he's all on his own in the raids?'

'Yes.' Francis said, as if it was obvious. There was no one else after all.

He pushed open the front door and it came home to Grace, from the odd odour inside, that the lower part of the house was of course the funeral parlour. There was a whiff of chemicals and other sickly smells she did not like to think about.

She pulled out her torch and switched it on.

'Don't!' Francis shouted louder than she had ever heard before. 'Turn that off! You should've stayed outside!' She realized he had not expected her to follow.

But it was too late. On a long table at the side of the room she had caught a terrible, half-lit glimpse of what seemed to be a macabre jigsaw puzzle: most of a torso, with parts of limbs laid in approximately the right places.

'Oh, my God.' Sick with shock she turned the light down towards the floor. 'Is that . . . ?'

'I told you,' he hissed quietly. 'They bring the remains to us. We have to try and make them decent.' His voice softened. 'I'm used to it. You just stay here a minute.'

'No!' Grace almost shouted. 'Don't you dare leave me on my own in here with that!' She followed right behind as he went to the back. Only then did it occur to Grace to wonder exactly what kind of long table Mr Paine senior might be lying under and what might occupy the top of it.

'Father?'

'Francis?' Mr Paine's baritone voice rang out from somewhere in the dark room. 'What're you doing here?' He sounded stern.

'Just checking you're all right, Father.'

'Of course I'm all right, you imbecile. Go along. Get out!'

Francis hurriedly retreated, stepping back on Grace's foot as he did so, and she couldn't help a yelp.

'Who's that with you?' Paine Senior demanded.

'Just one of the other wardens, Father,' Francis said. Grace was appalled by his subservient, almost cringing tone. Here he was looking out for his father's safety and the old man was nothing but a bully! 'Well – so long as you're all right.'

Followed by more insults from Francis's father, they went outside again. There seemed to be a lull, but the air was thick with burning masonry, rubber, everything – and Francis was immediately off coughing again.

'D'you think it might be over?' Grace said, peering at the sky. She felt so weary she could barely stand. Francis made no reply. He was walking with his head down, hands in his coat pockets and shoulders hunched as usual as he tried to draw in each breath. He looked like an old man.

'Is your father always like that?' she asked.

Francis nodded. She couldn't tell whether he was miserable or just so used to it that he hardly knew what she meant. She was trying to think of something kind to ask him, like how old was he when he mother died and how he must miss her, when her attention was caught by a sight along the street which wiped Francis Paine completely from her thoughts.

Violet had spent these endless, terrifying hours with Miss Holt in Archibald Street. Several adjacent houses had been hit. A cooked-meat shop and the hardware shop next door had gone up in flames. The road was wet and straggled with hosepipes and rubble, and added to the acrid stink of burning was the aroma of roasted meat.

By the time the last wave of planes of the raid came over, they were at the top end of Archibald Street, having seen flames shooting out of a building.

'It's at the back!' shouted Violet, who had run a little ahead of Miss Holt. 'In one of the courts – Oh!' She had a terrible realization. 'It's where Mrs Bright and Miss Snell are!'

They tore along into the backyard. Glass crunched underfoot, but the flames were coming from the neighbouring yard in Arthur Street. It looked perilously close to Lucy Snell's attic. Shouts came from the yard over the back, buckets being filled.

'It seems all right at the moment,' Miss Holt shouted. 'Nothing much we can do from here.'

As they were going along the entry back to the street, there was another series of explosions that took Violet's feet from under her. She fell against the wall and went down, her hip bashing on something hard. The breath sobbed out of her and she lay face down, stunned for a moment. It sounded close . . . Horribly close . . .

'Up you get, dear.' Miss Holt, who seemed to have stayed upright, helped Violet to her feet.

As they started back down the street, a most terrible sight met their eyes.

They could only see halfway along because the rest of the road was obscured by clouds of dust and smoke. Violet could see immediately that somewhere near the junction of Archibald and Butler Streets, what should have been there was no longer . . .

'Oh, no . . . No, no . . .' She was about to start running, but Miss Holt seemed rooted to the spot, transfixed by the sight.

She had never seen Miss Holt look like that before. She heard her murmur in a bleak, helpless tone. 'Dear God . . . Oh, dear God, no.'

The last lot of bombers had dropped some of their load on Archibald Street. And the house at the centre of the blast was number fifty-six – the home of Arthur and Mildred Oval.

Forty-Four

Everything gradually came into focus. There was the first hint of dawn in the sky. The two of them hurried closer and Violet saw Mr Powell standing aghast, one hand on his helmet as if he could not take in what was in front of him. It was quiet suddenly. Neighbours emerged on to the street and stood, appalled and helpless.

Violet suddenly spotted Grace with Francis Paine along the street, Grace taking in what was in front of her eyes, then breaking into a run. Seconds later she was beside Violet.

'We've got to get in there!' she panted, grabbing at Violet's arm, utterly frantic. 'She was in the house – with those little girls!'

'Who – what d'you mean?' Violet said. 'Not Mrs . . . ?'

'Yes.' Grace tore over to where Miss Holt was standing with Mr Powell, and Violet followed her.

'They're coming – I hope,' Mr Powell was saying. He looked dazed. 'As soon as they can be spared. In the meantime we can all make a start . . . I do hope Mrs Oval wasn't . . .'

'She *was*,' Grace cried. 'I . . . I took some girls in for her to look after. And little John . . .' She broke down in tears then, in front of all of them. 'Oh, this is all my fault . . .'

'Don't be ridiculous, dear,' Miss Holt said. Violet was startled to hear, though, that Miss Holt's voice was thick with tears. 'The only person to blame for all this is that *wicked* Adolf Hitler.'

'Oh, Grace.' Violet put her arm round her friend's heaving shoulders. Her throat was aching.

Grace shook her head, the tears running down her cheeks. 'I was the one asked her to come into the house. She was in the shelter – there were these two girls, you see, bombed out . . .'

'For heaven's sake, you can't blame yourself.' Violet pulled Grace into her arms. 'She offered, dain't she? It could've been any of us took those girls to her – and none of us could ever've known.' Suddenly she was crying as well, and for a few moments they clung to one another.

People were already getting started, calling to one another to get in line, to start moving stuff away.

'It's all right, Mrs Oval!' one of the neighbours shouted. 'We're coming to help you.' This made Violet's chest ache even more.

She and Grace released each other. They were making their way over to help when Dolly Oval appeared, followed by Charlie and Sylvie. They had emerged from the shelter and somehow managed to scramble round to the street.

Dolly took one look at the house from the front and started screaming.

'Mom! My mom's in there!' Her distraught cries filled the morning street and Sylvie ran to her, her own face full of distress. The three of them had stayed in the shelter – Mark, being in the Fire Service, was out elsewhere. Neighbours tried to comfort them and Grace went and put her arm round Dolly.

Soon after, the long, unwavering howl of the All Clear rose over the city.

'Oh, thank heaven,' Miss Holt said.

It was then that Violet caught sight of someone familiar coming towards them from the other end of the road, a stocky, barrel-like figure. She saw him stop for a second, as if rooted to the spot. And then Arthur Oval began to run, a stumbling, desperate scramble along the street.

'No-o-o!' The sound of his voice echoed between the houses. Never had she heard so much emotion in one word. 'No, no!'

He reached them, gasping for breath.

'Dad!' Dolly Oval broke away from Grace and ran to her stunned father, flinging her arms around him.

'Where's your mother?' Arthur kept saying. 'Was she with you, Dolly? Where's my Mildred?'

'She went inside,' Dolly was saying. Sylvie and Charlie stood nearby, their faces contorting. Violet saw Grace's face, set and white. She stood still as a stone.

'Mr Oval . . .' Miss Holt went to him. Violet felt terrible for her. What could any of them say?

'Miss Holt!' Violet thought he was going to grab her physically, as if to shake an answer out of her. 'Where's Mildred?'

'I'm afraid –' Miss Holt's voice was trembling in a way Violet had never heard before. 'She was looking after two girls who were bombed out. She came into the house . . .' Miss Holt trailed off, unable to say more.

Arthur's bewildered eyes met hers, trying to take it in.

'She had little John with her as well.'

'Mom!' Dolly was sobbing, shouting at the wreckage. 'Mom!'

Recovery people began to arrive as they stood there. Violet found her arm seized suddenly from behind.

'Vi! I see you're all right then?' It was her mother. Everyone was turning out now the All Clear had sounded. 'Oh, we've had a terrible night. You've no idea what it's like in there, just trapped in that filthy shelter like sitting ducks . . .'

Violet's emotions swelled and spilled over.

'For heaven's sake, will you just be quiet!' She exploded at her mother's self-pitying expression. 'Look – the Ovals' house. What the hell've *you* got to moan about?'

May folded her arms. 'Well, that's nice! Fine sort of daughter you are . . .'

But Violet stormed off away from her, going to Grace who she could see had turned away as if she could stand no more.

The next hour seemed to pass so slowly that it felt like an interminable, nightmarish dream. A Church Army van arrived and kind ladies handed out cups of tea and buns. The rescue team got to work and everyone else who could formed a chain to lift bits of rubble away from the horrific pile of destruction that, just a few hours earlier, had been the Ovals' home. They passed lumps of masonry, planks, bricks hand to hand until their palms were bleeding, but nobody cared. Violet and Grace both joined in.

Arthur was frantic. He worked at the front of the line and everyone let him because they knew he needed to. Sylvie, Charlie and Dorothy all did what they could. Arthur's hoarse voice kept calling out, 'Mildred! Mildred, lovey – can you hear us? We're gunna get you out, love – just answer me!'

Everyone else was mostly silent, weighed down by the distress of it all. But when Arthur called out, they would all stop for a second, especially quiet, to listen for what they were most desperate to hear. But all that came from the house was a creaking silence. The silence spoke volumes, but no one wanted to say anything – hopeful or not.

Today was Maundy Thursday and they were supposed

to be at work later on, but Violet knew she would not be hurrying off anywhere, not when this was going on.

'Oh God, look at Arthur,' Grace murmured to her in the middle of it all. She straightened up from lifting a length of snapped timber out of the way and Violet saw her face change. 'Someone'll have to tell Jimmy . . . D'you think there's any chance?' She stared desperately over the rubble.

Violet wiped her eyes. As time had gone on, the chance of any of them being alive seemed so very slim. She was just about to say that it didn't look very good, when she noticed Grace's attention shifting to someone who was now organizing the rescue team. It was the tall, handsome man she had seen Grace embracing the morning after the BSA was bombed. And her attention was fixed fully on him.

But this detail was torn from her attention by a cry going up from Arthur Oval, standing amid the remains of what had been his front room. Stooping down, he pulled out one of Mildred's stout, brown shoes. He stood up again very slowly, staring at it. Sobs began to break from him, as he pressed it to his chest.

They all waited, the sense of hopelessness growing all the time.

Mildred's body was brought out first. They found her lying very close to her youngest child, Little John, as he was known to everyone. At a short distance away were the two girls Grace had taken to the house for Mildred to give them shelter. As Violet stood with Grace, both of them watching and weeping, she saw how all of them were carried with care, with reverence, to the ambulance. The remaining Ovals stood in a huddle, their home destroyed and the heart having been ripped abruptly out of their family.

For a moment no one seemed to know what to do. Then Violet saw Mr Powell approach Miss Holt, who nodded. He guided the remaining Oval family gently across to Miss Holt's house. Violet watched them, Mr Powell like a gentle old sheepdog guiding a small flock who had no idea what to do or where to go, this family who had been at the heart of the neighbourhood as well, now stumbling, lost, across the rubble-choked street.

'Oh, my God!' Violet heard a voice at her elbow. June Perry had appeared. She looked shocked, grubby and exhausted and they didn't need to ask what sort of night she had had. 'Whose houses're those?'

'Mr and Mrs Oval – and the ones each side,' Violet said.

'Mrs Oval,' Grace said. 'Jimmy's mom.' Her eyes were wide, glassy, and Violet could not tell what she was thinking.

The man from the rescue team walked past them. He glanced in their direction, then stopped for a moment, as if an electric shock had gone through him.

What the hell's got into him? Violet thought as he stared almost in horror at herself, Grace and June – as if a ghost was standing behind them or something.

Grace and June were both staring back at him and she saw Grace lower her eyes first, a blush moving through her cheeks.

'Hello, Harry!' June called, her tone cheeky and provocative.

The man mumbled something and walked quickly away.

'Know him then, do you?' Grace asked, turning to June. Her voice was strange, almost menacing, Violet

343

thought. She put it down to Grace already being in such a state about Mrs Oval.

June gave a cackle of laughter. 'You could say that! Naughty boy 'e is, that one!'

Violet took one look at Grace's expression and decided this was something she was definitely going to keep out of. Grace seemed calmer now, and she slid away from the pair of them and went over to Miss Holt. She would go and meet George in a little while – but first they needed to check along the street. She also wanted to make sure that Miss Holt was all right. She had never before seen her look so distressed.

'I'll come along with you,' Miss Holt said. Her face was drawn with shock, but she was calm, in control. 'My house is really rather full at the moment in any case. I don't know if anyone'll be able to take Arthur and the family in – they'll have to go to Dixon Road otherwise.'

'Oh, no,' Violet said. 'It seems so wrong – them having to just . . .' She trailed off. Of course it was wrong. All of it was wrong. As they walked up the road, Violet felt exhaustion fall on her. She let out a sigh.

'I know what you mean,' Miss Holt said.

Violet glanced round, trying to force her lips into a smile but barely succeeding. After the night they had had, smiling just felt impossible. For the first time she wondered how old Miss Holt was. She had always seemed ancient and didn't seem any more so now than when Violet was small. But it was all such a strain for these older people like Miss Holt and Mr Powell. She was finding it hard enough herself.

'Perhaps we might check on Miss Snell again?' Miss Holt said. 'I feel concerned about that fire . . .'

Emerging into the yard where Lucy Snell lived, the

morning light showed them the mess of glass and smashed slates across the yard. A charred smell filled the chilly air.

Violet's eyes searched the roofs of the houses. So far as she could see, Lucy Snell's house was missing a few more tiles but was otherwise still in no worse state than usual. The front door had been blown off and was lying in the yard. She and Miss Holt exchanged glances and walked into the house.

'Hello?' Miss Holt called.

There was a faint sound from upstairs, hard to interpret, and they both hurried up to the bedroom.

Inside, they found Maud Bright and Lucy Snell in a powdery state of plaster dust and bits from the ceiling. There was no glass in the windows which were left as jagged holes. Otherwise, the pair of them seemed perfectly all right. Maud was bent over the bed, turning down the edge of the sheet, while Lucy was sitting up with a cup of tea.

'Good morning?' Miss Holt said. 'Are we all right?'

'I was just tidying Lucy up a bit,' Maud Bright said. 'As you can see, we're in a bit of a mess this morning.'

The way she spoke it was as if there had been a little bit of bad weather in the night, not one of the worst raids of the war. Miss Snell was smiling at them in her usual sweet way.

'Come and sit down a moment – unless you have things to hurry away to,' Maud Bright said. 'I believe there might be a drop of tea.' Briskly, she wiped the seat of a wooden chair for Miss Holt, who sank on to it as if she might never get up again. There was a great deal more work to do, checking along the street, but a few minutes' sit-down wouldn't do any harm.

'I can perch on the end of the bed,' Violet said.

It was so strange, after all the terror and tragedy of the

345

night, to find these two ladies so calm and unharmed. Violet almost wondered if she had fallen asleep on her feet and was now dreaming.

'I expect you've both had a dreadful night,' Lucy Snell said in her soft voice. 'You poor dears. Maud, why don't you pour these two ladies a nice glass of sherry?'

The dreamlike sensation only increased. Sherry – at seven-thirty in the morning? Miss Holt didn't drink, Violet thought, wondering what she would say, but a moment later she was accepting a sherry in a delicate little glass engraved with leaves, poured from Maud's precious bottle, which she brought out from the bottom drawer beside her.

'Purely medicinal,' Miss Holt said, raising her glass to Violet, who had a similar tot to warm her up. 'And very welcome – thank you, Miss Snell.'

'Oh, it's Maud's bottle,' Lucy Snell said. 'She always keeps a little supply.'

Maud and Lucy used the teacups, from which Maud tipped the dregs out through the broken window in such a matter-of-fact way that Violet nearly got the giggles, hoping no one was standing underneath. She poured a generous tot into each of them. They all sat sipping the potent amber liquid, which, Violet found, certainly brought her round again.

'I must say,' Lucy Snell remarked, 'I didn't sleep any too well last night.'

'It was a bit noisy,' Maud agreed. 'And they've made a dreadful mess. We'll have to see to it when we've got our strength back, won't we, Lucy?'

Violet caught Miss Holt's eye and the two of them gave each other a little, wondering smile.

Forty-Five

Violet had just enough time to dash home for a slice of bread and scrape, change into clean underclothes then hurry over to try and meet George before work.

The streets were heartbreaking. Bombed-out families looking for somewhere to go were carrying as many of their things as they had managed to salvage in their arms, in prams or strapped to bicycles if they had survived the fray. Others were picking over their soaked, filthy possessions in the remains of their ruined houses, mess and rubble everywhere and the burned, sodden stink hanging over it all. There was still a fire engine at the end of the street as she hurried up to her meeting place with George at the top of the Coventry Road. Hurrying along, trying not to turn her ankle on anything, she felt light-headed from lack of sleep, her stomach queasy and her mind still jarred by all the images of that terrible night.

She waited by McGauley's as they were opening up. The place was adorned as ever with posters advertising BSA bikes, the shop owner carrying them out into the smoke-hazy morning to be displayed in rows. Violet drew in a deep breath. After all the awfulness of that night, the horror and fear, the lack of sleep and raging thirst after rushing about for hours – all she needed now was to see George's face and everything would feel so much better.

She stood. And stood. She started to feel a little bit embarrassed, then uneasy and finally worried to death.

'Stood yer up, has 'e?' one of the men called who

worked in the bike shop. 'You can come out with me if you like, bab!'

Violet tried to smile at all his joking attempts to cheer her up, but she was close to tears now. George was never late – not this late, anyway. He was regular as clockwork and always pleased as punch to see her. Where had he got to? She started walking up and down. If she waited much longer, she'd be late for work. But she couldn't bear the thought of going and spending all day on the line at Hughes's not having seen George and not knowing where he was. Even getting the sack would be better than that!

'Come on, love, please,' she murmured to herself as she paced the pavement, now not caring who saw her and what they thought. She struggled not to just burst into tears. '*Please*, George, come on!' All she could think of was seeing him, trying to will him to come limping into view with his cheerful face.

But a cold feeling of dread took her over. He wasn't coming. And the way things were last night, anything could have happened.

As she turned back the other way, she caught sight of a man walking wearily, along the opposite side of the Coventry Road, still dressed in his ARP uniform.

Looking quickly each way, she ran across the road. ''Scuse me!'

The man turned, his dusty face seeming blank with exhaustion. He was not young and he looked all in.

'I'm one of the wardens from the Archibald Street post. I'm looking for – I mean, there's a policeman . . .' Hardly knowing it was coming, she burst into tears and it took her a moment to get enough of a grip to speak.

The man seemed to understand before she'd got a word out.

'What name is it, bab?' he said carefully, and that carefulness made her feel even more afraid.

'George Cherry. He's a volunteer policeman.'

He hesitated. 'Come with me, miss.' He was suddenly more formal. 'I'm going back down there now.' He seemed to brace himself before carrying on. 'It's not good news, I'm afraid. One of the houses that came down last night – it's off of Grange Road – well, he went in and he ain't been seen since.'

Violet felt everything slow. There was a feeling of unbelief. Her legs were no longer moving.

'You mean . . . ?'

'More of the house must've fell in while 'e was in there.' The man took her arm gently and propelled her forward. 'They're still clearing it. It's been a long job . . .' He tailed off. 'We think there was someone else in there – a woman. He must've been helping her. And we don't know . . . They've been working a good while so it can't be much longer now. But you'd best prepare yourself, love – I'm very sorry.'

Her legs now felt most peculiar, as if the air was thick suddenly, like mud, and she was trying to push through it. A sick, shaking feeling filled her. The man stopped.

'D'you think you'd best go home?'

'No!' she almost shouted. 'I'm coming with you!'

They turned into Grange Road and eventually into another side road, where she saw once again the heartbreaking mess of smashed houses, slabs of inner walls suddenly exposed, a picture still hanging lopsidedly on the pale green flank of an upper room.

The street was full of activity, the intense, purposeful teamwork she had now seen many times: rescue squads and locals hauling at the pile of rubble, a lorry with a hoist standing by to drag off bigger lumps of masonry.

349

Every now and then, as they stripped more away from the central core of the terraced house, there would be a call for silence.

'Hello? Anyone there? Can you hear us?'

Violet turned to a skinny woman who was standing nearby. She looked to be in her thirties, dark hair yanked back and pinned up somehow. She wore something pale, a sheet perhaps, swathed round her shoulders and held her arms wrapped tightly round her. Violet could see how tightly she was clenching her jaw.

'Have they heard anything?' she pleaded, desperate for reassurance that there had been voices, cries for help – any living sound.

The woman shook her head. 'That's Poll Gledhill's house,' she said shakily. 'My friend, she is . . . Was.'

Violet wanted to say, *My fiancé's under there too, with her, he was trying to save her.* But she didn't seem to have the strength to speak and what difference would it make? For a moment she wondered if George really had gone into that house or whether he was somewhere else.

But as this thought crossed her mind, she saw another ARP warden coming towards her.

'Was it you asking about George Cherry? You 'is missis?'

'Yes,' she said faintly. Missis. Well, she was, sort of. 'The other man said he was . . . In there.'

The man nodded grimly. 'Yeah. I think he must've been. We're doing our best.' He drifted off as if he couldn't face her any longer.

Violet stood with her gaze fixed unwaveringly on the middle of the house, which was still obscured by rubble. People moved around her. Any thought of getting to work had completely deserted her. Her fatigue forgotten, she felt she would stand there for days if that was what it took, if her lovely George was under there.

Most of the people moving rubble by hand had moved back now and a man was directing the lorry with the earth-moving hoist, reversing it carefully into position.

'Oh, Lord,' she heard the woman next to her say. She kept gnawing on her thumb. Violet felt her blood thump and surge round her body.

The chains of the machine were fastened round a hulk of masonry, unliftable by any person. Slowly, jerkily, one end was hauled upwards. She held her breath. Supposing it dropped again . . .

Inch by inch, they moved it, pivoting it on its end, guiding it round out of the way before letting it subside gradually to the ground. Everyone breathed out. Now, they could see the smashed mess of wood which had been the staircase. The heavy-rescue men started on that straight away, hauling on broken treads and throwing them aside, realizing they were at last getting close.

It was almost unbearable watching, yet she would never have wanted to be anywhere else. Violet felt her eyes rooted to the sight. More debris was thrown away from the place in the house they seemed fixed on – which must have been under the stairs.

'Here!' A shout went up and everyone was focused intently on the man squatting down in the rubble. Violet moved forwards, unable to stop herself, until one of the other men held his arm out as a barrier.

'Hold on, love. It's not safe.'

A few of them were digging about, throwing things off and she wanted to shout, *Tell us what you've found!*

'I think it's Mrs Gledhill!' one of them called out.

351

The woman beside Violet let out a whimpering sort of sigh.

'Her kids are with their nan,' she said, her face creasing. 'Oh, God – don't let her be dead . . .'

Helpless, they all watched as Mrs Gledhill's battered, crumpled body was brought out and gently laid on a stretcher by the ambulance people. As one of the men turned away from the stretcher, he looked at one of the others and Violet saw him shake his head.

They knew they had someone else to look for. The young policeman who had gone missing. Violet watched every move they made, every look in the eyes of people she could see. She could tell the moment they caught sight of something: their eyes all fixed on the same spot.

'Please – let me go closer,' she said to the warden. 'It's my fiancé under there.'

'Oh, my God,' he said unthinkingly. 'You sure you want to, bab?' But she insisted and he took her arm and they edged closer to the heart of the house, picking their way.

'It's her fiancé,' he said quietly to the others.

Amidst the wreckage she saw what it was they were working at. A leg clad in the deep blue of the police uniform. She broke away from the man's hold and went to kneel by him, not caring about skinning her knees or about anything except being near him.

'George! It's me, Vi. I'm here . . .'

They were working faster now. The leg, a boot on the foot. She saw him emerge, piece by piece, torso, other leg, his chest, his head, lying turned to one side to avoid what was coming from above. All of him was covered in dust as if he had been coated in flour. He was limp as they pulled him out, his eyes closed.

At last they were able to rest his body on a stretcher and Violet took his hand.

'George! It's Vi. Just open your eyes – look at me!' she cried, desperate just to see one tiny flicker of life.

But there was none. His eyes didn't open and he lay utterly still and silent.

Forty-Six

'Violet, dear! Goodness, whatever is the time?'

Miss Holt stood at her door in a pale cream nightdress, a cardigan thrown hastily over the top.

Violet stared at her, numb with shock and exhaustion. She had no idea what time it was, had forgotten that people needed everyday things like sleep after a night like the last one. After George's body was put in the ambulance she had come straight back here, by instinct, straight to Miss Holt's door.

'Mr Powell and I were just catching up on a bit of sleep . . . Separately, I mean, obviously,' Miss Holt added, flustered and lowering her voice to a whisper. 'He is on the put-you-up down here in the back.'

And Miss Holt was by now taking in the state of her.

'Oh, my dear . . . Whatever's happened? You look all in – now look, come in . . . That's it, let's get you sitting down.' Gently, she guided Violet across the room. 'Let me go and put the kettle on.'

'No, don't wake Mr . . .' Violet tried to protest, but Miss Holt was already on her way to the back, and Violet heard her pouring water into the kettle. The sound of little snores from Mr Powell also came from the back room.

'He's flat out,' Miss Holt she remarked when she came back.

In the moments since she had sat down, Violet had really started to get the shakes.

'Oh, my dear,' Miss Holt said, taking in the state of her. She drew a chair hurriedly up alongside her. 'What's happened? Is it your young man?' Miss Holt's eyes, behind the spectacles, looked more intimately kind than Violet had ever seen them before. Violet finally burst into tears then, utterly overwrought.

'He was trapped under a building last night – other side of the Coventry Road. I've been there ever since, and . . .'

Miss Holt made a convulsive movement forward, leaning to grasp both Violet's hands.

'Oh, dear Violet . . . Is it . . . The worst?'

Violet stared at her, haunted.

'I thought it was. I thought he was dead!' She put her hand over her mouth for a second, eyes stretched wide at the memory of George's limp, silent body on that stretcher. 'He'd been there so long and they brought the lady out, the one he'd gone in to rescue. And she was . . . And they were all calling to him and he didn't answer . . .' She sobbed for a moment. Managing not to give in to it, she went on speaking, feeling her eyes stretched wide, as she relived what had happened.

'He looked so bad – covered in mess. I thought he was dead. And I was waiting for them to shake their heads, the way they did when they got the lady out, and then one of the ambulance people, a man, he picked up George's wrist and . . . And he said, "There's a pulse. He's still with us!"'

She shook her head, unable to go on, her tears flowing.

'Oh!' Miss Holt gasped, sitting up straight again, loosing Violet's hands. 'Oh, thank heaven!'

'I thought he was dead.' She couldn't stop thinking of that moment, of all it would have meant if she had lost him. 'But I'm so scared, Miss Holt. They've taken him to hospital. He still hadn't come round . . . He's alive. But what if it's like with Mrs Strong? She was alive – she seemed all right and she was even talking to us and everything. And then . . . What if he's the same?'

'I think we have to hope,' Miss Holt said. She leaned forward again and patted Violet's hand, then clasped it gently in her own. 'You know, lightning doesn't strike twice in the same place. Or the same way.'

Violet gazed at her, stupefied with shock and exhaustion. She clung to Miss Holt's words, wanting to believe with every fibre of her being that everything was going to be all right. But seeing George like that, unconscious, unmoving, so unlike her George with his cheerful, lovely face, it felt as if he had already gone somewhere far away from her and she could not yet trust in him coming back.

'You'll go and see him later?'

'Yes – oh, yes, of course! They said he would be in the General. I'll go as soon as I'm allowed . . .' Her mind jumped from thing to thing. 'One of the other wardens went to tell Mrs Cherry . . . I think I'm on duty tonight, aren't I?'

'Let's wait and see,' Miss Holt said gently. 'Would you like that cup of tea now, dear?'

Truth to tell, Violet was so done in, she felt she might topple off the chair. But she had come barging in and woken Miss Holt up. She felt embarrassed now that she had come to her old teacher as if she was a friend or relative and she realized that these days it felt almost as if she was.

'If you're having one,' she said. 'Thanks, Miss Holt. I'd better have one – and then I'll go and try and sleep for a bit. I really don't think I can manage going to work . . .'

She was so exhausted that the light seemed too bright when she went outside. Violet knew her mother would be ensconced in the shop by now. She crept along the entry and into the house, pushed her shoes off and fell on to the bed.

When she got to the right ward in the hospital that afternoon, she found Mrs Cherry seated by George's bedside. For a moment she hardly recognized the normally plump, cheerful little woman. Sitting hunched over in her baggy coat, holding George's hand, she seemed shrivelled and suddenly much older. Catching sight of Violet, she seemed to gather herself and she stood up.

'Oh, bab, I'm glad you've come, but it'll be a shock for you, Violet, that it will . . .'

'I was there when they brought him out, Mrs Cherry,' Violet said. She still felt very strange and a bit dizzy. She had slept, deeply, but not for very long, her head swirling with dreams of the raids and a feeling of dark foreboding.

'Oh, you poor girl. Did 'e know you?'

Violet saw in Mrs Cherry's face a desperation for Violet to say, *Yes, he spoke to me, he opened his eyes.* Carefully, she shook her head.

'I wish I could say he did, Mrs Cherry. He was out cold. But they said he had a good pulse. They said they thought he'd be all right.'

She added this even though it wasn't quite true.

'I'm glad you're here, bab, because I need to get home soon. Will you sit with him a while?'

'Course I will.' Their eyes met in silent understanding for a moment. Mrs Cherry patted Violet's shoulder. She leaned to kiss George, before turning to walk slowly away along the ward, blowing her nose as she did so.

Violet sank on to the chair. George lay on his back, his eyes closed. A nurse must have washed his face at least and he looked more himself, though she could still see tidemarks of reddish dirt round his neck and ears. He looked peaceful. Asleep. Worse than asleep . . .

'George? Love?' Frightened, she seized his hand and pulled it to her, kissing it. It was warm. It was still him. She saw one of the nurses coming along the ward and the young woman met her desperate eyes. She came closer.

'Why won't he wake up?' Violet asked quietly.

'We think he will, given a bit of time,' the nurse said. Her voice was soothing. 'He's had a bad bang on the head and we're watching him very closely, please be assured of that. The best thing he can do at the moment is to lie still and rest.'

'I see.' Violet stared bleakly at him. 'Shall I just talk to him, or what?'

'I think that would be a very good idea,' the nurse said. She gave a kind smile and walked away.

'George – love?' Violet leaned forward, speaking quietly because she felt silly talking in front of strangers here on the ward. But after a moment she forgot about them and poured her heart out. 'It's me, Vi, holding your hand – can you feel it?' She raised his hand to her lips and kissed it again. 'They say you just need a bit of a rest – I'm not surprised after the night we had of it. And you being so brave and trying to help that lady.' She stopped, not wanting to mention that Mrs Gledhill had not in fact made it after all that.

'It's funny talking on to you and you not answering back. Not very nice really – I'm used to you teasing me and that. I've never seen you so quiet.' Her emotions all rose to the surface. 'Please, George – make sure you get better. Don't go and leave me, will you? Just when we've found each other. I can't stand to think of it. There's all these things we've never talked about, not properly. I know you asked me to marry you, and I'd marry you now if someone was here to do it. But there was all the future in front of us – you and me, and us having children and a home and all the things we dreamt of. Just ordinary things but they'd be the best because it'd be you and me.'

Tears ran down her cheeks.

'I love you so much, George. I'm not much good at saying things, I know that. But you're . . .' She was crying now, hardly able to speak. 'You're everything to me. You are. You've just made everything good – better than good. Don't leave me . . . Please, please, wake up . . .'

She lowered her head as she cried, wrung out and desperate, resting her forehead on his thigh. It was comforting, feeling the warm, solid body under the sheet and thin hospital blanket. She longed to just climb in beside him, snuggle up and pour all the force of her love and energy into him, as if she might make him better single-handedly.

In the warmth and the darkness of her closed eyes, she felt as if she might fall asleep again. That wouldn't do. I must sit up and pull myself together, she thought. Be strong for him. Be strong in case . . . But that thought, what her life would be like if he didn't ever wake again, she couldn't allow into her mind.

Opening her eyes, she was about to force herself up when she felt something pushing upwards under her head. She shot upright. He moved! Didn't he? She blinked and pressed her hand on to George's leg where her head had been. Again, she felt a movement. He was definitely stirring.

She sat watching, desperate with hope.

'George?' His head moved from side to side. His face creased in pain and his body moved, like a baby waking, not sure where its limbs are.

'Nurse!' she called along the ward, not caring now who heard. She saw the nurse get up from her station.

George was still fidgeting and as Violet bent over him, her heart thudding like a mad thing, he opened his eyes, wide, as if startled. He looked completely bewildered. Violet gasped.

'George – it's me, Vi. Can you see me?'

Just as the nurse reached his bedside he said, 'Yeah – I can see you, love.' His face contorted into another grimace of pain. 'God almighty,' he said, 'how much did I have to drink last night?'

Forty-Seven

'Don't cry, Dad, please don't!' Dolly Oval clung to her distraught father as he broke down once again on seeing Grace come hurrying in that dinner time.

The family were huddled in a corner of the crowded school hall in Dixon Road which was offering shelter to the bombed-out homeless. There were huddles of families on the floor, babies crying, overwrought mothers trying to keep track of young children and a sharp, sweaty, fusty smell of a lot of unwashed people gathered together. Of the Ovals, Arthur was sitting on the only available chair as Dolly hugged him, her face raw with weeping.

Mark Oval stood, in his fireman's uniform, filthy, exhausted, red-eyed. Sylvie, who was just turned eighteen, had gone off to see if they could get a cup of tea. She and Charlie, who was fifteen, had both stayed off work today.

The sight of what this loving family had been reduced to brought Grace to tears the moment she set eyes on them. All her life the Ovals had been the beating heart, certainly of their section of the street, both Arthur and Mildred the soul of kindness to anyone, Mildred who was hardly ever seen out, even in the rationing queues, without her boy John in his little chair. And now look at them. Arthur Oval was bent over, head in his hands and his shoulders shaking.

'Dad,' Charlie said gently. 'Grace's here.'

She went to them, crying. What was there to say? *I'm sorry.* There were no words that could reach this. Silently she wrapped her arms round both Arthur and Dolly and they wept together for a few moments before she stood back. Turning, she looked at Mark and Charlie, touched each of them on the shoulder, and they each nodded and said hello, looking stunned.

Sylvie came into view then, her dark-eyed face tight and determined. She was carrying two mugs and Grace saw, heartbreakingly, that young Sylvie had overnight become the little mother, the one trying to hold everything together.

'Here's some tea, Dad,' she said, handing him one. 'There ain't no sugar, though. The rest of us'll have to share this one. Hello, Grace.' Her greeting was not especially warm and Grace had a sinking feeling suddenly. Why should they greet her as part of the family when she had treated Jimmy so badly?

'Thanks, bab.' Arthur wiped his stubbly face, trying to pull himself together. ''Ere – you share mine, Dolly. Grace – want a sip?'

'No, you have it,' Grace said. She was about to ask, *What can I bring you in? What d'you need?* But she hesitated. How about, 'everything'?

'I thought the neighbours had offered to take you in?' she asked. She had been appalled to find out, from Miss Holt, that this was where they had gone.

'No one's got room for all of us,' Sylvie said. 'And we want to stick together. The house is . . .' She trailed off miserably.

No one spoke for a moment. The house was destroyed way beyond fixing up and they all knew it.

'I dunno where we're gunna go,' Arthur said. He

leaned forward, resting his elbows on his thighs. 'I don't care really. I'd live in a field if I could 'ave the missus back. And little John. My Mildred – that's all I want.' Tears rolled down his face and Grace felt more run down her own. Her heart hurt her, as if it was cleaving apart – it was true, what people said.

Arthur's shattered face turned up to hers. 'Now the only thing I can do is try and give 'em a decent funeral. How'm I s'posed to do that?'

'The church'll help you, I'm sure they will,' Grace said, clutching at straws. She didn't have much clue what Protestant churches did about anything but that must be right, surely? And people would rally round, neighbours.

'Me and Charlie're going to the house in a bit,' Mark said. 'Get what we can out of our bits and pieces, if there's anything left.'

'Before some other bugger nicks it,' Arthur said.

Grace wanted to ask whether anyone had told Jimmy, but she was ashamed to mention his name.

And then Mark said, 'I've sent telegrams to Jimmy and Luke.' He was rubbing his head as if it itched. He was used to having a twin, and an older brother, let alone a mom. He seemed lost. 'They'll be here, I reckon . . . Soon.'

All along the street there were destruction and mess to be swept out of the way. Some bombed houses could be patched up and lived in again, but the Ovals' house was in too bad a state. Grace looked at it again as she walked home. A battered chest of drawers was clinging to the remains of an upstairs floor and behind it, a yellow, flowery wallpaper that she had never seen before. Only then did she realize that in all the years she had known the Ovals, she had never been upstairs.

'Oh, Mom,' she said, bursting into tears again when she got home. 'I've just been to see the Ovals. It's so terrible – they're in Dixon Road school with nowhere else to go!'

She sank down, sobbing at the table. Gordon came toddling up, having at last, at the age of eighteen months, decided to shift himself and take the trouble to walk about.

'Gacie!' He pummelled at her leg and she reached down to cuddle the plump comfort of him.

'Oh, my Lord,' Cath said, coming over to the table. 'God now, I wish we had the room or we'd put them up here.' They both smiled faintly at the ridiculousness of this since they were already squeezed in like pilchards. 'I suppose the council'll have to find them a place?'

'Well, how long will that take?' Grace said. 'They're crammed into a hall and it's bedlam in there. And it's so, so awful seeing them without Mrs Oval – they're all just like lost sheep.' Through her tears, she added, 'We could take them some food at least.'

'Oh, they can come and have tea with us,' Cath said, leaping into action. 'We've little enough but it'll always stretch where there's a will. You go and ask them, Grace. We can't have them squatting in there all this time.'

Grace was proud of her family that night. Cath Templeton got all the little'uns fed first, filling them up with spuds and bread and gravy and sending them outside again so that the rest of them could squeeze in and eat. She'd thrown everything she could find in the way of the week's bacon ration and butter beans and vegetables to make a big pot of stew.

Grace watched as her father took Jimmy's dad to one

side. Dad, tall and kindly, leaned down to talk to Arthur in what seemed a quiet, tender, men's conversation over in the corner. Mom was fussing about, trying to make sure all the Oval children were fed and comfortable and offering cups of tea. Grace could hardly hold back her tears at the kindness and awfulness and sadness of it all.

She, Tony and Marie did their best to keep all the younger ones occupied with games of cards and charades. She kept watching poor little Dolly, looking so pale and forlorn as she tried to join in the games, doing her best to be brave. But every so often her face just crumpled and she could not stop the tears rolling down her cheeks. Of all of them she seemed the most heartbreaking and Grace kept putting her arm round her, pulling her close. Dolly would lay her head on Grace's shoulder and turn her face to her to sob for a while, before drying her eyes and trying to be brave again.

'You could all sleep down here, if you like,' Cath said as the evening wore on. The next day was Good Friday and she was all for telling the Ovals to stay on, even though the house was hopelessly crowded. 'I know it's not much but it's better than being in that hall, God love you. It's no trouble to us, Arthur, is it, Bill? We'll give you any help we can – though it's precious little and that's the truth.'

Arthur Oval thanked her, but said that if he and his family didn't show their faces in the hall and let everyone see they were homeless, they would end up never getting rehoused at all. So they took themselves off again.

The Templetons went to the Good Friday service that afternoon. Or at least the women did, and the boys who

Cath was able to strong-arm into it, who were Michael and Adie – and Gordon who was too young to argue.

It was a day for fasting and abstinence and Grace and her mother had had nothing but a cup of tea first thing. This, Grace found, only made her feel more emotional. As the priest came in and prostrated himself in front of the altar, she saw some women were crying around her and her own feelings were already rising to the surface. As the long, emotional Good Friday ritual went on, all of them queuing to kiss the crucifix, the Latin and Greek words curling round the church, the incense in her nostrils and this familiar, ancient promise of a better day, a redeemed world . . . All of it welled in her in a long ache of tears.

She kept calling to mind so many of the terrible sights they had seen in these months of the bombing. The crushed bodies of parents and children, the blood and mess, the terror and destruction. And now, of all people, the Ovals left homeless and Mildred and John dead – as well as the two little orphaned girls in their care. They had been such a lovely family and they would never, in any sense, be the same again.

She was full of sorrow for the past, for her – as she now saw it – silly younger self. For all that she had got up to in the past year, clinging on to the excitement of being with Harry Cobb. She had closed her mind to the truth of Harry – that he was married. And then had come the discovery that he was not only two-timing his wife, but her as well – with June Perry of all people. And who knew who else, for that matter? She sat with her cheeks hot and her heart full of pain.

I'll try and help to make things better, Lord, she prayed. *I'll do anything I can to try and help the Ovals and anyone else who needs it.*

The service was so long that when they all finally poured outside, it felt as if they had been on a serious journey and emerged in a different place.

'I'll go and see the Ovals again now, Mom,' Grace said.

Her mother turned from talking to one of her friends and touched her arm. 'All right now, Grace . . . Yes, you do that . . .'

Glad of a little while to be on her own, she walked through her smashed-up neighbourhood to Dixon Road, her mind still dwelling on the past. She kept thinking of all the Oval kids as children, of all the times she had gone into their house and Mildred would be there, peeling potatoes, cooking, cleaning, ever busy. She had treated Grace more or less like one of her own, tomboy that she was. She played mostly with Jimmy and the twins. If they had cake or there was a bag of sweets or a treat in summer, when the Italians came along the street calling out with an ice-cream barrow, she would have one too, just as if she was one of the family. It felt as if she had been destined to be in their family – could have been by now – with Jimmy. But all that was in the past. She had messed it up good and proper.

When she walked into the school hall, the Ovals were back in the corner where she had seen them before. Near them was a collection of things that Mark and Charlie must have salvaged from the house. Grace felt a pain where her heart was when she saw that one thing they had piled things on to carry them, was John's little chair.

The crowds had thinned out, some having to go to relatives if they had people nearby, a few possibly able to return to their homes and patch them up, some re-housed already. But the place smelt ranker than before. There were not many lavatories and it had been overwhelmed.

But as she was taking in these assaults on her senses, she saw there were two extra figures who stood out, in their army uniforms. Leaning down talking to their father was Mark's twin, Luke. And beside him, even now catching sight of her coming towards them, was Jimmy.

Forty-Eight

Jimmy's eyes met hers. Her heart thumped harder, her feelings a mixture of longing and shame. He was so familiar – dear old Jimmy, always there in her life. He was like something to cling to, something known and safe and ever present. But mixed with this was her shame – all that she had done in the way of evading him, hurting him. Her evenings spent in Harry Cobb's arms. How could she even face Jimmy now? But she knew she must.

There was a time when he would have hurried over to her immediately, his face lit up. But not now. In fact, once he had taken in that she was there, he turned away and carried on talking to his father. It was like a slap. She felt like nobody of any importance whatsoever. But that was exactly what she deserved, wasn't it?

What she did see in him, though, as he bent over to hear what Arthur was saying, was a great tenderness, a maturity she had not known in him before. She saw that the boy she had always known, now crop-haired and a year in the army, had truly become a man.

Bracing herself, she went over to them.

'Hello, Mr Oval. Hello, Jimmy . . . Luke.'

There was a coolness from both of them in the way they said hello, though Dolly came up and flung her arms round Grace's waist and buried her face against her.

'All right, Dolly, love?' she said gently, hugging her.

'It's horrible here,' Dolly said, seeming too miserable

369

even to cry. 'It stinks – and they keep giving us these rotten, stale sandwiches. When can we go home?'

'I'm not really sure, sweetheart,' Grace said, an ache spreading from her chest up to her throat. There was not even the familiarity of school – it was the Easter holidays. 'They'll find you somewhere soon, I hope.'

'Can you come with us, Auntie Grace?' Dolly clung to Grace's hands, her eyes pleading up into Grace's.

'I'm sure I'll be coming to see you, Dolly – course I will, darlin'.'

Grace could see that the poor girl was missing her mother desperately, God love her. She had Sylvie, but Sylvie looked hard-faced and remote, as if she was holding in all her emotions in order to get through this. She didn't seem to have much left to give her little sister. Dolly was hungry for the presence of another, older woman.

Luke and Mark were squatting down talking to Arthur Oval. It was nice to see the two of them together again, Grace thought, with another stab of nostalgia. Jimmy kept his distance, watching them, talking to Sylvie now. In the end it was Grace who had to go to him, with Dolly still clinging to her.

'Hello, Jimmy.'

'Grace,' he said gruffly, giving her a stiff nod.

'I'm ever so sorry.' Her eyes filled once again. 'All this – it's terrible.'

'When're they going to find Dad somewhere else to live, that's what I want to know!' Jimmy burst out furiously. 'It's a disgrace. All of them – us – stuck in this filthy dump for days on end! And there's all sorts to organize – Mom's funeral, and John's.'

He lowered his head for a second, fighting his emotions.

'Is there any sign of anything?' she asked carefully.

'Mark's been to the council. Someone was s'posed to

be coming out today. No sign yet,' he added bitterly. 'Now it's the holidays.'

'They can't just leave them all over Easter, surely?' Grace said.

And just as she spoke, they saw a man come into the hall, look around and head in their direction. Mark Oval saw him and went over.

'Jimmy,' Grace said. 'Can I have a word? Outside? Dolly, love – loose me a minute, will you?'

'Not now – I need to sort my dad out,' Jimmy said crossly.

'Mark's dealing with it,' she pointed out gently. 'He's the one who's been here. You need to let him . . .'

Jimmy looked furious for a moment, then conceded. He nodded and followed her out to the street. They walked round the side, stood at the edge of the school playground. Grace longed to light a cigarette but she restrained the urge.

'I just wanted to say sorry, Jimmy,' she said. In the better light she could see that he really had matured. His face looked broader, his neck thicker, strong. She wondered if she looked much older to him. She certainly felt it. 'I know I've not treated you very well.' Once again, her eyes filled. She was flooded with sorrow and remorse, a whole skein of mixed and sad feelings she could barely keep under control. She wiped her eyes and tried to keep calm.

'Yeah, well,' he said. 'I s'pose I should've stopped kidding myself. You never really wanted me, did you?'

She looked tenderly at him, unable to answer. Her younger, silly self had taken Jimmy for granted. She had treated him badly, it was true. She thought of the last time they had met, how her mind had been brimming with her infatuation with Harry Cobb. And now – what did she

371

feel? It was so good to see him again. She was filled with a longing to wipe out everything that had happened over these last months, for the war never to have happened and for them to begin again, pure and free . . .

'Any road,' Jimmy was saying. He spoke in a clipped way, not meeting her eye. 'You might be glad to know I won't be bothering you any more, Grace. I've found myself a girl down south. Name's Lisa.' His voice was stiff and proud. 'I've been walking out with her – when I get the chance – for a couple of months now.'

The way he said it was like another blow. He had wanted her to know, as if to shove her away.

'Well – that's good, Jimmy,' she managed. 'I'm glad for you.' She was surprised at what she felt, at how much this hurt. But she pushed her chin up and, in her own pride, did everything she could to sound brisk and unbothered. After all, what did she want – Jimmy always on a string even if she played with him and didn't really want him? Because she didn't – did she?

'I hope she makes you happy,' she said, keeping her voice steady. 'And everything turns out well for you.'

'Yeah. Well.' Jimmy looked away as if he was going to go back inside. But something in him could not let him just turn away so abruptly.

'How've you been?' he asked stiffly. 'Family all right?'

'I'm all right,' she said. 'We've had some terrible nights. Being in the ARP, we're all out in it. But even that feels better than being in the shelter like sitting ducks.'

Jimmy nodded, but she could feel him slipping away from her.

'I'd best go and see what that bloke's got to say. Nice to see yer, Grace.'

And he was gone, leaving her standing outside.

*

But she had promised to help the Ovals, and even if Jimmy didn't really want her there, helping was what she was going to do, at least while she could over Easter. She followed him back inside.

The man from the council told the Ovals that there was a place they could move into in Hall Green. Because of the housing emergency, some larger houses were having to be split up into smaller, makeshift flats to provide somewhere for people to go. The Ovals would have to squeeze themselves into one of these.

'I don't mind that so long as we've got a roof over our heads,' Arthur said. He just looked utterly exhausted, bludgeoned by the amount of change and loss he was having to endure all at once. He was straining to keep going for his family's sake. 'It's gunna take us all longer to get to work, but that's how it'll have to be for a bit, I s'pose.'

It was the last thing Grace wanted to ask, but she felt she must.

'Are you getting on all right with the funeral, and that?'

Arthur nodded. 'They knew her well in her church – and our John, of course. They've been very good.'

'We can go tonight, Dad, if we can get a van from somewhere,' Jimmy said. 'Mark's asking a couple of his pals.'

In the end they piled the Ovals and what they could manage of their remaining belongings into a green baker's van, its bumpers painted white to be seen better in the blackout. The family could only just fit and Jimmy, the last to climb in, glanced back at Grace as if to say, *What are you doing still here? You don't belong here, not now.*

'I want Grace to come!' Dolly argued. She had found

an ancient rag doll that had once been hers and was cuddling it as if she was many years younger than she really was.

'I'm sorry, Dolly,' Grace said, her heart aching. 'There's no room. But I'll come and see you tomorrow – all right?' After all, she thought, it wasn't just up to Jimmy. He was hardly ever here himself. 'See you, Sylvie – I'll come and give you a hand.'

Sylvie nodded, her face very pale in the dark interior.

'See yer, Grace,' Jimmy said. He banged on the side and slammed the van door. It revved away and she was left outside, waving them off.

'Bye, Jimmy,' she replied. Everything he said now made her feel he was reproaching her for all she had been and done since he'd last lived at home. And she felt she deserved every bit of it.

She stood in the road in the dying light, feeling small and foolish and aching with sorrow. The sight of that van disappearing along Dixon Road was like watching her past, her childhood – all those days and years of herself and Jimmy – passing away. Those things she had scarcely even noticed that she had, all disappearing in a matter of seconds as the van turned the corner.

Forty-Nine

Although that raid just before Easter was one of the worst they had had, it did not lead the way to others and the nights were quiet. Despite this, the mood at Post F was sombre.

Violet was on duty on the Saturday evening. Her feelings were still soured by a bitter argument she had had that day with her mother. There she was, worried to death about George, and May had said carelessly, 'Well – 'e won't be no good if 'e's had a bang on the head. Sends some people very queer. I remember when Fred What's-his-name from down the road fell off that roof – 'e were never the same again. Turned proper odd, 'e did. That was a bang on the head did that . . .'

These days Violet found it impossible to keep quiet when her mother started being such a mean cow.

'I'm not talking about Fred Whoever-he-was along the road – I'm talking about *my George*.' Her voice came out, overwrought. 'We're engaged and we're going to get married! So there's no need to be so horrible.'

May turned, looking mildly surprised.

'I'm not – I was only saying—'

'Saying – yes. That's what you were doing, with not a minute's thought as to my feelings!'

'There's no call to be mardy with me,' May said dismissively. 'Anyone'd think no one'd ever had a bang on the head before – or a man running after them, come to that.'

Violet stared at her. She wasn't frightened of her mother any more. She could see her truly as she was – someone selfish and insensitive. Next month she was going to be twenty-one, and she had George and she was going to get away. At least she was if George was going to be all right. And whenever she thought like that, a dreadful, cold feeling went through her.

'You never think much before you open that big mouth of yours, do you?' She almost spat the words out. 'I love George – and he loves me. Which is more than you've flaming well ever done.'

'Oh, don't talk so silly . . .'

But Violet was on her way out of the door.

And now she was at the ARP post. There was no Arthur, of course. Grace was not rostered and she found herself with Mr Powell, Miss Holt, and the other men – Reggie, Quentin and Francis, who was on despite the fact that he had his arm in plaster from an injury the other night.

They all asked after George, how he was getting on.

'He's still a bit wobbly,' Violet said.

She didn't want to make a fuss, but she was still so worried. She visited as often as she could manage, and she knew he wasn't right. He still kept feeling dizzy and saying things that didn't make sense. Even when she was there, he would doze off to sleep.

'They say it's early days. Even though he had his tin hat on, he had ever such a bang on the head. He's hurt his leg as well, I think.'

'He'll be all right, Vi,' Reggie said, patting his pockets for cigarettes. He looked up and suddenly directed a smile at her, a genuine, kind smile. 'Tough little bugger like that.'

Strangely, this made her feel better. 'Thanks, Reggie,'

she said. 'I hope you're right. He couldn't even remember my name for ages when I went in the other day. Kept calling me Nancy – that's his sister.'

'Surprising how the body will heal, given time,' Mr Powell said from the depths of his desk.

Again, Violet was grateful for these comforting words. As well as George, they were all deeply affected by what had happened to the Ovals – even more than they had been by all the other terrible events of the last months.

'I'd give them my house if it wasn't already given over to the ARP,' Miss Holt said passionately. 'Mr Oval and those poor children having to camp out in that place – it's barbaric. There's no other word for it.'

'I can think of a few words,' Reggie said savagely. 'Bet you can too, eh, Perce?'

Quentin looked up at him. He was perched on the chair, his legs all wound round each other as if he was made of rubber. He was smoking in an affected way, his arm held well out from his body.

'More refined than the ones you have in mind, no doubt,' he said loftily. But there was no malice in it and Reggie grinned. 'They've got somewhere to go to now,' Quentin said. 'But they have certainly been cast away on the wayward tide of events . . .'

Miss Holt snapped to attention. 'Who said that?'

'I believe I did,' Quentin said, on his dignity.

'It's not Shakespeare?' She liked to think she knew every bit of Shakespeare.

Quentin frowned. 'I don't think so, no. Only I, the Shakespeare of Small Heath, Birmingham.'

Miss Holt gave him one of her looks.

'You should be writing plays,' Violet said. 'Not trying to act in them.'

Quentin gave a dramatic sigh. 'Perhaps you're right, dear.'

'Nah,' Reggie said fondly. 'You're just a bit of a clot, ain't yer?' He eyed Miss Holt, careful what language he used in her presence.

'Anyone in?' A booming voice came from the front and Violet, without meaning to, rolled her eyes.

'Oi!' Reggie reproached her. 'What's that for? That's June! 'Er'll liven things up!'

'Oh, my Lord,' Quentin said. 'Batten down the hatches.' He always pretended to be terrified of June. Or maybe he wasn't pretending, Violet thought. It was hard to tell with him.

Francis Paine also seemed to shrink into himself, as if under some sort of assault.

'All right?' June came breezing in. She was dressed in a dark green skirt with tiers of ruffles down it, pulled very tight over her hips, and a buttoned, short-sleeved blouse which did something similarly noticeable over her large breasts. On her feet were a stout pair of black lace-up shoes. Her dark hair was loose and hanging in big curled rolls. Even Violet had to admit she looked pretty magnificent. She felt like a little twig in comparison.

'All right, Vi? How's your George?'

June just about listened to the answer before turning her attention to Reggie, who practically had his tongue hanging out at the sight of her. And to Violet's amazement at her brazenness, she said, 'When're you off, Reggie? I'm not on for the next two days – fancy a drink one of the nights? Where's yer favourite?'

There was nothing in the least private about this conversation and everyone watched, agog.

'Monday?' Reggie said meekly. 'The Oxford?'

'All right then, Reg – 'bout seven? See yer there.'

And off she breezed.

Reggie let out a rush of breath, eyes wide. 'Cor!' he said.

Violet sat holding George's hand while he slept.

He is sleeping a lot,' said the nurse who she'd dared to approach on the way in. 'It's the best thing for him, really. Part of nature's way of healing.'

She was a middle-aged woman with a couple of greying locks of hair showing at the edge of her veil. She was distant, but not starchy like some, and Violet felt she would be honest about how things were.

'We are keeping a close eye on him,' she added, her expression clouding a little. But she did not go into more detail.

Violet didn't think George looked right. He kept having headaches and said he felt dizzy. Even in his sleep his face would twitch, his features tightening as if he was in pain.

Please be all right, she kept saying desperately, over and over again in her head. Sometimes when she visited, she met Mrs Cherry or Nancy. They were all worried, even though they tried not to show it.

She looked across the ward. There was a man lying swathed in bandages who she had not seen before and she wondered what had happened to him. He was all alone at present and every so often he writhed and let out a low groan which dragged at her feelings. Oh, God, this war, this terrible, cruel war.

At last George stirred and opened his eyes. He looked bewildered and then realized someone was holding his hand and looked round.

'Vi!' He sounded so pleased to see her, almost like a child on Christmas Day. She was glad he at least remembered the right name, but there was something a bit odd about the way he said it, almost as if he was putting it on.

'Hello, love,' she said. 'How're you feeling?'

He winced. 'Head hurts. Quite a bit.' He gave an attempt at a chuckle. 'They got me up this morning – went to the bathroom.' He spoke haltingly. 'My right leg got a bit bashed up. Nothing broken, I don't think . . . but now I'm limping with both legs. So I s'pose that's not limping at all, then!'

She smiled. This sounded more like the old George.

'You still dizzy?' she asked.

'A bit, yeah. They say it'll pass.'

Violet pushed her lips into a smile. She hoped this was true. She had felt that the nurse was not telling her something, that they were more worried about George than they were letting on, but she didn't want to give away any of her fears to him.

'Never mind, eh,' he said, squeezing her hand. 'When you're my wife, you can look after me proper, like.'

'Course I will,' she said. She was filled with longing. If only she and George were married, with their own little house and a garden and flowers and she could help him outside to rest somewhere in the shade of a tree. In her fantasy there was no war and it was summer; there were big fluffy clouds in a bright blue sky, with birds singing and butterflies round the flowers. And she would come out carrying a tray with a big teapot and pretty cups and saucers and they would sit there, side by side . . .

But reality came crashing back in. She'd be frightened to death to be looking after him on her own, because what if something happened? And the war was not over and the Ovals were gone and things were so dark and sad. And even if she and George were to get married, there was nowhere to live anyway because of the housing shortage. But he was alive. That was the main thing. He was here . . .

She stroked and kissed George's hand with all the tenderness she felt inside her.

'I feel a right useless nit just lying here,' he said.

'All you need to do is get better,' she said. 'For me. That's the only thing that matters, love.'

George's eyes brightened. 'You're my wench, you are. You're everything to me, Vi.'

She smiled down into his face. For a while, she sat with him and chatted about this and that, keeping off the saddest subjects, trying to do everything she could to make him feel better.

But when she had been there for the best part of an hour, she could see that George was beginning to slide back into sleep again. She got up and kissed him goodbye.

'Come back soon,' he said drowsily.

On her way out, she turned and looked back at his still form on the bed, his eyes closed. He certainly wasn't right yet. One of the nurses had said before that every head injury is different, that they would just have to wait and see. But looking at this sweet man who she loved, so still and quiet, she was filled with a terrible feeling of dread.

Fifty

All through the Easter Vigil and the Mass on Easter Day, with its flowers and feeling of celebration and new life and spring, Grace could only think sad thoughts about how her brother Den was no longer here and about the Ovals and all the grief and upheaval they were suffering.

Seated beside her mother in the church on Sunday morning, trying to sing the Easter hymns, she could not hold back her tears and Cath, not needing an explanation, and with grief of her own, took Grace's hand and squeezed it. Their eyes met in sorrowful understanding.

'After dinner I'll go and see them,' Grace said to her afterwards. She would have preferred to be over there with the Ovals, cooking for them to save poor Sylvie the burden of being the one in charge, having to learn to be a mother and housewife to all of them at once. Did they even have any food? she wondered.

When the time came, her mother sent a small parcel of the remaining beef and a few slices of cake over with her – it was little enough but it was all they had.

She took the tram along the Stratford Road and found the place after walking back and forth for a bit. There was some bomb damage along here as well and everything looked dirty and down-at-heel.

The Ovals had been housed in a dingy flat above a butcher's shop and the stairs up to it stank of stale fat

and blood, which made her heart sink further. To think
the Ovals had been reduced to this. Where they lived
before was in no way grand. It was cramped and damp
and bug-ridden like all the other houses in the street.
But it was their family home and they had always been
part of the street. Now they were here in what felt like a
wasteland surrounded by strangers. Yet these days everyone was supposed to feel happy just to be left alive.

The shabby door was held on only by one hinge. She
knocked and Dolly came, managing to drag the door ajar.
Her face looked very strained, but she forced a tiny smile
when she saw Grace.

'Hello, love,' Grace said, squeezing into the room and
then hugging her. She felt so old suddenly. It seemed
hardly a blink since she was only Dolly's age herself,
but now Dolly saw her as a grown-up who she had to
look to.

'Dad!' Dolly called. 'It's Grace.'

'Come in, bab.' She heard Arthur's voice, friendly as
ever, but so tired and sad that he sounded like someone
else.

She went into the bare room, to a depressing smell of
tinned sardines. She saw there was a main living space
with a couple of rooms leading off it. The one grimy
window, with faded blackout curtains hanging each side,
looked over the street. A stove with a couple of gas rings
stood to one side on a table and there were a few other
sticks of furniture – a table and three wooden chairs. She
noticed, draped over the back of one, one of Mildred's
red-yellow-and-green crocheted blankets, all mucky. It
was one of the things they had managed to salvage.

There was nowhere to sit of any comfort and Arthur
was at the table with Jimmy. Grace saw that Arthur had

been slumped forward on his forearms and as she came in he sat up, trying to pull himself together for a visitor.

'Hello, Mr Oval,' Grace said carefully. She felt Jimmy watching her. 'Hello, Jimmy.'

'All right, bab – it's nice of you to come and see us,' Arthur said.

Never had she seen anyone's appearance change the way Arthur Oval's had in the space of a few days – this bustling, stocky man with his cropped salt-and-pepper hair. Now it was almost completely white and she could see stubble like salt grains all over his chin. His previously cheerful, fleshy face now sagged and his eyes were raw red. He looked at least ten years older.

'All right, Grace,' Sylvie said. She was busying herself washing up their few crocks.

'Where're the others?' Grace asked, since there was no sign of the twins, or of Charlie.

'Gone to catch us some dinner,' Arthur said, trying to make a joke of it. 'They managed to save Luke's fishing rod out of the house.'

Grace nodded, thinking this a good idea, even if bringing home dinner was not the most important thing it achieved. All these lads couldn't just sit staring at each other all day – it would be good for them to get out and for the twins to be together.

'We managed to find the ration books, see,' Arthur went on. 'Mildred kept 'em all safe in that biscuit tin, so's we knew where to look. 'Er was like that, my poor Mildred . . . Always so orderly . . .' And he was weeping again, quietly. All around them was the echo of absence: Mildred, little John and their lovely affectionate dog, Ginger – she had not survived either.

'Mom gave me a few bits for you all,' Grace said huskily. 'She said to tell you she was sorry it's not more.'

She handed the little parcel of leftovers to Sylvie.

'Thanks, Grace.' Her eyes filled.

'That's good of her,' Arthur said.

'We managed to bring a few tins,' Sylvie said. 'Sardines and that. That's all we've had. None of us feel like eating anyway.'

'How're you getting on?' Grace felt like a blunderbuss coming in and asking all these questions. How could they possibly be getting on except with horribly painful difficulty? She felt Jimmy's eyes on her and his gaze scraped at her as if everything he was thinking was a criticism. *What are you doing here? What's it got to do with you?*

But as she stood there, Grace felt Dolly come up and snake her arm round her waist, hungry for contact and affection. Grace put her arm round the girl's shoulders. She seemed smaller and bonier than before.

'Well – we're better than some,' Arthur said. 'We've got a roof over our heads at least.'

'Are there any beds?' Grace asked.

'Dad's got one,' Jimmy said. 'The rest of us are making do.' Their eyes met for the first time. 'He's the one needs it most.'

And she heard in his voice such a gentle concern for his father that she was moved to tears and had to swallow and look away for a moment to get herself under control. They all seemed so stranded in this bleak place – and soon Jimmy would be gone and Luke too, once the funeral was over.

'Is there anything I can do while I'm here?' Grace said. Everything looked as if it could do with a good scrub. But it was Easter Day – hardly the time to start – and she doubted there was as much as a bar of soap in the house, let alone Vim. She cursed herself for not thinking of this.

385

No one seemed to be able to suggest anything, so she said, 'Dolly, Sylvie – it's dry out. D'you want to come for a little walk?'

Sylvie shook her head but Dolly seemed to want anything that would mean the comfort of Grace. Grace realized they were not really close to any parks, so they meandered round the block. The overcast afternoon pulled Grace's spirits so low it was all she could do to try and remain strong for Dolly. What with those scruffy, dark rooms and the state of everyone and, under all this, the sad, antagonistic feelings between herself and Jimmy, it was all enough to break your heart. And here was little Dolly, in her ankle socks and her grey coat, too small on her and her dear, tender little face. Dolly, who she'd known since she was a baby. Grace held the girl's hand and tried to say cheerful, encouraging things, which was one of the most difficult challenges she had ever faced.

'D'you think the war will *ever* end?' Dolly asked as they headed back along the Stratford Road.

And Grace could see exactly what she meant. Eighteen months of it and already it had become their way of life.

'Course it will,' she said kindly. 'Everything has to end, Dolly. Like the last war – I bet no one thought that would ever end, but it did, didn't it?'

'D'you think our mom can see us from heaven?' Dolly asked suddenly.

It was all Grace could do not to howl. She leaned down and for a moment, took Dolly in her arms.

'I'm sure she can, Dolly love. She'll be up there with little John – and he'll be pleased to have Ginger with him, won't he? Because he really loved Ginger. And they're all looking down at you and waving, sending all their love, and they're proud as anything of you.'

Dolly looked up at her, so trusting and serious. 'Is that true?'

Grace straightened up. God, what a question. Gently, she said, 'I hope so, Dolly.' And as this didn't seem quite good enough, she added, 'I think it is, yes.'

Fifty-One

'D'you think it'll be quiet again tonight?' Violet asked Miss Holt as they patrolled the streets on Easter Monday night.

'I have a feeling it might be,' Miss Holt said. 'They seem to have got into the habit of really *coming* for us about once a month.'

Violet found it a relief being with Miss Holt. Last night she had gone out on patrol with Grace. She was happy to be a friend to Grace, to listen as she poured out all her grief about the Ovals, about how old Mr Oval looked and poor Sylvie and how she was managing . . . But her own mind was brimful of worry about George. He still didn't seem to be recovering quite right and Grace didn't even ask about him. Grace didn't say much about Jimmy either, Violet noticed, and at the moment she didn't really want to know. She had enough of her own to worry about.

Everyone missed the Ovals and felt for them. Post F was not the same without Arthur and Violet could see also how much all of this was telling on Mr Powell, who had also, quietly and without fuss, taken on such a lot of responsibility during this war. He too had aged visibly. Miss Holt, however, despite all the strain that went with these months, the lack of sleep and the toll taken on the nerves and the digestion, almost had a spring in her step. She seemed, if anything, younger than before. But it didn't feel quite the right thing to ask her if she was actually *enjoying* all this.

They had checked all along one side of the street and were crossing over at the top, when a girl of about nine years of age came running out of an entry a bit further down. She looked, with seeming urgency, each way along the road and seeing them in the dusk, came tearing towards them, her long hair flying.

'Where's the fire?' Violet said. 'You all right?'

Close up she could see an urgency in the child's expression.

'Can you come? Mrs Bright sent me to get someone.'

Violet and Miss Holt exchanged looks.

'Is she with Miss Snell?' Miss Holt asked.

The girl nodded. She seemed relieved to offload this responsibility.

They hurried into the yard and knocked on Lucy Snell's door, which someone had screwed back on its hinges. It was opened almost immediately and they saw Maud Bright's anxious face looking out.

'I sent the little girl – but what we need is someone to call the doctor. Lucy's not well at all.'

'I'll go and get Mr Powell to call him,' Violet said.

She raced down the road to the post, delivered the message and went straight back to Lucy Snell's. Climbing the stairs, she could hear Miss Holt with the two ladies in the bedroom.

Miss Holt and Mrs Bright stood side by side, talking softly. As soon as Violet caught a glimpse of Lucy Snell, she could see that the elderly lady was very ill indeed. She was breathing only with difficulty and she was shrunken and spare as a little insect.

'Sit down a minute, girls,' Maud Bright said. 'I'm sure you could do with being off your feet.'

They obeyed, Maud and Violet perching each side at the end of the bed and Miss Holt taking the chair.

'I was saying to Miss Holt,' Mrs Bright went on, 'that Lucy started to feel poorly a few days ago. Just a cold, we thought, but she's gone downhill fast. I'm afraid it's settled on her chest.'

Violet noticed that Maud Bright did not seem upset, exactly, but calm and resigned.

'The doctor will get here as soon as he can, I'm sure,' Violet said.

'I don't know as he'll be able to do anything,' Maud Bright said. 'I thought I could manage, but she's gone down ever such a lot since yesterday. I should have called for him earlier, I suppose – but Lucy's always bounced back before.'

'I'm sure you've done your level best,' Miss Holt said kindly. 'You've been a very staunch friend to her through all this time. You've put your own life in danger to be with her.'

Maud seemed indifferent to this, even as an idea. For a moment they all looked at Lucy Snell, who was sleeping as she seemed to do everything – quietly – and lying very still.

'Oh,' she said. 'You can call me a staunch friend if you like – but Lucy has been the staunch one. You're too young to remember what she did for me, aren't you?'

For a second it felt to Violet as if she and Miss Holt were children of the same age, the way Maud Bright was talking.

'She's always been a kind person. A real Christian. She believed in people helping each other carry their burdens.' Maud smiled, looking down at her friend. 'That's how we got to know each other. I had my boy, Rob, in '81 – in the February. Well, it turned out that my husband was . . . Well, let's just say that together we made babies rather quickly. And by Christmas I was expecting again. The end of August the next year I had Floss and Lizzie. I never knew it was twins until close to the end – although I started to suspect because it was a bad pregnancy. I was ever so sick and worn down and after it was all over I wasn't doing very well. Bert – that was my husband – he was at his wits' end and so was I. There we were with three babies under two years of age and I wasn't myself. He started threatening me with the asylum, I was that bad.'

She stopped, as if thinking for a second.

'Lucy lived with her mother on the yard across from us. They'd only come to live there quite recently, after Lucy's father died. Lucy wasn't married – she never did marry. But she was a good soul and she saw the state I was in. She and her mother said they'd take Floss off me and look after her – and Lizzie too some of the time if I wanted. So apart from feeding them which of course I had to do, they helped bring up our girls. And of course, within another couple of years I had Ernie as well. That was the end for me. No more, I said. Whatever it takes. I just couldn't do more, wasn't really made for it, I don't think. Bert didn't like it – someone else helping bring up our children. But there it was. Lucy was a friend in need and the girls always loved her. She's been like a sister to me ever since then. Floss and Lizzie come and see us both when they visit. I'd no problem with jealousy – nothing like that. Lucy never tried to play the girls off against me or anything – she was just kindness itself.'

She leaned forward and touched her friend's frail hand, giving a tender smile.

'We both moved on later to different houses, for one reason or another. We had a chimney fire in ours . . .

Almost burned the place to the ground, but that's another story. After fate made me a widow we thought about me moving in here with her. But then my grandson came back to live with me – he was here until the war began and he joined up. But Lucy and I stayed close. It got so we couldn't imagine not being neighbours. We've been more than that, for a long time – we're more like family.'

'What a lovely story,' Miss Holt said. Violet could see she was moved, as was Violet herself. She could hardly imagine Maud Bright's long, long life, all these grown-up children and grandchildren and she and Lucy always here, all this time, looking out for each other.

'Shall I make you a cup of tea, Mrs Bright?' Miss Holt said.

'I'll go if you like?' Violet offered.

Miss Holt indicated for her to stay where she was. 'I'll see if there's any sign of the doctor while I'm down there,' she said.

Violet stayed up with the two elderly ladies. She wondered about suggesting that Maud Bright now take the chair, but the genteel little woman seemed quite happy on the bed, holding her friend's hand.

'Yes, Lucy – you've been a friend to me, all right,' she said gently. 'There's not many like you, old girl.' Violet thought she might have forgotten that she was there, but then she looked up at her. 'I don't really know why she never got married herself. She would have made someone a marvellous wife. But there it is.' Lowering her voice, she added, 'It's a long while since she's really been well and herself, though. I don't want her to suffer. It'll be a sad world without Lucy, but we all have our time to go and perhaps she has reached hers.'

With both hands she cradled the little veined hand and stroked it. Violet watched Lucy Snell's face. She had shown no signs of life except for her shallow, laboured breathing. But as they both watched, a slight, sweet smile appeared on her face and she shifted her head on the pillow just a fraction. Violet and Maud exchanged glances, and Violet saw in Maud's eyes a glow of love and acceptance that moved her beyond words.

'I think she can hear us,' Maud said. 'Bless her sweet heart.'

And then the tiny rasp of Lucy Snell's breathing stopped. It took a moment to realize, as when a sound of distant hammering or an electrical hum in a room stops, and the silence is sudden and noticeable. Lucy Snell lay completely still, her face serene.

Maud leaned over her. 'Lucy? Lucy, my dear?' She reached frantically for her friend's pulse, listened again for her breathing. And then she said, in a most loving voice, 'Oh, my dear. You've left us, haven't you?'

By the time Miss Holt came up with the tea, they had arranged Lucy Snell's hands gently together on her chest and tidied the bed, and Maud had combed her hair in soft little tendrils each side of her cheeks, so that she was respectable and ready to be seen.

Fifty-Two

Violet hurried over to visit George the next evening.

It was a cold, leaden day and she was glad to get inside the warmth of the hospital, even though the place filled her with misgiving. She was grateful for all the attention George was receiving, but seeing so many other people with terrible injuries was upsetting. And even more, there was her worry that something so bad had happened to George, an injury to his head so profound, that he was never going to get better again.

She thought of her mother's doom-laden words. What if the worst happened and he never recovered? Because she knew, now, that the worst could happen – did happen, all the time.

The usual smells of the ward made her stomach clench with dread. She controlled herself, managing a kindly smile as she set off along the ward, instead of showing the dismay she actually felt, and prepared herself to be as cheerful as she could for George's sake.

Her gaze hurried along the row of beds to his. Half-way down on the right, wasn't it? Had they moved him? She couldn't see him lying there as he usually was. Wasn't that his bed, the one newly made, the sheet perfectly turned and tucked in with hospital corners? *That* bed, now prepared as if waiting for someone new to come into it?

Her heart picked up speed. He wasn't there. However much she looked wildly round the ward for him – was he in a new position, a new bed? – there was no sign of him. George was gone. The worst had happened. He had died in the night and she would never see him again . . . She stood stock-still in the middle of the ward, feeling as if every light in the world which had given meaning to her life, had gone out. In seconds she was cast into a dark place of utter grief and despair.

'Hello?' The voice was cautious.

She turned, dazed, to recognize one of George's nurses. Violet stared dumbly at her.

'You'll be looking for Mr Cherry? He's having a very good day today – he's gone down to the day room. You can go and see him in there, if you like? Oh – are you all right, miss? You look very pale.'

The nurse caught her arm as she staggered, catching hold of the end of the nearest bed, to stop herself falling.

'You wait there a moment, dear – I'll bring you a chair. That's it, pop your head down below your knees and you'll soon be better.'

The blood thumped in Violet's ears as she stared at the floor between her black lace-up shoes. She felt the colour flush back into her cheeks and soon, groggily, she was able to straighten up.

'I thought he was dead.'

'No, dear,' the nurse said gently. She did not pour scorn on this idea – they were in a hospital, after all. 'He really is looking better today. We have reason to be very hopeful.'

She found George sitting in a corner of the day room, where there were chairs, a table, a few newspapers. Violet couldn't help herself. Completely uncaring that there were a handful of other men in the room, she ran straight to him, flung her arms round him and burst into tears.

'Hey!' George protested. 'What's brought this on, love?'

'I thought you were dead!' she sobbed, clinging to him at one side of the chair. 'Your bed was empty and I thought they'd taken you away!'

'Oh, dear, oh, dear,' George said. 'Poor old Vi – what a fright. 'Ere – get that chair and come and sit next to me. I'm perfectly all right. In fact, I feel better than I have in a long time.'

One of the other men helped push a chair towards her from a seated position.

'She loves you to bits, mate, and no mistake,' he said to George. 'You want to hold on to that one! I don't think my missus'd carry on like that if I was to go missing.'

George grinned at him. 'Oh, you might be surprised,' he said.

The older man said, 'Huh,' with a sceptical roll of his eyes.

Violet brought her chair right up close and they formed a little huddle, oblivious to everyone else.

'I've brought you a few things.' She rummaged in her bag. 'A few barley sugars . . . Toffees . . . Razorblades . . . No *Sports Argus*, I'm afraid . . .' They made rueful faces at each other. Sports addicts were having to do without their Saturday fix of news now the war was on. 'But I'll take your book back to the library and change it for you, if you like?'

'Oh, I still haven't got through that yet,' George said. 'Has your mom been in?'

'Yes – yesterday. Hey . . .' He nudged her. Violet looked up from rummaging in her bag to find him just staring at her in utter, loving delight. 'Seeing you's the thing that really makes me better.' He took her hands again. 'Blimey, Vi – you're a smasher, you are, d'you know that?'

She blushed, smiles of happiness and relief and love for him finally breaking over her face.

'I just thought . . . It's been such a terrible week, with the Ovals going and then I got here and . . . But here you are.' Words gushed out of her. 'When I thought that . . . Just for a minute . . . It was . . . Well, it was terrible – the worst thing. I just felt as if my life was over without you, George.'

'Don't talk daft,' he said. But his face sobered. 'Mind you – that's how I'd feel without you.'

'Look,' she went on urgently. 'I'm going to be twenty-one in . . .' She calculated. 'In three weeks. Let's get married as soon as we possibly can, love – let's not waste a minute!'

'Your mom's not against us, is she?' he asked, frowning.

Violet sighed. 'I dunno. You never know with her. She can be one thing one minute and the next she's right the opposite. I know you've only seen the good side of her but she's not always like that, I can tell you. But these days I've got past caring whether she's for us or not. You're the one I really care about . . .'

George held her hands and looked so seriously at her that she felt fear chill through her again.

'You are going to be all right, aren't you?'

'I think so,' he said. 'Yes – course I am. It just takes a while. And when I get out of here, I don't want to waste a single moment of life without you by my side. You're everything to me, Vi.'

'I don't mind if we don't have much of a do,' she said emotionally. 'None of that's what matters – having a fancy wedding dress or a big cake or anything. I dunno where on earth we can live but even if it's in one tiny little box room, it doesn't matter. All I want is to know we're going to be promised, and together – for ever.'

Looking up, she saw George's eyes fill.

'Blimey,' he said, hurriedly wiping them. 'Blimey, Vi. I don't half love you.'

And they held each other tight, leaning forward on their chairs, and in that moment, nothing and nobody else mattered.

Fifty-Three

Everyone was there. Most of the street, as well as all the ARP post, turned out to St Aidan's Church in Herbert Road to give Mildred Oval and little John the finest send-off they could manage.

Grace saw Miss Holt with her upright stance, in a black coat and a proper hat, a felt thing with black gauze at the front, which seemed very strange after seeing her so often in a steel helmet. Mr Powell was sitting one side of her, likewise in a little bowler hat instead of his white Head Warden's helmet. On the other was Violet, in a neat blue hat with a brim.

From where she was sitting, Grace saw Quentin and Reggie come and settle in a pew, both looking abnormally smart. It took her a moment to realize that the solemn, hefty, black-clad figure beside Reggie was June Perry. They managed to find a seat amid all the neighbours from Archibald Street and people who had known Mildred from church or school.

Grace was halfway down on the right, sitting beside her mother who, uneasy as she was at being in a Protestant church (they mustn't mention this to Father O'Riordan, she'd cautioned earlier), was not going to stay away from the funeral of a friend.

All the Oval family were at the front. Grace could see Sylvie and Charlie and between them, Dolly, her hair taken up in a knot at the back. Her little neck looked pale and vulnerable, with a babyish curl of hair in the middle at the back, but her swept-back hairstyle made her look heartbreakingly grown-up.

As the organ played softly, Arthur Oval came in, walking unsteadily, as if his knees were buckling under him. Grace's heart buckled in turn. Arthur looked like someone who had been hit by a train, who was so hurt and bruised that he would never, ever be the same again. He was supported on each side by his boys – Jimmy in his army private's uniform and Mark in his fireman's one. Luke, also in khaki, walked close behind.

The sight of them all together as a family, especially today, made Grace feel unutterably sad – for herself as well as for them. She was on the outside, whereas before she had been almost a part of the family, swept up in the embracing Oval affection, which she had taken for granted. And whose fault was it that she was banished in this way?

She could not help watching Jimmy. She saw the way he supported his father, helping him into his seat, making sure he was all right. His expression was solemn and strong, and again she knew she was looking at a man, not at the boy who had gone away all those months ago. Seeing him, she felt moved and full of regret.

For a second, Jimmy's eyes cast along the church and seemed to find her. But as she looked back, his gaze swept over her and away and she thought, Of course he wasn't looking for me. He just caught my eye by mistake. I'm being stupid.

The organist launched into the first hymn and everyone got to their feet . . . *The day thou gavest Lord is ended* . . . They all stood, trying to sing, throats already strangled with emotion.

And then Grace became aware of movement and the procession brought in the coffins. She turned to see the bearers holding Mildred's coffin. Processing in front, to lead them in, she saw a familiar face – Francis Paine, skinny and slightly bowed, still with a cast on his arm – and another young man. Together, between them, they were carrying a much smaller coffin – that of little John Oval.

The older Mr Paine, Francis's father, lean and grim-looking, brought up the rear of the procession. Father and son were both dressed in their formal undertaker clothes of tailcoats and top hats. Both looked immaculate and stony-faced. They and the other pall-bearers bore the coffins along the aisle with an impeccable pace and solemnity. And Grace watched, thinking how odd a mixture people were. There was Francis, tongue-tied, sickly, inadequate – actually nasty in some ways, as she knew. And yet she also knew him to be dogged and brave as well, despite his wretched health and miserable family life. And there was his father, a growling, mean-spirited old misery in his home. Yet here, transformed, dignified, they could bring a sense of order and meaning to all this horror and sadness with their ceremonial forms and their own quiet seriousness.

Afterwards, Grace could hardly remember anything about the service. The vicar's voice rang out with the words, *I am the resurrection and the life, saith the Lord . . .* And there was a torrent of words which followed, and even though they were in English and not Latin, she could recall none of it afterwards. She realized that all of it had been so unbearable that she had blotted it out. She came back to herself only when the words of the last hymn rang around the packed church.

Heaven's morning breaks,
And earth's vain shadows flee,

In life, in death,
O Lord, abide with me.

And then she realized she was sobbing uncontrollably, but that no one around was likely to notice, because they were all doing the same.

Standing in the mothball-scented crowd, June Perry was crying.

When she first walked in and sat next to Reggie, her attention had been rather more fixed on him. Like everyone else, she had known the Ovals to some extent but she was not involved the way Grace was.

Through all the church blather, she spent a lot of the time peeping at Reggie's thighs out of the corner of her eye. She had never before sat side by side with him like this and it felt very nice. In fact, it rather tickled her fancy. As they were all squashed into the pew, she could feel Reggie's leg pressed against her own. His legs were quite a good shape, she thought, seeing the strong curved muscle against the black cloth of his trousers. He sat with them braced apart, the right one – not the leg pressing against her in such an interesting fashion – twitching up and down. He was not at all used to being in a church, she could tell. She wasn't either. She could feel energy coming from his body like a thrumming rhythm, as if all he wanted was to be up and away.

And it felt funny wearing these solemn clothes. She'd had to go to the rag market to find a black hat. That was where she had picked up the hairnet as well and all of it made her feel older and as if she was in fancy dress.

By the time she had sat there for a while, though, looking ahead of her at Mildred Oval's coffin, with little John's arranged close to it on a stand, and seen all the people who had come to give them a proper send-off, the sadness of it all began to sink deep into her. She had seen enough terrible sights over these months, seen people heartbroken or in agony in ways she had never known before in her life. She even thought about Harry Cobb and how unhappy he seemed, and even though she knew he had been using her and she had let him, she felt sad for him as well. So that by the time they all stood up to sing the final hymn with its sweet, melancholy tune and she could hear people's grief all round her, the sobs came heaving out of her and she couldn't stop them.

'Hey.' Reggie turned to her as everyone got ready to go out. He looked startled, taking in the state of her. 'You all right, June?'

'Yes,' June wailed, tears trickling down her face. She felt her nose running horribly and she could hardly wipe it on her sleeve. 'You got a hanky, Reggie?'

'No, I ain't. Eh, Molly-noo – got a snot-rag on yer?'

Quentin turned, with dignity. 'I do happen to have a handkerchief if that's what you mean, Reginald.' He pulled a remarkably clean-looking hanky from his jacket pocket.

'Cheers, pal,' Reggie said, passing it over.

June swabbed her face. 'Thanks,' she said quietly to Quentin.

'Come on, girl.' She was surprised and moved to find Reggie shepherding her out of the church in a most concerned way, threading an arm through hers.

'Goodness me,' she heard Quentin say quietly as they all shuffled out. 'It has a soul after all.'

Outside, away from the main mourners, Reggie put his arm round her shoulder. 'You all right now, bab?'

'Yeah. Ta.' She stuffed the hanky in her pocket. She

couldn't exactly hand it back to that Quentin bloke in that state. 'I will be.'

But Reggie didn't remove his arm. He leaned round and looked into her face, under the hat brim. Their eyes fixed on each other's.

'Drink?' he said.

June looked solemnly back at him, then her face broke into a smile. They'd had a good time last time they met up. This really seemed to be going somewhere.

'Yeah,' she said. 'Go on then.'

Grace and Cath Templeton stood outside. It felt as if something should have changed, but Herbert Road looked much as it ever had, barring some bomb damage. The day was grey and dull, everyone else going about their business as they stepped out from the religious drama of grief.

'That,' Cath said quietly, 'was terrible. God in heaven, what a wicked thing this war is.'

Grace couldn't keep her eyes off the family, people all clustering round them to offer their condolences. She wanted to be there beside them, an arm round Dolly, trying to support Sylvie and the boys. Above all, she wanted to comfort Jimmy. But she had no right. She didn't belong with them.

'You coming home then?' her mother said. She sounded flat with sorrow.

'I'll just stay a bit longer,' Grace said. 'Have a word with Dolly and . . . You know . . .' She drifted off.

He mother gave her what seemed a knowing look but she didn't say anything.

Grace stood to one side, trying to remain inconspicuous. It wasn't hard to blend into the black-coated-and-hatted crowd. She shrank back close to the shadowy front of the church and watched. The funeral had not been as grand as ones she had seen before the war, with horses with black plumes and big carriages. There was one carriage, waiting a little further along at the kerb, and she could see the twins helping their father into it. She was not sure what the family were planning to do next – were they going off to have a drink? Because she did not feel invited.

The crowd of neighbours was dispersing and Grace felt she ought to go as well. But somehow she could not tear herself away. She leaned against the blackened bricks of the church porch, taking comfort from the solidity of it, not caring if she got smuts on her coat.

And she watched Jimmy. Her eyes followed him as he talked to old neighbours and friends. He and his brothers stood out in the crowd, the only ones in uniform. And all she could feel was desperately sad. Not just about Mildred and little John, though that was sad beyond measure. But for herself. Here was this good man, who she had not given the chance to grow beside her into the man he was now. She had wasted it – wasted the chance they had had by being arrogant and silly and always wanting more.

By the time there was almost no one left and the last people were about to leave, she had still not managed to tear herself away. The family were getting into the carriages to go to the cemetery, but she saw Jimmy pause to light a cigarette, and then he glanced around and noticed her standing there, almost hidden in the church's shadow. He hesitated, then came slowly over to her.

'Grace.'

'All right, Jimmy?' She tried to keep her voice steady. 'Beautiful service.'

'Yeah.' He looked down at his feet. He had one hand

405

in his pocket, the other holding the cigarette. There was strained feeling between them.

She knew he would have to go, that there were seconds here, this snatch of time before he would say, *Well, I'd best be off then . . .*

'I'm sorry,' she said.

He looked up, guarded, but also startled.

'I was such a silly fool.' She wasn't going to tell him about Harry Cobb. That embarrassment would go with her to the grave. But the way she had been with Jimmy, so haughty, as if she deserved better.

'Couldn't see the good things under my nose, I s'pose,' she said. She sounded humble and she felt it. Very humble and foolish.

Jimmy was silent for a moment. He took a long drag on the cigarette.

'I thought you was getting married. That's what you said.' His voice was very bitter.

'No. It was a mistake, Jimmy,' she admitted softly, fighting back her tears. 'Worst mistake I've ever made.'

There was a silence. Jimmy blew out a lungful of smoke. After a few moments she felt him looking at her and, fearfully, she raised her eyes to meet his.

'You were always the girl for me, Grace,' he said sadly. 'I never knew what else to do.'

She licked her lips. Dare she say anything, dare she?

'But now . . .' She forced the words from her lips. 'There's someone else?'

Jimmy turned and looked away across the street and she felt he was withdrawing from her. A cold feeling of loss and failure began in her.

'She's a nice wench,' he said carefully. He paused for a final drag on the cigarette before stubbing it out on the church wall. Then he turned to her. 'But she ain't you, Grace.'

Her pulse flickered, moved faster.

'I . . . I mean . . . I'm so sorry, Jimmy,' she stammered. 'But I'm here. If you still feel . . . I mean, I hope I've grown up a bit. I'm just . . .' She shrugged. 'I can see what an idiot I was.'

He smiled, looking down at his feet. Cautiously, sardonically almost, he said, 'Is that so?'

'Yeah,' she said softly. 'It's so, Jimmy.'

'Look, I've gotta go. But – will you write to me again? Proper, I mean? So we can . . .' He didn't seem to know how to finish the sentence.

'Yeah – course I will,' she said gladly. 'So long as you write back?'

They looked at each other for a long moment. Jimmy stepped forward and leaned to give her a kiss on the cheek. He looked into her face as if trying to decide whether he could trust her. And in his eyes she saw hurt and pride and that he was wary of her. But at least he was looking at her.

'I dunno when I'll be back again. Let's take it from here, shall we?' And, gently, he touched her arm before moving away.

She watched him walk down to join his grieving family, his back very straight in the khaki uniform, and she thought what a fine man he was – strong, serious, kind. A man she loved. She knew that now.

'Bye, Jimmy,' she called.

He turned, just for a second, and smiling raised his hand.

407

Fifty-Four

May 1941

''Ere yer go, love . . .'

Violet woke feeling George's lips on her cheek. Her eyes snapped open and she rolled over, full of amazement. She was *here*! In their own awful, wonderful little home! A cup of tea was on the ancient tea chest which served as a table by the bed and George was now climbing back in beside her.

'Oh – thanks, love.'

She sat up, thinking how strange it was. They had tied the knot only a week ago and already she felt like a comfortable married old lady. Because living with George *was* comfortable. It was lovely, in fact!

As she settled her pillow against the wall a shower of musty plaster dust landed on her and she brushed it off, laughing.

'This house is about as bad as it gets,' George said.

They both sat looking at the cracks and holes in the wall opposite, the sagging ceiling, the rotten old floorboards. The two rooms above Quinn's had been uninhabited for years until they moved in. They had been used for storing old abandoned bundles, whose owners must have long died, as well as a collection of other old rubbish and bric-a-brac. They had begun to make a start

408

on the other room – their one living room except for the bedroom – trying to fill in cracks in the walls.

'It's terrible,' Violet agreed cheerfully, reaching for her teacup. 'But it's ours. Better than living with Mom, anyway!'

To her it was her little palace. She was with George and they had a door they could close. Even if the place was falling down round their ears, was bug-infested, and the only way to reach water or the lavatories was all the way round in the backyard – it was still a place to call home. And Mom was happy enough that she hadn't gone far away.

'I reckon the only way to hold that wall together is to wallpaper it,' George said.

'D'you know how?'

'No. Can't be that difficult, though, can it?'

Violet grinned at him. 'If you say so.' She took another sip of tea. 'I'll help you make a start later. But I do want to write that letter first – all right?'

There was nowhere else to sit so she got her pen and little pad of writing paper and sat on the bed, under the old flowery eiderdown.

It felt very strange writing her address:

> 22A Archibald Street,
> Small Heath,
> Birmingham.
> May 25th, 1941

Dear Tom,
  Sorry it's taken me so long to answer your letter. It was nice to receive it. Things have been so up and down here with all the raids but now I've got something to tell

409

you – I turned 21 on May 10th and now George, my husband, and I have just got married!

She sat back, thinking of her day, trying to think what to tell her far-away, almost unknown half-brother. This time it was her and George standing at the front at St Aidan's, with people smiling and being happy for them.

Since she didn't have a father, she had asked Mr Powell to give her away. He had led her along the aisle, carrying out his task with his usual quiet competence, and gave her a very nice smile once he had delivered her to George at the front. They had kept everything simple – she wore a short cream dress, one serviceable for other occasions.

Who really cared about dresses when she had George there – getting better by the day, it seemed – in his Special Constable's uniform, his smile almost as wide as his hat brim? And as she turned, freshly married, on George's arm, all those faces watching and wishing them well brought a smile just as wide to her own face.

There were a few girls from Hughes's Biscuits. But there were so many people who, had it not been for the war, she would never have known at all, let alone felt so close to or honoured by or grateful to. Some of them were neighbours who she had got to know by calling in to their houses or air-raid shelters time after time to see if they were all right. Among them she saw Maud Bright's sweet face smiling at her from under a little hat, her dentures a white band of happiness between her lips.

And of course, there was Grace, her lovely friend Grace, looking beautiful as ever. Grace had asked Violet jokingly whether she wanted her to come to the wedding in her tin hat.

'I don't care what you wear,' Violet said. 'You can come in a paper bag, so long as you're there!'

She had half-hoped Grace *might* wear her ARP helmet – but of course she was there in a beautiful deep red dress, her hair up, and a little blue hat perched at a cheeky angle on her hair.

Violet beamed at her as she looked along the church, holding George's arm. How shy she had been of Grace at first, when she ventured out of her lonely little life and into the ARP! Now they were equals, friends for life – maybe, she thought, like Maud and Lucy. That was quite something.

There were Reggie and June, who were now inseparable. Violet had heard Grace ticking June off afterwards for going on about the fact that she and Reggie were going to get married soon as well.

'Well, that's very nice, June,' Grace said. 'But this is Violet's wedding day today – so button it for another time, all right?'

All the rest of them were there too – Quentin and Francis, and Miss Holt, smiling proudly at her, probably, Violet thought, more proudly than her actual mother! And the Ovals came, all trying to look happy for her. Arthur Oval came up to her outside the church, his face full of emotion.

'This is a great day, bab,' he said, hugging her like a bear. 'A great thing, being wed – take my word. You make the most of it, young Violet. And you, young George – you'd best look after this one or there'll be trouble!'

'Oh, yes, Mr Oval,' George said, pretending to be scared. 'Right you are. I'll do my best!'

'Thanks, Arthur.' Violet smiled at him, her eyes filling.

Mom had managed to get herself a new frock and hat in emerald green and white and she looked the most glamorous of all of them.

'I never thought anyone'd take my mouse of a daughter off of me,' she said to George, at her most charming today. 'So this is a very happy day!'

'Thanks, Mrs S,' George said. He always treated her good-naturedly, even though he and Violet exchanged looks as she passed on. 'Mouse, eh?' George whispered to her. He rolled his eyes. 'More like a little tiger!'

They had already made a good start on clearing out the rooms above Quinn's before the wedding. Sitting here now, Violet still couldn't believe the loveliness of that day. They had finished off by going to the pub for a drink and then in the middle of that the air-raid siren went off and all the ARP people except for them had to dash off and go on duty. It wasn't much of a raid in their area in the end, but, as George said, it'd be something to tell the grandchildren.

She sat, dreamily, thinking of all the changes, good and bad, of the past year and a half. That life before the war – how very long ago it seemed now. How smashed up and wrecked was her home city and so many other places. How sad and exhausting and frightening it had been. And yet she would not have swapped the friendships that had come out of it for anything.

I hope you're all right, Tom, she wrote, after telling him a few lines about their day, about George being a special and about his injury.

I'm sorry we didn't get a chance to talk when you came but it was very emotional for you. Our mother is not an easy woman – never was, I'd imagine. But I'm like you – I've always wanted a brother or sister too. And we've got each other now.

Keep safe and when this awful war is over, come and see me. I won't be far from where you found us before.

412

There'll be a warm welcome from George and me – I promise you.

But for now, God bless you and keep you safe. From your little sister,

Violet Cherry

She wrote the navy's address on the envelope, sealed it, gave it a kiss and climbed out of bed to begin her day with George.

Acknowledgements

As usual there were a number of helpful books that enabled me build up a picture of Britain, and Birmingham in particular, at war. Joshua Levine's *The Secret History of the Blitz* is a new and very interesting study. Angus Calder's *The People's War*, Julia Gardiner's *Wartime: Britain 1939–1945*, Steve Hookins's *My Grandad: the Air Raid Warden* and Peter Doherty's *No. 13 Herbert Road* were all a help, as well as *Birmingham Blitz: Our Stories*, compiled by Brian Wright for BARRA, the Birmingham Air Raids Remembrance Association.

In addition I owe a huge thank you to Matt Felkin, keeper of documents for BARRA, who was so generous in supplying me with all sorts of pictures and details of Small Heath during the Blitz and answered emails almost straightaway at the oddest times of day. Thank you, Matt – the perfect research assistant.